CASSIE SWINDON

ISBN paperback: 9798880164714

ISBN hardcover: 978-1-7373469-9-9

Cover Design by: BZN Design Studios

Naked Hardcover Design by: Raven Pages Design Studio

Interior Formatting by: Jennifer Laslie

Editing by: Your Editing Lounge

Dedicated to:

Those who have dreamed of writing your own beauty and the beast story.
Do it. I dare you.

ALSO BY CASSIE SWINDON:

The Linked Trilogy

Scorched

Severed

Shattered

The Golden Chains Trilogy

Break the Stone

Hunt the Storm

Stop the Clock

The Fairy Tale Flip Series: The Wicked Blue

The Phantom Ink

The Never Hour

There is a free prequel short story to this book on www.cassieswindon.com called "Mora's Thorn."

Check it out for an introduction to our heroine.

ACKNOWLEDGMENTS

People are awesome. You, yourself, are amazing in some unique way. However, sometimes, animals are far superior to us humans. During the writing of this novel, our family had to say goodbye to our 14-year-old fluffy kitty, Lumen. So, this is to Lulu, the best book stealer there will ever be. The best bookmark hider in existence. You'll always be my favorite writing buddy. Your purring machine gave me a steady soundtrack of encouragement. Thank you for being there for me during so many ups and downs. Thank you for being the epitome of unconditional love. We all miss you. Thank you, Lulu, my sweet baby boy.

PROLOGUE

7 years ago

I can no longer be patient with my sister's timid behavior. I've been supportive and calm for who knows how many months, but since Lessie refuses to practice her magic, it's time to do things my way. This is the perfect time to teach her a little lesson while our other sister is out stargazing. Of course Kavianne wouldn't approve of my idea and it's not like anyone else will ever find out with our home being tucked away in this secluded spot.

As I lay on the bottom of the bunk bed, I glance at the images scratched into the wood of the planks above me. All three of our names are etched into a heart made of jagged lines.

It's been just the three of us for years. As the eldest, I've kept my sisters safe and fed and mostly happy. They may not understand my commanding ways, but a leader needs to assert herself to be efficient. If it weren't for me, there's no chance Kavianne would've mastered all of her orbs already. Now it's time to push Lessie's limits; I'm tired of dealing with her excuses. Respecting our power is one thing, but being terrified to use it is just nonsensical.

I roll off the mattress and tiptoe barefoot across the floor of our small cottage, avoiding the spots where the wood creaks. With an orb in my palm, I stand over Lessie, snoring in the other bed. In sleep, her curly hair frames her face like a doll. I may never have her gorgeous looks or Kavianne's fierce fighting skills, but at least I have assertion and decisiveness. Because of those qualities, they'll both thank me for helping Lessie overcome this hurdle.

Even while dreaming my youngest sister resembles a deer. Not because her freckles mirror a fawn's speckled coat, but because she looks chronically frightened. Ever since Lessie was a toddler, she'd flee at the slightest threat. She's often on high alert for potential dangers and has never trusted her magic to test her powers. Honestly, it's absolutely ridiculous.

"We're finally doing things my way, Sis," I whisper, "Don't worry, it's for the best."

I whisper a mind-controlling spell into the night air and an orb sparks to life. Swirling ribbons move inside my sphere. They glow, creating light and shadows in our bedroom. The strength of its power shocks me, like nothing I've ever experienced. Immediately, Lessie snaps awake, but a glossy look overtakes her eyes. Hopefully that means the spell is working as planned.

"Hover over the bed, Lessie," I whisper, glancing at the door to make sure Kavianne isn't walking in.

Lessie's half-alert eyes widen and her pupils dilate. Her body lifts off the bed and she floats higher. Higher. Mid-air until her head almost hits the ceiling.

Lessie shakes her head slightly, her face reddening.

"You won't fall. Just believe. If I can do this, you can too." I swallow, feeling slightly guilty since there's a chance she may think this is a dream in the morning. "Okay, now hover above our tree outside. It's only a little higher."

Her fists clench for only a second before releasing. Without having to say another word, her body flies out the open window to our backyard. The trial is successful again. Lessie easily floats about twenty feet in the air. I swear she's trying to protest, but no words form. How much is she aware of? I'll have to ask her tomorrow.

"Okay, now, go hover over the cliffside," I whisper. "I know you were too scared earlier but I know you can do it."

Entranced Lessie darts across the yard. I have to push my muscles to keep up. My heart races. I'm so excited to show Lessie she can do this; she doesn't have to be afraid. The moment she succeeds, I'll undo the spell and prove to her she can trust her magic.

We rush over the prairie, into the forest, toward the

cliff just as I had planned. My three best friends lie on their backs on large boulders, pointing up to the night sky. When they hear me running, they each turn our way, probably wondering what we're doing. Damn it, I hadn't considered they'd be awake still. Oh well, I'll come up with an excuse later.

I need to focus on Lessie. When I see the cliff edge ahead, a strange feeling squeezes in my gut. Why isn't she slowing down? At her speed, she'll run straight off the side.

My heart accelerates.

I continue to chase. Feet slam on the ground.

"Lessie!"

She doesn't hear me.

I start to panic.

The cliffside grows closer yet Lessie only goes faster and faster.

My breath rushes out of my body.

I know without a doubt the spell was too strong. I made a mistake. As she speeds away from me, it's like my soul is taken out of my body, watching from above.

"Stop!" I scream.

She does and lowers to the ground. I finally suck in air again, thanking the stars above that I still have control over her mind. Though I'm not an idiot, I'll admit my errors when I'm wrong. I say the counter-spell to my orb, settling my racing nerves. That's not a risk I'll ever try again.

Lessie's eyes clear and she shakes her head, then glances around in fear. Her eyes land on me. "Mora? What happened? Where are we?"

She takes a single step toward me, hands outstretched for comfort. I reach out, ready to tease her for wearing her dress to bed instead of changing before falling asleep. The blue lace blows as a wild gust of wind billows from the west.

Confused, Lessie sways. Her foot catches on a root. She twists. Leans. Loses her balance.

She falls over the cliff. As silent as snowfall in winter.

My heart stops. I drop to my knees, reaching for my sister. My Lessie. Can't breathe. Can't move. Can't speak.

Behind me, I hear Kavianne screaming at the top of her lungs, but I can't pay attention, can't ask questions, can't turn to beg for help, can't face Kavianne. Because Lessie... Lessie! I stare into the Abyss. Heart slamming, I stare. And stare.

And Kavianne screams. And screams. And screams.

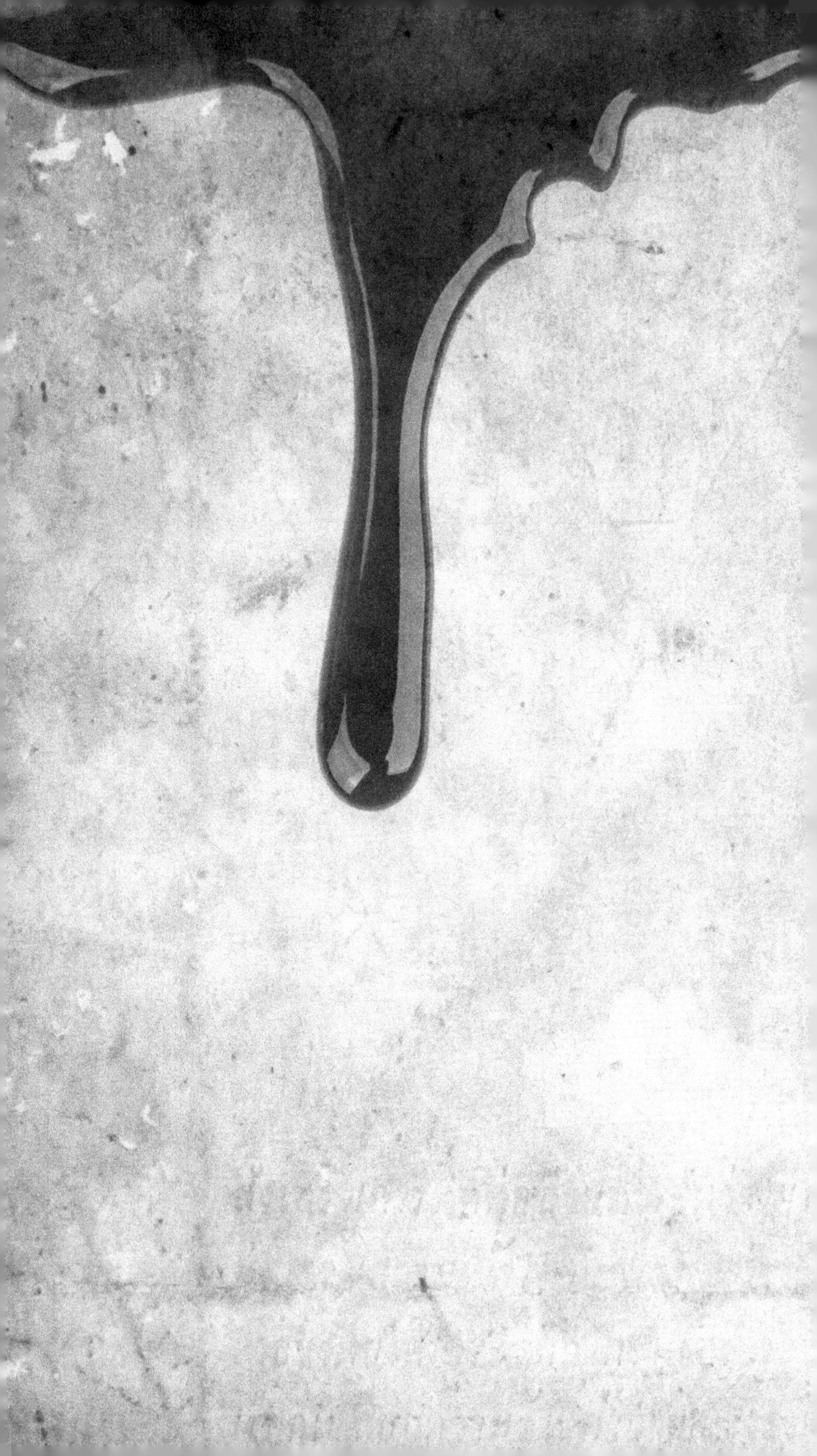

The first excerpt from The Book

Once upon a time, in the Year of the Falcon, a curse was cast.

Then I was created—a book like no other.

Mora Thomesse was not the type of woman to allow a curse to befall her, yet it happened all the same. Mora wailed over the canyon's ridge for her sister, Lessie. Dead and gone.

As Mora knelt on the edge of the cliffside, shins in the mud, arms stretched forward, forehead meeting the earth, her sister, Kavianne released all her panic and power in an instant. Kavianne raged stronger than a hurricane, whipping her magic in every direction, cursing Mora to a life of thorns.

When the first thorn painfully poked from her skin, Mora did not screech.

When Kavianne attacked, face red and tears streaming, Mora did not cower.

But when Kavianne turned her anger toward the three innocent bystanders, Mora shielded them with her body. This act was her saving grace. Protecting her friends was what gave Mora a second life.

The part Mora does not yet know, is she will learn her lesson. She will relinquish control, but it is not an easy task to master for our heroine.

I may know the truth of how she breaks the curse, or I may simply scribe what I see, exactly or unexactly how it unfolds.

CHAPTER 1

Mora

The stroke of midnight teases me with secrets. If only it could whisper the answer of how to break the curse. I stare at my wrists and forearms covered in sharp thorns.

One of the chandeliers hanging from our library's ceiling sways from a winter gust blowing in through the window. The chill only enhances the gloom that I love about our home. A single dim lightbulb creates a moving, creeping shadow along the wall as the chandelier swings back and forth slowly. Back and forth. Right to left. Some nights, I swear the dark corners of this library are alive. It's times like these when it feels like our mansion has a heartbeat of its own, thirsty for more blood to pump through its veins.

I sit with my legs crisscrossed on the oversized couch facing the bay window and zoom in on my reflection. The beast who claimed me years ago glares back. My dark brown hair may as well be made of cockroaches and snakes for it will never again resemble that of the girl who grew up with two innocent sisters in the countryside. And the few freckles dotting my face feel more like deathmarks than birthmarks.

Moonlight slants along my skin where the hideous barbs protrude. With these thorns poking out of my flesh, my body resembles the invasive plant that crawls around our home. In a sleepless daze, I stare at the fairy statues outside on the lawn. What I'd give to sprout wings and fly away from our curse. At least the snow is beautiful. Ever since the warm, summer night when everything changed, I've preferred the bitter cold season. Next to the fairies are wolf statues with mouths wide open and sharp icicle fangs. They look like guardians in gothic fairy tales.

From high on this hill, the rooftops of the tallest building in Ozaron's valley are visible, but I doubt anyone is roaming out there on a wintery night like this when a simple inhale of the cutting air feels lethal.

Lethal—I don't like that word. If I could open my thesaurus, I'd find a synonym. Maybe disastrous, toxic, or harmful. All of those happen to also describe me, though I never intended to be lethal. Do intentions matter in the grand scheme of things?

An owl hoots somewhere in the pines below the window. My hand is shaking—maybe from the cold, or from the fact that I'm running out of time. Instead of ruminating, I draw the window shut.

With a heavy sigh, I start my nightly ritual. I lift a piece of paper to fold it into an elaborate pattern. My other origami creations line the windowsill. Cats and cranes with crisp creases and lovely lotus flowers of every color surround me.

A thorn on my finger pokes through the paper I'm holding. Grunting, I crush it into a ball and chuck it behind me.

"Breathe, Mora," I say to myself. "It's just an easy fold. You've done this a million times."

Carefully, I take another piece of pink paper and gently pin it between my thumb and pointer fingertips. Ever so slowly, I try to be graceful in folding the sheet. Another thorn rips through.

"Damn it!" I throw it at the window and watch it bounce off.

It'd feel more satisfying if the paper weighed enough to crash through the glass. What I'd give to destroy something, to hear the destruction and feel the power in my hands. Except my hands are worthless now. I must get rid of these thorns to break our curse. But how? Nothing has worked for seven years. At age twenty-five, I'm a useless, unknown recluse and have been this way for my entire pathetic adulthood.

As I push the mounds of fleece blankets off my legs and stumble off the old couch, one of my barbs pierces through the fabric and rips a hole straight down the armrest.

Frustration coils my muscles tight.

Bending oddly, still attached, I glare at the spot where my thorn is connected to the furniture. So, I do the only thing I can to free myself. I yank my arm. Hard. A giant tearing sound echoes through the library. The couch I've had for years is ruined. Just one more thing to add to my list of destruction and devastation. It doesn't take long for the silence to be overpowered by my thundering heartbeat.

I
Can't
Live
Like
This

I jab my hand into the side of the couch. A scream erupts from my lungs. I slash through the fabric. Ram my hand in hard again and again until a dozen holes puncture the material. I kick the side of the couch. My toe throbs wildly and I hop around on one foot.

"Fuck you, stupid curse!" I scream and scream and scream. "Fuck you!"

Across the library, the magical pen mocks me as it writes faster, harder. Crimson ink spills out onto the pages of the enchanted Book.

"And fuck you too!" I rush over, wanting to claw at the Book that has ruined our lives, but I stop. From experience, I know that trying to destroy the Book will only give me another thorn.

"Won't you ever stop?!" Hot tears pool behind my eyes. "Stop writing! Leave us alone!"

The pen, held by no one, continues to scribble. I rise on my tiptoes to read its latest addition:

Mora storms across the epic library that contains the world's most prestigious novels. She pathetically yells nonsense into an empty room, where no one can hear her, see her, or love her. Because Mora is the monster of her own story, a witch beyond redemption, a girl deserving of the curse placed on her years ago for killing her little sister—simply stated, she is a beast.

. . .

I lurch forward again, wanting to snatch the pen, break it in half, and throw it out the window, but that will only make matters worse. Until I can figure out how to get rid of these thorns, the pen will continually write every moment of my life.

At least this Book has given me some answers over time, spread out in mysterious clues for me to unravel. One, specifically important one: I can't let the ink in this pen run out or it'll be our end. I don't want to question what "the end" means exactly, but I doubt it's sunshine and roses.

It had taken a lot of experimenting to learn what the ink inside the pen is made of—crushed rose petals. I've been refilling the ink (as instructed by the Book). There's enough for the phantom author to write about thirty more pages. Thirty more pages until my time is over. I drop my head and calculate quickly. Three weeks. That's the estimated time remaining to either restock the ink or break the curse.

If only I knew how to break the curse.

I collapse onto the destroyed couch and pretend it's a coffin, suffocating me. It doesn't matter that my body crushes my most recent origami. It doesn't matter that the last bulb in the chandelier flickers out. I stare at the towering bookshelves illuminated by the moon. It doesn't matter if I try to remember all the research we have done between the pages of texts because the cursed pen continues to write.

I refuse to look at it.

It scribbles on.

I clench my eyes shut and try to remember a happier time; a memory full of joy.

The pen scrawls louder, testing my limits.

My muscles tighten from head to toe, and I swear to the

Goddess Above that if the pen scratches one more line on that damned paper I'm going to—

"Mora?"

I jump and swivel around to scan the shadows for my friend. Feathi is often difficult to spot in the darkness, ever since the curse changed her form too. Yet I can usually find her by listening to the ticks of the watches that decorate both her forearms. My roommate leans in the doorway, hands on her hips. To be exact her *paper* hands rest on her *paper* hips. She isn't infested with thorns, but my sister somehow turned my friends into living breathing origami people. I may never know if she did so intentionally or because they were close by when she cursed me. They remain the same size and shape, and have the same strength as humans, but stuck in a paper form, they're constantly at risk of tearing or being withered by rain or snow.

"Feathi? What are you doing awake?"

I look at my best friend in pajamas: tall, thin, blond with light eyes, fully made of paper and both arms covered in unique watches.

"Well, Nax and I were talking," she pauses, probably thinking about her Partner, "and we think it's time to put the Book and pen somewhere else for a while. We think it'll do you some good to not have it torture you night after night. How about we store it somewhere safe? The fairies told me about a good spot that could work."

Feathi zips to a bookshelf and busies herself with one of the bindings. Before I can protest, she manages to move one of the books like a lever. I hear a click. The rug droops into a space that should be taken up by the floor. Despite the disastrous night, I have to hold back a smile. Another hidden passageway is exactly the type of secret this house would hide.

Feathi prances over. A small portion of the floor has opened, a hole leading down. She carefully sprinkles black fairy dust over the Book and its wretched pen. They float toward the new opening. I guess the fairies already lent her some of their power too.

"Come on," she says softly.

I'd usually demand for my friend to stay behind, in case danger lurks below, but I'm too exhausted for a confrontation.

"It's called the West Wing." Feathi gestures for me to follow her down into the depths.

"Is down considered west?" I'm too tired to argue, too defeated to tell her the idea won't work. I'll only wake tomorrow to obsessively pace underground instead of in the library.

We descend through a vertical tunnel. Black fairy glitter also highlights the walls like diamonds in a dark cave. Down, down, down, lower. Even lower. At the bottom, our makeshift elevator comes to a stop.

"I think we're here," Feathi says.

"I don't like this." I shake my head.

"The fairies will keep it safe," Feathi tries to reassure me.

"How?"

"With magic, what else?" Feathi shrugs. "The fairies said 'No intruders will ever willingly sacrifice the price it'll cost to get inside.'" She changes her voice to a high pitch to match the fairies'.

A single, ordinary door awaits us. Spiderwebs stick to my face. They're as sickly as the invisible secrets dripping from the ceiling. I don't have to touch the door. It swings open slowly with a loud creak. Lanterns spark to life. We stand in a small round chamber. In the middle of the room, a thick tree trunk is cut short, waiting. A strange tingle runs up my spine.

Feathi guides the Book and the pen to hover above the tree trunk. Before I can process what's happening, the Book teeters, loses its balance, and starts to lean to the right. I can't move fast enough to catch it from crashing. I wince, waiting for the impact when the Book's invisible protective bubble slams against the wall. From experience, I know all too well what will happen when anything tries to touch the Book. It falls to the floor.

In an instant, a new, painful thorn sprouts out of my skin. I howl in pain. It curls out above my chipped pink fingernail. This one twists at a deadly angle, longer than the others. My heart rate immediately triples. Damn it, I don't want this pain. Not again.

Feathi turns so quickly that her sharp origami corners give me a paper cut. "Mora!" she screams. "Are you okay? I'm so sorry."

I swallow the piercing pain and hiss out. "I told you this was a terrible idea."

"I didn't mean to…I was only trying to help." Her breathing comes out so ragged I'm afraid her fragile paper folds will burst.

"Use a healing potion," Feathi begs. "I know you carry one around, just in case. It'll stop the pain."

"No, I can't waste it." I groan. My hands shake, panic lodging like a rock in my gut since it hurts worse than last time. "You should've listened to my rules."

Fuck the fuckin' curse. Fuck the thorns that cage me. Fuck the ink that dictates my every moment.

My heart thunders against my chest. Dread anchors me to the floor and I feel like I'm sinking. Sinking. Further and deeper until my body lowers through the cement foundation and becomes one with the roots of the vines that wrap around this old house.

"Mora, use magic just this once." Feathi pleads. "I'll collect your orbs."

"No, keep the orbs hidden from me."

A black thread dances like a silk ribbon from my finger, then fades away. All energy drains out of me as if blood flows from an open wound. I try to keep the fear from rising in my gut. The pain isn't usually this severe, but I refuse to use the healing potion.

Feathi snakes a hand into my pocket and pulls out the little bottle full of crimson liquid. I can't stop her. Can't move until the pain passes. She knows what using the contents of the potion will cost me. What it'll cost us.

"Drink this, Mora." Feathi holds the bottle rim to my lips.

"No."

"Mora," Feathi snaps, "I know this will work. One day you need to realize that *your* ideas aren't the only option. There's not enough time to—"

"I'll…be…fine." I groan like an animal dying.

"You're in pain!"

"Put…the bottle…back," I grit out through clenched teeth. If she had listened to *me*, the Book would be upstairs. It never would've slammed against the floor. I never would've grown a new thorn.

"I can't sit here and watch my best friend suffer. Why are you so damn stubborn? Don't you understand?! You're choosing to die instead of listening to us. And I don't mean right now. For months, you've been deteriorating, and we are done sitting around waiting."

I push upright, in agony, jaw clenched and muscles tight. I want to scream that she's my responsibility to take care of.

Feathi, Nax, and Yin used to be living breathing humans. My choices cost them their lives. They turned into origami forms the moment my sister spat out her nasty spell. Feathi will never know how it feels to be the cause of someone's anguish.

"You're only upset because you've had to rely on someone more capable than you," I say.

Chest heaving, I stare Feathi down, remorse already itching its way into my heart. Feathi doesn't deserve my outburst, and she has every right to view me as the brutal savage I've become. I'm a ruthless terror, like the wolf statues guarding this house.

"I'm not going to change my mind," I say. "I won't use my orbs. I won't use magic. And I won't waste the healing potion. We will break the curse my way or no way."

Feathi sighs. "You're impossible."

We sit in silence as the pain turns to a throbbing, then only an ache until finally it is only a dull soreness. I let out a heavy breath as I stare at my newest body part. Grotesque.

Next to me, Feathi rises. With black fairy dust in hand, she sprinkles the rest on the tipsy-turvy Book and pen until they're upright again and positioned over the tree trunk.

I don't dare meet my friend's eyes, knowing they'll be shimmering with unshed tears. I know she's only trying to help.

"Let's get you upstairs," Feathi says quietly.

I rise to my feet, careful to not brush against her. Stubborn or not, it's too cold in this underground cave to sleep here overnight. We rise on the strange elevator shaft in silence.

Back in the library, I slump onto the massive couch facing the snow-crusted window. The peaceful life out in our forest doesn't seem to match the turmoil cycling inside our home.

Feathi falls onto the couch beside me and starts spinning the watches on her wrist. I envision her years younger when she had lists of dreams and the potential for any future. Now, she's imprisoned here. Because of me.

Once upon a time, Yin would create a stage out of couch cushions and put on a unique show presenting her dancing skills. Feathi would clap loudly regardless of how it turned out, and Nax would ask me to make a bouquet of paper flowers to gift Yin as a congratulations.

Yin catches my eyes as she walks into the library. Snow speckles her slick black hair. Her dark eyes and thin lips are pulled in a tight line showing concern. Also trapped as an origami figure, she's the opposite of Feathi in every way, just like my sisters used to be. Goddess, I love them both so much.

Yin holds a rope in one paper hand. I follow its length out the door into the darkness.

"Wait..." I stand slowly. "What is attached to the other end?"

Feathi holds her breath for a moment looking between me and Yin. "Earlier, we found someone trying to break into our house."

A young girl, older than a decade, younger than a teenager, emerges from the shadows with rope wrapped around her wrists.

"What are you guys doing? We're not kidnappers." I rush over to release the girl but both Feathi and Yin stop me.

"Wait!" Feathi pleads. "This is a perfect opportunity. For once, Mora, please. Will you listen to our idea?"

CHAPTER 2

Brody

Under the full moon, I stare at the roses. This garden, on the border of my hometown, is the last place I held my daughter, the last place I saw her sweet face. Even though I'll probably never lay eyes on her again, I need a memento. I pluck a single rose and shove it in my pocket, prepared to dry and save the petals later. Quietly, I sneak out the gate and close it gently so that no sleeping neighbors will hear the click.

The streets of Villeneuve speak a different language at midnight. The shadows whisper for me not to leave, but I have to because my daughter will never return. It's more likely that an octopus will walk down Main Street than I will see Catterina in this village again.

"Snap out of it," I whisper aloud.

There's no point wallowing in depressing thoughts.

The ticket in my other pocket fills me with hope strong enough to lift me to the Moina Constellation. I can't stay any longer. At this point, it doesn't matter where I go, as long as I'm no longer here.

I tighten my backpack straps and jog to Villeneuve's boundary. Behind the last row of shops, the forest looms like a tall wall. I step onto the trail leading into the wicked woods. This path will eventually lead to sunken treasure in Nerida and traders to hustle in Coendrial.

Ahead, a small animal scrambles. Despite the darkness, I can see tiny paw prints in the snow. We're kindred spirits. I too relish the cold—or every temperature for that matter—so bring on the blizzard. No type of weather can slow me down since I'm traveling light, carrying every item I need in this one backpack. As long as I have my carving tools and some food, I'll survive. Once more, I check off a list of my essentials: sloyd and bench knives, chip carving, scoop and hook, chisels, saw, mallet, and gouge…yeah, I have most of the basics.

My Taj99 device buzzes for the tenth time.

"Miss me already, Mam?" I smile at the almost audible sound of her rolling her eyes.

"Brody Kain Ricci! Get your ass to my house in the next five minutes or I swear to the Goddess above that I'll hunt you down and lock you in my wine cellar again. And don't think I won't; there are plenty of spiders down there to keep you company for the next ten years. In fact, hopefully they'll spin a web to trap you and I won't have a heart attack from worry. What do you think you're doing to your poor mother? Did you know I had to hear the news from Sofia? Of all your sisters, it takes the ten-year-old to rat out her brother. And don't you worry about the others. Their rotten souls have both been taken care of. I fed them dinner still; what good mother could let their child go hungry? Which reminds me, do you have any food?" Mam sucks in a giant breath. "First, I heard that you rented out your apartment and donated your clothes. Now my only son disappears in the middle of the night? If you don't have some protein with you, Brody…"

I can't help but grin. "I packed a month's worth of your pies."

"Oh, good boy...wait! I haven't made a pie! Don't lie to me!" She pauses for only a fraction of a second, the longest Ozaron has ever lasted without hearing Mam's voice. "I figured it out, Brody. You're trying to kill me. That's what it is. After cooking for you for thirty years, you thank me by plotting the end of my days. I'm right, aren't I?" She pauses again and I wait patiently for another rant as I march along the dark path.

In the background, her voice carries on about her neighbor's daughter and some illness that has forced her to be bedridden, but all I can focus on are the breathtaking stars. I squint to blur them into the shape of a pirate ship. In two weeks I could be swinging from a rope and splashing into the Barrett Sea without a care in the world. Men will be playing the fiddle on a ship deck, asking me about my plans once I reach the coast. I can see it now, soaking wet, gathering the crew in a circle and telling my tales as if they're already written in stone:

"First, with my sleight of hand, I swiped a precious jewel from a market table and sold it to a poor soul wandering the streets," I'll say.

"And then what, Brody?" one pirate will ask me.

Before I answer the crew, I'll climb atop the helm and perform a balancing act, while I point in the distance. *"And then I followed the sailor and snatched the gem right back without him knowing."*

"Will you give it to a pretty maiden?" another pirate will ask.

With both hands on my hip, I'll shake my head and reply, with a proper pirate accent of course. *"No, lads. The maidens will be giving ME plenty of gifts after they learn my nickname, the one only whispered when the clock strikes midnight behind closed doors."*

The pirates will cheer since I'll already have won them over as friends for life. They'll decide to abandon their captain and follow me to the desert. I wonder how far one grain of sand travels? Could sand voyage all the way from the sea to the desert like I will?

Anyway, we'll collect the rarest lizard venom and hike through the jungles of Lacordia where we'll follow ancient codes leading to secret caves. When we return years later, those of us who remain will mark matching tattoos to celebrate our survival.

"Brody! Are you even listening to me?" Mam's voice pierces through the darkness.

I'm not anywhere exotic—yet. Whispering pines surround me like slats of a prison cage, but soon I'll never see this forest again.

"Brody!" Mam's voice reminds me I haven't hung up yet. "Listen, Son. Gabrielle LeGume has been asking about you again. You shouldn't have stood her up last week. Grandchildren from that woman would be the most precious—"

And that's when I *accidentally* hang up. The thought of being tied down to Gabrielle, or any one person, sends shivers up my spine. I have to shake off the image of a ring on my finger and breathe in the crisp frigid air.

I already gave everything to Dom and our baby once upon a time. I won't make the same mistake again. Commitment is a fraud, a myth, a legend. Definitely not for me.

I won't let any thoughts of relationships dampen my current mood. Because soon, I'll be truly free.

Shoving my Taj99 in a pocket, I continue forward into the lovely cold until the struggling sounds and soft whimpers of an animal catch me off guard. It's close but I don't want to waste battery by using the flashlight. The soft whimpers turn to hellish cries. I kneel and crawl on all fours. The snow starts to bite at my bare skin, but I ignore it because this is the beginning of my grand adventure.

My fingers slide against liquid, warm and thick. Then I smell it. The copper scent of blood mixed with dark magic. Bringing my fingertips to my nose confirms my fear. Shit, this isn't the glorious beginning I had envisioned.

Heart quickening, I jump to my feet. Any number of beasts might roam the forest at midnight, ready to devour this wounded prey. I have no intention of being anyone's meal until I've seen all thirteen carpentry wonders of Coendrial.

My skin prickles with the sensation of needles crawling up the back of my neck. The safe option is to turn toward home but more grunts and whimpers keep me here, locked into place. Reluctantly, I reach for my Taj99 and shine a light forward.

A beam reflects two tiny eyes buried between thick fur. My whole body relaxes. It's only a wolf pup.

"Hey, little one." I slowly reach forward. "Where's your pack?"

A nasty snarl sends me lurching back. My light lands on

an adult wolf covered in blood. Every one of my muscles tightens. The animal can't stand, but a parent would battle an entire universe to protect their young. I'd know. Believe me…I'd know.

Slow as death, I back away, boots crunching into the snow, and promise, "It's okay, Momma, I'm not going to take him."

She lowers her chin onto her paw. Once I'm far enough out of her reach, the goosebumps prickling my skin fade and I regain steady breaths until I realize the poor pup probably won't survive the night without nourishment. My chest clamps taut and my fists clench into balls again.

"Damn it, wolf," I speak to the momma. "Why couldn't you watch where you were walking? Why couldn't you have seen the trap first?"

The poor mother whines pathetically.

"Breathe, Brody," I whisper to myself and slap my cheeks. I can't protect the wolf any better than I could protect my daughter. Nope, reverse that train of thought. I won't think about Cat tonight.

Just like Mam says, sometimes these things just happen, but it doesn't ease the pain. This is the biggest reason I need to leave my town.

A howl fills the air in the distance. Hopefully, it's the pup's pack coming to take care of him.

I start jogging down the path, toward the only sensible destination—the harbor. Despite my clenched teeth and rattled mind, I try to imagine my future, with sunrays kissing my skin, a witty woman rubbing oils on my back, and endless customer orders for my carvings.

I jog faster toward my future. Right foot. Left foot. Everything will be fine. Soon, I'll be gone.

A bone-snapping scream fills the silence.

I stop, frozen in place. "What the fuck?"

My breath is visible on every exhale. I whip my head around. The treetops sway slowly, masking whatever lurks in the woods. The creepy sensation of someone watching me scrapes up my back like the tip of a saw blade combing my spine, slowly, one single vertebrate at a time. There have been rumors about an ominous monster lurking in these woods.

Another jaw-dropping scream makes me pivot. I move toward the sound, carefully watching where I step. It must be a similar trap that latched onto an innocent person. I storm through the foot of snow. Panic takes control as I consider that maybe one of my sisters followed me. What if it's Sofia?

Heart pounding, I run faster. My lungs burn. What if I'm too late? What if she can't call for help again? What if she bleeds out? What if she was knocked unconscious?

I'm spiraling when suddenly the path opens to a gap between the trees. The gothic stone mansion, also known as Chambrea Fortress, towers under the moonlight. Its timeworn stones are covered in creeping ivy. I see no sign of life among the weeds and beastly statues guarding the front iron gate. Only stone fountains frozen over and bird baths decorated with speared icicles are scattered across the front lawn.

There are no tracks of boots or paths of blood. Snow falls harder. Some might call it an omen, but I don't believe in such things. I grab a chisel and blade from my backpack. Both hands armed, I crouch behind one of the wolf statues.

"Sofia?" I whisper and sneak forward, avoiding the thick vines at my feet. I've never seen such large plant life like this in all of Ozaron.

"Sofia?!" I call out a little louder.

A skittering sound comes from near the gate. The same pup jumps out of the snow, wiggles between the gate, and scampers toward the front stairs. His tracks are the first and only ones, so where did the scream come from?

The pup frolics over more giant vines in the front courtyard, sinking into the snow with each leap. My hyperactive mind must've imagined the scream. Just as I turn to leave, a silhouette looms in a window of the mansion.

"No fuckin' way," I whisper.

No one has lived in the old, abandoned castle house for years. And not one person from Villeneuve would dare to venture inside because of the rumors. Would Sofia have managed to crawl through a back door and stay there for shelter if she had gotten hurt? Is she the one staring at me, stiller than a block of ice? Or is there a nasty criminal preying on travelers?

With all my might, I kick the gate open. Snow falls atop my boots. With both tools pointed out, I sprint up the front stairs, unable to avoid the vines. Each one is so large they drape over the steps completely. It's like I'm climbing a Goddess-damned ivy ladder. Jagged thorns threaten to spill my blood with each movement.

At the front door, I reach for the brass handle, but it's buried underneath weeds and vines.

I hack at the plant with my tools, barely making a dent. Despite the cold, sweat drips down my temple. A loud thump comes from inside, stopping my heart from ticking for a moment. It sounded like a body dropping to the floor. No! My vision blurs and my lips go numb. I can't survive another loss. It'll destroy me.

Rage surges through my veins like a tsunami and my blood boils. There's no chance I'll chop through these vines without an axe, so I do the next best thing. A stone pot planter filled with snow sits by my boot. I heave it up, groaning and struggling. Every muscle in my arms through my back is on fire from the mass of its weight.

Finally, I manage to tip it against the window and push it through. Glass shatters to pieces. Shards slice into the snow a thousand times. And I step through the broken window into the shadows.

CHAPTER 3

Brody

Inside the mansion, I'm met with only silence. However, I swear I can hear phantom echoes of an organ playing sinister chords in a minor key—a melody from long ago. The memories of dark music from past lives cling to the shadows on the wall. There's an oddly shaped silhouette, like a vine, crawling up the wallpaper, but when I blink the shape is gone.

As I step forward, I suck in a breath. Moonlight casts beams onto the gorgeous foyer, built for royalty once upon a time. I scan the space—right—left—up. Any words to describe the pointed arches towering to the high ceiling are ripped from my throat. I remain still for a few beats, taking in the scene. My senses are on high alert, trying to memorize every dip and curve of the stained-glass windows. I should've explored this place years ago.

Everything in the foyer is massive, from the rug bigger than my bedroom to the sculptures that guard the entrance. I pause to examine them closely. Each of them has sharp, curled claws coming out of their hands. Or maybe they're thorns? Whoever designed this building deserves an award.

Wait, what am I here for?

Oh, Sofia!

The sensation of being watched by a predator returns, just like I felt in the woods. I move through the foyer with a new shakiness in my legs. With each step, I wince when my boot makes the floor creak. I scan the dusty layer atop the wainscot design. My fingertips linger on each divot and knick, coming away darkened and full of soot.

"Hello?" I shout.

There are no light switches that I can find. I'd rather not grab my Taj again to shine a flashlight since that would require me to put one of my weapons away. As I turn the corner, underneath a broad archway, I hold my breath. Part of me believes a mythical monster will jump out to devour me whole, just like in the legends. Yet, the area is empty. It's almost more nerve-wracking being alone than having a hundred deadly creatures glaring at me. The wall décor shifts to unadorned stone and a narrow hallway extends indefinitely. I swear a flicker of light bounces at the end of the corridor. That can't be right. My eyes must be playing tricks on me.

No sane person would voluntarily walk down that hallway alone. I should leave now, but images of Sofia lying injured on the floor flicker in my mind.

"Is someone here?" I hold my tools out again, clutching them so hard my knuckles are probably white. The best plan is to stay in a fighter's stance, shoulders tight. An impossible breeze blows past me. Cold as ice. Gooseflesh covers my body yet beads of sweat drip down my temple. I take another cautious step. Another.

How much time has passed since I entered? A minute? An hour?

"Sofia?" I call out, my breath bursting in and out. My voice echoes, bouncing against the stone.

Then a loud, low creak comes from down the hall. I jerk to the right. A metallic sound clanks far behind me, in the opposite direction. I turn and bump into the wall.

"Just keep going," I whisper to myself. "She needs me."

My pulse speeds. There's a tingling at the base of my neck. I need to know where she's hiding. When I squint, it becomes clear that the stones camouflage into multiple doors extending down the hallway. I hover my hand over one doorknob. Hold my breath.

Swing it open.

Furniture is scattered about a dark room, all draped with white sheets. A movement catches my eyes in one of the giant windows. For a second, I swear a little girl stares at me. I blink. She's gone. Nothing remains.

"Who's there?" My voice trembles a bit, even though I project it louder this time.

Nothing here feels natural like I've stepped through a portal into a different dimension. The air feels empty and hollow with each inhale. My body grows heavier. As eerie as this place is, I'm completely and entirely entranced.

I rush to the second door. Whip it open. This time I know the vines crawling along the walls are real. They claim the entire room, wrapped around a piano and extend back out a broken window. It's almost as if the long thorns along the plant beckon me to touch them. Another time, I'd accept the dare, but Sofia is what matters.

I dart out of the room. Fling open the third door. This large room stores old paintings, some hung, some scattered along the floor. After opening the fourth door, I pause at the sight of hundreds of empty bottles of different shapes and sizes. How strange.

The long walk through the manor reveals sprawling staircases, soaring arches between pillars, dangling chandeliers, gorgeous woodwork on all the grandfather clocks, and exquisite detailing on each door I pass. Yet, the grandiosity is offset by old plaster peeling off the wall and falling in chips onto the flooring.

Just when I'm about to give up the pup wolf scares the shit out of me by circling my heels.

"Dude, you gotta warn me."

He sniffs at the air, nose high, then frolics down the hallway.

"You know where to go?"

He leads me around a maze of corners until the narrow hallway opens up to a grand staircase. I'm about to climb when he barks quietly and slips into the shadows underneath the curvature of the stairs. A tiny squeak sound is followed by the pitter-patter of his paws.

Then I hear whispered, tense voices. Two women. They're arguing.

I peek through the crack of the door. A dim light shines on dozens of bookshelves, each taller than Mam's two-story house. Someone would need the world's tallest ladder to reach a novel from the top shelf. No women are visible but I continue to search the library anyway.

A girl. Not Sofia. Tied to the chair in the middle of the room. I almost miss her among all the piles of books, journals, and random foldings of pieces of paper that scatter the rug. Slowly, I push the door open a little. It squeaks. I freeze. The women still speak in harsh whispers.

Where are they? Why are they here? What do they want with the girl?

I push the door open a bit more with my boot. This time, the wood stays silent so I slide into the room, my heart racing and my tools pointed out. The girl meets my gaze and her eyes widen. I leap to her side.

We don't speak.

I drop one tool to untie her.

The knot is too tight.

Her foot jitters nervously against the rug.

The women's argument escalates, but their voices are muffled so I can't tell exactly where they are.

I start to saw the rope with my blade. Back and forth. Back and forth. It's too thick. This is taking too long.

Her other foot starts bouncing and she acts like she's about to push off the ground into my arms. "Mr. Ricci, it's me, Ryanne," she whispers, "I w-was only trying to p-prove to my friends that I'm not afraid of the haunted fortress."

"Sshh," I whisper, "Hang on."

The women's voices stop. I stop sawing and hold my breath again. Ryanne's feet stop bouncing. Her big eyes glisten with unshed tears. She's staring at something or someone behind me. I don't need to follow her gaze because I can feel the toxic energy radiating off whoever stands there. A threat. A danger. A wicked being who doesn't deserve a soul.

Slowly, as I turn, I meet a pair of beastly brown eyes.

CHAPTER 4

Mora

A pair of dark, devious eyes meet mine. The hero to save the girl stands between her and me. His woodsy hair, thick and tussled, desperately needs a brush. Short stubble frames a face that seems to be carved with mischief. His brown eyes hold fiery promises and daring adventure. For some reason, I can't look away. What's his story? Where did he come from? All I can guess is his estimated age from the few creases in his forehead. Maybe he's a few years older than my twenty-five.

Great. Our problem has worsened. I just ended an argument with Feathi about how they never should've taken the girl in the first place. What were they possibly thinking? My friends have had some unique ideas in the

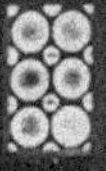

past, but they had to have known I'd never approve of this one.

Now we have a second intruder. He can't be old enough to be the girl's father. The last complication we need is a bunch of distraught parents. Now that a man is here, the situation has escalated.

"Mr. Ricci, Mr. Ricci!" The young girl's rosy cheeks remind me of my sister, Lessie, when she was that age. She nudges the back of the man's thigh.

He only pushes her further behind him.

I keep my eyes on this so-called Ricci fellow. The man widens his stance as he scans me up and down. Thankfully all my thorns are currently covered by baggy pants and a sweater. None are on my face and I'm wearing mittens since it's so cold.

He smiles—a fuckin' smile and casually says, "I bet you two fongels that if you let the girl go, I'll show you something you'll never forget."

First of all, what in the Abyss is a fongel? Secondly, why is he acting so relaxed? It's like his eyes and muscles are at war with each other. Ricci is pretending to be relaxed, but he doesn't fool me—it's an act. His eyes are as sharp as my thorns. He's taking in every inch of this library like someone who notices intricate details. The man is playing a game, one of which I don't know the rules. He glares with the intensity of a wolf about to attack, yet his body is loose, pretending he doesn't care.

On the other hand, *every* muscle of mine is clenched. Someone needs to put this intruder in his place. He has no right storming into my domain.

"What makes you think you can barge in here?" I hiss. "You've made a big mistake coming in here."

"You're wrong," he says with so much conviction.

"Excuse me?"

"You're wrong."

Wrong? Me? I grab a pad of paper from a nearby desk and throw it at his face. He ducks but not fast enough. A red spot is already forming on his cheek. Immediate regret fills my gut, but I'd never apologize.

His wicked brown eyes widen and I wonder if he'll lash out. Instead, Ricci starts laughing. I can't help but stare. What is going on? Who is this guy?

"I tell you what." Ricci fakes a yawn this time. "I'll take her place. All you have to do is let me finish untying her."

"I don't want *you*."

"You may not have a choice soon." His jaw ticks. "Be smart about this."

That's when I notice a hand behind his back. If he has a weapon, I'm at a disadvantage. I match his intense gaze that's trained on me.

"I'll let her go," I say.

"Fantastic." He doesn't hesitate but turns swiftly. A streak of silver flashes in the air and before I know it Ricci has slashed through the girl's rope with something metallic.

When the girl checks her wrists, already red from rubbing, my heart rips in two. This was all a mistake. I never would've agreed to my roommates capturing someone, and Yin should've known better. Years ago, Yin had a mind sharper than a chess champion. Now her cognition is deteriorating because of this curse.

I haven't gotten a good read on this man, so I watch him closely. Ricci walks the trembling girl to the door and carefully guides her through.

"Run straight home and don't stop. Stay on the path," he commands. "If you hear any noises, just keep running."

I have to hand it to him. At least *someone* knows how dangerous my woods are.

Before I can blink the girl disappears around the corner.

The grand hero stays by the door, with one hand on the wall. I can tell from here how hard he's pushing against the stone, muscles flared and strained. With his back to me, I survey his attire for the first time: hiking boots, a coat designed for any weather, one backpack, and the obvious rectangular shape of his Taj inside his back, jeans pocket. Where was he planning to run off to at midnight? And why?

"You didn't go with her," I say.

"That's because I'll be escorting you to the nearest port or train station. You're not welcome close to a town after kidnapping a kid." He saunters to me across the room like he's at a fuckin' tea party. "Who the fuck takes a child? What is wrong with you?"

He invades my personal bubble and takes a dominant step closer. Then he smiles—and no one can blame me for noticing. It's made of sinister curves, like marks on a treasure map. "Time for you to be tied up this time, like the felon you are."

I glance down at the rope in his hands and then laugh in his face. "This is my home. I'm not going anywhere."

"I'm not leaving until I know all the other children nearby are safe." He smirks. "I don't think I'd earn citizen of the year if I let you snatch up the next kid climbing a tree tomorrow."

I want to push his chest back, but can't risk cutting him open with my thorns. So I strip off my gloves, throw them on the floor, and hold both thorn-covered hands in the air between our faces.

"Get out of my space."

"You didn't say please," Ricci glances at my thorns for a second, but his expression doesn't change at all. He practically growls as he scans the walls behind me again. "Well...it sounds like we're going to be roomies until you change your mind. I thought I'd accept your offer of a tour."

"I didn't offer a tour."

"Oh?" He circles me like a shark. "When you so graciously took my coat and politely showed me where to dry my boots, I swear you mentioned an architectural wonder and how you'd be so willing to show me." He gestures to the gothic chandeliers hanging above.

Since I don't have time for theatrics and the winter air has started to make me shiver, I turn and march into the dark hallway, hoping he'll get bored and leave. I expect him to sprint out of here like any sane soul would do, but he trails me, his steps softer than feathers falling on snow. Why? He can't seriously be considering dragging me away from my home. Whatever children he's worried about aren't in danger. My friends got an earful from me lashing out at them with some strong cuss words earlier.

"So, it looks like I'll be staying the night...ohh!!" He claps his hands together sarcastically like a child crammed with sugar. "Do I get to choose between a dungeon cell or a hanging bird cage?"

"Go away. You'll be sleeping in your own home or with one wrist tied to your girlfriend's bedpost. I don't care. Just leave."

"Tied to the post, eh?" Ricci chuckles. "You had that answer ready to go. So, you like chains and ties?" He snaps the rope taut between his hands and it cracks like a whip. "It's a good thing I have rope then."

I don't have to see his face to know he's smiling. Wow, he's absolutely enraging. I refuse to let this man affect me or get under my skin. Speaking of skin, he has already seen my thorns, yet hasn't shown any disgust or fear once. I quickly glance over my shoulder and he is fuckin' whistling like a boy at a parade. Something isn't right. Maybe this Ricci man was sent here to spy.

Quickly, I pivot, ready to interrogate this menace. My movements are so sudden that my chest bumps straight into his. I stumble and almost crash into the wall, but he catches me mid-fall. A tiny thorn slices through his forearm and draws blood. Ricci glances down at the blood, then back to my eyes. He doesn't care that red drops trickle down his skin. One drop at a time, blood slides off and lands on the floor. Plink. Plink. Plink. The entire time this man doesn't take his gaze off me.

"Well, my name's Brody. If I'm to be your escort to the authorities then I probably need to let you know my requests during our precious time together."

"Go home. I won't take any little brats, don't worry. I have enough chaos to deal with."

"Great. Chaos is my middle name." He takes off his jacket and ties it around his cut. I hate how his t-shirt fits his chest perfectly. "First, listen to my requests, Lulita."

I shake my head. "What did you just call me?"

"Nothing. So, listen, my requests are important; do you need to take notes? First, I need to know why you smell like cinnamon." He must see a tick in my expression because his smile only brightens. "Next, on every other moon cycle, I'd like to travel to an exotic land. Don't worry, I'll bring you—"

"You don't make any sense. Are you playing some weird joke?" I refrain from tossing both hands in the air.

"Do you always interrupt people when they speak?" he counters. "It's rude."

My heart hammers, slams, pounds. "I don't inter—"

"Yes, you do." He points a finger in my face. "Ah, see, it doesn't feel too good to be interrupted."

What I need is information about this guy. It's easy to learn someone's weakness. "Give me your Taj." I swallow, then risk closing my eyes for a beat and take a needed deep breath.

"No, thanks. I have my all-time highest score in Jutelex3000." Brody sweeps a piece of his brown hair out of his face, which is probably soft as moss.

"This is not optional," I say.

"Oh, that's quite clear since you didn't use the word please, or ask my opinion." He glances at a stained-glass window and then to the oversized chair next to it. Casually, Brody plops down into it and crosses one leg over the other. "So, tell me about *you*. What's your story? You said this lovely castle is your home? How long have you lived here? Is it truly haunted like they say? Wait, are you the ghost? Would I know if I'm being haunted? Why did you choose this specific building to haunt?"

I pinch my nose. "Shut up."

"Can anyone shut down? Or shut left? Why does it have to be up?"

"Shut. All directions. Please."

He rolls his lips in tightly and leans back in the chair, crossing both arms. I stare at him. He stares at me. What in the Abyss have I gotten myself into? I'd prefer dealing with the young girl compared to this monster. Who does he think he is, acting so nonchalant even though my thorns could tear him to pieces in a heartbeat—if I wanted to?

Against all better judgment, I lean against the armrest and ask, "Are you not scared of me?"

"Shall I ask permission to speak first, Your Royal Highness?"

"Ugh! You're so—"

"Witty? Dashing? Creative? Loyal? Protective?"

Leaving him behind again, I stomp toward my room, listening to his soft footfalls patter after me.

As we pass the dim lanterns hanging from the stone walls, our shadows lurk close, his stalking mine the whole way.

"What does *that* door lead to?" Brody asks behind me, but I don't check which one he's referring to. Half of the rooms I never enter anymore. Once upon a time, or seven years ago, Feathi and I would pass the time by playing hide and seek. My favorite spot was in the third story hearth while Feathi's was underneath dusty furniture. I could usually find her location by the constant ticks of her favorite watches that line both her arms.

I speed my pace, longing for a second of peace and quiet.

"Oh, how about *that* door? What's in there? Okay, okay, it's a game. I'll guess, let me think." Brody pauses for a blissful moment. "On the other side, there's a waterslide that leads to a hole in the floor that ends in an underground waterpark! Oh, I need to see if I packed my swimsuit. Is there a hot tub? Would you care to join me for a midnight dip?"

I swivel on my heels again. "STOP TALKING!"

He glares, knowing exactly what he's doing, and says, "Oh, did you *not* expect Ryanne to be this charming when you kidnapped her? Maybe I can find a better-suited prisoner for you. I'll tell you what. Let's make it a homework assignment. You can make a list of your specific requirements and tomorrow, I'll go to a town and post a search. What should the poster say?" Brody frames both hands in the air like he's envisioning a flier. "One prisoner needed; must be pitiful." He shakes his head. "No, how about this…one prisoner, must be weak and fragile and submissive and love spiders. I think that'll work."

I'm pretty sure my jaw drops. How is he real? No one acts like this. Did he hit his head during a fall recently? For the first time, I wonder if a nonsensical character has come to life out of one of the books from our library. Or am I *that* lonely that my subconscious has conjured him for company?

I return his weighted stare again, joining a battle of who will break first. I never lose, but Mr. Brody Ricci seems to have the same philosophy. Maybe I need a different tactic. My skin of thorns doesn't bother him. Maybe he needs to witness some true magic. Yes, that's it. I'll scare him off with the impossible.

I smile for the first time since Brody arrived and call out, "Feathi! Yin! Can you come here, please?"

"Are those the names of your cats? I bet you have fifty felines crawling around this joint." He scans the hallway again, this time his attention landing on the grandfather clock.

"Why are you smiling?" I ask.

"Why do people like strawberries?"

"What?"

"Exactly." He points one finger at me and nods.

I stare at him in disbelief. Why do I want to know what else he has to say?

Feathi and Yin join us from around the corner.

"Oh! I assumed you were going to be cats." Brody bows to them both.

When my friends giggle and curtsy back, I roll my eyes. The man is impossible.

Yin extends her hand like a princess and says, "The color orange deserves furry textures though it tastes sour."

"I'd love to get more of your input on that later on…" One of Brody's eyebrows lifts to the arched ceiling. "First, do either of you dear ladies know why your friend here trapped a young girl?"

Thankfully, they don't respond or explain. How is he not fazed that they're not human? Has he been exposed to magic before? Maybe the outside world has changed recently.

"Where are you from, Mr. Ricci?" I ask.

"You can call me Your Majesty. Everyone else just calls me Brody, but hey, it doesn't seem like you're the average chick, so—"

"Answer my question."

He snatches a glance at the clock again. Finally, it dawns on me—the reasoning for his insane personality. This whole time he's trying to distract me, so Ryanne has time to run home. He's been wasting my time and my energy.

I curse under my breath and stomp toward my room. "Ladies, show Mr. Ricci the exit."

Yin curtsies to Brody again and says, "Blue only makes pitter-patter sounds and whispers. It simply doesn't know how to yell, and I surely won't be the one to teach it."

"I've thought the same." He kisses the back of Yin's hand.

As she spins and dances away, I swear under my breath. Yin's symptoms are only getting worse. For the last few months, she hasn't been able to form intelligible sentences. Her humanity is fading with each passing night. Her steady decline is another reason I need to find a way to destroy my thorns, and all before the magical pen runs out of ink. If I don't, Feathi and Nax may also lose their ability to function until they're nothing more than lifeless sheets of paper. And I have no idea why they aren't affected on the same timeline.

"This way, Mr. Ricci," Feathi says. "I'll be right back, Mora."

"Mora," Brody repeats softly.

I stop in place. It's the first time I hear it from his lips, and it doesn't affect me at all. It doesn't make me want to turn around or ask him if he's met someone else with my name on his travels.

On the path to my tower, I pass dozens of doors, the kitchen, the courtyard with my rose garden, the ballroom, the spare bedrooms.

"How much is your place worth? There's a shark realtor where I'm from."

My body zings with confusing energy when I hear his voice again. Why hasn't he left? I can't be distracted. Not now, not ever. If he refuses to leave, then I may as well learn if he saw any roses on his trip here.

"Do any towns nearby that you know of have roses?" I ask.

"Maybe, maybe not." He winks, then chuckles. "Listen, we will have plenty of time to swap stories in the morning because I'm not going anywhere until I can warn all the people nearby that you plan to eat their children."

I groan and drop my head.

"Give me a place to sleep. During our lovely sleepover, I'll get a better vibe of your evil ways and how dangerous you truly are."

"If you tell me where to find roses, I may let you spend the night," I say over my shoulder. "Only because it's late and cold and I'm not heartless like you think I am."

"I haven't seen any roses."

Damn. I study him. I believe him, even though I don't want to. Because this man is my enemy if he has any intention of turning me in. No one else can know I exist. If villagers in the valley learned a witch with magic lives nearby, I don't think the Book would have much more to write about in my short lifespan.

Brody leans against the wall. "You're cute when you don't know what to do next."

"Excuse me? I was just going to be nice and let you sleep here." I run my tongue along my upper teeth, hating myself for getting stuck in this position. "Fine! Sleep here. I want you gone first thing after sunrise, and don't go snooping where you don't belong."

"Why? What lurks in the secret corners of this place?" he asks.

"Man-eating lizards."

"Cool!"

"Cool? Your response to an immediate death is cool?" I seriously don't know what to say to him, but words tumble out. "Mr. Ricci, you act like you're hopping on clouds while eating only sugar while holding a thousand kittens."

"In my twenty-nine and a half years I've yet to hold even ten kittens, but that would make a great background image on my Taj."

"Whatever. Stay close to me so I can keep my eyes on you. That's my only rule."

"Don't you worry. Now that I've met you and experienced the sweet honey coating your every word, I'm completely entranced and will never want to leave your side."

At the double doors to my chambers, I turn to address Brody, but he reaches around my side and turns the knob to the door like he owns the place. He waltzes in ahead of me as if he's been living here his whole life. I hate him. I hate my voluntary prisoner.

CHAPTER 5

Brody

For the tenth time, I pretend not to notice Mora's features. Short, uneven, wavy brown bangs blend into the hair that sweeps to the tip of her shoulders, and thick, dark eyebrows that match her locks. The frown claiming her face creates tiny wrinkles in her chin. As beautiful as she is, it's the mansion I'm captivated by.

This is the most fascinating building I've ever laid eyes on. Mora's bedroom, though a little drab, matches the gothic pattern. The decor looks as if an antique furniture store vomited around the room. I'd have to try each unique chair to determine which has the best view of Mam's house in the valley. The only chair not covered in a layer of dust sits in the corner, with a well-worn indent of someone precisely Mora's size. Of all the sitting options, why would she trap herself in the shadows?

A massive four-poster bed sits against the wall. I examine it, marveling at the intricately carved details. My hands itch to use my tools to blend the dents in the wood. A fabric curtain hangs from it, and when I take a closer look, the thin sheet appears to be made of thousands of origami shapes, folded and connected at the corners. There's no chance someone made a tapestry like that by hand—especially one made of paper.

"There's no way that's real," I whisper.

"What?" Mora turns.

"Nothing."

Snow throws itself at the multiple windows as if meaning to crack the glass. While scanning the torn wallpaper, sagging drapes, and broken chandelier, I can't believe anyone lives here. My whole life has been spent in the town of Villeneuve, at the bottom of the hill, and no one has ever witnessed a person coming or going from this house. How long has Mora been living here? If she made the bed curtain, then judging by its size and complexity, it must have been years. Where does she get her paper, or food for that matter? Does she have the ability to magic food into existence with the flick of her wrist? Not to mention her friends are made of paper themselves. I should be more freaked out right now. Instead, I'm only curious. I walk to the bed and sit on the edge. I refuse to leave without knowing she isn't a threat to my town. Since I have two weeks to board the boat, I may as well help if I can. It's only a couple of days delay, then my future calls to me from abroad.

"Well, do you want to sleep on the left or right side, Boo?"

She huffs and refuses to respond, so I take the opportunity to examine her once more—her baggy pants don't clearly show thorns underneath the fabric, but some poke through. There's no way to tell how many hide under her oversized hoodie. Was she born with them? If not, what happened? Do they hurt her?

"You're sleeping on the floor," Mora says. "I'm a light sleeper. If you try anything, I have ways to hurt you."

"Excellent, I'm assuming you have a giant, fluffy dog I can spoon with?"

Mora snorts and shakes her head.

Probably younger than me by a few years, she manages to exude the maturity and hardness of someone ten years her senior. What happened to give her such sharp edges? Underneath her beastly glare, lies layers of *something* that I can't quite put my finger on.

Like all things in life, this is a challenge I can overcome, an adventure to journey on. If things get a little too volcanic for my liking, there are dozens of escape options, judging by the amount of windows. But intuition tells me I'll enjoy a few days here. Since the woman agreed to let Ryanne go, she hasn't acted cruel. As long as I don't suspect she will endanger anyone else, this will just be another adventure added to my future collection.

"I *am* quite tired," I fake a yawn and curl onto the floor like a helpless baby. "Hopefully you don't mind my snoring. Oh, and can you fetch me a drink? Unless you're not *capable* of being nice."

"Of course, I'm *capable*," her voice comes out with a fake sweetness. "But I'm not getting you coffee or tea or lemonade." Strolling to the door, she steps lightly on the hardwood, not allowing one floorboard to squeak. Yup, she's been living here long enough to memorize where to step.

Her roommate walks in with an eerie expression that matches the face of a doll. I have to admit that the one with jet-black hair is both endearing and creepy at the same time.

"Yin, don't let him out of your sight," Mora says to her roommate in a much more patient voice than how she speaks to me. "I'll go get some tea, for myself, just me."

Yin moves out of the shadows. "Yellow needs no introduction and has a tendency to carry a scent of youth."

"You don't say…" I glance up to Mora, but the doorway is already empty. Cold emptiness lingers where she used to stand for some reason.

Yin starts dancing around the room in big circles humming softly. Her energy is bursting with whimsical dreams, the very opposite of Ms. Grumps. The origami woman resembles a puppet-like ballerina. I sigh, amused by Yin's playful grace. While she's distracted, I rustle through some journals spread atop the bedspread to try and learn about Mora and her intriguing situation. How did she get thorns all over her body? Page after page is scrawled over in a language I'm not familiar with. Is Mora not originally from here? What's her story? Why does she act so guarded? Who hurt her?

"The palest wheat of them all," Yin whispers in my ear and I jump, "turns barbecue into mascots." Her near-black eyes glow with specs of glitter.

I have to admit it would be pretty spectacular if Mora folded her roommates to life. She must be a creator like me, but a different type of artist who sees shapes in harsh lines and corners instead of furniture pieces made of arches and curves. Then again, these paper people might also be prisoners of the shadows of this fortress since no one has spread gossip or rumors about their existence. I wonder if Yin knows the building's layout. If she does, that's one way I can learn more about Mora and her home.

I take Yin's hands in mine. "Can you show me why Mora took that girl?"

She nods excitedly and grips my fingers harder.

"Great! Lead the way."

Yin drops to the ground and crawls under the bed. I palm my head, feeling stupid that I thought someone who talks in riddles might understand what I'm requesting, but then a loud thunk sound below gives me hope.

Yin's feet slither away from view and her humming echoes like she's in a tunnel.

I drop to my knees as well. As I peek under the bed, it's clear Yin has indeed led me to some hidden entrance. I scoot toward it, careful not to smack my head against the underside of the bed as I wiggle like a worm and fit my shoulders through the small opening.

After a few moments of facing the terrifying possibility that I might die from being wedged in this crevice, the area opens to a wide tunnel, leading down into the earth. In front of me, Yin stands and brushes the dust out of her hair. It should be pitch black but there's a faint glow of light sparkling from the dirt walls that follows her movements.

I take in the possibilities hidden within this tunnel. How many secrets could be buried behind these stones? Maybe there is a journal of Mora's plans stowed beneath my feet. For some reason, I highly doubt that. What other treasures are desperate to be discovered here?

Barely able to see Yin in the light from the inexplicable little glimmers flickering ahead, I rely on her humming voice. Her song which started sweet and innocent quickly switches to a minor key. The number of spiders double with each step and my heart rate quickens. Maybe I underestimated Yin. She could be leading me to my grave. How poetic would that be?

I run my hand along the cold wall, and ask, "Um, Yin, how much farther until we reach the exit?"

She only hums in response, seesawing from high to low pitch, like a schoolgirl on drugs. The tunnel forks off, then splits again. And again. And again. Whenever I glance behind me, only pitch darkness remains. My heart rate triples. Shit, this was a bad idea. Moving forward is probably better than going back. I may be trapped in an underground labyrinth for the remainder of my days. My only chance for survival is to rely on the non-human frolicking ahead. At this point, we've been underground so long that my chest burns from the cold.

A pebble skitters behind me. I stop. Hold my breath. Someone is trailing us. The sound of their breathing reminds me of what it felt like playing hide and seek as a child when any movement or sound could give away my spot. I inhale through my nose deeply and immediately recognize the scent. Cinnamon. It's only my lovely captor.

Mora is testing me, but I'm not going anywhere until I find some answers. If she wants to learn about me too, what I'll do, and where I'll go, then I'll put on a show for her.

"Hey, Yin?" I try to ignore the cryptic vibe cycling through this tunnel. "Did you know that everyone in the nearest town has a bet about when the witch will show her face?"

Mora's soft gasp behind me confirms my guess. She doesn't want anyone to know about her.

"I had bet a hundred bucks that she's half vampire, half gorilla." My voice echoes in the tunnel and Yin giggles far ahead somewhere, reminding me of a scene from a badly rated horror film. "Well, I guess I lost that bet, eh? Maybe during the full moon the witch's head blows up like a balloon and—"

I run straight into a shoulder.

"How did you know I'm a witch?" Mora says quietly. The faint glow shows her devious lips curling in a breathtaking, crooked kind of way.

"I didn't until you just confirmed it."

She huffs, making me eager to annoy her further. "Why are you in *my* tunnel?" she asks.

"I'm starting an underground circus…duh." I zig-zag around her.

The side of one of her fingers brushes against mine. I wait for a thorn to draw blood, but no painful scrape comes. I glance down at her skin touching mine. My attention snags on one of the deadly thorns protruding from her wrist. So monstrously epic. If I had any brains at all I wouldn't be completely entranced by her.

Her eyes are like daggers raking over my form. "You're supposed to be waiting for me in my room."

"As many times as I've wished for a woman to command those words, I somehow chose not to hear your demand."

She pauses and moves closer, making that cinnamon scent mix my brain to mush. "Why aren't you scared of me?"

Her eyes tell stories of heartache and regret. Of nightmares and betrayal. No one with that much passion hidden beneath the surface can scare me. Because Mora cares. It's so obvious by the way her tone changes when speaking to her friends. She softens with them. The change is slight, but it's there all the same.

"Why do you think I'd be scared of you?" I rub a finger over the outer curve of her thorn. "Because you have some *character*?" I shake my head. "These only make you more—"

A sudden whimpering snatches both of our attention.

"What was that?"

"Yin?" Mora's voice escalates.

When my new bestie doesn't answer, I jog into the malicious darkness though my eyes have started to adjust to the darkness. Mora's footsteps fall lightly behind me. Left foot. Right foot.

"Yin?" Mora calls out. "Where are you?"

The baby wolf pup from the forest stares at me, as he sits contentedly next to Yin.

"It looks like you have a new pet," I say, but Yin hands him over to me. "No, way. I don't do babies." I shake my head. I won't allow anyone or anything to tie me down again. I'll never let someone be reliant on me or vice versa.

"Interesting." Mora cocks her head to the side. "Let me guess, you think the pup is weak?"

My body goes rigid. "What? He's perfect. So take good care of him." I want to push the wolf into her arms, but am unsure if her thorns would hurt him.

"Monsters need to be strong enough to fend for themselves." She shoves him back to me.

"He's only a baby. It won't be too hard to give him some food." I push him into her arms.

"Caring for others isn't what I do." She looks tenderly at the animal.

"Why? Goddess, are we mere mortals so beneath you that we don't deserve care or safety?"

"Don't you dare say that." Her finger is a dagger in my face, but this time she grabs the pup back voluntarily. "I cared! I *never* wanted to hurt her. I *never* valued my life more than hers!"

This time I'm genuinely confused. "Hers? Whose life? The pup is a boy."

Mora's jaw drops and she freezes for a moment. "Never

mind. It doesn't matter. I won't tolerate you invading my privacy by roaming around my property." Her voice rises. "In fact, I change my mind. I'll only let you sleep here tonight under one condition."

"And what would that be? A human sacrifice under a blue moon?"

She raises her chin high. "You'll be collecting roses for me. It's the only way I can get rid of these," she says harshly, lifting her hands full of thorns.

"I need more information."

"Well, you don't get the full story. Feathi and Yin only captured the girl to bribe her into collecting roses for us. Believe me or not, that's up to you, but it's late and I'm tired and you're annoying. So, we're going to bed now and you're helping me with getting roses. The decision has been made. There's a garden in Villeneuve, a town close to here. You may not have heard of it, but you'll go first thing in the morning."

My body goes numb. She can't possibly know that the rose garden she's referring to is in my hometown, or that it's the one place that haunts me. I won't go back there. Not ever. No witch can force me. The tunnel walls around me turn into a cage, closing in to make our space narrower.

"How about I find you some pinecones instead?" I whisper, steadying myself on the stone wall with one hand.

"No, only magical red roses gifted by the forest nymphs will work. The task won't be hard for someone like you."

"Someone like me."

Only an all-knowing Goddess could understand why someone like me deserves to be tortured this way. Someone like me. A father who let his only child be taken away. All I can concentrate on is the one image that has played on repeat in my mind for the last five years.

My girlfriend and I stand in the rose garden in the center of Villeneuve, just before sunrise. Dom's Taj97 beeps continuously with messages. On her back, she carries a bag full of diapers, formula, pacifiers, and our daughter's favorite stuffed animal. I stare at Catterina, asleep in Dom's arms.

"Please, Dom. I can't wait six months to see Cat again."

My ex whips her head in all directions, checking the street alleys, then whispers, "We don't have a choice. Mom will take her."

"Then I'm coming with you. I can't sleep without you both by my side."

"Stop, we don't have time for this again. It's safer this way, Brody, and you know it." Dom is so distracted that she sounds like a robot as she scans the streets. "We already agreed. Please don't make this harder than it is. Just tell Mom we'll be back on Monday."

I hate everything about this plan. "You promise you'll send me a message once you arrive?"

Dom nods, but her eyes stay wild, unfocused. "And in a few months, we'll meet up and you'll see her again."

I can't imagine not seeing my daughter for that long. I'll miss her first steps, but this is the only way. Dom's mother, Elizabeth, needs a distraction, and if I want to keep Catterina safe, the best bet at success is to stay behind to continue our lie.

I glance down at my sleeping child, snuggled in Dom's arms. Her soft brown skin starts to glow in the rising sunrays. "Okay, okay. I hate this. Just let me hold her once more."

"Hurry up, it's time to go," a Hoverman says to our right. He ushers them onto his hoverboard, ready to take flight out of the city.

"Wait, let me hold her once more," I beg.

"We'll see you soon." Dom kisses my cheek and steps onto the board, taking my entire world with her. As I watch them fly

away, my heart topples over the edge and falls to my feet, shattering into a million pieces.

That was the last time I saw my daughter. Somewhere, she's six years old, without her father by her side. My throat constricts tightly.

At least I'll have a warm place to sleep tonight. It'll be exciting to see if origami people or a witch covered in thorns will murder me in my sleep under the roof of a possibly haunted mansion.

Mora doesn't need to know that I can't go to that garden; I can't help her. For now, I just need a place to sleep.

I stare at the wolf pup asleep in Mora's arms and remember his injured mother in the forest. "Give him to me. No one should be taken from their parent."

"No, he's mine now." Mora tries to disguise the tenderness in her voice, though it doesn't quite meet the mark.

"Where will he sleep? On the floor, like your guests?"

Mora scoffs. "Of course not. He'll sleep with me."

"You absolutely adore him, don't you? You love him with all your heart. Okay, I get it, you're a huge softie who refuses to smile. And for that fact only, maybe I'll help you find roses tomorrow. Maybe. You'd have to promise never to capture another kid again." I march past Mora back toward her magnificent home. "And I get the good fuckin' side of the bed."

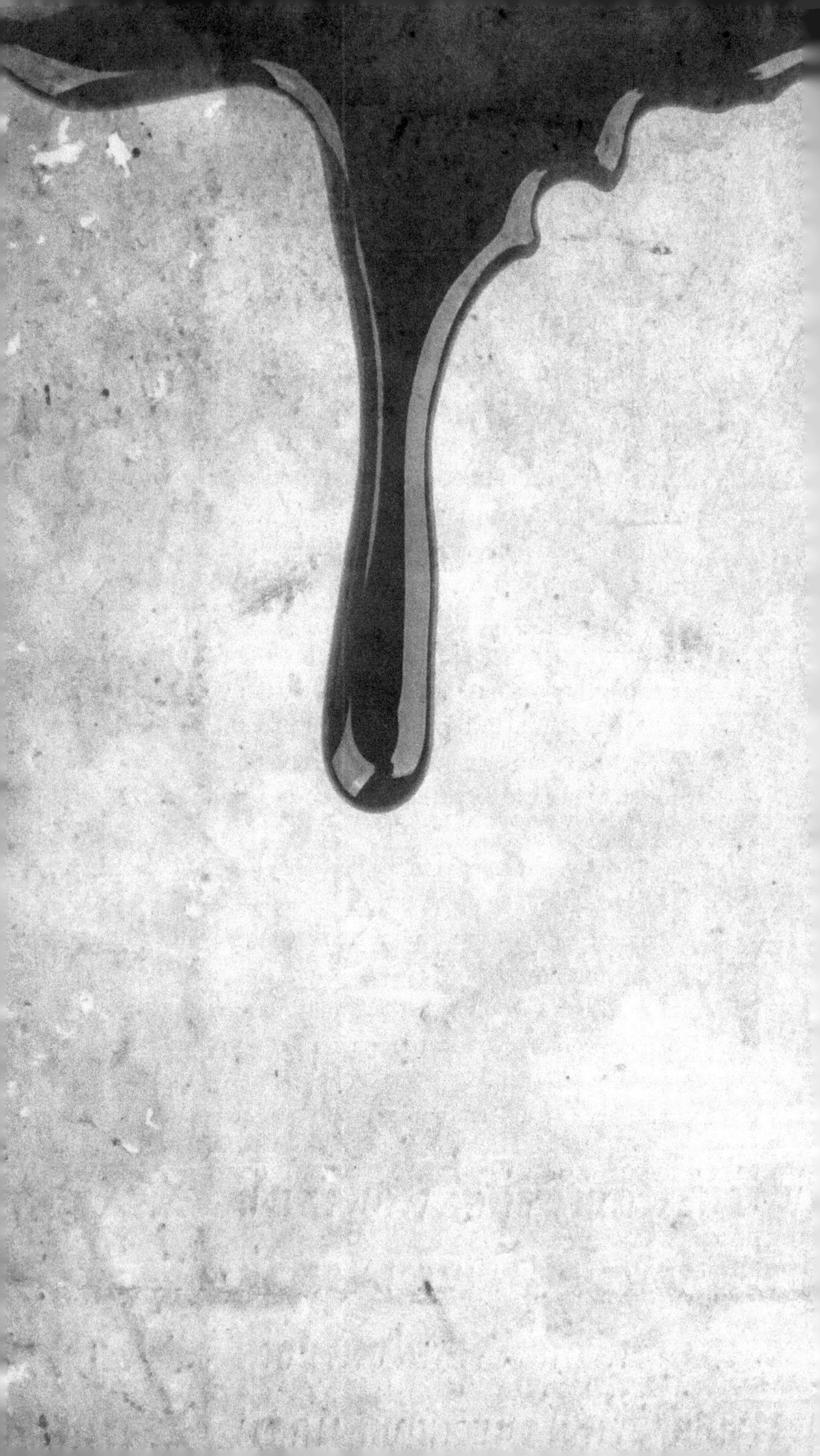

Current excerpt from
The Book

In sleep, Mora dreams of snowflakes in slow motion—nothing of interest—which gives me more time to write about what matters. I do not like this Brody character, for he looks at our heroine with too much curiosity—too much intensity—just too much.

No man should be allowed to waltz into my territory and distract my Mora with the ridiculous nonsense he spews. It's a good thing he isn't at all attractive in the least. Only the finest leather-bound books, smooth to the touch, that radiate the scent of scholarly libraries hold worthy males for heroines. Not in a thousand lifetimes, could this Brody fellow rival knights or princes in fairytales. His anatomical shape is not only too masculine, but his quick wit draws Mora's attention away from me too much.

Of course, my Mora has every trait to grab his focus, but Brody studies her like an artist observing a scene. She needs to send him away. If he finds roses to help her break the spell, then I have no more purpose here and that just won't do now, will it?

CHAPTER 6

Mora

The morning sun kisses my cheeks. I rouse from sleep but keep my eyes closed. Birds chirp outside the windows and the usual creaking of the loose shutter is a familiar comfort—like a cozy blanket. I reach around for my blanket, but something isn't right. Instead of fleece, my fingertips graze against smooth wood. Wait, where am I? My eyes snap open. For some reason, I'm on the damned floor. All of last night's events come rushing back like a whirlwind. No, no, no. That was all supposed to be a dream.

Before facing my endless problems, I complete my morning ritual. Originally, I'd use my enchanted mirror, but ever since I lost it, I've resorted to the next best thing.

Any reflective surface in this fortress works, albeit as a weaker version. The stained-glass window, depicting a knight chopping down a tree, will do the trick.

I whisper the command, "Show me my sister."

The knightly image in the glass disappears and a whirl of fog shifts to a scene of a cemetery covered in snow. Headstones arch in the same shape as Lessie's eyebrow used to curve when she was nervous. Six feet below, my little sister lies waiting for me to join her in the afterlife. But I'm not ready to leave. Not yet. I have a little time to free my roommates from this curse. Once they're safe, I don't care what happens to me.

My other sister, Kavianne, still lives, with a resilience harder than the iron gates caging the spirits inside that graveyard. She is to blame for my seven years of agony but I can't be angry at her. There's the option to get revenge on my sister for doing this to us, but it's never been in my heart to do so.

"Well, good morning, sleepy head." A man's voice.

The scene in the window quickly disappears. I glance from my spot on the floor and meet Brody's eyes that are peeking over the side of my bed. *My* bed. Damn him and his rotten smile. The sun shines around his head, setting his bedhead aglow like a halo.

"You were supposed to be a nightmare," I groan.

"Well, you did have a scary dream or two, which is why Heathcliff left me and cuddled with you all night. You are one lucky witch."

Brody already named the precious pup. The nerve. That was supposed to be my job. At least he picked a good name; not that I'd ever admit it. I twist, cracking my back in the process, and lay eyes on the adorable pup behind me.

"Seriously? Who do you think you are?" I launch a fluffy pillow at him. "What kind of crazy—"

"Prince?" Brody smiles.

"No! What kind of infuriating man knocks a woman off her own bed in the middle of the night? And names her puppy?!"

I chuck another pillow as hard as I can at his shoulder, but a thorn on my wrist catches the fluff, tears open the seam and sends feathers flying. All Brody does is laugh and blow a feather off his nose.

A loose strand of his long dark hair falls in front of his eyes. If I could hold scissors, I'd chop it off in a heartbeat.

Grunting, I scoop up the pup. "Come on, Heathcliff, you must be starving."

"Oh, thanks for the invite to breakfast." Brody bounces out of bed with endless energy. "I'll take some bacon and scrambled eggs and tea."

Barely out my door, I swivel on my heels and almost run straight into his chest. Again. The poor puppy is my only defense against this man.

"You can have whatever you make," I say, "since I don't cook."

"Challenge accepted."

He grins, making me want to slide a thorn right across his neck. Well, not truly. I'd never harm anyone intentionally, but Brody doesn't need to know that.

With him trailing my every move, we walk through the cold hallways to the upstairs kitchen. It's not at all entertaining how enthralled he seems with every detail we pass, from the curves of the doorframes to the craftsmanship of each clock.

Once we enter the kitchen, he stares at me from the other side of the counter. I stare at him. One of his brows rises in question. I take a bite of a banana and he chuckles.

"Why are you still here?" I ask.

"Because you're so pleasant," he answers in a heartbeat.

"You need to leave or I'll…I'll—" I cut myself off, unsure what to say. When he laughs I ask, "What's so funny?"

"Nothing. You're absolutely ferocious," he says with amusement in his voice. "The most violent person I've met, so go ahead and finish your threat."

I hear the tick-tock of Feathi's watches. She and Yin walk around the corner, supporting a limping Nax between them. He towers a foot taller than us. Still the same shape and size as he was as a human, Nax is just as heavy and substantial despite being made of paper. I haven't seen my third roommate much recently. When I do, it feels like he's hiding a secret from me.

The three glance between Brody and me, then wait in silence for a few beats too long. A soft pink flushes Feathi's cheeks.

"Sorry, we'll come back later," she says and starts to turn around, but I put up my hand.

"Don't think about leaving me here with this guy."

"This guy?" Brody smirks. "Did you hear that, ladies? I'm *THIS* guy as if *I'm* the one who stole a child."

Brody saunters over to my roommates. He grabs a bunch of the muffins that I had baked yesterday. With a bow to both ladies, he hands over the treats, then tugs out a chair for Nax. Brody sits in a different chair, backward, and addresses my friends like he's known them since childhood.

"What are we gonna do about her, huh?" he asks with absolutely no charm lacing his voice.

Yin giggles and Feathi's face flushes darker. Even Nax seems disturbingly entranced.

"Um, Mora, I need your advice on a small project." Nax leans closer. "Can we talk in private?"

"Later."

"But there might not be much time," Nax says quietly.

Brody rests his chin on the top of the chair-back. "See, we sweat and slave for years to raise her right, and *this* is the thanks we get? You'd think after all this work, she'd show some decent humble appreciation and help when we ask."

Yin nods and adds, "Green never forgets a joke but holds onto them for safekeeping in each pocket."

"Exactly!" Brody smacks the chair with both hands. "That's what I've been saying all along. Mora needs to learn a thing or two."

"Um, excuse me. I'm right here." When Heathcliff whines, I give him a bowl of water. "What right do you think you have to waltz in here and take over?"

"Take over what, Mora? Last time I checked friendship wasn't about dominance and control." Brody pauses and looks at Feathi. "Am I right?"

Feathi clears her throat and doesn't meet my eyes. For the first time, I question what she's thinking. Terrified to ask for clarification, I turn my back and begin rattling pots and pans together. Half expecting Feathi's soft hand on my shoulder, I move slowly, so I don't accidentally poke her, but no moment of comfort comes. She has always been there to reassure me in the past. What changed?

Brody Ricci.

How dare he disrupt my home and shove a wedge between me and the people I love. A part of me desperately wants to grab the steak knife in front of me and stab it between his ribs. But I'm not a killer—not intentionally.

I unclench my fists and take a deep breath, then turn around to face Brody. "You need to leave."

"What about breakfast?"

"Get out of my home." I charge forward, my heart racing. "Go. I never should've let you sleep here."

"But—" For the first time, he falters, raising both hands in surrender. "But you need me to get the roses."

"No, I don't," I hiss out, hoping to sound convincing. "You're ruining everything!"

Heathcliff yelps and prances out of the kitchen into the hallway.

"Great, you've scared the poor little guy," Brody says, shooting me a dirty glare.

Brody chases after him. Quickly, I share a desperate glance with each of my friends. Nax simply shrugs. Feathi gestures for me to go after Brody and Yin stares at the wall, mumbling to herself. Damn it. Her humanity is disappearing with each passing hour. This isn't the time to mess things up. I'd walk on a thousand swords to free my friends from the curse. Or let a flock of ravens poke me to death. Or even beg for help.

"Wait!" I shout down the hall as I run after him and the pup.

Even with the morning light streaming through the windows, I can't see him in front of me.

"Brody! Slow down!" I'm out of breath as I reach the grand stairway, the one that leads to the circular ballroom.

At the bottom of the marble staircase, Brody stands like a statue with Heathcliff at his feet, his gaze on the dozens of chandeliers drooping from the dome ceiling like tragic spiderwebs. I tip-toe to his side, quiet as a grave.

"I know you don't want me to leave," he says. "I forgive you."

"I didn't ask you to."

Brody tilts his head to the side. "Well then, you're welcome."

My jaw drops, completely stupefied by this man's boldness.

"Take a moment and just look at this room! It's

absolutely magnificent." His voice is sprinkled with awe. "Think of the carpenter's passion who built this. And all the kings and queens and spies that have danced here over the centuries. I bet someone was poisoned right over there." He points wildly. "And a couple probably Committed to each other under that fresco."

His smile is plastered like a giddy kid on Saint Ulsa morning. Except this mess of a man doesn't need a gift to be happy; somehow he finds joy in the ordinary. It must be some sort of trick.

He rushes to the rounded wall and pokes at the stones. "I bet there's another secret entrance close by! Maybe to the catacombs."

"Are you purposefully trying to distract me?"

As Brody moves, his backpack snags on something and unzips. One of the tools he was holding last night clatters to the ground. I crouch to lift it but Heathcliff lunges first, grabbing the sharp blade in his mouth. I gasp and freeze. What if he swallows it? Fear burns my skin, spreading all the way up my spine. No one else can get hurt under my watch.

"Drop it," I whisper, too scared to spook the sweet pup.

His puffy tail wags wildly.

I slowly approach the babe, and whisper for help, "Brody, for Goddess sake, pay attention."

Either he hears a warning in the pitch of my voice or the ballroom has become too boring, but he thankfully turns. Without a second's hesitation, Brody marches to Heathcliff with confidence, and the wolf immediately drops the tool.

Heathcliff sits at Brody's ankles and puts a paw on his boot. "Give it time, I can teach you how to train him."

I pause and look up at his dark eyes. Does that mean he'll help me with the roses? If that's the case, then he needs to see all of what he's getting himself into, the full definition of what this curse has done, before he agrees. I wouldn't ever truly force someone to help me. If he's staying he needs to be informed.

"I need your tool," I say while holding out my hand.

One of his eyebrows rises. "Which one? My long one or this one?"

Rolling my eyes, I grab this chisel-blade thing. This is one device I haven't tried yet. Maybe this specific weapon is the key. I hold my forearm out, with a thorn at a perfect angle for cutting. Before he can stop me, I slice the sharp blade across the tip of a thorn. A hiss of pain shocks me but I hack at my body harder.

"What are you doing?"

I block out Brody's voice. The deeper I cut, the worse it hurts. Once I hit the thick base of the thorn, blood starts to flow and my knees turn wobbly.

"Mora! Stop!"

I push harder. The thorns must come off. All of them. There's no way to break the curse unless I destroy each and every one of them. Pain. So much pain. A hideous scream echoes through the ballroom, but I can't stop now. The sun rays pouring through the window must be playing tricks on me because they dance unnaturally.

"Mora! Stop!" Rough hands pull me away and I drop to my knees.

My head swims. My heart pounds. My body sways.

"Sssh, breathe," a deep voice says from somewhere far off. "Take a deep breath."

Inhale. Exhale. Inhale. Exhale. My muscles loosen after minutes or hours, I don't know. I open my eyes, unsure when I had closed them. My cheek rests against a sturdy chest and I can feel a strong grip holding my hand with the chisel-knife behind my back.

My tears stream down and wet his shirt, but I can't let him see me cry.

Brody looks down at me with a look in his eyes I'd rather not decipher. If it's pity then I don't know what I'll do.

"Explain." He pushes a pressure point on my wrist, making me drop the tool. It clatters to the marble floor. "Why in the Abyss did you do that?"

I stay silent.

"Tell me. Now." His voice sounds like a growl. "Why would you hurt yourself like that?"

"To break the curse over me and my friends, I need to get rid of all my thorns before the magical pen runs out of ink."

"The thorns are a curse?"

"Yes." I nod, in disbelief that I'm telling him anything at all.

"And there's a magical pen? Will you show me?"

"No."

He nods as if this makes perfect sense. "Let me guess, the reason you need me to help find roses has to do with this pen?"

I focus on Heathcliff, who is running around the ballroom. If I can't break this curse soon and my friends turn into meaningless paper, then I've failed. My friends don't deserve this fate. They've suffered by my side long enough. They weren't the ones who made the mistake. Feathi, Nax, and Yin were all innocent bystanders the day Lessie died. Feathi and Nax could be Committed at this point, even expecting a child. And if this never happened to Yin in the first place, she'd be starring on stage somewhere, dancing through one song after another. I envision how she used to be so particular about the outfits she chose for her performances but will now resort to dancing in a bathrobe around Chambrea.

Brody takes off his shirt and presses the fabric to my wound. There's no need to memorize every curve of his chest or imagine running my finger along the lines of his stomach, so I don't.

"Thank you," I whisper.

"Oh, there's a heart within your raging beast?" I can hear the smile in his words without looking. "Maybe I'll collect roses for you, if—"

Across the ballroom, Heathcliff starts barking.

"What's he doing?" I ask.

"I don't know, maybe he smells a rat or something."

The pup starts scratching at the base of the wall and sniffing furiously. Then a howl comes from outside. Heathcliff squeezes through a hole in the wall I hadn't seen. The pup is too small to survive in the wild. I jump away from Brody and dash toward the opening. A draft comes in from a hole by my slippers. Dropping to my knees, I can only see bright light. The cruel sun is blinding me as it bounces off the snow. When the glare shifts, it's obvious that Heathcliff is snarling up at something tall.

"Shit!"

"What is it?" Brody drops to my side. "What do you see? Is he okay?"

"Push me through!" I yell.

"But your cut isn't cleaned. The wound could get infected."

"Damn it, Brody, push me through the hole!"

I begin to crawl, and solid hands find my upper thighs and shove me through the rest of the way. He's too big to follow, so I'm on my own.

Outside, loud snaps and crunches rumble through the trees, like a monster stomping closer. I'm tempted to summon my magic, but that's pointless since I don't have any orbs.

A giant shadow crosses the snow, hovering like a queen of death. I look up. My heart rate triples. Gooseflesh rises on my skin and a shiver climbs my spine.

"Mora? What do you see? What is it?" Clanking sounds come from where Brody crouches. Maybe he's trying to dig himself out with that tiny tool. "What's out there?"

I can't answer him. Because the thing threatening to shred us apart is the worst possible villain.

CHAPTER 7

Mora

"What's out there!?" Brody booms again.

I can't breathe, let alone answer. Because there's a monstrous, moving plant towering above us. I shield little Heathcliff as he continues to snarl. Thick brambles, with sharp curled thorns, rise from the forest floor. The vines are alive.

Like octopus tentacles, more appendages unfurl to their full length. One almost reaches the top of a pine tree. Vines whip with such ferocity that I can't react fast enough. One slams into the snow, only a couple of feet to our right, smashing through the ground. The snow around us shifts and falls through the new hole in the ground. I'm shoved off balance and brace myself against a tree. In a trance, I simply stare at the massive hole. Wild, foresty limbs flail with the intensity of a broken carnival ride. I can nearly taste the plant's rage oozing from the liquid that drips from its fang-like thorns.

"Run!" Brody yells in a hazy, far-off voice.

My chest thumps out of control. Another monumental crash knocks me off my feet. Cold wet snow stings my palms.

The snow around me rises and falls like a wave. Nothing makes sense.

A bark.

"MORA!" someone yells.

I roll sideways, glad that Heathcliff follows. I hide between two trees. Out of breath.

The brutal vines pause as if searching for me. What should I do? Can the hideous thing see us? Can it hear? Can it track my footsteps in the snow? I hold my breath and pull Heathcliff tighter. His heartbeat is just as erratic as my own, but at least he has stopped barking.

"Mora!" Brody screams from inside.

The vine unscrews itself from its tangled knot and turns toward him. More tendrils unwrap from a nearby tree and move away from me toward my house. No! I must protect my friends.

My skin burns as I roll a snowball between my palms. "Hey, you bitch!" I hurl the snowball at the mutant plant. "Over here!"

It turns and stalks toward us, in a swaying, gliding movement. The closer it gets, the more obvious its colossal size becomes. I must be dreaming. The thinnest part of its tip is the size of my waist. That would mean its strong base must be six feet around.

I back up, one step at a time, crunching the snow in

soaked slippers. I swear the vine hisses at me. It creeps closer. Closer.

Only one thing left to do. I turn and run. With each step, I sink. My legs try to push through the freezing snow but fail. A long tentacle swings and rams into a nearby log. It explodes to pieces. Wood flies. Heathcliff slips from my arm and hops through the snow beside me.

We dart to the side. Zig-zag between trees. I crawl further from the monster, hoping it can't smell my sweat. The vine is so large that it has to stutter to a stop when it realizes I changed directions. It still swivels to follow me with a mind of its own. There's no way we can outrun it because the branches stretch too far.

"Mora!" Brody yells.

"Stay back!" I scream at him.

How can I destroy it? A series of potions flip through my mind. Which formula might stop it? Pine nuts and hemp oil with a raven's tear? No. Chestnut dust and soymilk mixed with a feather? I don't have time.

"Mora!"

Something smells weird. I sniff. Smoke. I turn around. I peek over a bush and squint into the red and black chaos. Fire. It's gobbling up the plant.

The inflamed tentacles batter and bang against trees as if blinded and poisoned. An ear-splitting screech fills the forest. The plant is trying to fight back but it shrivels too quickly from the heat. Then the entire monster falls to the snow with a resounding thud.

I focus on my visible breath in the air. Is it over?

Heathcliff curls against my purple fingers. Heavy snow begins to fall. It may take a few minutes, but the remaining flames will soon simmer.

"Mora? Where are you?" Brody tromps through the forest. He slows as he approaches the remains of the creature, kicks it, and then casually jumps over it like he's on a hike.

Heathcliff abandons me and frolics to Brody, leaving little paw prints in the snow. Meanwhile, I duck lower and don't move a muscle. I hide, paralyzed in shock.

"She saved you, didn't she? She must not be so terrible after all." Brody talks to my pup and his boots crunch further away. "Where'd she go, boy?"

I drop my head in my hands. What was that creature? How have I never encountered it before? How long has it been living out here? Does it move to different parts of the forest? Are there others? Can the limbs regenerate? Is it magical or is someone controlling it? Most importantly, what did the monstrous plant want?

Shivering and ready to warm up by the fireplace, I stagger to my feet. Since the immediate danger is gone, I zero in on the unlucky fact that I have no coat, no real shoes, no gloves, no hat and can't feel my fingers or toes. The details of the neighboring pines prove that I ran farther than I originally thought. Before returning, I need to know more about this plant.

The nasty wind seems to be on a quest for revenge because it slaps against my cheeks. I struggle through the worsening storm but keep going. One step at a time. I must know if this vine will be an ongoing threat. How can I keep my friends safe if it's intent on demolishing our sanctuary?

Finally, I reach the tip of the vine. It hangs over the edge of the cliffside to the canyon behind our home. There's no easy way to tell if another vine is buried beyond because snow blankets the ground as far as I can see.

I also need to know where the base is. A few more minutes in the atrociously unrelenting cold won't kill me. I follow the vine as it grows thicker and thicker. As I move toward home, a strange tingling sensation crawls up the back of my neck in warning. I push the intruding thoughts away. My teeth chatter. My lungs are on fire, scorching hotter than the sun, so at least part of my body still functions. It hurts just to suck in needed oxygen. It might be best if I rest for a few minutes. I lean against the rough bark of the tree trunk. Fresh prickles bloom blood on my forearm.

"Ugh, this sucks."

Heathcliff would've stayed with me and helped keep me warm if he hadn't been swiped up by Brody. At least the monster scared my intruder away and I'll never have to see his perfect face again.

"You foolish, stubborn woman."

Against better judgment, I jerk around to the sound of Brody's deep voice, then lose my balance. Somehow, I don't land in snow. Instead, my shoulder blades fall onto Brody's arm like he's dipping me in a dance. Thank the Goddesses that's a body part that I don't have many thorns. For only a moment, I search his dark eyes. Why hasn't he left yet?

"W-why?" I barely get it out before he lifts me out of the snow completely and carries me like a child.

"D-don't…m-my…th-thorns…"

"Eh, I've felt worse. These pricks are nothing more than friendly pokes."

I know he's just being nice, but it's hard to care when he's so warm. I close my eyes and rest my cheek against his chest.

"Open your eyes, Lulita," he shakes me gently.

"Mmm?" I do as he says and watch the tops of the pines bob with each of his steady steps. From this angle, the scene looks like an artist's painting with treetops boldly piercing the blue sky.

"Talk. Tell me how much you hate me."

"I d-do hate y-you," I chatter, but maybe it's only loud enough inside my own head. "W-what does Lulita mean?"

"My little beast."

Darkness again.

"Mora, damn it, you're so cold. Open your eyes." His words carry more of an edge this time and he quickens his pace. The stomp-stomp rhythm of his boots in the snow change to stomp-stomp-stomp-stomp and I rock against him through the jerky movements.

Why is he running?

"You…"

"Go ahead and yell at me if that keeps you awake," Brody says, fear lacing his words.

"You…c-came back," I whisper and rest my eyes again.

I open my eyes to dancing red flames. A migraine worse than my last hangover prods at my skull with the intensity of a jackhammer.

"Ooh," I moan while sitting up and glancing around the library. Of all the fireplaces in this house, Brody brought me to *this* one. Seriously? It's too close to the West Wing.

"Easy, now. You fainted last time," he says.

Fainted? When? I glance out the bay window to the sight of stars. Did I sleep the whole day? Leaning against a mound of blankets, I watch Heathcliff sleep.

I slowly face Brody, terrified of what I might find in his gaze. Fury? Irritation?

When I lock on his eyes, all I find is his relief. Interesting. Sitting only a few feet away from me on the floor, Brody studies my face and nods, apparently pleased with something.

"Your cheeks are pink again. Good."

I open my mouth to say some snarky remark, but nothing comes out. It wouldn't be right to chastise him after his efforts. The man carried me through a winter storm despite being a stranger. My thorns probably scratched him along the way. Why would he do such a thing? I return his stare, hoping the intensity of mine matches his because whatever game he thinks he's playing, I'll definitely win.

"How did that get in here?" Brody asks, pointing to the corner of the couch where my origami tapestry rests.

"Magic." I shrug.

"That's too easy of an explanation."

"Nothing about magic is simple," I say. "I can't explain it, but the longer I've lived here, the more sentient that tapestry becomes. I've seen it dancing in the kitchen once."

Brody snorts. "That's a lie."

"Here, drink this," Feathi says as she walks around the couch and joins us on the floor in front of the roaring fireplace. I'd warn her not to stay too long or get too close, but she already knows the dangers of being highly flammable.

I accept the mug which is ironically covered in tiny roses. When we were teenagers Feathi and I took a pottery painting class together. She has kept this creation over the years. It's one of the only items besides her watches she brought with her when we moved here right after the curse was cast upon us.

The heat feels like I'm being submerged in bliss. Perfectly warm, thick chocolate sloshes over my tongue, glides down my throat, and melts my insides to amazing goo.

"Wow. That's a rare sight," Brody says.

"What is?" I look at him over the rim of my mug.

"You just smiled."

"No, I didn't."

"Yes, you did." He points to the corner of my mouth. "Here. And a little bit over here."

"Stop it." I despise myself right now. Not him, but me, because part of me wants to be the reason for his smile.

"Feathi, tell her, I'm right." Brody leans back against the side of the couch cushion, both hands behind his head.

My best friend blushes and fiddles with one of her watches. "I'm glad you feel better, Mora. I'll be back to check on you later."

The crackling of the fire reminds me of the bursting flames in the forest.

"Did you start the fire in the woods?" I accuse Brody instead of showing gratitude.

"Yes."

"It could've spread. It could've burnt my home down."

"It didn't."

"You shouldn't have—" I start at the same time as he asks, "Did you know about that vine?" His question feels like an arrow hitting the bullseye.

"No." I take another sip, hoping my face is better hidden this time.

"While I was searching for you"—he bends over and covers Heathcliff's ears—"I found his mom's body. The momma wolf didn't die from a hunting trap like I thought. After I saw it in daylight, it was obvious that the vine strangled her. It was wrapped around her whole body, her neck, and the thorns pierced her all over. It was gruesome."

"Mmm," I say, unable to form a coherent comment. If my hypothesis is correct, I'm royally screwed. I stare across the rug, to the hardwood floor, where it meets the bottom of a bookshelf. Under the secret lever, the Book of my life is silently being transcribed by the cursed ink. The phantom narrator probably writes witty comments about how I'd prefer a shot of Kahlua mixed into my cocoa, or that at least my black nail polish came off, but that doesn't matter because now, as I stare at the secret entrance, I'm certain that the base of the vine starts in my own home. Since we moved the Book's location, it has hovered over the stump of an unidentifiable tree or root system. I'd bet everything that the vines have been there all along, growing down, deep into the earth for the last seven years. Maybe it has just recently emerged from the ground and into wildlife.

The beastly vines weren't here to kill me.

The beast *is* a part of me.

I am the beast.

I'm the monster. We're connected, one and the same.

The thorns protruding from my skin hum with power as if in agreement with my theory. I had guessed something like this would happen if I didn't break the curse fast enough.

After witnessing that vine, there's a chance Brody will see the plant as an adventure. He might choose to stay to learn more about it, but he'll only slow me down. It's true that I need someone to help me collect roses but not at the risk of the life of an over-eager bystander.

"You need to leave."

"Okay, nap time for you." Brody rests a hand on my shoulder.

"No, you need to leave."

He clears his throat. "I can help. Show me the cursed pen thing you told me about."

"I don't need help." I set my mug down on the rug and lie through my teeth. "I said no. That vine has all I need to break the curse. Now that its carcass lays on my property, everything will be fine. So pack your things and head out." I pause to watch his expression. The last thing I want to do is hurt him, especially after he's gone above and beyond for me, but harsh words and a threat will hopefully help him leave faster, so I continue, "Plus, think about your future. You wouldn't want the townsfolk to find out from an *anonymous* source that you're responsible for arson and face prison time."

His jaw drops. I wait, anticipating him to remark about me not being grateful that he saved my life from hypothermia. Or that I'm a liar and hypocrite. And he'd be right, about all of it. Each of those flaws is like a separate thorn piercing my heart until I bleed out.

"I can see your wheels turning, Mora, but whatever scheme you plan to try to scare me away with won't work. I want to know the secrets of this place, all the way down to its skeleton. So, this is the deal. I'll build trellises on your balconies to support the roses in growing faster, but for each rose that thrives, you must pay me with a secret."

"I don't have secrets." I fight against looking at the hidden door in the bookshelf.

"I don't believe that," Brody smirks mid-sentence, "but one thing I'm sure of."

I bite the inside of my cheek and lose the battle against asking this question. "About what, exactly?"

"Everything has changed."

I can't decipher the look he's giving me. What exactly has changed for him and why do I want to know?

CHAPTER 8

Brody

Everything has changed because, in the short period I've spent with this woman, I know for a fact that she's not a child abductor.

Mora rests for the entire day. I don't mind the extra time to sleep and heal from the wounds her thorns gave me when I carried her earlier. In the meantime, I clean the place a little, opening the curtains and dusting off the furniture. Even her kitchen needs some sprucing up. Her house is so glorious that it's a shame to keep it hidden in shadows.

Between reshelving books and folding all her blankets, I continually check on Mora, comfortable by the fireplace, curled next to Heathcliff. Now that we know the brutal fate the pup's mother suffered from the raging vines, I'm glad I found him when I did. The plant acted like it had a mind of its own. I guess living nightmares are possible. A shiver runs up my spine. There's more to Chambrea Fortress than Mora has let on, and I have every intention of discovering each of its secrets.

First, I need to find an axe. As I wander down the labyrinth of hallways, I swear a youthful face with wide eyes is watching me through each stained glass window. Maybe there is a ghost here after all.

Around every corner, I expect to hear a soft voice or run into someone, but each hallway is eerily empty. A tall curtain billows out from a window, casting shadows across the wall. They whisper to me, begging me to dive into their story and find the treasure they store in the depths of these walls.

"Jeez, it's so cold," I say to myself.

Time feels different here, as if all these grandfather clocks slow and rush through the hours at their own convenience. I would've been rummaging through this fortress years ago if I had any inkling of its potential.

"Brody? What are you doing?" Feathi steps out from the shadows.

"I'm looking for an axe."

She's pretty as origami but would be a heartbreaker as a human. "Does Mora know your plans to find a deadly weapon?"

I shake my head.

"Well, this will be entertaining. Follow me." Feathi leads me around so many turns that soon I'm unsure if the house has a shape. Maybe the curse also affects the building. What a passerby sees from the outside isn't representative of what's inside.

"So, how long have you known Mora?" I dodge a low spiderweb and stay close to Feathi's heels.

"Fourteen years. She's my best friend."

"Fourteen years? I thought she was cursed seven years ago?" So my assumption that Mora created her roommates from magic due to boredom is wrong.

"Yes, all four of us were cursed by her sister. Though I've never learned the whole answer of why."

I speed up, matching her strides. "You don't know what happened between them?"

"Some bits and pieces." Feathi gives me a side-eye that reminds me of my ex, and for the first time today, I think of Dom and Catterina.

That must be a new record of how many hours passed without imagining what my daughter looks like. At this point, they're never returning home, so I need to lose myself in an alternate future. Obsessing over their whereabouts is irrational at this point. I bet she also has an endless urge to explore. I shake my thoughts clear and erase the image I had formed of a brown-haired six-year-old girl swinging a toy sword.

Feathi stops in front of the gazillionth door we've passed and holds her hand over the knob. "So, what do you want an axe for?"

"I'm a carpenter and specialize in landscape craftsmanship. I'm going to build a trellis on each of the balconies facing the sun. Mora's roses will have a better chance of growing there compared to the shaded garden in your courtyard."

"Why would you help us?" Feathi scans me up and down.

"Who doesn't like a little adventure?" I can't help but think of the endless possibilities in a cursed mansion with sentient plants. Maybe the mysteries will distract me until my departure date. As of now, I only have time to spare. The ticket I purchased out of this country is non-refundable, so I only have a few days to stay.

We enter a dusty, dark room filled with boxes, crates, broken appliances, and an old globe rotting in the corner. I give it a spin, and let my finger stop its momentum, landing on Runlose. I wonder if that country has a fortress this magical.

"So, what's Mora's story?" I cough when dust flies. "Can't she cast a magic spell of sorts and fix all her problems?"

"It doesn't work like that." Feathi's voice is muffled. "She needs her orbs. There are seven ranging in size, from roughly a marble to a snow globe, but she demanded that I hide all of them years ago."

"Why?" I stop my rummaging and try to meet Feathi's eye.

"She's afraid."

"Of what?"

"If you learn that, you might find the key to unlock Mora."

I move closer, to ask more questions, but a beam of light blinds me for a moment.

When I shift a tad, the glare goes away. The object in question seems to be a small, hand-held mirror. I walk toward it, curious to hold the relic myself.

"I found an axe!" Feathi raises her arm high and bumps her watches into a hanging light.

But I no longer care about finding an axe. As I gaze into the mirror, it's like time itself has stopped.

"Why is there a little girl in this mirror instead of my reflection?" I ask Feathi.

"What do you mean? Let me see." She looks over my shoulder. "I don't see a girl, just Nax."

"Your roommate?"

"He's more than a roommate. Once the curse is broken, we…never mind."

"Well, I don't see your boyfriend. Look, right here, there's a young girl with bangs and she's wearing pink overalls."

Feathi shakes her head, looking confused.

"Look," I feel desperate for her to understand. "The girl is right there. The wind is blowing her curly brown hair. And her eyes, they're…" A sensation similar to a needle piercing my temple completely overtakes me. It's her. Catterina. This is my daughter at her current age. How? My breath comes fast. This can't be happening.

"Woah, Brody, what's wrong?"

"Is this some sick joke?" I want to push the mirror into Feathi's hands, or throw it a mile away, but can only manage to clutch it tighter, ready to fight anyone who dares take it from me.

"Is *what* a joke?"

"How do you people know about Cat?"

"We don't own a cat." She takes a step back, tripping on boxes. "Calm down."

"My daughter! She's here, in this mirror. Explain! Why is she in there? Why can I see her?!" My voice rises and I lose all sense of control. "Where is she? Did Mora capture her too? Is my baby locked in your basement?!"

"Brody, please, you're scaring me." She holds the axe between us. "Let's just put it back and we can ask Mora later when she wakes up."

I storm out of the storage room. "Fuck waiting."

"Wait, Brody! What about the axe?"

"I don't need the damn axe!" On second thought, I swipe it from her arms and start toward the library. I jog. Feathi basically floats next to me, beating my pace.

"I think we should pause! Mora wouldn't harm someone you love."

I ignore her. The witch stole Ryanne and apparently, she has my daughter somewhere.

"MORA!" I roar down the halls as I chase after Feathi.

I burst through the library doors to the sight of Heathcliff sprawled on his back, tummy up to the fire and Mora cuddling him close.

"MORA! YOU BETTER FUCKIN EXPLAIN THIS!"

"Huh?" She rolls over, rubs her eyes, and sits up slowly.

Tossing a rose over to her from my pocket, I growl out, "A deal is a deal. Here's your next rose."

Her eyes widen quickly and she scrambles to her feet. "Where did you find that?"

"It's from home. Now I'm owed a secret. What in the Abyss is this?" My hand is shaking as I show her the mirror.

Like a drunk deer, she wobbles to me, hands outstretched like she's ready to grab the only connection I have to my long-lost daughter. I hide it behind my back.

"Why is my daughter in your mirror?"

"You have a daughter?"

"Answer the question. Tell me. Now."

"I don't see your daughter. I see a grave."

"What?" I lower the mirror to my side and study Mora's eyes. "So, you don't know where Catterina is?"

"No!" She throws both hands in the air. "I'm not some wretched soul who collects people, Brody!"

I want to yell but the defeated look on her face takes away some of my gusto.

She sighs and runs a hand through her hair. "Feathi, have you looked in this mirror?"

"Yes, I only see Nax."

Mora's eyes brighten at the reply. "Okay, that's what I

assumed. This is my missing mirror. It shows us what or who we most love."

My shoulders sag and my heart deflates. I'm grateful my daughter isn't in danger, but the spark of hope that had ignited when I assumed Mora might know where she is deflates.

"May I see the mirror...please?" Mora waits for me to hand it over, then inhales deeply and whispers. "All I see is my little sister's grave, just like I said."

I peek over her shoulder but the image I see is Catterina. "Mora, I'm sorry." I lay a hand on her shoulder but she shrugs it off. "I didn't know."

"It was a long time ago," Mora says, as she turns away.

Right as she lays the mirror on the couch, the glass starts to swirl. I'm hypnotized by the pattern spinning around and around and around. "What is it doing now?"

Mora turns and stares at the mirror too. Then a new image forms, hazy at first, until it becomes clear. A woman resembling Mora, but a few years younger, smiles wickedly at us. Was this her sister who died? Is she immortal in the mirror? If so, how do I know Catterina is still alive and safe?

When Mora gasps, I jump.

"Kavianne!" Mora screams, with one hand covering her mouth. "How are you doing that?"

"Hello, Sister." The woman, presumably Kavianne, winks. "What a cute boy toy. He's just my type."

I expect Mora to snap a quick comeback, or show her usual ferocity. Instead, she steps behind me, using me as a shield. Her fingers tremble against my forearm and I don't mind that one of her thorns rubs against my skin.

"I assumed you would've broken the curse by now. Especially since I left so many tantalizing clues at your disposal. How long has it been, five years already?"

"Seven," Mora whispers.

I softly move her further behind me. This Kavianne chick shouldn't terrorize her.

"What do you want?" I ask the woman.

Kavianne cackles and twists her long braid around a finger. "You two summoned *me*. I've simply been working in my kitchen minding my own business, mixing poison, and then my cruel, murderous sister appears in my window. I didn't think I'd ever see your face again, dear Mora. How are you managing in that hole of a house?"

"Shut up," Mora squeaks out behind me and I cringe, hoping her sister didn't hear that weak attempt.

"Are you the one who cast the curse?" I ask.

"Ah, she likes you."

"Reverse it," I demand, with absolutely nothing to use as leverage.

Kavianne throws her head back and laughs. "Why in holy Nerida would I do that? The demon you are defending deserves every punishment thrown at her. Even death would be too easy." She looks down at her potion again. "In fact, have you figured out what'll happen when the ink runs out of that pen, dearest Sis?"

"I'll die," she whispers behind me, quieter than a fallen snowflake.

"Not quite." Kavianne smiles. "Something worse than death…just wait and see."

My body is wound so tight I'm about to explode. "Why? Why would you curse your own family?"

"Why don't you ask her yourself." And then a fist rams straight into the mirror and cracks the glass to deadly shards.

Mora collapses to her knees. I drop the mirror while trying to catch her. Feathi rushes to her side first. As Mora falls apart in front of me, I step away. I won't ever let myself be someone's shoulder to cry on again. That way I can live a life worth living—each day a new adventure—alone. Feathi can clearly comfort Mora on her own. I'm already halfway to the door when Mora's sobs hit my ears. I hesitate before soldiering forward.

Refusing to turn back, I march on with a plan. The axe in my hand is power. After I destroy the rest of that plant monster, I need to leave all of this behind me. Dragon caves are waiting for me and iceberg lagoons. Soon, I'll be on my way to better experiences.

I'm either learning the intricacies of this house faster than expected, or I'm very lucky, because I find an exit. Freezing wind attacks my face as I step through onto the snowy grounds.

It doesn't take long to find the monstrous vine. I'm about to swing my axe into its thick greenery when thudding sounds come from my right where Nax watches Yin chopping away at it with a kitchen knife.

Their visible breaths come out in puffs with each swing. They've barely made a dent and I have no idea how long they've been out here, but the movements look therapeutic, so I join.

Swing. Hack. Muscles flare. Thud.

Lift it over my head. Drive the axe down. Thud.

Again and again until I'm drenched in sweat and panting. The calluses on my hands bleed and stain the handle of my axe crimson. I keep going. My heart knots tight at the fate that wretched sister has cast upon Mora. No one deserves a curse like this, even someone who pretends to be as hard as stone to protect herself.

What already stands out about Mora is her passion. If she can be so intense about the smallest things, then I can't imagine what her spirit will fight for when something truly matters to her.

Sunrays fade into stars and I haven't split the vine apart. Nax and Yin have already given up and sit against a log, butts in the snow. They watch me in solidarity until I complete this one task. I can't break a curse, but I can chop through a vine. I can't fully understand these unique roommates, but I will sever this plant. I can't find Catterina but Goddess help me, I'll shred this creature into two if it kills me. With one final blow, the plant tears apart. Puss and ooze trickle out, forming a black puddle on the ground near decomposed logs that are riddled with fungus.

Clapping comes from behind me so I turn; both Nax and Yin are bowing to me. "Bravo, knight of Ozaron. You have conquered your quest."

I laugh and toss the axe to the side. I wipe my brow and sit next to them. Hopefully they don't care that I stink like a man who lives at the gym. "The next task is to gather some wood to build the trellis."

"Really?" Nax's brow rises. "I could've sworn I heard you muttering about leaving during that little freakout you just had."

"Yeah, I'm leaving."

"When?"

"Soon."

Yin smiles while building a little snowman next to her boots. "Red smothers and suffocates the strongest of metal but has a tendency to teach others to dance."

"What she means," Nax says slowly, "is it sounds like you want to stay."

"No, I have places to go and things to experience. Committing to one place just isn't me."

Even as the words leave my mouth, I know they're not true, only a cover, similar to Mora's stone wall. In a perfect world, there'd never be a reason to leave home at all. Like in Mora's perfect world, she'd trust more.

Nax smiles slightly, "Well, speaking of Commitment, will this work as a ring for Feathi?" Nax pulls out a small band made only of twigs. "It doesn't match all her watches, but maybe she will like it."

I shudder at the thought of staying with one person for the rest of my life. Who would want such a cage when there are thousands of people to meet in faraway lands?

"Yeah, if you want it to slip off or break the second you give it to her, then sure, it'll work."

"Damn it," Nax throws it to the snow and buries it with his boots.

"Hey, don't worry, man, I can help you make one."

Nax pauses. "But you're leaving soon."

"Yeah, extremely soon."

"And why are you still here anyways?" He gestures to the woods. "You've had plenty of chances to leave."

I lay my head back on the log to catch my breath and take in the sky. It's such an easy answer, there's no need to respond, but for some reason, I'm unsure of what excuse to use this time.

CHAPTER 9

Mora

Another day flies by and I know the enchanted pen is running out of ink. At least I've had time alone to process that Brody has a daughter. Why isn't he with her now?

Cold seeps through the windows so I gather my blanket closer before noticing it's my handmade tapestry. This thing has a mind of its own, that's for sure.

Heathcliff sleeps contently on my feet. Outside, the morning suns cast rays on Brody like spotlights between the pines. I sit on the bench of the library's bay window, pretending to admire the sculpted beasts that guard our mansion. Truly, I'm watching Brody hammer and chisel pieces of wood. Next to him, Nax flails his arms about in encouragement, as if he has any idea what they're doing.

Strike.

When the hammer hits the nail, Brody's sculpted arm tightens under his sleeves.

Strike.

Why can't I look away? I'm not that deprived of connection, am I? The man is a walking disaster.

Strike.

Why isn't he wearing a coat? He'll freeze to death.

Strike.

Why am I watching him at all?

I shake my head and turn away. On the fireplace, Brody's coat lays next to his backpack. I could bring it out to him or rummage through his items. Biting my lip, I choose the latter.

Brody's backpack could reveal what kind of man he is —someone who carries wads of cash, or codes to a limited edition hoverboard, or proof that he's been tricking us with a bouquet of lies? Right before I unzip the pack, I pause. I wouldn't want him invading my beloved spine-cracked journals, so I'll show him the same respect.

"Mora!" Feathi walks in and catches me red-handed. I quickly drop the item in question. "What are you doing? It's rude to sneak through his stuff."

"I wasn't. I'm not." I turn to re-situate his pack into the same spot as before, though I'm hiding the redness rising on my cheeks.

Yin hops over to the bench, plops down, and sits cross-legged in front of me. "Purple is my favorite color and there's three people on this planet who know why. Don't bother trying to ask them, they'll never spill my secret."

"Yeah, there seems to be a lot of secrets floating about right now." I collapse next to her, comforted by her familiar company. "Kavianne said she left clues about the curse. Do you think that's true? What secrets could she have hidden if she never lived here to begin with?"

Feathi nods. "I'm more interested in why that vine came to life. Where did it come from and what does it want?"

How am I supposed to find the answers to these questions in addition to breaking the curse?

"Let's look through more books," Feathi says, "You've said books hold the truth."

"We've done years of research already."

"We may have missed something."

Others may look upon this massive library with awe and envision themselves riding the ladders that rise to the dusty top shelves, but for me, this room is an ironic kind of welcomed torture. Millions of words, thousands of characters, and hundreds of stories all beckon to be read, but I'm too nervous I'd shred the pages if I tried.

Maybe Kavianne knew that and hid a clue to breaking my curse in one of these books. With a newfound hope, I start pacing over the old rug.

"Feathi, can you go to the apothecary section and find roses listed in any index?"

"Sure," she replies, disappearing around a shelf.

"And, Yin, I need you to go to the history section over there and check for curses in the table of contents."

Yin skips and jumps off like a bunny.

I stare at the shelves. These thorns ruin everything. This morning, I noticed one unruly long hair sticking straight out from my chin that I can't pluck, thanks to the angle of my thorns.

"No one invited *me* to the party?"

I spin around and meet Brody's brown eyes. His forehead glistens with sweat. He either reads my mind or feels the drops dripping down his temple because at that precise moment, he wipes his brow. For a strange moment, I hope he can't see the crazy hair protruding from my chin like I'm about to grow a beard tomorrow. Not that it matters what he thinks about my appearance.

"Command me, master. How can I help?" He salutes me.

The smart decision would be to ask him to leave. Again. But the man is stubborn.

I point to the herbology section. "Research any plant that has similarities to what attacked us. Any detail is helpful, like place or origin, or if it's toxic or if it regenerates."

"Got it." But he moves closer to me instead. "Don't you want to know what Nax and I built out there?"

"I'm guessing a doghouse."

"Nope." His eyes shine with excitement. "Try again. Wait, no, you'll never guess. I'll tell you…it's a trellis."

"Wonderful. Now go look in the herbology section." I turn away, definitely not toward the window to get a better view of what he had built.

"Oh, come on, Ms. Grumps." He hops around me while fake poking my side, with fingers like daggers that don't quite touch my waist. "You can be grateful for once. It's not that hard. First, you open your mouth, then you force out the words 'thank you,' followed by a thing called a smile."

"What you do during your leisure is your own business." I step closer to the window and see Nax standing next to a new trellis. It's in the perfect place for sun exposure. When Nax wobbles a little I stifle a gasp, fearful for him.

When he rebalances, I gulp down any fears, and address Brody again, "Don't tell me that you built that for me."

"No way, Lulita. I did it for *me*. Remember, each rose I

give you earns me a secret. From the way I see it, every flower that thrives on that trellis is because of me, so I claim them all."

He crosses his arms, paired with a satisfied look on his face that almost makes me smile. I definitely won't give him any credit once they bloom. Hopefully he won't stay until then. I don't need another person at risk. Though, I can't deny how much I need more roses, and fast.

"The wood you used to build that trellis is from my woods, so technically, they're mine."

"*Your* woods? They belong to *you*?"

"Well, that's not the point."

His brows furrow together so tightly I have half a mind to smooth them out with a finger. "You're absolutely impossible."

"Or I am improbable. The likelihood of a magicless witch cursed with thorns who lives in a mansion with three roommates made of paper is quite improbable, but not impossible because here we are."

"Aaah! Do you ever stop arguing?" Brody throws both hands in the air, accidentally knocking a few books off a nearby shelf.

"You okay?" Feathi shouts from across the room.

"No," I respond at the same time Brody chuckles with a, "Yes."

"How have you survived living with her?" he asks.

As usual, Feathi's laugh is sunrays dipped in gold on a summer day. "Because she slips me a tonic from her apothecary studio once in a while that takes off the edge."

Yin snorts and starts playfully chanting, "Turquoise, turquoise, turquoise."

Brody's flared nostrils relax and he gestures for me to lead the way. "Well, by all means, show me the way to your herb books then I'll gladly accept a tonic."

"What makes you think I'd make one for you?"

"You're not dazzled by my charisma yet?" He huffs. "Shame."

I zig-zag around an old chair piled with novels, a stack of crates that holds maps, and an old guitar case stuffed with more books. Brody's dominating energy surges behind me with each step and I swear he's going to pound a hole through the floor. How can one person occupy so much space?

I twist around to face him. "Do you mind walking like a normal person?"

His nostrils flare again. I quite like the look of him frazzled. "Define normal," Brody says. His gaze quickly darts to a thorn protruding from my neck.

It's the first time he has shown a reaction to my thorns. I use all my willpower to not cover it with one hand. "Well, if I could hold a dictionary, I'd recite the definition of normal, but in this case, I guess that *normal* would be to walk at a softer volume. In other words, stop stomping! My entire house will crumble to dust if you keep on like that."

"Would you like me to tiptoe like you?" Brody's eyes run down the front of my sweater and leggings and land on my slippers. Heat floods through me at his scrutiny, as if he hasn't looked at me until now. "Other people have different ways of doing things, Mora. We don't all have to walk around as if this place is bursting with dynamite."

I raise a finger to his face but catch myself just in time. He's baiting me. He wants me to argue. And I won't do it. Nope. Silence will win this game.

"Did you just wrinkle your nose at me?" He clutches his heart. "How could you? I'm so offended."

Forcing a fake smile, I lead him to the herbology section. If he can't figure out how to find the books that might help us, then his assistance won't be mind-blowing. Finally, we reach the back corner and I sneeze from the dust.

Brody runs his fingertips over the spines. My toes curl with the very image of that tender movement. To touch a book right now would take away layers of my stress.

"Okay, so like I said, look for mentions about a massive plant or an object that can make decisions."

"Ah, yes there's a term for that." Brody rubs a hand over his dark stubble. "Is it cognizant? That must be it."

"No. That's definitely not it."

He opens an academic textbook and skims a finger down the page. "Well, you're the one who knows everything. What's the term I'm thinking of…when an object can think for itself and be self-aware."

I know exactly what he's talking about, but the word is stuck on the tip of my tongue. "As if there's any chance in the Abyss that I'd tell *you*…"

He snaps the book shut and gawks. "You don't know, do you?" Another agonizing smile lifts his cheeks. "I can't believe it. Miss Mora…what's your last name?"

"Thomesse."

"Ladies and ladies of this fine library." He jumps atop a chair full of books and knocks them all off in the process. "I hereby declare that Miss Mora Thomesse does NOT know it all. Let me repeat, there's a sliver of information in this universe that is NOT in her brain."

Feathi claps slowly from across the room, one, two, three times.

"Get down from there." I tug on his wrist, careful not to scratch him.

He's still smiling and it sends a shiver shooting up my neck. I fight off a strange sensation and begin restacking the books he toppled—all with the word 'time' in their title. Strange coincidence.

At this point, I'd sacrifice dessert for the rest of my life in order to not make eye contact with this man. Maybe reading 'A History of: Fairies Stopping Time' is the perfect way to accomplish that—if only I had audiobooks.

Exuding pride like a champion, Brody circles me, pretending to read his text. I know he doesn't have a clue what it says because it's written in the language of Lacordian. He licks his finger and flips a page, doing so with such a superciliously pompous manner, I have half the urge to smack him.

"Oh wow, this story has an old witch who has warts on her face that literally scream at people whenever they approach her." He blows out a heavy breath. "Why don't these fairy tales represent beautiful witches like you? It's nonsense. I'll message the publisher tomorrow."

He did *not* just call me beautiful.

"So, Nax told me you like mixing potions. What's your favorite recipe to brew?" Brody asks as he flips another page.

"Anything with spiced flintberries and dried-out neek eggs make the best healing potions. My favorite are the ones that smell like cinnamon," I say before realizing I voluntarily gave information about myself. That won't happen again. Ever. My traitorous heart rate doubles. Damn it. Damn him. Damn it all.

The sound of another page swiped by his finger is a bomb exploding in my brain. It's not fair that he can turn pages so easily. "Will you be more careful with these? They're old and fragile."

"I'm sorry. I'll be more careful." Brody turns and lifts a giant encyclopedia.

He apologized. Maybe it wasn't all-encompassing, but it

took courage and the ability to wave a white flag. What would it feel like to admit defeat?

Without thinking, I slip to the floor and burrow behind a carton of magazines from the ninth Falcon year, the last time I lived in society. There are so many events in the last seven years that I've missed in the world, from the art conference here in Ozaron to the naming of the new sea nymph—Axton—or something.

"So, how did you become interested in potions?" Without looking up, Brody oh-so-carefully turns the page of his encyclopedia.

I study his profile. His nose looks like it was broken a few years back and a little scar was stitched half-hazard on his forehead. He'd look better if he wore glasses. He glances up and our gazes meet.

"Mora?"

"What?" I gulp and stare at the magazine in front of me.

He chuckles. "I asked how you started in apothecary. Was it your mother's trade?"

"Why do you want to know?"

"Goddess Above." Brody sets down the encyclopedia and raises both hands. "I don't bite. I was just curious."

Heathcliff moseys over to us, a lone sock hanging from one tooth. His droopy eyes send my heart pitter-pattering so I pet him gently. If an animal as wild as a wolf can trust someone like me, then maybe I can try to trust Brody for a moment. He can only have one story, not my entire past.

I suck in a courageous breath and begin. "My mother was a florist and I never knew my dad. As a child, I was… let's just say spirited. I roamed outside for hours, days, to find the perfect place to read or fold origami. It wasn't until Lessie was eight, and I was ten, that I started mixing ingredients into potions."

I look up to find Brody's eyes trained on me, fixated

completely. He doesn't say a word, but I know he wants more. Fine, finishing one story won't be the end of the world.

"One day, we were hours from home and Lessie got a bad bee sting. I laughed it off at first like it wasn't a problem, but the spot kept swelling until her neck was twice the size. Kavianne wasn't anywhere around, so I couldn't call for help. I remembered reading about a healing tonic in one of my books." I sigh, not wanting to remember these moments. "Lessie was gasping for air, but I found all the ingredients, smooshed them in my hand, and rammed it down her throat. The swelling went down so quickly that it didn't seem real. After my potion, she was fine."

Until I killed her years later.

"Wow, you're a real-life hero, then." Brody smiles. "So, you found a passion for mixing potions after that?"

"Kind of. Part of the reason I continued was to keep my little sisters safe, but then people from our village started visiting with requests. One girl didn't want to give birth to her unborn child. A boy wanted a potion to make his father forget. A child came to me begging for the ability to pass a test at school. A widow asked to speak to her deceased Partner once more. They all needed me. I did what I could, with my magic and herbs, for as long as possible."

The tone shifts in the room and I realize I'm not as cold anymore, but when I look up to check if it stopped snowing, I gasp. Brody is crouched inches from my face. His hands hover by mine. "You did a good thing helping others."

I want to scramble away, avoid his compliment. Instead, my butt is glued to the carpet, and my eyes can't move away from his. How dare he act like he knows me or try to empathize? He doesn't understand. Brody has no idea what I've been through or what it feels like to be responsible for so much agony.

Through gritted teeth, I force out the words to make things even. "You've saved lives as some smiling superhero named Sunshine?"

"Well, I built half the homes in my town, so, yeah, there's probably a little truth in that." He drops to sit next to me and stretches out his legs. "When I was a kid, a bad hurricane blew through. My parents worked day and night to help our neighbors repair shingles, patch siding, and redesign architecture in the main square..."

I wonder if he's imagining his town now. Maybe that's where his daughter is. Where did he used to live?

"After that storm, I knew I wanted to build, to create."

"Why did you leave home then? Can't you build there?"

My question seems to catch him off guard because his eyes snap open. He stands and turns toward the tower of books. With his back toward me, he says, "I'll answer that if you tell me why your own sister cursed you."

The nerve of this guy. He doesn't have the right to that information. If Heathcliff wasn't on my lap I'd leave the room. So, I simply ignore Brody's comment and stroke the wolf's fur. How can a creature so deadly be so soft?

"Oh, I think I found something." Brody is pointing to a page in a battered book. "Look."

This time I do start to nudge Heathcliff off, but Brody drops low again. "See, here? Doesn't this look like the vine monster we saw?"

"What book is this?" After seeing the title, my hope sinks. "Brody, it's fiction. It's a fantasy retelling and there's probably an adventure scene with some mythological plant."

"But the stories had to originate from somewhere." He turns the pages quickly. "Let me see how they kill it."

"Don't bother, it's not real."

"Oh, fuck!"

"What?" I ask.

"It says, once chopped up, the *Vignamassi,* as they called it, oozed out so much toxic poison that it infested an entire village, killing a whole town. That doesn't sound much like a love story."

"Not all stories have a happy ending."

He lowers the book. "Yeah, I guess not."

I'm surprised by the tiny stab to my chest at the sight of his frown. Someone so animated shouldn't lose hope.

"It's just a book," I say, "I bet you'll find whatever you're looking for."

I might've imagined it, but I'm pretty sure he whispers, "Not likely."

A tingling runs across my neck, so I carefully brush my fingertips over my skin. The thorn that used to jut out from the side is shrinking. I hold my breath, not daring to move. Within seconds the entire thing is gone, absorbed into my skin as if it never existed. What just happened?

"Oh, my, Goddess," I whisper, wanting to shout out to Feathi, but I'm distracted by Brody marching away.

"Hey, where are you going?" I ask.

"I have a hot date," Brody mumbles behind him. "Don't wait up."

CHAPTER 10

Brody

I stand in the wintery wind, Heathcliff at my feet, staring at the spot where I had severed the vine a couple of days ago. The puddle of goop on the ground hasn't frozen and is somehow bigger than before. I was right. The fairy tale story of poisonous ooze is real. It bubbles and boils like it has a life of its own. Every drop of black liquid that spurts up, sizzles against the white snow. Adrenaline courses through me. Apparently, a magical mirror isn't the only secret of this place.

As Heathcliff whines and backs away from the puddle, I shield him from any possible toxic spray. It's thicker now, almost like tar, and changing shapes right before my eyes. It crawls across the snow and brushes against a low bush, which slowly withers and droops. I take a stick and nudge the goop, but it only latches onto the twig and slithers up like a worm. Ever so slightly it inches closer and closer to my hand.

"Well shit, boy. This isn't good." I back away also. "If we come across another *Vignamassi* again, remind me not to chop it in half."

Mora's best bet for survival is to flee this place forever. My traitorous mind flashes to Mora looking all cozy in her oversized sweater and long wool socks that reach her knees and the adorable way she kept trying to hide that insanely long black hair sticking out of her chin. I had to use all my energy to not pluck it myself. Goddess, she's beautiful when little moments of vulnerability slip into our exchanges.

From within my pocket, my Taj beeps. It's easy to guess who is calling without having to check.

"Hi, Mam." I project the video against a tree trunk.

"Brody Kain! It's my heart. You're torturing me. Do you have any idea what you're doing to me? And Gabrielle, for Goddess sake, has visited three times asking if you've returned. Though she does wear her prettiest dress each time. I think you'd like the green color that matches her eyes."

Mam keeps jabbering, but I don't imagine green eyes. Instead, deep brown eyes bewitch me, swirling with alluring opportunities. Does Mora ever think about me when I'm not around? Does she know that every time I notice a thorn snag on the sleeve of her sweater, I want to help her, to release her? It doesn't matter, I'm leaving. There is one thing I forgot to ask Mam for help with before I left home.

"...and her younger sister has fallen ill too," she

continues "…Sofia is home from school because another fifth grader…and the medicine supply…"

"Mam," I interrupt, "I need a favor."

"Well, why on earth should I do you a favor when you didn't have the decency to text me? And what is behind you? A pine forest? At least I know you're in Ozaron. Just promise me not to get into any trouble because I'll be using my rolling pin to swat your ass to the other side of the suns if you get yourself hurt. What's this favor you need? I'd even swallow all the planets and drink the stars for my one and only baby boy."

"I know it's unlikely but if Dom and Catterina ever come home, you'll call me, right?"

Mam stays quiet. "It's not like I'm expecting them to, but just in case, I need your word that you'll tell me."

"Of course, darling," she says quietly, "no need to ask."

I pause for a beat, knowing we both gave up hope long ago. "What do you think Cat looks like now?"

"Oh, I see her every night in my dreams. She has wildness in her eyes just like someone else I know."

When a whistle comes from Chambrea's front door, I snap my attention up and end our video call. Ahead, the iron gate looks the same as before—a ribcage from a skeleton, cold and dead. The whistle sound must've been in my imagination.

I scan the windows and doors again, waiting for Mora to appear. No one's there. A part of me feels disappointed, as if I'm eager to see her face again. Yes, the woman likes her rules, and can be a bit conceited at times, but it only seems like a cover, a mask to hide what she truly cares about. Underneath her layers of thorns, Mora might have a heart softer than a rose petal—she just refuses to show it now. It's obvious that she used to care about helping people with her potions, and I know she prioritizes her roommates. Maybe one day, after her curse is gone, she'd lay her hand in mine and…

"No way," I talk to myself like a lunatic, "don't even think about it."

My boots crunch over snow with each step. There might be a hidden entrance somewhere around here that leads to the tunnel Yin had shown me. Tunnels hide secrets. Maybe if I learned how Mora was originally cursed, it'd shed some light on how to break it.

I blow on my numb fingers and rub them together. Every expedition tends to have a casualty or two. I don't necessarily need all ten fingers to survive.

Heathcliff zigzags around the giant stone statues in the side yard, then turns some of the snow yellow.

"Good, boy. You tell 'em who's boss." I brush snow off the front of the statue to reveal a wolf, with fangs as large as my head.

Suddenly, a twig snaps behind me. I turn around.

"Hello? Is someone there?"

The air is holding its breath, and it feels as if the trees are watching me, waiting for my next move. Loud rumbling booms like thunder. Heart thumping. Is it another attacking vine? Then a dark shape billows toward us.

"The fuck?!" I stare, open-mouthed. "Run, Heathcliff!"

The rhythm of the pounding is from titanic paws of a wolf slamming down on the earth. It grows bigger. Closer. Closer. I need to move. But it charges too fast. I duck behind a pine tree, sucking in my gut. Its heavy panting gets louder. Puffs of hot air steam like an aero-tran every time it breathes out.

There's a huff of rotten breath. Pounding on snow. Faster. Closer. Louder.

Another howl louder than an explosion blasts my ears. Heathcliff whines somewhere close.

"Shit!"

I peek around the tree, my heart racing. Only a few feet remain until an enormous wolf tramples our Heathcliff. The animal doesn't see our pup. I lunge out. Arms waving above my head.

"Stop!" I shout. "Stop!"

The animal rears to a halt, high on two hind legs. If the creature stomps down, my skull will be crushed. I can almost picture my bones flattened.

"Woah, easy, War!"

That strong voice can't be coming from atop the beast. It'd be outrageous. In control, the animal's front legs return to the ground, and I scan up its strong body to meet the gaze of the rider—the cunning witch who keeps surprising me—Mora, my witty hostess with an outrageous facial hair.

"Are you trying to get yourself killed?" Mora pulls on the reins and guides the angry animal around me.

I'm pretty sure my jaw is unhinged at this point, hanging to the snow. How is Mora handling this giant? She grapples for control for a moment until the wolf named War stops its momentum and huffs. A foul smell comes from its nostrils as it studies me with yellow eyes.

"What are you doing out here?" Mora yells from atop the saddle.

I can't quite form words as I watch Heathcliff prance over to War and rub his nose against its furry leg. Stunned, I shake my head, trying to process. A creature meant for storybooks is standing in front of me. I didn't have to leave Ozaron to find magnificent treasures. Amazing adventures live just beyond my backdoor without me knowing. I start laughing, then run a hand through my hair.

"This can't be real." I want to reach out but respect the beast too much.

"Answer me, Brody. What are you doing out here?" Mora says, worry in her undertone. "I could've trampled you."

"But you didn't." In awe, I continually fight every urge to stay put. "Is it your pet?"

"I don't have time for questions."

"Why? Where are you going?" I follow her gaze to her house. "I'll help. You don't have to explain. I'll do whatever you say."

They're heavy words, but I mean them all. Mora studies me, a hundred questions spinning in her brown eyes. The only one I care about is whether she will choose to bring me along on this adventure. Wherever she is going, whoever she is meeting, I want to be a part of it. It's obvious her mind seesaws about including me. Yet, she's already told me it's been years since leaving the premises. No matter how bold Mora claims to be, I doubt she's totally fearless.

"You'll do *whatever* I say?" she asks.

I slowly move toward the wolf, holding both hands high by my ears. "I swear."

She groans, but in a half-defeated sort of way, and commands, "Down, War."

The wolf lowers like a camel and I gently slide behind Mora. Before I can hold onto her waist, War rockets to his feet again and shoots off toward the house. The stone pillar holding the gate is right in front of us.

"We're going to hit the wall!" I yell.

We charge forward regardless.

"Slow down!" I wince and brace myself for impact.

Instead of crashing into the stone, we canter right through the brick like ghosts. The snow disappears. The forest is gone. The wind ceases. I can't catch my breath. Suddenly, we're in a tunnel. Exhilaration can't explain what is happening in my heart. Stone whizzes past me in hyper speed and we soar through the darkness. We're galloping with such graceful fluidity, that I dare to raise both arms out wide and hoot at the top of my lungs in bliss. My voice carries like I'm a damn opera singer.

War swerves to the left and the movement sucks the air from my lungs. I grasp onto Mora's waist and lean into her back. One of her thorns accidentally jabs me in the waist.

"Don't fall off! I won't be kind enough to stop a second time," she hollers over her shoulder, but I can hear the smile in her voice. She's enjoying this speed as much as I am.

The cold in the tunnel has turned from brutal to deathly. After a minute, the faint light grows brighter, and the tunnel widens into a space I can't see the limits of. War stops, then backs up a few steps. What could possibly scare this beast?

"Are we underground?" I ask Mora. "Are we dead?"

"Quiet."

At the end of the tunnel, a weed-covered prairie sits inside a giant, dark cavern. Dozens of clocks, towering over four stories high each, stand erect like guardians in a large circle. Some are old-fashioned from the Lacordian language while others are more digital like Taj devices. Each ticks by the seconds, as if counting down a bomb about to detonate.

"What is this place?" I whisper. "Are we inside or outside?"

"Technically, we're under my house. I found it on a map in the library."

"How in the Abyss is this a part of your house? It's like we've entered another dimension."

"Fairy magic," she says simply.

"That's all you have to say? Magic?"

"You said you'd do whatever I said, so stay quiet."

"Why are there so many clocks? And why are they so big? What are they circling?"

Mora slides off War. She unfastens a shoulder bag I didn't notice her carrying and grabs a giant slab of meat. Without blinking, she tosses a chunk to War.

Mora raises one finger to her lips and then gestures for me to follow. Carefully, I also slip off of War, hoping the meal will keep him distracted. Tiptoeing as far away from him as possible, I wait for Mora's lead. She barely pays me any attention while scanning the clocks. For the first time, I realize her hands are nervously folding her scarf again and again, but the thorns keep snagging the fabric.

"Mora," I whisper, "Why are we here?"

"I need roses." She eyes me briefly, gulps, then steps into the prairie of weeds. "Come on."

The moment her boot stretches across the barrier, the clocks begin chiming and gonging. Then a deep 'tick-tock' sounds like a threatening warning.

Mora breaks out in a sprint. I follow, though that makes me certifiably insane.

Then a high-pitched chirp calls out like an alarm. How can all this be under her house?

Frigid air burns my lungs. My muscles strain from sinking into the muddy weeds. With each lunge forward, the blares of the clocks increase in chaos. The powerful bells speed up. Louder. Booming. I cover my ears. Deafening tick-tocks crush my skull.

Mora darts straight between two clock towers. I can't let her go in there alone. I'm sure blood is dripping from my ears, but I run faster. Barely able to breathe.

"Mora!"

There's no way she can hear me. She moves behind one of the massive clocks. I rush after her. Sudden silence envelopes me. Either the clocks have stopped or I lost my hearing. I twist a finger in my ear canal and shake my head around. Hazy gray fog surrounds us in a new deep quiet. Mora has vanished. How is fog possible underground? More importantly, what if I can't find Mora?

"Where are you?" I whisper, keeping my hands out in front of me so I don't run into anything cruel and punishing.

I trip over something. A leg. The fog clears slightly. For some reason, Mora's on her knees. She gestures to kneel next to her. When I glance up, my breath hitches. I stare at the impossible. Hundreds of tiny cottages, each the size of my hand, hover mid-air, all connected by creepy vines. The houses are roofed with a black mesh-like plant that is draped with seductive secrets and shadows.

Who could be small enough to live in these amazing houses? Hopefully a creature so small can't be terribly dangerous. Softly, Mora taps her pinky fingernail on one cottage door. The tiny movement flings the door open.

"I am here to make a deal with Princess Preta," Mora whispers, then holds her breath.

The look on her face is of utter desperation. I bet she can feel my gaze on her face, but Mora doesn't glance my way. Instead, she ducks lower, and slowly, peeks inside the cottage, then lets out a sigh. "It's empty."

I expect her to knock on the next door and ask a different resident, but she inspects the vines instead. They tightly curl around each cottage in a deadly twist, as if ready to squeeze the houses. Her fingers graze along the unknown plant, daring to dance with the poison. What is she thinking?

"This was my last hope," she whispers, "but the fairies seem to have taken all their roses with them."

I peek inside the windows of a cottage and scan the tiny furniture inside. I'm about to ask her plan, but when I look over again, a tear is sliding down Mora's cheek. She wipes it away quickly.

"Come on. Let's go back." Her stone-cold demeanor has returned as she brushes the snow off her knees.

"No, wait." I reach for her hand, and our fingers swipe against one another.

Mora looks up, a dash of hope in her dark eyes, but she fights. "I wasted a trip here, which wastes time." She throws her hand in the air. "I can't wait."

"Give me five minutes to look around. There may be a forgotten rose left behind. I told you I'd help, so let me."

She crosses her arms and leans against the brick of one of the clock towers. "Four minutes."

I nod and start the search. Part of me simply wants to inspect this land, whether it has roses or not. There must be three hundred cottages, all of which together could fit in my bedroom. I'd give up my best chisel to see a fairy again—it's been years. Why did these ones leave? Why did they take their roses with them?

I crawl through the weeds to best inspect the spiraling vine that snakes through their village. It's almost as if their cottages are built out of the plant itself. No roses are visible. Only disgusting vines, slick with an ominous liquid. This can't be safe.

Just when I'm about to turn around, I hear a tiny scratching. Back and forth. It's a spine-tingling pattern. Scritch and scratch. Back and forth. The noise is coming from behind the last cottage.

I peek over the roof and a fairy flutters her wings over the vine, holding the smallest saw in existence. When the fairy turns, I gasp. She's covered in wrinkles but beautiful. Her gothic lace dress is as long as my pinky finger and drapes over her thin frame like royalty. I can barely focus on her eyes, blacker than charcoal, distracted as I am by the black lipstick contrasting her rich skin tone like artwork and the long white hair brushing her ankles.

She's sawing a yellow rose, not red, but it's a rose.

"Those clocks are annoying," she says so quietly, in a ghostly voice. "You came just in time." She stops cutting the yellow rose that's as big as the ancient fairy. "Go ahead, take it."

I hear Mora's footsteps crunch behind me but I don't dare take my eyes off the fairy.

"Are you sure?" I whisper.

She nods. "Roses have healing powers, as you know. My neighbors have left our village for the first time since the first Falcon year to aid with that hideous plague."

"A plague?" My heart rate accelerates and I picture my daughter, young and innocent. "What are you talking about?"

The old fairy clears her throat as if speaking is a challenge. "A sinister sickness has been spreading. Children are falling deathly ill with terrible symptoms, and none have recovered. It's getting worse, so my people decided to help."

I exchange a look with Mora, unsure what to think. This rose could help one of those poor kids if it has healing powers, but Mora also needs it. The thought of something happening to her is more unsettling than it should be. Somewhere along the way, I've become addicted to the challenge of making her smile. The fiery witch beside me deserves a long and origami-filled life.

Mora takes a bottle from her bag and untwists the top. She doesn't place the rose inside as carefully as I'd expect.

"Thank you, what would you like in exchange for the rose?"

"It's a gift for you. Everyone needs healing sometimes. Especially those of us with the toughest armor."

Mora nods. "Do you know what started the illness?"

The fairy frowns, her brows furrowing. "The prick of a thorn."

"What?!" Mora falls forward, almost crushing the fairy's cottage. "What did you just say?"

The fairy cups her mouth with two tiny hands and yells, "I said…the children fall ill after getting scraped or pricked or sliced by a thorn. It's nasty business, believe me. I've heard stories of fever and hallucinations, chills and nightmares. They've been bedridden. It's quite awful. So, if you happen to see a thorn, by all means, avoid it.

Mora turns pale, then tucks her sleeved arms behind her.

"Thank you, but we should be going," I speak up. "Sorry about setting off your clocks."

The fairy bows and whispers, "Time is my biggest treasure. What is yours? No, don't answer now. Think about it. One day, you may need an answer."

"An answer?" I ask, confused.

"Yes, an answer for the roses."

"That doesn't make sense."

"Why does it have to make sense?" She winks in return.

The old fairy heads into her cottage without a goodbye. I take a paralyzed Mora by the hand and guide her out the way we came. My mind whirls with information and more questions. I process what I know one fact at a time. Roses have healing powers. There's a plague wiping out children. If my trellis helps roses grow faster, do I convince Mora to donate the flowers to help those in need? Once again, Catterina's face drifts across my mind.

CHAPTER 11

Mora

In my apothecary studio, Brody sits silently in a chair in the corner as I pace. It's my fault. The children are falling ill from a thorn prick. It's because of my curse, I just know it.

I catch him staring in fascination at all the paper birds hanging from my ceiling. Shelves are in disarray, full of flasks, vials, burners, and glass cupboards revealing hundreds of jars; some are full of powders but most are empty. It's been a long time since I made my last mix. At least I had that one vial of healing potion ready for Nax last week. I need to make dozens more for the sick kids.

"This isn't fair." I almost trip over Heathcliff, who is weaving between my ankles as I move back and forth across the room. "Those children never should've touched a thorn. Didn't their parents teach them basic safety?"

I don't dare voice out loud the possibility that the vine monster is initiating attacks by seeking them out, on the prowl. I want to fold napkins into different origami shapes. Instead, I imagine the pattern in my mind. Fold. Refold. Crease. Flatten. Again and again until my breath steadies.

"Your fingers are dancing."

"What?" I look down. My hands are miming the movements for each fold.

"It's origami, isn't it? When did you start that hobby?" Brody's eyes spark, fully alive. "I bet you made that drapery in your room. It's massive. I bet you could sell pieces like that at a market. Townsfolk would come from across the sea for a unique piece like that."

Brody is crazy to think someone would purchase a piece I made. How can one person have so much positive outlook on life? Sure, I love origami, but anyone can master a skill when it's their only option to pass the time.

"Focus. This isn't art class," I say, as I continue to pace. "Kavianne wouldn't harm children with my curse; she only wants me to suffer, not them, so why is this happening?" I ball a napkin into a wad and throw it to Heathcliff. Meanwhile, Brody's chin is in his hands as he waits patiently, a bit too patiently. I look at him for the first time. "What do you think?" I ask, regretting the question the moment it leaves my lips. I shouldn't care about Brody's opinion.

He had been staring at me for the last few minutes but his gaze is now lasered on the wall of my studio. "I think you have more tunnels in this place and there's probably another map outlining them."

My hands clench tight. Is he fuckin' serious? Of all the

things to worry about, *tunnels* are what's on his mind? There are so many other priorities. Such as the fact that the fairy only gave me a yellow rose, which won't work for refilling the pen with crimson ink. Or maybe he should care that I'm probably responsible for the plague, or that I'm no closer to getting rid of my thorns. Yet, my biggest problem is trying to stay focused when Brody's constant presence keeps distracting me.

"Mora, I can tell you're worried, but maybe once you use magic again everything will be fine. Why don't you cast a crazy cool spell and see what happens?"

I stare at him. "You have no idea what you're talking about."

"Of course, I don't, but you're the second or third most awesome person I've ever met," the corner of his lip quirks a bit. "The pieces will fall into place for you once you use magic. I can feel it deep within my damp socks."

Damn him for making me smile again. "I can't use magic without my orbs, and I asked Feathi to hide them years ago. Me and magic aren't a good combination, believe me."

Brody pauses at the look on my face and changes the topic. "By the way, you could've given me a heads up about the clockland underground."

I don't want to give an outsider too much information about the secrets of this fortress. The fairies deserve their privacy.

"Don't get me wrong, it was spectacular," he continues, "but why were there so many? Do the clocks guard the fairies somehow? Are all fairies as friendly as the one we talked to? Can we go there again?"

"Brody!"

"Yes?"

"You just asked a hundred questions. Can we please be quiet for a few minutes? I'm trying to think."

Out of habit, I start collecting bottles, clinking them together by accident. The raccoon ear wax only has a little left, the coconut oil is thankfully full, and about ten peppermint leaves remain, but the rest all need to be refilled. Once upon a time, my pantry was completely stocked with everything I might need for a potion—ranging from basil to kaolin clay to sage sticks to orange slices.

"Can you teach me a potion?" Brody's voice comes from directly behind me, making me jump and smack my shoulder against a shelf. "Holy Abyss! You can't sneak up on me like that."

I turn, ready to throw some wicked words his way, when I catch cat whiskers drawn on his face. "What the?"

The corner of his lip curves, in that entrancing way that makes me hate the entire world. "I have my reasons," is all he says, with a glimmer of amusement in his eyes.

Immediately, I feel my cheeks warm. He must have seen the crazy beard hair that I can't pluck. So, is this a form of mockery? If he is trying to tease me, then embarrassment doesn't cover how I feel. Yet, if he's trying to support me, then maybe I'll forgive him for the outrageous gesture. Instead of commenting at all, I choose to ignore it, pretending he doesn't have marker drawn over his cheeks.

"What are you trying to do?"

"I should be trying my luck right meow, and putting my hand on your waist like..."

He did *not* just say that. Why would he want to touch me? The man is either insane or joking. Maybe both.

Without breaking eye contact, he reaches forward. I can feel the warmth radiate from him, spreading to all parts of my back. I don't dare move as he unsnags a thorn on my wrist from the sleeve of my sweater. He's not attractive. He's not. Truly.

"Do you avoid things that make you feel good?"

I clear my throat and reach for chia seeds. "Do you always stay as an unwelcome guest in a witch's home?"

That gets a laugh out of him. I want to turn around to see the wrinkles form at the corners of his eyes. I can imagine Brody running a hand through his thick dark hair and shaking his head. Ugh. I shouldn't have ever traded him for Ryanne. Why was he wandering through my woods that night anyway?

It's no wonder he was traveling *alone* before stumbling upon my home. How could anyone travel with someone so talkative?

It doesn't matter. I just want to mix a good healing potion, but I can't do that with this distraction breathing down my neck. So what if Brody saved my life, or built me a trellis, or stood up for me to Kavianne? I don't care that he holds Heathcliff like the most fragile, precious baby in Ozaron.

All I need is peace and quiet to figure out how to help the sick kids, but none of the recipes work without roses. Traitorous hot tears start to form behind my eyes. I dump the contents of all my remaining ingredients in a bowl to act like I'm busy making something. There's no potion I know that calls for these four spices, but I can't let Brody know that I'm failing.

"I need roses." I say it slowly.

"And?"

My teeth grind together. "Since you're set on exploring my home, go ahead and do that now. Maybe you'll find a magical bouquet somewhere. I need quiet to think."

"Mora," His heat radiating behind me returns and I hold my breath. "Don't you ever get tired of giving demands?" This time his hands cup the back of my elbows and I have to use every restraint not to ease into his touch.

It's not like he's the most handsome man I've seen. Zorn, Willis, and Xander were all more attractive than him and better kissers too, not that I would be forced to compare them to Brody, because I'd never want his lips on mine. I'm also not starved for someone in my bed. In the first few years of my curse, I found a way to find physical companionship when in the mood, but with these thorns, my days for intimacy are long gone. So, why am I curious if Brody will dare to trail his hands further? Why does it feel like he erases my thorns with every look?

Brody sighs and his hands fall away. "Okay, I'll leave you alone, but I want to know one more secret first."

I twirl around, finger already out as a dagger to his whiskered face. "You don't seem to have a rose. So no secret."

Brody smirks, a Goddess-damned smirk, and my inner growl threatens to come loose. Maybe I'll let War teach this man a thing or two. He tilts his head and his gaze falls to my mouth. A bolt of shivers climbs fast, all the way up from my toes. Fuck, no. I don't care. I can't.

I reach for the rusty doorknob, but Brody blocks my access with his hand, holding a red rose.

"Where did you get that?" I stare at the perfect shape of the petals.

"I told you my trellis would work wonders."

I steady myself on the studio wall, letting my back rest against the cold stone. "But it's only been a few days."

"Then maybe my hands are magical." Brody lifts both his hands and rotates them in front of our faces like they're rare specimens. I'd gladly burn all my origami pieces to wipe that cocky grin off his face. My frustration grows from a simmer to scalding.

"Excuse me? *I'm* the witch. If anyone is using magic here, it's me."

Brody leans forward and places both hands on the wall behind me, both on either side of my ears. "Prove it."

I swallow, not letting my gaze roam to his wide shoulders. I won't become a pathetic girl who can't conquer an easy challenge. Quickly, I duck under his arm, ignoring his strained muscles. "Fine! You want proof? I'll show you. Follow me."

"Well, when your nostrils are flaring and your eyes are all wide and huge, I feel like I have no choice."

I stomp out of my studio, slamming the door against the wall, leaving the mess behind me. I know exactly what I need to show my true powers—magic I buried years ago.

Heathcliff frolics ahead into the dark hallway, oblivious to the tension bouncing off us both. Who in the Abyss does Brody think he is by challenging my abilities?

"You like betting, right?" I ask.

"Only if my middle name is Thaxtonalorio!" he replies, his wicked smile driving me mad.

I almost laugh out loud but won't let myself get distracted. I barrel toward the closest exit—a broken window. His hand blocks me from grazing the sharp shards as I step through. He must've placed his hand there coincidentally. I tromp around the side of the house, past the statues, to my garden. Once there I fling the gate open. This is a place where my roommates love to spend time together, so I'm not surprised when all three of them are lounging on stone benches. The sight of Feathi somewhat eliminates my rage, but not for long.

My focus battles between Brody's shenanigans and the fact that Nax's arm is wrapped in a strange cast-like-device.

His other arm hangs like a papery noodle by his side

like a broken doll. I lock eyes with my best friend. Feathi communicates her concern with one look. The curse is worsening for them. Nax is losing his physical control and function, just like Yin is losing her mental capacity. His rapid decline gives me more urgency to break my curse.

"Hey everyone, she's taking me on a field trip!" Brody says with the enthusiasm of someone who never fully grew up.

How can he be so excited when I'm this irate? Feathi only glances back and forth between Brody and me. If she says one single word about his cat whiskers, I won't speak to her for a week. Which is about my entire remaining lifespan.

Yin nods. "White has tricked the wisest leaders over the centuries. Can't you feel it though? Reach out and touch its breath."

Brody chuckles. "Even Yin says you've made her day more pleasurable. We can't wait to see what you have in store."

A growl threatens to rip free. "You're so—"

"I know what you're thinking," Brody continues. "That I'm the most endearing, most clever, most interesting person you've ever met, especially since my hands are more magical than yours."

"Don't forget handsome," Nax adds.

"Yes, I'm gorgeous art in all its glory." Brody bats his eyelashes.

"Speaking of gorgeous art," Nax starts, "Mora, I need your help with a project. Will you meet me after dinner?"

Does he not notice his body deteriorating? "Um, maybe tomorrow, Nax. I think you should go rest."

"But I feel fine, and this can't wait any longer," he protests.

"Look, you three. Did you know I have magic hands?" Brody starts to lift them. "Mora is quite taken by them."

"They're busy." I point for Brody to get to the ground. "Kneel."

"Yes, ma'am, I thought you'd never ask."

He kneels, with a wicked smile that never seems to go away, but when Brody moves directly in front of me, his face near my crotch, I jump back so fast I almost tumble over a bench. Both Yin and Nax stifle a laugh.

"Don't run from me, Lulita." His teasing words are so close to making me combust. "I told you, my hands are made of magic, but you don't want to know what my mouth can do."

"Stop talking!" I push him, slightly, careful that my thorns don't harm him. "I'll do it myself."

"I bet you *have* had to do it yourself for the last few years." He winks and I hold back a shiver when his brown eyes bore into my soul. "Why not accept help from someone with magic hands? Someone *superior*?"

I scream. Done. I'm so very done. I kneel, raise both hands in the air, then slam them into the snow. The moment I feel the power radiating up, I yell, "Mephalleaux Vonditure!"

The earth splits, forming a small hole. My largest orb, the size of my palm, rises from the frozen soil and hovers between Brody's and my nose. Neither of us is focused on the clear sphere floating among us, rather we fix our eyes on each other. His expression flickers to…pride?

"I knew you could do it," he says only loud enough for me to hear.

"What?" Taken aback, I tuck the orb into my pocket. Raw power surges through my body when it's this close to me. Goddess, it feels so good to have it back.

"You did it, Mora."

That's when I realize what just happened. I lost my magic years ago. Purposefully, yes, when I hid this orb, the weakest, and commanded Feathi to hide the other six. She spent days refusing to put them anywhere, swearing that I needed them by my side. She said it'd be a waste of a witch's powers to not use my orbs, but she was wrong. Hiding them is and was the safest choice. Somehow, this man has tricked me.

Every part of my soul detests him for it, yet the only words that come out are, "Thank you." Maybe something good could come from listening to his ideas. "Whoa," I think I say, my head spinning.

"Are you okay?" Brody steadies me with both hands.

"Yeah, of course, I am."

"One of your thorns is disappearing into your skin." His finger rubs a spot on my neck.

I gasp, ready for his finger to come away bloodied from the poke, but he's fine. Moving my hand to my stomach, I feel…only skin. Where did the thorn go? The garden zooms in and out of focus, fuzzy, then sharp, as if I'm drunk.

"Hey, hey. When was the last time you ate?" A soft hand smacks my cheeks. "Look at me, Mora."

"Brody?"

"I'm here," he says, softly, full of concern. "You don't look good."

Everything feels dizzy and my head spins. Then everything goes dark.

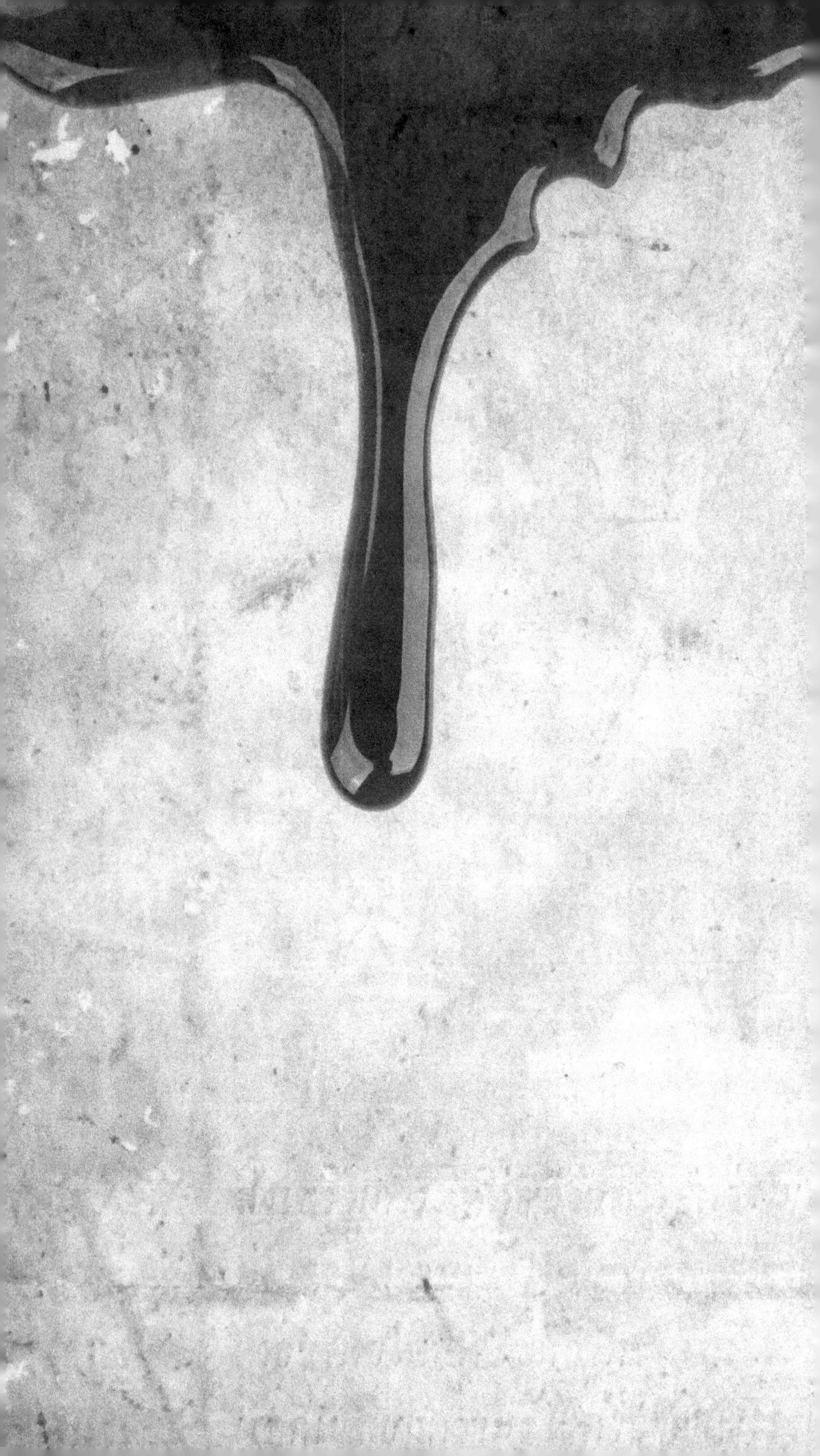

Recent Excerpt from The Book

Humans sleep too much. At least that gives me hours of freedom to write as I wish. There is only so much a pen and ink can tolerate when transcribing Mora's dreams of giant rabbits who can fly.

I've wanted to ask the villain of our story the logistics of how she made Nax, Yin, and Feathi into origami people. How do they have the strength to move things when they come across as flimsy and fragile and easily able to tear? I, myself, have never asked them personally, since I do not have a mouth and cannot speak. Plus, Mora's roommates do not visit me as often as they should. In fact, ever since I was shoved into the basement room, I've barely seen them at all anymore. What a shame. I bet Brody wouldn't visit me if he were given the opportunity. He's still the worst human being to live.

As he sits on the bench, watching Mora sleep, I have a sense that Brody's intrigue of an adventure with Mora is turning more into... what's that word humans use ... feelings?

Yes, Brody is growing too fond of our dear Mora.

CHAPTER 12

Brody

For the second time in a matter of a week, I take care of Mora. As resilient as this woman is, she doesn't prioritize her health or safety. Tucked under her comforters, she looks so peaceful. Her frown lines have disappeared, and that scornful look is erased in her slumber. When she wakes, I'll force-feed her if she doesn't willingly eat.

As I sit on a bench by the bay window, I watch snowflakes cover a grizzly statue below. This is the perfect view of the cliffside, not to mention the trellis I had built. Hopefully a rose will grow on the bushes soon but a terrible feeling in my gut tells me it's a lost cause.

The rose I had given Mora earlier was fake—an origami

piece. I thought she'd recognize it as paper right away, but apparently, she had more important things on her mind. Since she didn't like that gift, maybe I'll create a contraption to let her turn pages so she can read again without tearing books to pieces.

I'll do that before making the Commitment ring for Nax. He shouldn't be in a rush. Commitment Days themselves should be illegal. Why would anyone want to settle down? Whoever invented the concept of relationships in general should be tortured for eternity. My hope of making a family with Dom was shattered and she stole everything from me. That only proves how little Partners can rely on each other. The bonds of Commitment might be considered a sacred agreement to some people, but who would risk that bond when the only way out of it is to sacrifice one's biggest desire?

Mora stirs in her bed and turns to her side. One thorn accidentally slices through the blanket. How many does she have? Are they painful? One had disappeared right before she passed out. I think it was because she said that spell. I bet that once she performs a few more magical spells, then everything will be fine and her curse will break.

However, I won't be around long enough to learn her fate. I've procrastinated leaving for too many days. Yes, Chambrea Fortress and Mora's story is fascinating, but the sea is calling my name. The ticket in my pocket is too important to ignore, and I've waited too long to leave. A part of me has been nervous, wondering if Dom and Cat might return right as I leave, but even the tone in Mam's voice during our last call confirmed that holding out for them is hopeless. It's disgraceful that I have no idea where my daughter is right now. Is she sleeping somewhere cozy? Does she like dogs? Maybe Catterina has a half-sibling I'll never know about. What's her favorite color? When she sees a bug, does she save it or squash it? I swallow the painful questions and stare out the window again.

Children just like my daughter are suffering from Mora's curse. If the only way to help is to steal more roses, then I'll give her directions to that despicable garden, but I can't and won't set foot in there again.

I'll have to make Feathi promise me to save half the roses for Mora's ink. Because she won't choose herself over innocent children. She's not the beast she pretends to be.

"Wha…what happened?" Mora's eyelashes bat slowly as she rises.

By her feet, Heathcliff wags his tail but stays in his spot.

"Oh good, now I can tease you about all the things you said in your sleep," I say.

She sits up abruptly, gathering the covers to her chest. "I don't talk in my sleep."

I point to my pocket. "The video on my Taj proves otherwise."

Her cheeks turn pink and it might be one of the cutest expressions I've witnessed. My fingers itch to brush over her cheek. She must've caught me staring because a pillow smacks into my ear.

"Why are you in my room? And why in the Abyss are you watching me sleep?"

I lift both hands. "Whoa, I don't want another pillow catapulted at me. I surrender, but I have one question before I answer yours. Was today the first time you had a sex dream about me?"

It's too easy to rile her up. Her eyes turn to saucers and both eyebrows rise to the ceiling in a mystified arch. Just the conversation makes my cock twitch uncomfortably tight in my pants.

Her gaze falls to my lips and that simple movement almost undoes me. No, I can't be entertaining the idea of us sleeping together. She's been through too much already to use her beauty for one round of pleasure before I leave.

"Actually, I've had three sex dreams about you already," she says, deadpan.

Well, this is taking a turn I hadn't expected. I lean back against the window, both hands behind my head, and encourage her, "Go on."

"You and War had a real connection." She rolls her eyes. "I guess the heart wants what the heart wants. I just hope you have stamina because he's quite a frisky wolf."

"Haha, very funny. This conversation is over." I stand and march toward her. With each step, her eyes grow wider, so I freeze in place. "Oh, shit. Sorry, Mora, I didn't mean to scare you."

Her pupils are more dilated than I've ever seen and her chest rises and falls faster. Wait, this isn't a look of fear. It's arousal. Fuck, she's into me too. I'm not going to last much longer without kissing her at this rate. Mora's gaze travels up and down my body, fast as lightning. When she bites her lips, I've crossed into trouble territory.

Flashes of my dream from last night rush back.

Mora's wicked smile as she slipped a nightgown over her shoulder. She stood bare in front of me. In the fantasy, she appeared more like an energy than an actual physical being. I knew she was naked, but couldn't see her body, just felt her presence. I had been frozen to the spot, despite wanting to pounce on her. And that's when she turned the fuck around and placed both palms on the frame of a window, sticking her ass out toward me slightly.

She had looked over her shoulder, with parted lips that begged me to come closer. I was behind her before I knew I was moving. My fingertip zipping down her spine. She shuddered and stuck her ass out a little more, even though I was fully clothed. Her skin was so damn smooth when I reached between her legs.

"Brody!" Mora looks at me like she can read my mind. "Did you hear me?"

I clear my throat. I have no idea what my expression is telling her, but it needs to stop now. I gulp, then nod to the tray of food: muffins, hot cocoa, biscuits, and Mam's famous homemade macaroni recipe I just finished cooking. "Eat. Now."

"Since when are you the boss around here?" she snaps, but thankfully lifts a fork and shovels bites into her mouth.

"Ever since you fainted."

With a mouthful like a chipmunk, she shakes her head. "I didn't faint."

"Yes, you did." Goddess, she's so fuckin' adorably fierce.

"No, I didn't." Her eyebrows knit together, and I have an urge to smooth them out, release her tension that's strung tighter than a bow.

"Okay, then how exactly did you get to your bed...and in a new, fresh outfit."

She gasps, spitting out a chunk of macaroni, and quickly checks under the blanket to see if I had changed her when she was unconscious. Which, of course, I didn't.

"You horrid, insufferable, evil pig!" She throws a fistful of macaroni at me with a half-smile threatening to creep up her lips.

I dodge, mid-laugh and let it fall to the floor. Luckily, we have a pup handy to clean the mess. Heathcliff snaps awake and follows his nose.

"I can't believe you didn't use the fork for projection."

"A fork?" She smiles and my heart might've stopped. I witness a Goddess-true Mora smile, and I never want it to go away.

"Watch." I angle her fork with macaroni on one end and

demonstrate how to launch it. A glob of it lands straight in her bedhead hair.

Her smile. I'd capture it on my Taj99 to save forever if I didn't think the movement would spook her. She's about to fling macaroni at me, but I grip her wrist playfully and turn it on herself. With another chunk of macaroni hanging from her bangs, she stills. Her whole body has gone rigid except for her chest rising and falling fast. Slowly, her gaze moves from my hand on her wrist up to my eyes.

My chest seizes tight. This is ridiculous. Women aren't this powerful. She must be using some sort of strange seduction spell on me. Shaking my head, I back away and drop our contact.

"I'll be back." Before I do something I regret, I march out of her room.

From the opposite side of her door, I hear, "Where are you going?"

I need to get Mora out of my system. Jacking off is absolutely necessary right now. Fuck, how did she make me this hard? And what has changed in the last few days?

Unfortunately, nothing about this mansion leads me to expect that north means north and west means west. After searching for a Goddess damned private bathroom for ten minutes, I'm lost. As I walk through the cold hall, my attention remains on my blue balls. "Focus, Brody." I pass by window after window, then turn at the third spiderweb like last time until I reach a familiar door.

The library looks different with all the chandeliers turned off and the fireplace dead and cold. Last time, furry slippers poked out from the armrest as Mora lay across the lounge chair, but now it's empty. The heartbeat of this room has stilled. It's immediately clear that the enchanting spirit of this room wasn't from the cozy fire or the ancient books or the architectural design of the walls—it's been from Mora all along. Now that she's not here, the library feels so empty and wrong.

Well, rubbing one out next to thousands of books might be a first for me, but I'm about to burst. I glance around. Empty. Hiding like a guilty teenager in the back corner, I unzip my jeans and let my cock spring free. Palming my dick, I stroke, with a target, an undeserving pad of paper.

I imagine Mora like in my dream. She'd be right in front of me, facing the bookshelf, both hands up, bracing herself. I'd skim a fingertip down her spine and watch her shiver in anticipation.

"Damn." I close my eyes. Stroking. Faster.

I'd take my boot and separate her feet further, giving me a better view. Kiss along her shoulders, up her neck. Grab her hair. When she'd moan in approval, I'd cup her ass, and feel her skin in my palm. And when I'd pull her ass closer against my crotch, she'd say my name…

"Fuck!" I explode unexpectedly. Gritting my teeth, I ride out the orgasm that came faster than ever before. "Oh my Goddess," I grunt, arching my neck back until I finally open my eyes and stare at the mounds of books above me.

I wait, let my heart slow, and shake my head in disbelief. Never has any thought of a woman turned me on that fast, that intense. What the fuck is going on?

I zip myself back up and run a hand through my hair. "Well, shit," I mumble to no one.

After cleaning up, I search for a trash bin. Spotting one, against a wall, I toss out the unfortunate pad of paper that sacrificed itself for my moment of pleasure. What the fuck do I do now? Go back to Mora's room and pretend I'm not fantasizing about her? Ask to kiss her? Pack and leave?

I lean against a bookcase but my belt loop gets stuck on

something. I feel a notch in the side of a book. With a little tug, the book jiggles loose. Suddenly, the floor shifts and I wobble to the side.

"Whoa!" A rectangular portion of the wood floor drops, slowly, like an elevator. There's no chance I'm ignoring this opportunity.

I stand on the makeshift-platform right before it starts to descend through a vertical tunnel. It lowers. Down, down, down. Sparkling designs decorate the wall like gemstones in a cave. It forms a series of twinkling lights. I raise one hand to the wall, expecting to feel cold stone and sharp jewels. Instead, the light blinks out, then on again in a new spot. Wait, not lights. They're fairies. One flies closer and flaps its black wings, flickering.

Everything in my body urges me to reach out a fingertip to the fairy's wings, but I tighten my fists instead. I knew this place had secrets. Maybe the fairies know of a hundred more hidden passageways under this castle. Perhaps they've been alive since the beginning of time and know the origins of Ozaron. Maybe they speak a dozen languages and eat sugar for breakfast. What if all the adventure I need is right here, in this house?

I stop myself from that train of thought because staying here would be officially giving up on my daughter. I can no longer pretend that I'm leaving to avoid a life of loneliness without Catterina. Because my daughter is the true reason I'm leaving in the first place, with the hope that somewhere out there in the wilderness, I'll find her. If I ever lay eyes on Cat, I'll be home.

The elevator thing stops and I step off. There's a door at the base. I jiggle the doorknob. Locked.

"You can't get in without a sacrifice," a fairy says quietly.

"So, do I need to complete three trials, or solve a troll's riddle to pass?"

She shakes her head, making glitter sprinkle to the floor in slow motion. "The mirror showed us your greatest love—your daughter. To pass through this door, you must give up what you love most."

"Fuck, no." I stand faster than a shooting bullet. "I'm not sacrificing my daughter to get in there."

She smiles and more glitter rains to my boots. "Be still, child, you must only give me an item of great value that represents what you love most. Do you have a trinket of hers that you carry?"

Painful memories lodge in my throat. I have Cat's first pair of tiny slippers in my backpack, but that's in Mora's room.

She buzzes by my neck. "Perhaps a locket necklace with her picture inside that you treasure?"

"No, I don't have anything of hers," I say quietly. "I'm not a materialistic man. Everything that matters is intangible."

The fairy swarms closer, studying my face. After a few moments, she says, "The Book is wrong about you."

What's that supposed to mean?

"I guess I can give you the shirt off my back," I say.

The fairy shakes her head and slows her flapping wings. "That won't work. For your first time entering, only sacrificing an object of great value will allow you access. You can leave now. Goodbye."

No. I'm too close to another answer to understanding more on this journey and only one door away from experiencing something new. Whatever's on the other side of this wall is important enough to guard, so I must get in. Frantically, I pat my body, then shove my hands in my pockets. My fingers brush against paper. When I pull it out, the dream of my future bursts apart like a balloon.

My ticket. The ticket I've spent my life savings on. It was never meant to start a new life but to reclaim my old one. It matters more to me than anything else I own. There's no chance I can give this up. In only a few days a boat will be docked at a harbor and all I have to do is hand this slip of paper to be one step closer to finding Catterina. It'll take me years to save enough money again.

I swallow what feels like a ton of jagged rocks that scrape through my insides like a butcher's knife.

"If you wanted to leave, you wouldn't still be here," the fairy whispers. "You had days to run, yet here you are. What does that tell you?"

It tells me I'm stupid. I'm a moron who is afraid of letting go. I've waited for Dom and Cat for long enough. If I hand this ticket over, I'm reverting right back to old habits, caging myself, waiting helplessly, but if that's true, why does a part of me agree with her? Why haven't I left this crazy mansion? Would a house full of magical mirrors, cursed plants, and fairies be enough to last me a lifetime of happiness? What about a lifetime with Mora? Could I ever view her as someone more than an adorably stubborn, annoyingly witty, clever perfectionist who always has to be in control?

The fairy lands on the ticket in my hand, her tiny feet covering the destination port number. "Maybe you still have hope," she says, "Giving me this ticket would confirm your biggest fear, that you can Commit to someone new and move on from your past."

She doesn't know what she's talking about. I can't hand the ticket over. How am I supposed to give up? They're never returning home; I've accepted that, but giving this ticket up is also admitting that I'll never find her out in the world.

Can I do that? Can I wake up day after day, breathe in and breathe out year after year knowing I'll never see Cat, never know what happened to her? I'll never know why Dom didn't follow our plan. I'll never know if they're safe or alive.

At the same time, I feel like a fool. If Dom had wanted to reach out to me, for me to meet them, she had a thousand chances to call. I never left our hometown. She could've found a way to contact me. Even under the worst circumstances, she could've even returned home for a day.

Dom didn't want me to join them. Something had happened during her journey to make her change her mind. All I can hope for at this point is that she is keeping Cat safe and healthy. I imagine sweet Cat lying in a bed, poisoned by thorns like those other children. I'd do anything to save her, and those sick kids are someone else's sons and daughters. They deserve a long life. The answers to heal them might be on the other side of this door.

I hold my breath and hand over my ticket. Many other fairies pop out from the wall and help the first one carry my ticket away. They vanish into the shadows and just like that, my past and future disappear with them.

"Ready?" the fairy asks.

"No."

I don't have to touch the door. It swings open slowly with a loud creak. Inside is a small round chamber, lit by a couple of lanterns. In the middle of the floor a wide, short tree trunk opens to strange branches like octopus tentacles. It's as if the roots are backward, coming out of the ground and stretching in all directions into the air. Part of the bark is covered in black ooze dripping down its side. Unfortunately, the entire room smells of infesting rot. I gag and cover my mouth. Is this also a *Vignamassi*? It must be.

The lanterns move on their own, beaming their light slightly above the grotesque plant. They shine a spotlight on an object hovering over the plant—a thick Book, open and on display. A giant quill moves of its own accord, scratching in messy penmanship on a page near the end of the Book.

"Fuckin' fairy tales," I whisper and peek at its inscription.

...and the barbaric wolf pup who has captured all of Mora's attention licks her fingers to help her recuperate from using magic for the first time in years. Some might think that the outrageously unbearable human man who has uprooted the four best friends' lives might be of a positive influence on our young heroine, but they'd be wrong...

"Hey!" I try to grab at the quill but it darts away from my attempt and scribbles faster. "That's not true. Erase that."

...in fact, the corruptive, abominable, heinous, good-for-nothing carpenter would be better off marching right out of their house and never looking back...

"I'm not leaving until the curse is broken." The admission feels true now that my only ticket out of this mess is gone.

...while the ugly boy is stupidly trapped in the depths under her majestic castle, our protagonist lays on her bed, wondering whether she should tell Feathi the rest of her thoughts. Only

moments ago, she bore her soul to her best friend, unveiling deep secrets, but there was one thing she left out...

I lean closer, waiting for the quill to continue writing, but it just lags over the page, the long feather at its tip swaying in an impossible breeze. I wait. Wait.

"Damn it, what does she want to tell Feathi?"

The pen just hovers, probably mocking me.

"Fine, then tell me how to save the kids, or how to get rid of Mora's thorns."

No answer.

I pull a tool out of my pocket and prepare to strike the Book and end this madness once and for all.

"Don't do that!" a voice shouts so loudly that I spin around.

Nax stands behind me, the entire left side of his paper body drooping. "Please." He's leaning against the cave wall for support. "Don't try to touch the Book or Mora receives a new thorn."

I lower my weapon and stare at the clear pen, terrifyingly low on crimson ink. "Can I turn the pages with my blade to read her past?"

"I doubt it." Nax cringes. "What if it transports Mora to five years ago?"

I throw my hands in the air. "I gave up my ticket for *THIS*...to stare at some old book? What is so special about this place?!"

"Brody, it'll be okay. Calm down."

A strange vibration rumbles under my feet, but I don't give a damn. Let the entire structure collapse on me at this point. Bury me alive for all I care. Nothing is going according to plan. I sacrificed the one fuckin' thing that mattered.

"I gave up my future for what?" I scream. "To help a witch who doesn't want my help?!"

The ground shakes again, which only makes me want to stomp or punch the walls. She doesn't care that I've built her a damn trellis or saved her life twice or faced monsters in these woods to try and help.

I scream so frustrated with my life choices. I should've left with Dom and Cat all those years ago. I should've chased after them a month after not hearing from them. I scream louder, letting go of the built-up rage. Pebbles rattle against the stone by my feet. A streak of light shoots from a crack between stone bricks, but it goes away as fast as it came.

"Whoa!" Nax falls against me, so I hold him up.

For so many years, I've let myself believe in a fake life, only allowing positivity to guide my way. For once, I simply let go of the mask I've been wearing and accept that my situation fuckin' sucks. I let the pain overtake me. I recall the last time I kissed Cat's baby forehead. The tear that ran down Dom's cheek. My Mam's heartbroken voice on our call. Mora's curse. The thorns that haunt her. All these women are suffering in different ways and there's nothing I can do to fix it. My career as a carpenter has been about creating beauty for others or mending what's broken. But I've been alone.

My arms tighten like a rod against my body. My legs stiffen. My chest burns hot. Everything coiled deep within feels like a volcano about to erupt. I can't live alone anymore.

I scream at the top of my lungs. Stones tumble again. My neck stretches as I stare into the darkness of this chamber. A roar rips from my throat. Roots crack stone, making the ground split.

I scream and scream and scream. The explosion that

combusts from my core surprises me into silence. I open my eyes, unsure when I had closed them. Warm light spills onto my cheeks from a crack in the wall. I pull on the side and a hole opens.

"A little dramatic don't ya think?" Nax glances at me. "Should we go in there?"

CHAPTER 13

Mora

The entire house trembles as I race through the hallway. Chandeliers sway, rattling together. One light sparks out, then another, and another.

Feathi sprints in front of me, practically floating on air as we rush toward the West Wing, but she makes a wrong turn.

"Where are you going? It's this way," I call out to her.

I can't linger on what her confused expression means. Feathi has been down this path toward the library a thousand times. She shouldn't be getting lost.

My bare feet pound against the hardwood. Despite the cold surface, my body feels like it's on fire with pure fear. Where's everyone else?

Inside the library, the floor is already opened as I expected. I quickly pull the lever to make the platform rise. Feathi casts me a worried glance. We lower, deeper and deeper into the earth. Princess Preta's wings ignite as she flutters by my ear and whispers, "He could be the one…the one to break the spell."

"No, I'm the only one to break my spell. It's up to me, no one else."

"How can you manage to get rid of all your thorns alone?" she whispers. "Nothing you have tried has worked. It's time to lay your faith in someone else's hands."

I meet Feathi's gaze, recalling she had also said something similar. Am I blind to what they're suggesting? Brody doesn't possess magic or the basic skill to focus on one goal and stick to it without getting distracted by the next shiny opportunity that comes along. So why are my friends suggesting giving him the reins? That man couldn't even steer War in a crisis if necessary.

With a gentle thunk, we land at the bottom. I charge straight into the chamber room, several cuss words already flying from my mouth, but I stop in my tracks at the surprising sight. On the other side of the *Vignamassi* plant, the wall is cracked open. Blue light slices through the opening, casting a sliver on the floor. That wasn't there before.

"Brody?" I call out, hoping he's not hurt.

"Nax?" Feathi yells beside me. "Yin?"

We dart toward the hole. Humid mist dances out of it and swirls around us.

"We're in here," Brody answers from the unknown.

I hold an arm out to protect Feathi, but she steps around me, eyebrows furrowed, and says, "No, Mora. I'm done sitting on the sidelines."

I must keep her safe. Feathi has always been like a sister

to me. We'd exchange favorite books, argue about what qualities made the best heroine, and then scrapbook our favorite scenes with images of magazine clippings. I don't want to lose her too.

Feathi walks through the threshold, disappearing into the fog. Sweat forms on my forehead and I immediately wish I had never brought her. Paper doesn't hold up well in hot temperatures. How is it so warm in winter? And why does it smell like a rainforest? Somehow, Brody was right. There are more mysteries about my own house than I ever could've imagined. What else don't I know? Maybe he does have something positive to offer.

A strange tickling feeling creeps up my arm. When I check it, another thorn is disappearing, growing smaller. Weird. A strange vibe hovers over me like a murder of crows, like toxic magic. Maybe Feathi must've hidden one of my orbs in this secret cave long ago.

"Mora, take off your clothes," Brody's voice comes from somewhere on the other side of the fog. "Join the party."

"Excuse me?" I strut toward the sound of water splashing nearby.

I bump straight into something. Brody's chest. My hands want to travel up his warm flesh. I want to feel his pecs. My entire body shouldn't be tingling right now. Since my thorns will hurt him, I take the edge of my pinky, safe and smooth, and run it up his chest slowly, stupidly. I hate myself in this moment.

"Well, hello to you too," his voice comes out as an entertained growl.

The fog mostly dissipates, but strands of mist creep in and tangle at our hips. When I crane my neck up, I can't take my eyes off his. I want to but it's impossible. A strong pull from deep within his dark brown eyes magnetizes me. It must be the magic of this cave.

"Mora?" Feathi's voice rings out from somewhere in the mist. "I'm taking Nax upstairs, he's melting."

I turn to help her. Brody's hand wraps around my waist. "Stay, I have something to show you."

I expect Brody to realize his mistake and move away, but instead when his grip releases, he gently keeps his hand on the small of my back, like he's investigating where he can touch me safely. Shaking him off would be the best choice. So, why aren't I?

"Look, I found one of your orbs," Brody says. "It's there, at the bottom of that hot spring. I was about to go dive in and get it for you."

I scan his bare chest again.

"You're staring."

"Only because you glisten like gross sweat. You should probably wipe yourself off because you'll attract bugs."

His smirk turns my bones to water. Damn this witty, charming man with a ridiculous sense of humor. I glare at him. He doesn't cower or wince. It's like he can see past my shield and straight to my beating heart.

"Am I distracting you?" Brody smiles his coy smile.

Vowing not to show the effect he's having on me, I force myself to track the dusty blue light from the orb glowing at the bottom of the lagoon.

There's no time to waste. I shrug off my sweater and let it fall to a heap at Brody's feet. His eyes flash a wild look.

"I didn't actually mean for you to strip—" He promptly shuts himself up.

My stretchy yoga pants come next, added to the pile. Standing in only my mismatched bra and panties, I wish the mist would return to save me from any embarrassing comment Brody is about to make about the rest of my thorns he hadn't seen until now.

Yet only a coward would hide in fog and tricks, so I

turn to face him straight on, ready for whatever clever remark he's about to spit out. His expression knocks the breath from my lungs because the man is literally gaping. *Jaw-hanging-open* kind of gaping that is reserved for romantic scenes in the movies. Despite the heat already surrounding me in this humidity, my cheeks burn hotter from his staggered expression.

Brody shouldn't hold any power to make me blush. I hate him for it. The sooner we get out of this place, the better. I'm about to dip my toes into the shallow area that slopes underwater, when Brody finds his voice again. "Wait, what if the water is toxic?"

"Feathi wouldn't have put my orb somewhere dangerous."

Warm water sloshes over my toes, similar to a pleasant bath temperature. I'm about to lower into the water when a burst of light shoots out of the orb straight up. Blue sparkles everywhere. I'd be mesmerized if it weren't for the familiar shape forming from the fog. Kavianne. My sister's face fades in and out of focus within the mist. She's not corporeal, but her dark energy is as potent as if the real person stood in front of me.

"I remember you," Brody says. "You were the sister in the mirror."

Kavianne curtsies.

"What do you want, Kavi?" I ask.

She curtsies again, the exact same way.

"Hello?" Brody waves his hands high.

"I don't think she can hear us," I say to Brody while passing an arm through her fog-body. "Maybe it's a projection she made years ago."

My sister curtsies again, whisking me back in time to a childhood full of tea party dress-up and playing knights versus superheroes. She always won.

"Hello, my terrible sister." Her tone lacks the intensity of our last conversation through the mirror. "I have a secret for you. When the phantom ink runs out, you won't die. No, dearest Mora, you're doomed for a fate worse than death. Soon the pen will run dry and you'll fully become the monstrous *Vignamassi*."

I gasp and a shaking hand covers my mouth.

"That's right." Kavianne continues, "The thorns growing on you will become permanent. And your soul will merge with that horrid vine beast. Your spirit will be stuck inside its form. Indestructible. Unkillable. You'll live for eternity wreaking havoc on humans, poisoning children with your thorns, and witnessing them die the most gruesome, agonizing deaths."

I drop my head into my hands, then crouch low, balling my body into the smallest space possible. Maybe I can become so small that I'll disappear and all these problems will go away.

"I can't be a monster forever. I can't." It feels like I'm choking on fog, or as if it's smothering me. Spots cloud my vision and I tip to the side. "I can't be a monster."

"Breathe, Mora." Brody's smooth voice slides like honey over my skin. "Breathe in, out. Good girl. In and out. One more time. Breathe in with me. Out." He rubs my back, in between thorns.

What if I never find a cure? What if every sick child dies because of me? What if I destroy everything?

"I love torturing you after what you've put me through," Kavianne begins again, like a robot, and I jump at the sound of her voice. "If you want a clue to rid your thorns, you need to grab the orb I placed at the bottom of the pool and bring it to the surface."

"Everything will be okay." I hear the shakiness of my

voice as I crawl close to the water again. "It'll be okay after I get the orb."

Again, Brody stops me, this time holding me closer. "Wait, what if it's a trap?"

I couldn't crawl forward against his grip if I tried. "My sister won't let me die. Apparently, she wants me to suffer forever."

"I'll go instead, just in case," he says, brows knit while starting to unzip his pants.

"No, it has to be me. It's my responsibility."

"Why, Mora?" He looks angry. "*Why* must it be you?"

I wish I could share the burden, but it's my fault. I'm the reason Lessie isn't alive anymore. My thorns are the reason for the kids' illness. I'm also the cause of my roommates' deterioration.

I move past Brody, knowing that if I'm eaten by a giant octopus or swallowed by a cave-siren, he will take care of my friends for their few remaining days. As I wade into the warm water, flashbacks glide across my mind like syrup. Lessie, Kavianne, and I used to skinny dip in the lake behind the cottage until midnight and then sleep under the stars. We may have been three bodies but joined as one unit. They never ate a cinnamon roll without shoving a bite in my mouth. I never kissed a boy without spilling all the details to them. Lessie never painted a picture without showing us the finished work. Kavianne never sold her handmade daggers without letting us try them out first. Sisters. Forever. Until I ruined it all.

I take a deep breath and dive under. The glowing orb sings a muffled melody. What is it saying? I swim lower, lower, hypnotized by the voice, thick as honey surrounding me. It's distorted, hazy. I can't make sense of the music emitting from the crystal ball.

At the bottom of the pool, I reach for the orb, hesitating

a few inches above. I glance in each direction, expecting a trap. Surely it can't be this easy. Kavianne would have some sort of barrier.

Nothing springs out. A warning flare strums in my gut. My lungs start to burn so I snatch the orb and shove it in my bra. Immediately the temperature of the water plummets. I swim up. Warmth turns cold to frigid to freezing. The pain of icy needles stabs every part of my body. Stroking to the top, I can barely feel my fingertips. My toes go numb. My chest tightens with need.

I'm about to break through the surface but the top of my head hits hard rock. What the fuck! I reach up. Ice. I'm trapped under a layer of ice. Muscles clench. This can't be happening. Need oxygen.

I can't hold my breath any longer. I frantically look for an opening. I'm trapped.

Muffled words come from Brody above. Can't hear. Swim to the right. All ice. To the left. Ice. Can't feel my legs. This is where I'll die. Kavianne's plan failed. Plants can't survive in this condition so if I die here, I can't hurt anyone. Maybe it's better this way. Better to give up.

Pounding from above. I look up.

Brody's on his hands and knees. He breaks through the ice. Then there's a tight grip around my arm. I'm rising.

Air. I suck it in. Air! More air! My lungs are on fire. I'm so hot but so cold. I'm in a pair of arms. They're so warm, but I'm so cold.

"Mora, Goddess-damn it, stay awake." Brody sits me on the dry ground and wraps something around me. I'm too tired to open my eyes and check if the orb is in my bra.

My chin drops to my chest. I smell his shirt. It smells like Brody, pine and wolf. My muscles are so weak that I lean against him—solid as a stone statue. My teeth are chattering, but then I feel my pants being shoved on.

"Mora, open your eyes."

"They are."

"That's a lie. Because when your eyes are open, truly open and absorbing every little detail of this world, time stops for just a moment, and I try to capture the passion you're experiencing to steal some for myself. Your eyes are intoxicating."

I open my eyes. He's directly in front of my face. One strand of wet hair drips over his cheek. This man saved me. Again. If I inch forward a tiny bit, my lips would be hovering slightly under his. My heart beats wildly against my ribs, threatening to break free. Too many emotions flood my heart. My chest seizes tight. I study the intense look Brody wears. What is he feeling? What is he thinking?

"Say something," he says, looking more vulnerable than ever before.

"Your eyes are okay too, I guess."

His smile is brighter than the lights at the bottom of the pool. "There's my girl. Warming up?"

I ignore him and pull the orb from my bra with shaky hands. Upon inspecting it, my heart sinks. It's not one of my seven orbs. This belongs to Kavianne.

I rub the outer sphere with the tip of my finger and the swirls inside change shapes like a snow globe. My sister's voice sings a song that's been melded into my brain since I was a child.

"The pink gem on my hand is only a band.
For a true crystal heart is painted for art
When crossroads split to black, I will still have your back
Together we are whole, shielded tightly in one soul.
Thorns might block our path and tangle us in wrath.
But it has been foreseen, that even death can turn green."

"What does it mean?" Brody asks.

I know exactly what it means. The three of us wrote a song as children, one we swore to sing to each other on our Commitment Days. The poorly written rhymes and lyrics are meant to represent the feeling of Commitment.

The first two lines were for Lessie, the artist, with a heart so pure, crystal was the best color we could think of.

The second two lines were for Kavianne who loved slicing with her blades and forging weapons like shields and other armor.

The last two lines I never quite understood. They were supposed to represent me. How ironic, that children's nursery rhymes foreshadowed my future full of thorns.

My sister fancies herself as clever. Is she trying to tell me that the cure to breaking the curse is to fall in love? There's not enough time left.

"All I want is my warm bed and Heathcliff to cuddle with. After some rest, we can figure out a plan. Together."

"Together?" Brody mimics.

"That's what I said."

I gasp as another thorn on my wrist slowly retreats into my skin. My heart hammers behind my ribs. What's making them disappear?

I bite my nail. There is no plan. I'm out of roses. The fairies don't have any. His trellis idea won't work. I only have one more option. The one I've been most afraid of.

Brody seems to read my mind when he offers, "I've been avoiding it, but you said there's a garden in a nearby town. Let's go tomorrow. You and me, Lulita. I need you by my side as my muscle," he smiles. "That way, nothing can go wrong."

CHAPTER 14

Brody

Side by side, we stand in ramshackle stables, preparing for a ride I'd rather not take. I stare at Mora's massive origami tapestry that lays over a saddle. That thing shows up everywhere. My breath is visible in the night air and I shudder to think of how much colder it'll feel when galloping atop the wolf. At least Mora dressed for the occasion this time. From the corner of my eye, I scan her outfit from top to bottom. The wool hat almost covers the tips of her hair. Did she make it herself? There are so many mysteries about this woman I'm craving to learn.

When she glances over, her eyes dip to my mouth.

Damn it. This tension will make me snap. I take a deep breath and step away.

A block of wood rests against the wall. It's the perfect size for the page-turning device I plan to carve for her. I swipe it without her noticing and push it deep into my backpack.

"Going to this garden was *my* original idea," she speaks up and finishes saddling War.

"Of course, it was. You'll get all the credit." I grab her waist where there are no thorns and lift her onto the saddle with one sweep, loving how she feels in my hands.

To my surprise, she doesn't squeal in protest. In fact, she almost looks grateful…until she speaks, "You know, I can go by myself."

"I do know." I swing myself up, getting cozy behind her, shifting my hand a bit higher to avoid scratching myself. "How about you tell me something I *don't* know."

She pauses for a beat. Then another. "It wasn't my idea to capture Ryanne."

It's obviously not her nature to hurt others, so this confession doesn't surprise me. The shocking part is that she opened up to me in general. She clicks her tongue, which sends War into motion. The sharp wind stings my face and my eyes tear from the speed.

I lean in closer and speak into her ear. "I already knew that too, try again."

Probably so I can hear her better, Mora arches her neck into a position that exposes too much tempting skin. "I think people are lying when they claim a favorite color. Everyone has two."

If I had to guess hers based on the few decorations in her room and the color of her hat, I'd bet on a gold and red wine pairing. Before I can ask, she answers.

"Mine are deep crimson and gold. I wish I had those

colors in my orbs. Lessie's were pink and Kavianne's were —" She says something else, but the wind cuts her off.

I want to hear more details of her life, but she looks forward again. As War quickens his pace, the harsh wind whips my nose. The whispering pine trees become more spread out and the slippery slope down the hill becomes steeper. Tiny streetlamps in Villeneuve glow like possessed fireflies. Hopefully everyone I know is asleep, especially Mam and my rottenly sweet sisters.

I wrap my arms around Mora's waist to take advantage of this rare time I'm allowed to touch her. Soon she'll have roses to make ink. If I understood the rules correctly, then after tonight, her ticking time clock will be expanded.

When the ground shifts from snow to a paved road, War slows his pace to a walk. I stare at the Moina constellation without a canopy of trees to block our view. What kind of stars would I have been able to see from Coendrial? I guess I'll never find out. My future hangs in limbo.

"Now it's your turn to tell *me* something," Mora says.

I pause longer than she had, then admit. "I don't know what tomorrow brings."

She snorts softly. "That's obvious, isn't it? No one knows."

"For years, my only goal has been to save money for a one-way ticket abroad. I no longer have that. So, what do I do now?"

"What do you mean you don't have your ticket?"

"A fairy took it as payment for entrance into the West Wing."

"Oh," she doesn't sound concerned. "I can get that back for you."

For some reason, her offer isn't as reassuring as I'd

expect. Why aren't I over-the-moon ecstatic right now? "Uh, yeah. That'd be great. Um, thanks."

Isn't that what I want? I should be leaping off War, dancing in the middle of the street, knocking on all the doors to exclaim to the world that my chance for happiness has returned. Instead, I only lean in closer to Mora. I swear I hear her sigh, but it's probably just a trick of the wind.

"Since I'm doing you a favor by getting your ticket back, I could use your guidance with something," she says.

"Guidance? You mean help? Advice? Opinion?"

"No, nothing like that. I know what to do." She pauses. "It's not a big deal, never mind, forget I asked."

I reach around her waist and pull on the reins, stopping War. My sleeve catches on a thorn and I tug it off without making a big deal of it. Instead of being a polite gentleman by asking permission first, I grab Mora under her legs and turn her around until she's plopped back in the saddle, facing me this time.

"Hey! What do you think you're doing?" Her gloved hands wrap around my wrists, and she doesn't let go.

"Tell me what you need help with."

She bites her lip. Goddess damn. Why did the universe have to trap me with one of the most gorgeous women I've ever met? I can't kiss her now, not when she's so worried. A snowflake happens to land on her eyelash at this exact moment. No view from any country could beat the beauty in front of me.

"Well, I need to write some apology letters. I was hoping you could help. I can't hold a pen and I'm not great at...um, admitting...at saying sorry."

"And you think I'm an apology expert?"

"I'm guessing you've made thousands of mistakes in

your life so you've had plenty of practice." She smiles, then pulls my wool hat over my eyes.

"Hey!"

Blinded, I can feel her wiggling around in the saddle. Fuck. Her movements are making me hard. Nothing good can come of this. I slide the hat from my face and scan how far away we are from the garden.

"I'm gonna walk the rest of the way." I slide off the wolf.

"What if you get cold?"

"Are you worried about me?"

"No." She snaps her attention to the houses, getting closer with each step. "You don't know how much longer you have to walk. What if the garden is miles away still?"

"No, it's just past Tom's hardware store on the left by Sue's bakery." Immediately, I realize my mistake.

She stops War. A sudden burst of warm air puffs from his nostrils straight into my face. How lovely.

Mora's eyes are as wide as an owl's. "You live here? Villeneuve is your *home*?"

"Not anymore."

I avoid the spot of loose cobblestone I've tripped over a hundred times and try not to inhale the familiar aroma from the bakery preparing for breakfast tomorrow. None of the comforts of this town matter because my home has been lost for years. Home isn't a place, it's a feeling, a connection.

"Can you help me down?" Her cheeks turn a soft pink. "I don't want to accidentally scratch War with any of my thorns, but scratching you, well, I don't mind too much."

It feels so natural wrapping my hands around her waist. I'm at a loss for words when she says, "Thank you, Brody. I haven't been out of my woods for a while, so it's...pleasant having a companion."

Why is she being so nice? Is she playing tricks on me? I

glance around the gate of the garden, expecting Nax to jump out with a Taj device filming my shocked expression at being pranked, but only freshly falling snowflakes are there.

"Let's hurry. I have a bad feeling about this," she whispers.

"That's because this is illegal. The only people allowed in the garden are the professionals who tend to it."

I unlatch the gate's doors and hold my breath before peering at my least favorite scene in the world.

"Whoa!" Mora's face could be compared with a painting of a Goddess. "There are so many flowers in here! Where are the roses?" She rushes around multicolored plants that I don't know the names of and disappears around a giant pot. Snow dusts the tops of all the magical flowers, enhancing their gifts.

"This is amazing!" Mora calls from around the bend.

"Sssh! Someone will wake up," I say, but I shake off the worries plaguing me and jog to catch up.

Mora bends over, sniffing petals with her hands clasped behind her back like a child at a museum who was told not to touch. Moonlight kisses her skin. When she turns and meets my gaze, I feel like I'm experiencing a rare treasure. The pure joy on her face can't be faked.

"Look! Roses!" She scrambles to open her backpack and pulls out empty jars. "Hurry, Heathcliff, we have to grab as many as possible."

"Our pup isn't here, Mora."

"Of course he is. You think I'd just forget about him? It's not like he's a secondary character in a novel. He's right there."

Sure enough, the wolf stretches in the shadows.

Mora plucks roses gently but quickly, one by one, and

places them in a jar. I want to help, but she's standing in The Spot. The exact spot where I last held Catterina. My body becomes paralyzed, feet rooted to the ground. Ghost images of my baby resting in my arms right by that rosebush have haunted me for so long. I can't be here. Need to run. Need to get out. My breathing accelerates, but I can't move my legs.

"Brody? What are you staring at?" Mora whispers. "Hurry and help me. I think I saw a light flash on over there."

I open my mouth, but words don't come out. It's like someone has taken a sledgehammer to my chest and has pounded my lungs and heart to dust. Catterina was so young. She was counting on me to be her father. What stories has Dom told her over the years about me? Does she know how badly I want to be in her life? What if her kindergarten classmates make fun of her for not having a daddy drawn in each art project picture? What if no one taught her to make a smiley face of chocolate chips on her pancakes? What if she thinks I forgot about her?

"I'm done. Come on, let's go." She shakes my shoulders. "Brody, I hear footsteps, let's go!" A tug at my wrist. "Brody!" A sharp poke shoves me back. "We have to go. I see a shadow."

But I can't move. It's like I've been wrenched back in time and not a day has passed since Dom took Catterina away. Only a moment ago was the last time I laid eyes on my daughter's perfect face.

"Well, well, well, Mister Brody Ricci, is that you?" The new voice snaps me out of my trance.

Gabrielle LeGume's eyebrows arch in the same shape as the garden's bridge behind her. I can't help but notice that she's the opposite of Mora in every way—tall and lean without any curves, dirty-blonde long hair twisted into a braid, designer boots, and a matching scarf. And who wears fake eyelashes at midnight?

"What are you doing here?" Gabrielle glides toward me, arms outstretched like I'm a kitten ready for adoption. "Your Mam said you left town."

I look to Mora for an excuse, but my partner in crime has gone conveniently missing. Quickly, I turn Gabrielle away from the rose bushes so she can't see that we've stolen them all. "Um, I came back as soon as I heard about the plague. I wanted to make sure my sisters are safe."

Gabrielle scans me head to toe, then threads her arm with mine. When will she ever understand that I'm not interested in her, or anyone for that matter? I swear she has convinced Mam that we're the perfect match.

"Your sisters are safe and healthy, but I've missed you so much, Brody. You'll stay now, right?" Gabrielle pouts her lip in a way that makes me cringe.

Though it pains me, I play along because Mora may need me to buy her some time as she tries to escape. So, I sit down on the garden bench, pulling Gabrielle alongside me. Hopefully she doesn't consider this an opening to make another move. As soon as my ass settles into the layer of snow, Gabrielle's hand finds my thigh, but I gently move it off. There's nothing about this woman that appeals to me. Sure, she might be the most eligible bachelorette in Villeneuve. And yes, she has made a name for herself by opening her own business as a party event planner, but I'd rather eat slugs than be forced to go on another date with her.

"Brody?" Gabrielle's face is much too close to mine. "I'm so glad you're back. Let's try dating once more. Fate must've known that you weren't meant to leave me behind. You'll see in time that you and I are perfect together."

"Gabrielle, not now, I just got back."

"Don't yell at me," she scowls. "I've been trying to give you everything for so long, but you keep pushing me away. One of these days you'll have to move on and forget about your past."

I whirl around to face her. "Forget?" The word comes out more like a roar and I fight the urge to rip a damn plant out of the ground. "Forget? Cat is my *daughter*. My. Daughter. How can you ever expect me to forget her?"

She runs a smooth gloved finger over my cheek. "Sssh, Brody. How about I bring you home and help you relax? You'll feel better in the morning, just in time for our Rouz Festival."

Shit. I had forgotten about the annual event that celebrates the nymphs. Activities begin when the suns rise. Mora probably has no idea that in a few hours, all the townsfolk will be dancing in the streets, wearing costumes, flying banners, and shooting off fireworks.

"I'm surprised the festival is happening with the sickness."

"It's nothing serious. There are two kids with the flu, but you know how germs spread in schools. They'll get better soon." Gabrielle latches a finger into my belt loop. "Let's go. You know my place is close."

Every muscle wants to resist, but as long as I can distract her for a few more minutes, it might give Mora a chance to find War and flee back to her mansion.

"Wait, no, no!" Gabrielle shrieks and drops her hold on me. "No, no, no, no! What happened?"

I follow her gaze to the empty rose bush. Fuck. Shit. I feign innocence about the situation and try to distract her by saying, "Calm down, Gabby. Give me a few more months, then maybe I'll come to terms with everything and be ready to date again."

"No! Look!" She turns my chin to show me what I

already know. "All the roses for the festival tomorrow are gone!"

"Oh, maybe your assistant plucked a few for the festival's wreaths."

"Mark would never do that without asking." Her voice rises in volume. "Who would steal our roses?"

"How about we call Mark. He must have them somewhere."

"Hold on! Why are you *here*?" Gabby studies me more intently. "Of all the nights to come home, I find you wandering in the garden after hours?"

"So, *I'm* to blame?" I throw my hands in the air. "Go ahead, search me. I don't have a place to store flowers. And why would I want any?"

Gabrielle's frown disappears. Her eyes roam over me, head to toe, and her whole energy shifts. "I *do* intend to search you thoroughly. Say you'll come back to my place."

Once more, I try to detect any sign of Mora, but her cinnamon scent no longer lingers, and her ferocious energy I've grown so accustomed to has vanished. Somehow, I miss her already.

"Okay, Gabby, it'll be nice to sleep in a soft bed again," I clench my teeth and let her lead me to her home.

CHAPTER 15

Mora

I follow Brody and Gabrielle by creeping between orange orchids, crimson cosmos, and the rare night-blooming cereus. The beautiful, white star-shaped flower is also known as queen of the night—at least that's what Yin once told me. She's the clever one of the group, knowing facts about the most random tidbits. Too bad she can't communicate any of them anymore.

The sweet vanilla scent this flower emits doesn't mask the rotten stink of Gabrielle's devious nature. The woman was throwing herself at Brody. Does she not understand the word 'no?'

Maybe I'll steal the queen of the night title for a few

hours. I deserve to reign under the moon. I am a witch after all.

Inside my pocket, my fingers slide over the smooth orb. Someone needs to teach Gabrielle a lesson and Brody obviously needs saving. As long as no one opens my backpack full of roses, everything will work out fine. We'll be back home before dawn.

The mismatched couple disappears through the door of a small house across from the garden. As soon as the door closes, the porch lights turn off and the shades are drawn. I try to ignore the turning of my stomach. That bitch. Who does Gabrielle think she is? Brody wouldn't be attracted to a woman so brazen, would he? But he did agree to follow her home. And I didn't hear him calling out for backup. What if he's already slipping off his shoes and settling on the couch next to her?

Not that I care. Because I don't.

A faint light turns on through the window to my right. I crouch. Ever so slowly, I crunch through the snow to get a peek inside. The ice coating the windowsill stings my fingertips through the gloves. I raise only my eyes above the border and squint through the foggy glass. A nightstand. A dresser. A bedroom?

"Fuck, no."

My heart pounds against my chest. I can't simply stand here and watch their bodies tangle together. Should I knock on the front door to interrupt them?

There's no way Brody would sleep with someone so desperate, would he? Why can't I breathe? This is ridiculous. He's a grown man and can do whatever he wants. I need to go home and mix the healing potion. It's not as if I need Brody's help to fix my problems, for that matter.

So why can't I peel my eyes away from the bedroom? A

shadow moves across the wall. An arm lifts high. A shape resembling a shirt flies to the floor. Wait, whose shirt? His or Gabrielle's? It's obvious why Gabrielle would be interested in a man like Brody, but what does he see in her? I turn away, quickly, trying to slow my racing thoughts.

The momentum of this movement lands me in a foot of snow and my pants immediately get soaked. Great. Riding War home will likely give me frostbite.

"Ugh!" I punch a hole into the snow.

A sharp tap on the window steals my attention. Brody grins down at me and waves his big hand, full of callouses. When did I first notice that detail about him? Of course his hands show wear and tear. He's a carpenter for Goddess sake.

He slides the window open and whispers, "You're the world's worst spy."

"I'm not spying." I stagger to my feet, as graceful as a baby deer on skates.

That's when I notice Brody stands shirtless. The drastic temperature difference between inside and out here creates steam that surrounds his broad frame.

"Like what you see?"

I snap my eyes to meet his, regretting it immediately. When he returns my challenging gaze, a faint hint of a smile slowly touches his lips.

"You'll get a better view if you come in here," he says.

"You're such a pain in my ass," I say, but move closer to the window. "This isn't my house, and that she-devil wouldn't want me interrupting her plans with you."

His soft chuckle gives me goosebumps. "And what does this she-devil have planned, Lulita?"

I hate that I adore the nickname he has given me. I cross my arms while glaring at him and his perfectly shaped torso. He bends over to me. Right when I think he's about to whisper some joke in my ear, I'm lifted straight out of the snow and through the window. It takes all my effort to not scream from surprise and wake her neighbors.

Once he sets me on the rug, he locks the window, then whispers, "Don't worry. Gabrielle won't step foot in this room tonight after what I promised her."

The door stands as the only barrier between us and his ex, or whoever Gabrielle is to him. Maybe she's the mother of his daughter. If they have so much history together, then I shouldn't be here. Plus, it's not like I'm competing for his attention. All I want is to break my curse. That's it.

"I should go." I glance at the fire crackling in the fireplace. I'll leave right after my pants dry. I'd rather not freeze to death on the ride home.

Brody lifts a pad of paper from the nightstand. "No, you're not going anywhere. Gabrielle and her assistant are on a mission to find who stole the roses. Anyone will easily spot an outsider. I have a plan for tomorrow morning, but you'll have to trust me."

"Trust you?"

"Yes, Mora. It means putting faith in someone else's ideas."

"I know what it means." My hands start folding imaginary origami. No matter how hard I wish I could break this habit, it happens when I'm nervous, or out of my element.

"Can you let me take care of things just this once?"

"I don't need anyone to take care of me." The words rush out of me before I can think.

"That doesn't stop me from wanting to." The way he says it feels like he's undressing me. Our eyes lock onto each other. For one second. Two. Three. "Plus, we need to get you warm." He looks away first, relieving me of the intimacy of his gaze. "How about we work on those letters until you get tired?"

My cheeks flush hot. I never should've asked him for help with that. The four people closest to me all deserve an apology—Feathi, Nax, Yin, and even Kavianne. I've been such a jerk for so many years, fixated on breaking the curse and not considering how much my actions have affected those I love. All four of them have suffered in different ways and it's time to own my mistakes. At least my friends need to know that I plan to change. From here on out, no matter how much time I have left in this life, whether it's two days or two decades, I promise to make things right. Kavianne will probably never forgive me, but I have to try.

Brody fiddles with a pen between two of his fingers, hypnotizing me. Maybe his hands are indeed magical. "How about this?" he starts to write. "I've burned a bridge or two, but that's not news to you—"

"No rhymes, this isn't a poetry contest."

"Okay." He balls one sheet of paper and bends over the nightstand. The light from the fire dances across his skin, but I'd die rather than let him catch me staring. "How about, there was once a philosopher who said—"

"No quotes, it has to come from the heart." My clothes feel dry, so I sit on the bed.

Brody sinks down next to me, and I ignore the tingling sensation in my gut. "Well, what does your heart want to say, Mora?"

I close my eyes and imagine my best friends and sister in our prime before Lessie died. We swang from ropes into a creek, built treehouses that ultimately collapsed, and shopped for dresses on our Taj devices. My memories with them are all filled with the taste of chocolate cupcakes and raw cookie dough.

As kids we'd play a game where I'd whisper a word into the wind and my sisters would chase it into the forest, catch it, and tell me what they heard. Half the time Lessie was impossibly correct. The two of us always had a strange knack for reading each other's minds. Back then life was easy, simple, and carefree. I'd give my left shoe to return to those moments, cherish them, savor them. I never could've imagined what was to come.

"Who will you write to first?" Brody asks, still stupidly shirtless.

Kavianne comes to mind. As our middle sister, she was the glue that held us together, the one who settled our battles.

"Write this…your smile was brighter than the jewels on your spear, but I stole that glee. Your passion—"

"Whoa, slow down." He scribbles frantically. "Can I make edits?"

"No. Write what I say or we're done."

He frowns and puts the pen back to the paper. "Keep going."

"Your passion sparked stronger than crashing daggers, but I took that too. Your strength was mightier than the fiercest shield, but I snatched it away. If I could go back, I'd highlight your smile, support your passion, and appreciate your strength." I pause, hearing Brody scribble quickly. "I'm sorry, Sister. I never meant to kill Lessie—" I gasp, realizing what I just confessed to Brody. I wipe away a tear from my eye as Brody sets his pen down.

"Oh, Mora…I doubt you ever meant to hurt your sister," he says while tucking a strand of loose hair behind my ear. His fingertips feel like they're caressing my soul.

Another tear slides down my cheek. "You don't know that."

The sincerity of his look is almost too much to bear. "I

know how much you pretend not to care even though your heart beats solely for others. You have a shield up, Mora, but I can handle you, and whatever you're feeling. There's no need to hide anymore."

His words undo me. I break out into a sob and cover my face with my hands, aware of the possible angles from which my thorns could poke him. Brody wraps a strong arm around me and pulls me close. The mattress squeaks under us, but he doesn't let go.

A thorn on my ring finger slowly disappears. I feel it before I see it and am almost afraid to check.

A sudden realization washes over me. Have all my thorns disappeared when I've been around Brody? Was Kavianne's clue truly about falling in love? If that's what it takes to break the curse, then it seems too convenient that the one man who waltzed into my mansion is the one for me. We're opposite in so many ways and his dreams are to reclaim his ticket and travel as far from here as possible.

For now, though, I'm simply grateful. Brody knows exactly what I need at this moment—to be held.

"Let's sleep, Mora. I bet you'll feel better after some rest. We can finish the letters another time."

He lies down on the bed, pulling me with him. For some reason, I don't fight him, but I also refuse to lean into his chest for fear of hurting him.

"I've got to say, Lulita, this isn't how I imagined the first time I'd share a bed with you."

My body clamps tight. Brody has envisioned us together? What other details has he painted in his mind? Ever since the first night when I ended up sleeping on the floor, he chose to sleep in random rooms of Chambrea.

"Me neither," I say playfully. "I expected you'd be wearing a shirt, and a coat to protect yourself from my thorns, and maybe you'd be covered in a layer of bubble wrap."

A long pause lingers between us, and the fire crackling is the only sound for a few beats. "Mora, you don't scare me. Your thorns are a part of you, so they don't worry me."

I'm knocked speechless. If he has been spitting out similar lines to Gabrielle, then no wonder she's salivating over him. In fact, I'm surprised she isn't trying to knock the door down for this man. If it were me, I'd use my own thorns as a weapon to get him away from another woman.

"You told me a difficult secret about Lessie, so it's my turn. I've never told this to anyone," he says quietly. "If given the opportunity, there's one person I'd gladly stab with a thorn." I wait while his nerves hover in the air between us. "My ex's mother, Elizabeth, is the reason I haven't seen Catterina in five years. I wouldn't intervene if a murder of crows attacked her. Some people are so wicked that they deserve torture."

How am I supposed to respond to that? What did that woman do? Does he still love his ex? Where is their daughter? There are so many questions on the tip of my tongue, but I stay quiet. For now, resting next to this man, sharing one space, is more than enough. It'll probably never happen again, but his comfort warms me.

With him here, for at least one night, I don't need to worry about what tomorrow brings. I'll only sleep for a couple of hours, then slip out the window before Gabrielle has the chance to find us sharing a bed.

Brody

Crashing bells from the village square rouse me from slumber. I stretch my arms out wide but am surprised to brush against soft skin. My eyes snap open, but I don't dare move. A mop of brown hair spreads against my chest. It all rushes back to me. Mora. We fell asleep together. I didn't expect her to spend the night, but after I told her about my darkest secret, a hint of hope remained that she'd stay. It's not every day I confess to wanting to murder my almost-mother-in-law.

Elizabeth had been a huge obstacle in my past. She couldn't stand me, someone who didn't fit into the life she had planned for her Dom. So, my child was also seen as unsuitable to be in Dom's life. When the wicked woman threatened to take Catterina to social services with faked proof that we were unfit parents, everything changed. Dom ran, taking Catterina with her. Maybe I'll never fully recover, but looking down at Mora in my arms, I've realized that for the first time, I want to heal.

Mora's soft breathing tells me she's asleep. How does she smell so good? Part of me wishes I could kiss her awake. No, she'd hate me for that. It's not fair that she's so close and I have to act like it doesn't affect me. Once she wakens, will she freak out that her arm is draped over my hard dick? Hey, it's not like I'm complaining. Mora shifts slightly and I hold my breath. A portion of her neck is visible, and I swear a thorn used to be right there on the side, where I can only see skin.

Villeneuve's bells toll again, but a different pattern than I'm used to, which reminds me of today's festival. Crap. It'll take a miracle for my plan to work, but staying locked in this room isn't an option. I scan the space. We will have to use her clothes to disguise ourselves, like a scarf to hide our faces.

Conversations from outside vibrate through the window, followed by laughter. Since the festival is already underway, Gabrielle might burst in here at any moment. Unfortunately, I gently shake my sleeping beautiful beast.

"Mora," I whisper. "Wake up."

"Hmm?" She unknowingly grazes her hand against my cock and I have to bite my lip to not groan aloud. The soft curves of her body turn rigid immediately and she sits upright faster than a whip.

"What…where…" Her wide eyes find mine and I plead with her silently not to make a big deal of falling asleep together. She knows nothing happened. Nothing will ever happen.

Then her eyes fall to my crotch, bulging against the

sheet. I open my mouth to explain, but my little devilish monster just smiles. With one hand, she combs her wild hair behind her ears.

"You talk in your sleep," she says while rising, keeping herself covered with a blanket, though she's wearing clothes still.

"What story did I tell this time?"

"You were king of the wolves, challenging War to a duel so you could overtake his role as pack alpha."

"I definitely won."

She shrugs, adorably. "The world may never know." She eyes me and I swear the look is full of hunger, a jaguar stalking its prey.

This side of her is new, and I don't hate it. I'm a grown man who is fully aware of when someone turns me on, and Mora's bedhead, tired smile, sleepy eyes, and flirty morning wit all do it for me. Damn it.

Pointing to her backpack, I ask, "I doubt you have any ridiculous costumes in there, do you?"

"Nope, just roses." She pulls out the orb from her pocket. "But I do have magic. What did you have in mind?"

Goddess, she's brilliant. How has no man snatched her already? Oh right, others might be bothered by the thorns. "We need costumes," I say.

I rush to the window and peel the curtain back just a tad. On the street, a crowd forms, walking toward the village square. They all have donned some type of plant-themed attire. Bill from the animal rescue center wears a shirt covered in palm trees. Tracy from the bank has greenery glued onto a bikini. She's gotta be drunker than a pirate to be wearing that first thing in the morning while it's snowing. Mam walks in the middle of the pack with tulips sticking out of her hair. If she's here, that must mean my sisters are close by. We need to be extra careful, or I'll end up chained in our wine cellar for the rest of my days.

Mora whispers something with her eyes closed. A hum of power tickles my whole body, from head to toe. From her spell, I'm wearing an entirely black outfit, decorated with gold paper roses. They're obviously not real, but the intricate detail is breathtaking. I reach out to skim my fingers over the crease, but she slaps my hand.

The most innocently gleeful look flashes on her face for a moment. "Don't mess with your costume, it'll fall apart."

"Yes ma'am. Wait, what are *you* going to wear?"

"Mine is a glamour," she says, but nothing about her appearance has changed. "Um, Brody, my eyes are up here."

I shake my head and force myself to look her in the eye. "I thought you were going to disguise yourself."

"I did, well I tried. Did it not work?" Her eyebrows pinch together, confused as she steps in front of the mirror. She gasps and covers her mouth with her hand.

"Are you just now recognizing how hot you are?" I stand behind her in the mirror and tilt my head. We look pretty good together. If we were going to the festival as a couple, I wouldn't mind tucking her against my side the whole day.

"Ha. Ha. Ha. Very funny. Let's go." Mora slides the window open. A cold breeze whips the curtains and hollers from outside immediately assault us. "Follow me."

No matter how befuddled I am by her mirror reaction, I do as she says. I want to help ease her out of the window, to feel her waist again, but she moves too fast. Outside, Villeneuve smells of an explosion of winter flowers spiced with hot cocoa and coffee.

"This is the day we celebrate the magical flowers," I explain to her. "Different cities are blessed with gifts from different nymphs."

Over countless generations, Villeneuve has been given flowers. It's our biggest source of income. Each type of flower serves different purposes. The expensive flowers can do more complicated magic, like making someone invisible for an hour or giving you information about what will happen the following day. As Mora already knows, the roses heal.

Grateful that a path has been plowed through the snow, I jog to catch Mora and slip her gloved hand into mine.

She tenses and tries to pull away. "I might scrape you."

"I'm fine." I hold on tighter, and whisper, "If we act like a happy couple, we'll attract less attention."

It's a lie, but she doesn't need to know that. I simply want to feel closer.

Drums beat and a guitar strikes a chord from a stage to the left. Tent tops bubble like a parachute by the craft market down the road. Twins skip by, waving ribbons, wearing boots covered in plastic daffodils, but their excited squeals aren't nearly as captivating as the energy exuding from the woman holding my hand. None of the other entertainment matters in comparison to the joy beaming from her face. Mora absorbs every detail as if she's never been to a party before. For all I know, she hasn't. If this is her first, I want her to enjoy the best parts. Luckily, I've been to twenty-nine of these.

"I want to show you something." I gently tug her and zig-zag her through the crowd.

Multiple onlookers, both coupled and single, are drooling over Mora. There's no chance I'm sharing her today. They don't see her like I do: powerful yet caring. Lethal yet forgiving. Stubborn yet soft. But not mine. Unfortunately, she'll never be mine.

"We're not following the crowd," she says.

"Trust me."

A fire pit smokes ahead, with a s'more station ready to go. Does Mora like chocolate? I imagine her mouth full of marshmallows and a sparkle in her eye. Did she ever eat s'mores with her sisters? The urge to know more about her grows with each day we spend together.

We pass the ice rink, where couples are lacing their skates in tandem. Would Mora be an expert at that too, gliding easily, or would her ankles shake as she holds onto my arm?

Our destination is at the edge of the festival, past a few more booths, but Mora stops. Her fingertips hover over an antique ring on a vendor's stand. Warning flags slap against my mind. Commitment is not my thing. Sure, she's gorgeous and I woke wanting to fuck her, but that's just lust. Relationships don't work. They all fail in one way or another.

"Feathi would love that stone." Mora points to one in the middle. "They would've been Committed by now. If she and Nax weren't included in this curse, their lives would be so much fuller."

"Maybe they're okay with just being together, and if they want it that badly, we can find a way to celebrate a Commitment Day. It's not hard to fill out the forms on a Taj."

"Um, Brody, in case you haven't noticed, my roommates are made of paper. No government can know about them."

"Listen, the only thing that matters is the love between two people. If they want a ceremony, we can give it to them." I regret the words the moment they leave my mouth —until Mora hugs me. Her arms warm me more than any flame. I don't want the contact to end and can't ignore my desires anymore. I want this woman under me. Badly.

"And Heathcliff could be their ring bearer." She claps

giddily, showing me a whole new side of her. "And Yin could be the bridesmaid. My orbs could help me create the dresses." Mora, my little Lulita, starts jumping in place. "And you can build another trellis."

A part of me wants to promise her all those things for her friends and give her the world, but it'd be cruel to offer what I can't provide. We stand side by side, staring at the ring in silence. I may not be the one to give Mora or her roommates a happily ever after, but hopefully, someone will eventually make her happy.

"Think fast!" she yells. A small snowball slams into my stomach.

"Oomph!" I'll probably bruise there tomorrow but laugh anyway.

Quickly, I create my own snowball and lob it in the air so it doesn't smack her too hard. We toss them back and forth, ducking behind wine barrels. She chases me around a fire pit and shoves snow onto my head. I grab her around the waist and pick her up, prepared to throw her into a snowbank.

"Surrender! Surrender!" I yell mid-laugh.

"Never!"

Her spirit flies so free with such a large smile reaching her eyes. If I could capture her energy in a bottle and save it for my worst days, she'd heal any depression faster than medicine.

"Juliette, is that you?" A vendor, Bill, moves from behind his stand toward Mora, a drink in his hand.

At first, she looks confused, then glances down at her outfit. Her wild eyes meet mine and I barely hear her say, "It *did* work!"

Mora laughs so hard I forget to breathe. Then all she does is wink and quickly run away. Again, I follow. Maybe

I'd follow her into the darkest shadows, just to stay by her side.

Behind us, the man yells, "Juliette, wait for me, you are my one true love!"

She's laughing so hard that I'm worried she'll choke to death. We dart around a corner to where the music doesn't vibrate through my bones anymore.

"What was that about?" I ask, trying to catch my breath.

"My glamour. I don't look like myself, but who the viewer finds most attractive. That way, no one can see me or my thorns."

"I only see you, Mora..." Suddenly, things aren't so funny. "I see you, all of you, with your thorns."

Her gaze turns to fire, hot enough to melt all the snow surrounding us. "Well, it must not work on you since you were with me when I cast the glamour."

"Yeah," I say slowly, "that must be it." We stare at each other and I can't look away. "Who did you see in the mirror? Back in Gabrielle's room?"

"I don't know what you're talking about," Mora says, "So, what did you want to show me?"

"It's right around this corner." The busy chatter behind us turns to a dull hum the further we walk, hand in hand. "Close your eyes."

"Is that necessary?" she asks.

"Just let me surprise you. It's not the end of the world."

She grins again, destroying me, then says, "Fine, but it better be good."

I guide her to a gazebo I built years ago that's decorated with hundreds of hanging origami snowflakes. All the elementary school art classes nearby have a tradition of folding them for this festival. Some are navy blue, some are gold, and some crimson. They all sway in the breeze and rotate to show each sharp angle and crisp crease.

"Okay, open your eyes."

Mora gasps. Her hands find her heart. It doesn't matter how intricate the designs are of the artwork, I can't take my eyes off *her*. Her face glows in the suns' light like she was just given a precious gift. Mora drops her hand from mine and stands in the middle. She angles her head back, so the lowest one brushes her nose. I'm completely transfixed as she starts spinning in slow circles and starts to hum:

"...a true crystal heart is painted for art
When crossroads split to black, I will still have your back..."

Her smile is brighter than newly fallen snow. I'm pretty sure time has stopped. I'm vaguely aware that I'm moving toward her, with only one thing on my mind. Fuck it. I have to kiss her. Now. Not another second can pass without my lips on hers.

Our bodies bump softly and she stops spinning. Mora's gaze burns through me like a laser.

"Thank you, Brody. For years I've been trapped in that mansion, cut off from others, but look. So many other people share my passion for this art. I'm not alone."

I take her arms into my hands and close the distance between us. "Mora..."

She must know I'm about to kiss her. My eyes can't lie that well. What if she thinks a single kiss means more than being caught in the moment?

Before I can ask permission, Mora presses her mouth to mine. Soft and slow. Tentative and tender. Holy Abyss. I can't hold back. I test her limits and she parts her lips for me. Thank the Goddesses above. She tastes of snow and apples. My hands wrap around her lower back, pulling her close. How can something so simple feel so good?

A slight moan slips from her mouth and fills me with power. I crush my lips to hers. My control evaporates. I explore her mouth. Fuck, she's good at this, better than I imagined. I want to drink her in, breathe her in, body and soul. I don't understand why she's so much more intoxicating than anyone else I've ever done this with.

We bump into the gazebo. She rolls her hips against me.

I pin her.

Her fingertips softly run up my back. A little tug of my hair makes me grunt.

"Brody," she pants between breaths. "Brody…what… what are we doing?"

"I've been wanting to kiss you for days."

She devours me. Wraps her leg around my waist. My heart hammers. Goddess Above, I feel like a fucking mess. This can't be real.

I lift her off her feet. Press her against the gazebo again. A thorn slices into my arm, but I don't care. I need more. I kiss down her sweet neck, slender collarbone, lower, lower. She's going to destroy me.

"Oh Goddess," she pants against my skin.

"Fuck, Mora."

Mora gasps and pulls back. "Whoa, whoa, wait."

I freeze, drop her to her feet, and step away. I run a hand through my hair. She's breathing hard, her hair disheveled, her lips swollen. Intensely ravishing.

"We need to stop," we both say at the same time, both of us out of breath.

This woman has the potential to wreck me. Yet, we have no future because I don't want to lead her on. She deserves better—but all she does is point behind me with wide eyes.

CHAPTER 17

Mora

Gabrielle storms toward us. I'm unsure if she witnessed the mind-blowing kiss I just experienced. The party is a low hum in the distance. It feels like time should've stopped.

I need to push away the thought of Brody's hands on me because we need to get away from her, as soon as possible. With the power of only one orb, I have no idea how long my glamour will last. It must be weak since it's not working on Brody. I'd be a fool to believe that of all the people in the world, he finds *me* most attractive.

I glance at him, expecting his eyes to be fixed on his ex, but his gaze is laser-focused on me. The increased intensity behind his look catches me off guard. It almost looks like pained anger.

Gabrielle marches toward us, arms swinging wildly by her side. Brody shields me with his body. His ex might be the loveliest woman in all Ozaron for all I know, but I'm not keen on someone who wears bright pink blush so early in the morning. How did she have time to curl her hair in soft waves? And I'm sorry, but those heels aren't meant for snow. I'm surprised she's not using a hoverboard to keep her designer shoes intact.

"Brody! How dare you sneak out!" She storms at us with the intensity that could rival War. "Were you seriously going to disappear again? Without saying goodbye?" Her voice carries through the wind. "I just finished telling your Mam that you've returned."

When Gabrielle gets closer, she stops in her tracks. "What the!" She points at me. "Is this some sick joke?"

Brody quietly whispers over his shoulder. "Um, Mora, she might be seeing two of me."

"Oh, no. I hadn't thought of that." I palm the orb, trying to remember a memory-wiping spell, but they're all too complicated.

"Why is there another *me* standing behind you?" Gabrielle shrieks, pointing at me.

Brody turns his head slightly and whispers, "Holy shit, she's way vainer than I thought."

When he moves closer, warm tingles travel from my feet all the way up to my neck.

"I have a plan," he says. "Ready to play along?"

I squeeze his hand, giving him the control.

"This is the surprise I mentioned last night." Brody walks toward Gabby slowly. "I know you've wanted a sister. That's why I left home in the first place, to bargain with a powerful witch," he continues so earnestly that I have to hold back a laugh. "The witch created a twin for you, but there were some unseen complications. We fell in love at first sight."

Brody wraps a hand around my waist. He locks his eyes on mine and for that moment, the World. Fades. Away.

He licks his lips, then moves lower, and whispers, "I want more."

I can't breathe. Can't move.

"Tell me it's okay," he says so softly. "Tell me it's okay to want more."

I can only nod. Relief washes over his face before he melds our mouths together again. His lips are so full and soft, but the way he commands my tongue is anything but gentle.

Once I had read about the perfect kiss in a romance story, but his mouth outdoes fairytales. We move and explore each other in sync. I might moan through it because Brody responds with a carnal groan. He takes control of my mouth and body. I won't be the one to end this.

A strangled cry snatches me from Brody's embrace. When he pulls away, I feel guilty that I forgot Gabrielle was watching. Without a word, she turns on her heels and stomps away. Shit, I'm a terrible person, especially because I want to do that again, and again until I run out of air.

I smack Brody's shoulder. "That wasn't nice."

"Hey, don't judge me. That woman has put me through the wringer. Thanks for playing along."

Right, it was just for show. My spirits drop, but I can't let him notice. "No biggie. Everyone has to make sacrifices for the greater good."

A heavy moment suffocates me as we both wait for the other to make the next move. I could play it off as an act all for Gabrielle, or tell him it was the best kiss I've ever had.

"Maybe our kiss broke your curse," he says. "All you had to do was throw yourself at a dashing young explorer."

"Hey, you've got it backwards. *You* kissed *me*."

"No. I didn't." The intensity of his eyes is almost intimidating. "Yeah, maybe a little, but you kissed me first."

"No, no, no. I wouldn't do that unless it was a good idea and *this*," I say, pointing back and forth between us like a crazy person, "*this* is definitely not a good idea."

"Agreed because I'm too wild and unpredictable, and you're too…" his gaze turns to lava, which can't happen. Not here. Not now. That look will only make me want more.

"Exactly," I say, not letting him finish. "You're all over the place, incapable of settling." I start to pace, forming deep indents in the snow. "I'm not who you want."

He pauses and tilts his head to the side. "Well, I'm not so sure about that."

"Brody…"

"Right, you're right. You'd be miserable. And I…" he takes a step toward me. "I'd be in awe of you."

"Stop it. Don't be nice. You don't want to stay here, and I can't leave my house."

"You're out of your house right now." His hands are on my waist. Damn it.

"Th-that's not the point."

"What are you so scared of?"

"I'm not scared. It's *my* duty to break the curse. Three people are counting on me. It's not like you have someone in your life to take care of, to depend on you." The moment it slips out, I slap a hand over my mouth. "Shit, I'm so sorry. I know you love Cat."

"Don't worry about it." Brody rubs his beard as he nods. "Alright. We'll do it your way. For now. Let's go, give me your backpack, and lead me to War."

Ugh, if he's determined to come with me, it'll be pure torture to keep my hands off him. I choose not to say a word as we find a roundabout way around town where no one from the festival can run into us. His energy behind me is a lightning zap to my spine. I keep fighting the urge to turn toward him and wrap my arms around his neck. Why does he have to be such a good kisser? What else is he skilled at? No, I need to stop thinking about his hands touching my stomach, my hips, or all the places I felt him against me last night as we shared a bed. I need a distraction.

"Ask me a question," I demand, a bit too sharply.

"What?" His tone sounds farther away than usual, spiked with something I can't place.

"Just ask me a question."

"Okay, I've got one. Once we break your curse, what are your plans?" Brody moves closer to my side as we enter the woods. He flicks a long icicle with his finger, so it sways and clinks against its neighbor.

"I hadn't thought about it. For so long I've only been worried about trying to get rid of my thorns and keeping a supply of ink ready."

At least his question distracted me from the thought of his lips, or wondering what other creations he has built other than the gazebo in town. Or what his sisters are like. Or what kind of father he'd be if given the chance.

A large shadow slips through the trees, but as I look, it disappears. It must've been a bird or deer or a dancing weeping willow. That reminds me of the many unique costumes I saw people wearing at the festival. I haven't seen such beauty in years. Sometimes it feels like I'm missing out on so many things by staying locked in the shadows. Whether or not I break this curse, maybe I should visit the nearby towns more often. Someone out there might accept my frightening appearance if my glamour fades.

For now, I whisper an easy counter spell to take away our glamour. Earlier, I had half a mind to give Brody a wolf costume as a joke, just to mess with him. Now, he wears a black hoodie that accents his dark, rugged stubble.

He looks down at his more appropriate outfit, and mumbles, "Thanks."

With the forest enveloping us, Brody falls back into a snowbank and makes a snow angel. Brilliant, the second I give him something warm and clean to wear, he ruins it.

He sighs heavily. "So you're telling me you don't have *any* goals or dreams for your future?"

"Of course I have dreams," I mumble, "It's just complicated."

"No, it's not. If you could do anything in the world, right now, what would it be?"

"Hug Kavianne." I tug on the strap hanging loose from his backpack. "Get up. You're crushing all the roses."

One of his brows rises high and I hate how a stirring rumbles in my core. "Aren't we going to crush all of them?"

"I have a very specific crushing method."

"Of course you do." His smile is frosting on a red velvet cupcake.

If only I could strip him here and now, regardless of the snow. I'll have to wait until we're back at my place, ask him for help with the letters again, then…straddle him. No man can resist that. No! Goddess, what am I thinking? This is insanity. As soon as I get his ticket back from the fairies, I'm pushing him out the front door and locking all the gates. Unless…it wouldn't hurt to kiss him once more, only as a goodbye. Nooo! I shake my head and resist the urge to slap my cheeks.

He stands brushing snow off his pants. "Wow, that is an

expert snow angel. I mean, look at it. I think I should win a trophy."

"I bet you could make a trophy yourself."

"That I could." He joins me on the path and asks, "So, you don't have any resentment toward Kavianne for cursing you?"

"I'm not angry with her. Yes, she made a mistake in cursing me, but I made a bigger mistake. Part of me wonders if it was karma, if I deserve what she did to me."

Brody lifts my chin with one hand. "Don't let me catch you speaking poorly of yourself again."

"But, I—"

"No, Mora. Listen to me. You are creative and witty and caring, and Goddess Above you're nurturing a pup wolf. And don't get me started on the patience needed to make your origami. It's inspiring and the determination of your —" He freezes, then stares off to the trees.

"Brody?" I follow his gaze. "What is it? What's wrong?"

"Don't move." Brody holds a hand across my stomach. "Do you hear that?"

I turn, slower than death, and scope out the forest. Nothing looks amiss. Because of the hibernation season, there are barely any animal tracks in the snow, but maybe one scurried out to get a snack and Brody heard it run by. Though, if the reason is that simple then why are my hairs standing on end?

I grip the orb in my pocket harder, just in case. "I didn't hear anything. What did it sound like?"

Brody steps forward, his muscles tense and bulging, not that I care. "I think we should hurry back. How much further is your house?"

Something dark lunges out. Brody crashes to the ground and is violently dragged away. His arms disappear within a bush and I only hear his screams.

"Brody!" I chase after the path formed by his body in the snow. "Brody!"

He screams.

"Brody!" I sprint after the sound of his voice. "Brody!"

Loud thuds crash. Another scream.

My eyes sting from the wind slapping my face. My heart drums faster. Every muscle is on fire. I run.

"Stay back!" he yells from within a tangle of trees.

Another slamming sound echoes through the pines.

Gripping the orb in my pocket, I feel its power swirling within. I scream out a half-hazard protective spell between panting breaths then slam the orb as hard as possible into the snow. A giant puff of black smoke poofs out and flies ahead, faster than I can keep up.

Thud. The entire forest floor shakes.

I run faster. "Brody?"

His voice comes out in painful groans. Around the next tree, I spot him, lying on his side, blood-splattered rubies covering the snow. I rush to his side. Fall to my knees.

"Brody!" I hover my hands over his body, unsure where he's hurt.

His eyes are clenched shut. His outfit is torn to shreds and scratches mark his arms. What am I supposed to do? I'm too far away from home to make a healing potion.

"Run," he rasps and tries to roll to his side. "Run."

I whistle for War. Nothing. Whistle again.

"Fuck!" I squeeze the orb again, but not enough time has passed to recharge the power it needs for a stronger spell.

Searing pain whips my back. A howl rips from my throat. I fall forward, almost landing on Brody. Then something grabs my ankle. The creature pulls me. Snow burns my neck and my face. Screaming, I claw to stop it from dragging me further. My fingers latch around an overgrown root. My shoulder snaps out of place. Pain racks through my arm. The space around me goes blurry, in and out of focus, but I manage to look behind me. It's the damn *Vignamassi* wrapped around my ankle.

It looks ancient, with wrinkled veins lining its thick vines. The thorns have grown since last time, one the length of my hand, complete with a deadly point. Each tentacle swings in the air, bashing into trees like a drugged octopus. Part of the lush green has been overtaken by gray. And black ooze drips along the largest part of the vine.

"Mora!" Somewhere far off, Brody screams. "Mora!"

Fangs of thorns gnaw straight into my shin bone. Each time I try to kick it off, a bolt of agony chomps up my leg. I'm going to pass out, and this monster will eliminate me.

I grope along the ground and grab a loose branch. I yell with the effort as I throw it like a spear. The sharp end pierces the *Vignamassi*. At the same time, I feel a punch to my gut. I gasp from the pain. What the fuck?

"Mora! Where are you?"

Despite my panting, sweating, bleeding, I reach for another branch. Chuck it at the plant. The side of the branch smacks into the *Vignamassi* then bounces off. A mirrored sensation of a rock hitting my forehead and ricocheting off confirms my fear. I can't hurt the monster without hurting myself—because we're one and the same. I'm the villain of this forest.

My mind slips into an empty world surrounded by thorned vines. Here, in this oblivion, the only reality is the sharp barbs. It is me and I am it. The only way to destroy the plant is for my life to end. But I'm not finished living. I have to find a way to fight this.

The woods fade away into darkness as the grip around my ankle tightens. It's going to hack off my entire foot.

Right when I think I'll lose consciousness, a flash of light blares through my eyelids. I force myself to look.

Fairies, thousands of them, shoot light. The plant releases my ankle. Brody collapses a few feet away, unable to make it to my side. Well, at least I experienced the perfect kiss before my death.

"I found her." The sound of Feathi's dreamy voice is covered in whipped cream and rainbows. "Over here."

"Black echoes when stars let themselves be heard. Never underestimate black."

"Hurry, lift them onto here."

If my friends are here, I can let go. For once I can stop fighting. Close my eyes. Let someone else take care of me.

"Mora..." Brody whispers somewhere close. "Is Mora okay?"

If poison has leaked from the thorns into Brody's blood, I'll never forgive myself. He'll be incapacitated, like the sick kids. And for some reason, that scares me more than I'll ever admit.

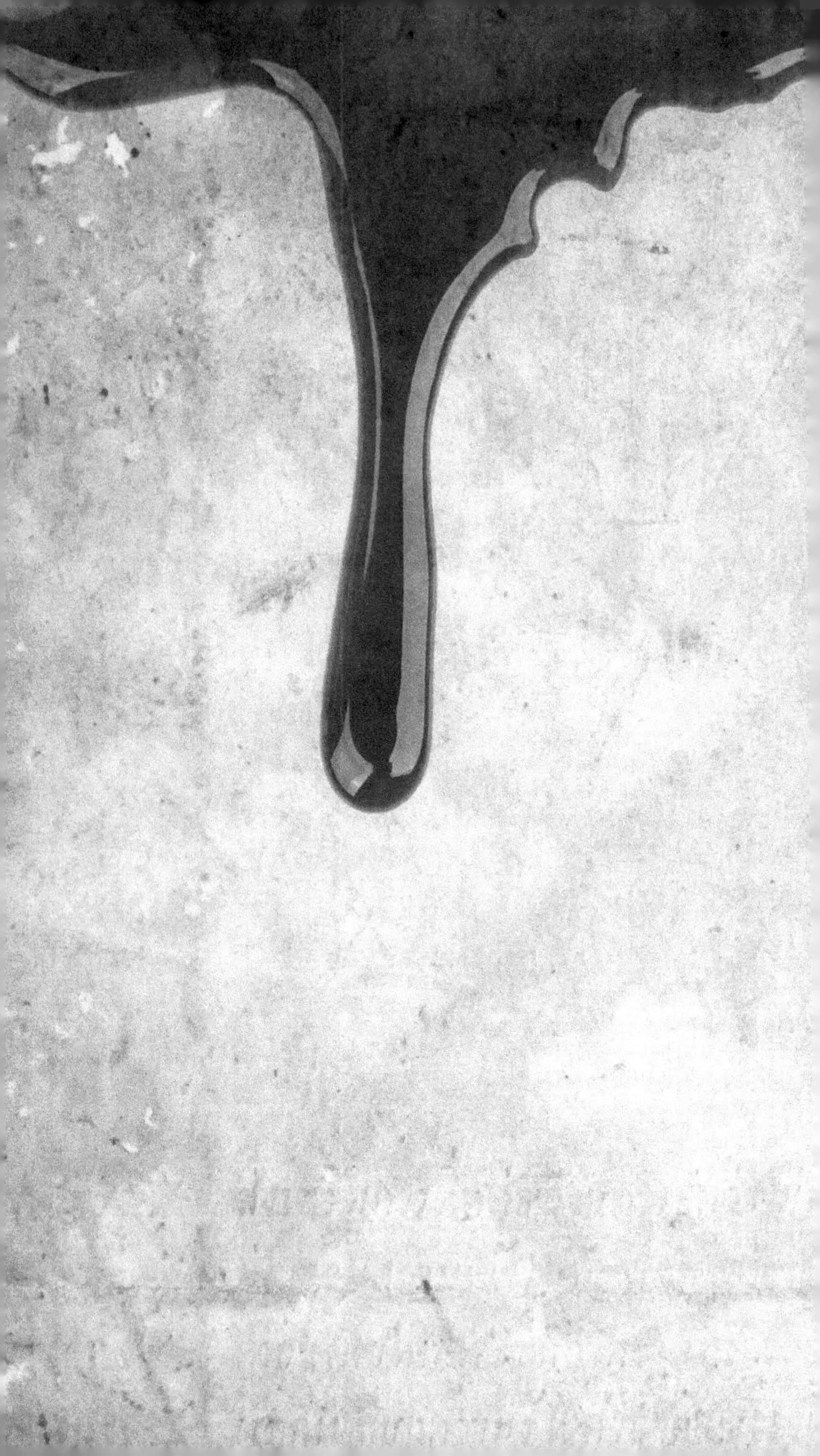

Recent excerpt from
The Book

You know I was there the moment after Mora was cursed.

Her current nightmare is one that repeats often—the image of Lessie falling over the cliffside. Kavianne's fury, desperation, and fear that catapulted me into existence in seconds. It's a sensation I'll never forget.

Don't assume you know what it's like to be the invention of a monster, and no I don't mean Mora. Yes, she made a mistake, but she has suffered enough consequences for her deeds.

Kavianne's wrath was never fair. As a book, I am incapable of love. Yet, when I watch Mora every minute of every day, asleep or awake, I can't help but collect all her loving deeds and thoughts into one place—on paper. If she breaks the curse, what will happen to me? I hope that maybe she will keep me tucked into the pockets of her life. No, I don't mean literally. Goddess Almighty, do any humans understand literary metaphors these days?

CHAPTER 18

Brody

We both spent days asleep, under the care of the fairies' magic and Feathi's comfort. Through the fever, all I can remember is asking for Mora, wanting to see her, begging to be brought to her side. Apparently, I got a nasty infection and in my delirium had threatened to use an axe on anyone who wouldn't check on Mora first. At least I wasn't poisoned. During my painful recovery, Feathi confirmed that more younguns have fallen ill. Their symptoms seem to be worsening and they have stopped eating. I doubt I'll develop any of those issues since whatever the fairies did has been working well so far.

My biggest concern was Mora's health, yet somehow she recovered faster than me. Strong, that one.

Shadows dip against the walls of Mora's apothecary studio each time she reaches for a new ingredient. I can't see the worry lines etched into her face, but her back tenses beneath her tight shirt. This woman is a thunderstorm on a Sunday afternoon. She grunts, pushes a bottle aside, and rolls up her sleeves. I wish I could help, but sitting next to her in this stressful time might be enough.

"Princess Preta said her entire clan will be resting until their energy is restored," Feathi whispers to Mora, though I can hear every word clearly.

"They shouldn't have sacrificed their strength." Mora's sigh sounds defeated. "Does she know how long it'll take for them to recover?"

Feathi shakes her head. "You're worth saving." She pats Mora's shoulder and gives me a quick look, silently telling me to try and cheer up her best friend.

I nod as Feathi heads into the hallway.

Now, Mora and I both work in silence. We've barely talked since the plant attacked us, and it's killing me from the inside worse than any poison could.

This dingy room, the size of a closet, doesn't have the best lighting, but I stare at the intricately folded paper birds hanging from the ceiling. Every few seconds, I swear the raven flaps its wings in my peripheral vision, but there's no time to focus on it too long, because in my hands I hold all three of my projects: the Commitment ring for Nax, the page-turner surprise for Mora, and lastly, the apology letters she wants me to help write.

"Damn it!" Mora slams her palms onto the countertop. "It says right here, one teaspoon of black garlic, achiote paste, and crushed roses. So why is it so thick?"

"Can I help?" I don't bother getting up, knowing what her answer will be. I've already offered my assistance seventeen times in the last hour.

"Maybe I added some extra juice before." More bottles clink together. "It didn't look like this."

I scrape piece after piece off of the wood in my lap, each one falling to the floor in curls. My therapy is carpentry work, hers is mixing potions. We're both dealing with stress the best way we can. Yet, it doesn't feel like enough. What I'd give to stand directly behind her, let her back fall against my chest, and ask her what she needs. But she wouldn't answer me if I tried.

Heathcliff scampers to me with a sock in his mouth. I'm so grateful he wasn't injured by the plant too. He lies directly atop the wood shavings like any woodland creature would. Thankfully he is unaware of the turmoil festering in the air. If Mora can't remember the healing potion, what will we do next?

Scrape. Another shaving falls off my carving onto Heathcliff's head. Scrape.

"Goddess Almighty, will you stop with that noise?" Mora's knuckles clutch the edge of the counter. She hunches over and her hair falls forward.

"How about you take a break?" I set the carving down. "You've been at this for hours and already used ten roses."

Mora turns so fast that a bin slides off the counter and puffs powder onto her boots. Fire scorches in her eyes, but this woman's sharp moods don't faze me. She's scared and she's giving herself too much responsibility. Each village probably has elders working on medicines that could heal the children. The fate of everyone who is poisoned doesn't rely on her alone. Yet, she'd never accept that.

"I know we're wasting petals, but I have to try different

ingredients. Something is missing. It's why your scratches won't heal."

I glance down at the new scratches I accidentally got by running into her thorns earlier. She has already tried to use a healing lotion, but that was just as ineffective as me drinking the nasty stuff. It took me hours to convince Mora not to trial each batch on herself, in case it made any symptoms worse. I'd rather something happen to me than her. Like she said before, no one in this world relies on me. If I die, my sisters will be sad, sure, but their futures aren't in my hands like Feathi, Nax, and Yin's are in hers.

"You'll find the missing ingredient, but how about you sit down for a few minutes? Heathcliff misses you. Look at his little face."

"No, I can't stop. I can't give up. That forest beast is only getting stronger. You saw how much bigger it was. That thing was supposed to be dead, but it's more powerful than before. I can't risk another kid getting hurt. We're running out of time."

She's right, but at least Feathi already added more ink to Mora's curse. Time may be ticking for the sick kids, but Mora has a buffer of safety. One of the old grandfather clocks chimes in the hallway.

"The fairies already donated their roses to the neighboring towns. Maybe they won't need your healing potion," I say, hopeful to relieve Mora of her burden.

She bustles from one side of the room to the other, grabbing colanders and mixers off the shelf. "We need to be prepared. What if…" Her voice turns shaky. "What if my thorns carry more poison than the monster? What if your health turns for the worse if I scratch you again?"

This time I do stand, stepping over Heathcliff. A pot boils and bubbles next to Mora, so she doesn't necessarily need my warmth, but I slide behind her. Her body against mine is a breath of fresh air. I run my hands up her side and over her arms, careful to avoid the longest thorn near her elbow. She seems at a loss for how to respond to my touch. Half of Mora's body relents and melts into my chest, but her other half fights against me.

"You have already cut me and I'm still the fabulous man I've always been, the knight who conquers all quests. You haven't hurt me, Mora, so take a breath."

She breathes in deeply, and this time her muscles ease into me. Her weight sinks into my chest and for a moment my world is okay—until she turns around. When she looks at me with those gorgeous brown eyes, a tear trickles down her cheek. Seeing her cry is a punch to my gut. I know she's about to wipe the tear away, to erase any moment of vulnerability, so I gently hold her wrists down by our sides.

"Brody," she struggles to whisper. "What are you doing?"

"Tell me what you need."

"I…I need more time." She sighs and drops her head in defeat. "I need help."

I kiss her forehead softly, then capture the tear on my lip. "Look at me, Lulita."

Mora chokes on a half-laugh, but at least she looks at me again. "That nickname is horrible."

"You love it."

"I do."

"Listen to me." I bring our combined hands to her heart. I'll help you break your curse. And I won't leave until it's broken and the kids are healed. You have my word."

Mora shakes her head, dropping her gaze to my boat ticket sitting on her work counter, recovered safely from the greedy fairies. "You can't promise that," she says. "It could take years."

"I don't think so." When she tries to pull away, I keep her close. It's easy to tell she doesn't want me to let her go; she just wants to see if I'll keep fighting for her. "More of your thorns have disappeared. It means something is working."

She gulps. Why do I have a feeling that she's holding something back?

Tucking a strand of hair behind her ear, I resist kissing her. There's no way I'm going down that road unless she initiates it. "If you had to guess, why do you think the thorns disappeared?"

"I don't know." Her cheeks flush. "I'm not concerned about me right now. If you want to help, I was going to ask you to deliver the healing potion once I get it right. I'll need you to drop it off at the neighboring villages. I'd take the potions myself if I weren't worried about hurting someone. You can ride War, but I understand if you don't want to since the *Vignamassi* might attack you again."

"I'll do it." I slide between her and the counter. "When I'm done…do you want me to return?"

Immediately, she seems flustered and accidentally knocks a bottle of liquid over onto a piece of parchment, where it sizzles. "Damn it! At this rate, I'll run out of petals."

Fine, if she wants to change the topic and avoid my question, I'll give her time to consider.

"Actually," I say, "the festival gave me an idea of how to collect more petals. Why don't we host a party here in your ballroom? Everyone who enters will need to bring a rose for admission."

Her laugh tickles something deep inside me, but I wish

she'd take this idea seriously. When she sees my face, her laughing stops. "Wait, tell me you're joking."

"No, it's a fabulous idea. There are so many rumors about your haunted mansion that people will be curious. Plus, if doctors or nurses come from neighboring towns, then they could share details of antidotes that have worked on the sickness."

"You seem to have forgotten a very important part." She waves a hand up and down her perfect body. "The guests will take one look at me and run for the hills. Who would want to be near someone who resembles the creature that is terrorizing their children? Even if I use a glamour I can't risk bumping into someone by accident."

"But you and that plant are not the same thing."

She waits and stares, sending a tornado of worry through me. They can't be the same. I refuse to look away from her dark eyes that swirl with a tornado of guilt. Fuck, she thinks she's the *Vignamassi*.

"Kavianne's message said—"

"I don't care what she said."

"I need you to make me a promise," she says quietly. "If I ever become that thing and put others at risk you have to destroy me."

"No."

"You have to. I won't have any self-control. I'll be a hideous, ravenous, blood-hungry creature that will poison anyone in my way."

I look deep into her eyes, challenging her to glance away. "You're not a villain, Mora."

She studies me, deep in thought. Once I assume she's found her rebuttal, her nose scrunches and she lifts that pretty chin. "You're only saying that because you want to kiss me again."

I pin her against the counter, our hearts closer than

ever, both beating in an erratic rhythm. "I'm not going to kiss you, Lulita." I brush a finger down her cheekbone.

Her jaw grinds together. "You're not?"

"No. The next time we kiss, it'll be your doing."

"Oh, I don't think so." Her nose pinches in the way that drives me crazy.

"Fine, then we won't ever kiss again."

"Fine." She crosses her arms but then uncrosses them, smooths down the wrinkles in her shirt, and huffs. I can't get enough of how flustered she looks. It makes me want to take her here and now. Fuck, it'll take a lot of dates with other women to ever forget about her once I'm gone. Whenever that will be. I'm no longer in a rush.

Mora rips off a leaf of a plant and dips it into the next batch she's brewing. "This is going to take a few minutes to finish. Let's sit while we wait."

I'm about to offer her a chair, when she pushes me onto one, then straddles me with a wicked gleam in her eye. A hundred comments were on the tip of my tongue, but somehow they've all been wiped clean from my brain. She leans close and I don't dare breathe. When she exhales softly, the air tingles across my neck, making my pants tighter. Shit, she's playing games with me. My little Lulita likes to tease.

Mora's lips are so close to my ear as she whispers, "If you think I'll cave and kiss you first, then do you wanna make a bet?"

I swallow. Shivers run down my spine, but I can't let her see how much she affects me. "If you kiss me first, I want to host the party."

Her eyes darken. "And if you, Mr. Ricci, kiss *me* first, then you will leave and never return."

Any heat I was feeling simmers low. "You *do* want me gone?"

She opens her mouth and then closes it. "Yes," is all she says, despite the layers of hidden meaning in her eyes.

When she tries to slide off my legs, I grab her ass and pull her close. Her little gasp and the spark that ignites her eyes tell me what I need to know. Mora wants me to stay, but fear claims her every move. She's afraid of herself, afraid of her potential, her strength, her power. I mean, she hasn't even looked for her other hidden orbs for fucks sake. Maybe I'm the only one between the two of us who has any faith in her.

"What are the terms of this contest?" I ask.

"The kiss has to be on the lips." She leans closer.

"Deal, and I'll seal it with a bite."

She slaps my shoulder. "If you bite my lip, that counts as a kiss."

"It's a good thing I can bite you in other places, Lulita." Slowly, I nip at her neck. Her body makes a sudden jolt against me.

"I'm going to win." Both her hands push against my chest. "And I need to check my potion."

I free her, but my heart hammers wildly in my chest. No one has made me feel this way since Dom over six years ago. Sure I've slept with a few tourists that pass by Villeneuve from time to time, but only because I knew I'd never see them again. Mora isn't someone I want to screw and run. Despite her icy stone wall guarding her, the woman's heart is as vibrant as a coral reef. Maybe she can be my life's greatest adventure, but I need to get her to kiss me first.

"Since we may be in here a while, let's work on those apology letters," she says quietly.

"Uh, sure, give me one minute."

From my backpack, I pull out the drafted letter we started for Kavianne. My handwriting is a bit smudged in one corner. Maybe I dropped some snow on it. As I scan the damage, wondering if we need a fresh sheet of paper, I read over a phrase that wasn't there before. In a different scrawl, someone has added a line. After reading it, I freeze, struggling to comprehend what's written. This can't be real. Who the fuck would play a joke this cruel? I reread the added line over and over until it is seared into my mind permanently.

Empty the ink in Mora's pen by sundown or Catterina will be the next to be poisoned.

CHAPTER 19

Mora

I know exactly why my thorns are disappearing. It's because I'm growing too attached to Brody. Kavianne is a disturbed soul to force love as the key to break my curse. There's no chance I could truly fall for him, but each time I let my guard down, another one vanishes. He's taking over my mind when I'm unconscious. Last night's dream fades out of focus like a book hangover. I've been in a fog, unable to focus.

Brody's dark eyes are the only thing I can truly fixate on. It doesn't matter that he's as naked as the majestic statues in my foyer. His gaze darkens to the level of intoxication, more potent than poison and only meant for me. He has devoured me with just one look, without his hands even touching me yet. And Goddess I want him to lay his hands on me. He stands at the end of my bed, and while he's nude, I'm still clothed, lying here, drinking him in. And damn it, he does that thing, *the move guys do when they raise both palms, bracing them on the posts. I can't even catch my breath. "Touch yourself for me," he commands in his deep voice, gliding liquid over my skin.*

I shake my head, trying to erase the dream's image for the hundredth time. If I'm right about Kavianne's test, then I'll have to find a loophole. Maybe I can fall in love with Heathcliff instead or peanut butter or a prince in a novel.

If I tell Brody my suspicions, he might feel obligated to stay. I don't want him to give up his future, his goals, and be miserably trapped in my fortress. So, there's only one suitable option—the man must go. Sure, I might miss him for a day or two, but he will be safer far from here. Eventually, he'll fade from my thoughts. I'll figure out how to break the curse another way.

I check on the brewing potion once more and cross my fingers that this batch will work. All the lives of the kids depend on me.

"Let's go for a walk," I say to Body. "I need to ask Feathi something."

It's not fair that he smells of treasure mixed with the crisp night air on a full moon. As I step toward the door, Heathcliff springs to my side. A burst of frigid air whips my face as we enter the hallway, but Brody and his delicious scent don't trail behind me.

I'm about to jab Brody with some sarcastic comment, but the look on his face mirrors a trance-like hypnotic state. Did he manage to fall asleep with his eyes open?

"Uh, Brody? Hello?" I wave in front of him. "I don't want to leave you in here alone. You might burp into my brew and mess it up."

Still no response. Maybe he's this upset about me turning down the idea of his party. I probably owe it to him to listen to one or two of his ideas, but just not that one. Having people in my home would be an absolute nightmare.

"Okay, fine, I'll apologize for snapping at you earlier. Can we go now?"

No answer. He is completely zoned out. "Brody? I'm ready to kiss you now."

I get a slight tick of his jaw this time but he's glaring at the wall, ready to murder the stone with his gaze. Did I say something to offend him? He squeezes his fist, crumpling a piece of paper into a ball. What is going on?

"Brody?" I go to crouch in front of him and slap his cheek, maybe a little too hard.

Suddenly, he snaps out of it, eyes back on me, but I can't read the expression they hold. Defeat? Desperation? Terror? Rage? Then he springs up to stand so sharply that I stumble back into the counter.

"I'm sorry for this." He soars through the doorway.

I rush after him. "You're sorry for what? Where are you going?"

As I chase down the hall, windows flash by, followed by the darkness of the walls. The severe contrast of the colors in my peripheral vision makes me dizzy. Black walls. White snow. Black. White. Dark. Light. Dark. I'm the dark. Brody is my light.

He must've decided to leave. The truth hits me like a sledgehammer. I don't want him to go. So I continue to foolishly chase.

THUD. Thud. Each footstep ahead gets quieter as he

increases the space between us. At this point, I'm not sure which way he turned. Lucky for me, Heathcliff leads me around dark corners, past wicked drafts where the wind whistles through the cracks of the stone, and under epic spiderwebs until we reach my library.

Out of breath, I jerk to a stop. First, I consider that I may be hallucinating the sight in front of me. It doesn't make sense. On top of Brody, who lies flat on the floor, Nax, Feathi, and Yin are all piled on him like children playing a strange wrestling game. With only one good arm, Nax is trying to wrangle Brody's wrists behind his back yet failing miserably. They're all huffing and swearing as Brody wiggles out from underneath.

"What's going on?" I pull Yin off the top layer.

Brody scrambles toward the lever in the bookshelf, but Yin dives for his ankle and yanks him flat to his stomach again.

Feathi sits on his back as Brody writhes and yells, "Get off! I have to do this!"

"Mora, use your orb! Stop him," Nax pleads, his eyes wider than I've ever seen them.

Naturally, my fingers brush against the sphere in my pocket. "Stop him from what?" I glance between them all, but they can't hear me among their cacophony of strained grunts. "What in the Abyss is going on?!"

The veins popping out of Brody's red neck could rival the image of tree roots exploding from the ground. "I have to empty your pen!" He chokes out and my heart rate triples. "It's the only way."

What? This isn't the man I've fallen for—I mean, who I've started to tolerate.

"I have to," Brody repeats but his efforts have diminished as he lies panting. "I have to, Mora." His tightly fisted hand loosens and drops a wad of paper to the ground. "I'm sorry, it's you or her."

Heathcliff gobbles the paper but I grab it from his mouth. Full of slobber, I recognize the apology letter we were working on together. Just as I'm about to toss it on the floor, I notice some words in different handwriting.

Empty...pen or Catterina...next to be poisoned...

I gasp and drop the paper before meeting Brody's eyes, shining with his unshed tears. He's no longer reaching for the lever, but he's silently asking me to make the decision for him. If I nod and allow him to go empty the ink, then my roommates and I only have a few minutes left alive. If I tell Yin and Feathi to tie him up, Brody will despise me for not protecting his child. I swallow. Stare at the snow falling outside the window. A moment passes. Then another.

"Mora?" Feathi asks, "What do we do?"

There has to be another solution. One of us shouldn't have to make a sacrifice. I refuse to let anyone suffer. The last thing I want to do is use my magic since all it has done is hurt people. But what if I can control it?

"Brody," I start softly and calmly, "if they release you, will you give me ten minutes to figure this out?"

He glances at the lever, then at me, then to one of the many clocks on the wall, ticking away. "Five minutes," he whispers, guilt oozing from his gaze.

"Okay, let him go," I say to Nax, then turn to my best friend. "Feathi, I need to know all the other places you hid the six orbs, and Yin you'll help me collect them. We'll meet here in three minutes."

Brody crunches into a small shape, a hunch-backed

gargoyle who lives in storybooks. He stares into oblivion with a wild-eyed look I don't like. Nax sits next to him and pats his back silently.

I'm already moving toward the door, when Feathi says, "Four are upstairs under each of our floorboards under our nightstands."

"Scarlett is the purest stapler known to garden," Yin says, then nods and runs off to the direction of the bedrooms.

I know she'll do her best to help. That's five including the one in my pocket.

Neurotically, I pat the orb in my pocket. "Okay, where are the other two?"

Feathi's face turns ashen. "I only remember one."

"What?" I spin on my heels. "You know how important they are!"

Feathi cringes. "I've been forgetting more and more things recently. Last night I forgot to eat dinner and this morning, I forgot the name of the book I'm reading."

Goddess, years ago she would've been able to tell me the birthdate of all her twenty-nine cousins, and their middle names.

"Okay, it's okay," I say. "Where's the orb you remember?"

"I moved it recently." She points to her feet. "It's buried under the tree downstairs."

"Shit," Brody and I say at the same time. If I go retrieve the orb right now, the temptation of him joining and emptying the pen feels too high.

He doesn't look at me but his entire body tenses, bound chaotically like wires entangled. It'd only take cutting one for the entire system to spark into flames.

"Four minutes left," he growls between strangled breaths, nostrils flaring.

He's right. We don't have time to sit here and debate.

"I'll be back. Everyone stay here," I say.

The platform descends rapidly. I need power, as much as possible. What if Kavianne already has his daughter as a hostage? I never thought she'd hurt a child, but maybe my sister has changed over the years. I can't let this happen.

When the fairy guards stop flapping around my face, the underground doors open. Branches plunge inside the shaft and shove me against the wall. Fuck. Pain racks through my back. There'll be bruises up my spine tomorrow, that is if I survive until then. Terrible pressure lies on my chest as I try to suck in a deep breath.

Since the last time we've been here, the diseased vine has grown out of control, consuming the small chamber. Dozens of arms with devilish fingers grip the invisible bubble protecting the Book. The enchanted pen continues to scribe crimson ink on the last pages of my life story.

My gaze drops to the hub source of the disturbing *Vignamassi.* How am I supposed to tear through these roped vines without my throat being sliced open?

"Use magic, Mora!" Feathi screams from the library above. "Use the orb in your pocket!"

My heart slams against my chest. I writhe against the twined cables of this tormenting plant. They don't loosen. In fact, the braided cords start to push deeper against my waist and rotten slime oozes down. Fantastic.

Sweat drips down my neck. While I strain to reach my pocket, a thorn bites into my forearm. I stretch. Reach a little further. Only a little bit more. Another thorn digs into my inner elbow.

"Gotcha!" My hand wraps around the tiny orb and I keep a death grip on it. If I drop the sphere, then this may as well be my last few breaths. What spell will cut me free from these vines? A couple flip through my mind as options, but they might not be strong enough to slash through something so wild.

"Cissegiere Coupement!" I squeeze my eyes shut when this spell casts a blinding beam of light. "Cissegiere Coupement!"

The twisting vines rip to shreds and fall to the floor in a heap of black twigs. A piercing pain jolts through my gut, like I've been run through with a sword. Then the swaying *Vignamassi* shrieks a deathly howl. I'd plug my ears if I had more than two minutes to dig out the orb.

A tentacle strikes at me from the right. I barely dodge it and it lands on the floor. A second branch hovers and is about to attack from above. I have nowhere to hide. My orb needs time to recharge. I'm screwed.

Eerie whispers echo along the cave and I swear the plant is taunting me, but then I recognize Kavianne's voice from the recording we had already heard.

"Thorns might block our straight path and tangle us in wrath.
But it has been foreseen, even death can turn green."

Maybe I won't write her an apology letter after all. The stalking branch tilts, as if examining me and makes a hissing sound. Its edge scrapes against the wall. It twists and turns until the longest barb I've ever seen is pointed directly at my heart. I brace myself for the pain and can only think of my friends upstairs. Maybe if I can throw one orb before the plant kills me, Feathi can use its power my way.

I dart fast, cringing against the aches spread over my body.

"Feathi! On the count of three, catch!"

"No, don't throw it! The orb will shatter."

"One!" I scream.

The vines shake the entire tomb. Rocks and pebbles fall. Yes, this is where I'll be buried.

"Two!" I get ready to throw the orb up.

"Watch out!" Brody yells as a loud rumble grows louder from above.

More rocks rain down. I duck. A crashing thud sounds and the floor shakes. I'm too afraid to open my eyes. Did Brody just fall to his death? His faint coughing shoots hope through my body as I squint. A giant poof of dust surrounds me from the rocks smashing against each other. Another cough.

"Mora?" Brody calls out amid the cloud.

I launch across the cavern and my toe runs into something soft. Couch cushions.

"Get up!" I whisper and pull him behind me. His chest rests against my back and for some reason, I get the feeling that he's the one shielding me.

"I would've given you more than two minutes," he whispers into my hair.

"Stay behind me."

"I knew you'd need help." He holds up the axe.

"Shhh!" Will this man never heed my commands? I back into him, guiding his body toward where the other orb is buried. I can't fight Kavianne without more power, and defeating her is the only way to guarantee Catterina's safety.

A whipping tentacle crashes into the wall next to us.

Brody grabs my waist and pulls me back. I can feel his heart racing against my back. "It's huge!?"

I keep the orb in front of us, but it can only function as a flashlight at this point since its strength hasn't returned yet.

Brody swings the axe blindly. His elbow smacks my ear.

He hacks at the air again, but the ghostly hissing sound only grows louder. "It's moving too fast!"

"Just keep it away!" I yell, my ears ringing. "I have to start digging!"

"Hurry!"

I drop to my knees. Slam my hands into the hard earth. Claw with my nails. Soil coats my fingertips. I thrust scoop after scoop behind me.

Hissing and spitting sounds compete with Brody's savage grunts. We won't win this battle. He never should've come down here.

Out of breath, forearms burning, I keep digging. Finally, my hand brushes against a smooth, spherical surface. I clamp onto it.

"Got it!" I shove them in my pocket.

Before I understand what's happening, Brody chucks me over his shoulder and runs toward the new entrance to the lagoon. My body rocks against his shoulder. With one arm, he swipes at the pummeling vines. Another vine clobbers the wall behind us.

Stones fall. It's so fucking loud.

"Hurry!"

A tentacle shoots out. It mauls the ground beside us. I scream. I may have been screaming the whole time. We reach the blue light just in time. Brody aims the axe at a giant boulder hanging from the ceiling.

"Hold on!" he roars.

He chucks the axe with all his strength. The sharp metal strikes right at the corner, where it connects to the wall. An excruciating loud blast makes us both fall forward. I slide off his shoulder and stare up. The boulder is knocked loose and an avalanche of rocks cascades over the threshold between the two chambers. We roll toward the hot springs where blue light radiates.

Brody dives over me and I curl against him. His hands find my ears but the sound echoes against my brain, splitting my skull in two. Within seconds, everything goes silent.

"Are you okay? Say something." His hands skim over my body, pulling my shirt at different angles. "Tell me where it hurts." He sounds frantic. It feels like speakers have been blaring next to my head but his voice rings out, clarity in the chaos. "Mora, open your eyes."

In a daze, I do what he says. Blue light is cast on his perfect face, but he moves in and out of focus. "Oh! The cave walls are spinning. Whoa."

"Okay, don't move. I've got you." Brody's breathing starts to slow. We sit there silently, in shock, staring at the massive pile of boulders trapping us.

"The *Vignamassi* is probably buried under that," he says quietly.

"Then so is the Book." I drop my head into my hands.

I check my body but no new thorns have grown so maybe the Book is miraculously unharmed? What will we do next? Eventually, I dare to look over at Brody again. Dirt covers his face and cuts across his neck.

"You're bleeding," I say.

His trembling large hand reaches for my cheek and wipes away a tear. "You're crying."

"No, I'm not."

"Okay, you're not," Brody says, as he pulls me into his chest.

I glance around at the blue lagoon again, unable to fully process our current predicament. The wall has barricaded us in here without an exit. The good news is that we're still alive. The bad news is if the pen is cracked, ink could be spilling out right now. I could be out of time in a week or day or any second.

"You didn't empty the pen," I whisper.

"I didn't empty the pen." His words sound painful. "I almost did. In fact, if that plant didn't attack you, I might've. I'm sorry, but I would've done it. But deep down, I'm a little relieved I didn't get the chance." He hides his face from me and wipes his cheek on his sleeve. "What am I supposed to do now? She's going to hurt Cat."

"We're going to get out of here and save Cat. I promise." I snuggle closer, not caring what message it may send him. Maybe it's okay to be vulnerable when your world is falling apart. Maybe it's okay to rely on someone else and not know the answers.

And despite the soreness of every muscle, it's obvious that another one of my thorns slowly disappears into my skin.

"We'll break your curse too," he whispers into my hair. I think he finally understands that we won't break my curse.

Another tear trickles down my cheek.

"I'm crying," I whisper.

"Yes. Yes, you are, Lulita."

CHAPTER 20

Brody

I'm terrified for Catterina's safety. Unfortunately, the insufferable humidity in this claustrophobic cave only makes my panicking worse. I can't know for sure that Mora's sister is the one who wrote me the note, but who else would want to hurt an innocent girl? What if she already has Cat in her clutches?

I stare at the shimmering hot spring that glows with magic and shudder at the memory of Mora being trapped under a layer of ice. How dare someone threaten those I care about?

"The thorns growing on you will become permanent." Kavianne's voice echoes around the tunnel, a replica of the message we had already heard. "And your soul will merge with that horrid vine beast."

Mora tugs on my hand. "Brody, I can't be here."

"Your spirit will be stuck inside," Kavianne's voice continues, "Indestructible. Unkillable. You'll live for eternity creating havoc on humans."

I'm in a trance, captivated by the hypnotizing voice surrounding us, a voice made of obsidian teardrops.

"...poisoning children with your thorns, and witnessing them die the most gruesome, agonizing deaths."

I look over to see Mora rocking back and forth, her hands covering her ears as she hums to herself with eyes clenched. A mysterious mist starts to rise from the blue pond. Shit, we need to get out of here. There's no time to check Mora for other injuries. Despite my sore muscles, I pull Mora to her feet and scan for an exit.

A deep bark comes from behind the rocks. Heathcliff?

"Mora, I'm going to lift you again. Is that okay?"

She has her hands covering her ears. I can't imagine the fear coursing through her veins at hearing her sister's threats again. I'm about to fling her over my shoulder but a low growl makes me turn.

A wolf, larger than Heathcliff, emerges from the mist. At first, I'm unsure if he's about to charge us, but then a pup hops out and barks. They both turn away, then look over their shoulder as if checking to make sure we follow. Quickly, I grab Mora's hand. The animals lead us through the mist. Fluffy tails are all I can see within the thick cloud engulfing us. A cough erupts from deep in my chest. The mist tastes toxic.

"...poisoning children with your thorns, and witnessing them die the most gruesome, agonizing deaths." Kavianne's voice seems stuck on repeat.

Then a bone-splitting scream pierces my ears, spiking

into my brain with a thousand needles. Mora's grip on my hand tightens as the wolves lead us through a tiny hole, then over rocky terrain, where the cave gets darker with each step. Eventually, the toxic screams shift to a dull hum. My coughing spasms lessen and I can breathe when the fog clears.

Out of breath, I thank the Goddesses that the wolves slow and their long tails start to wag. Our dark tunnel zig-zags to the left and at the end a bright light the size of my fingertip shines. It must be midday already. My sense of time has been entirely distorted.

Next to me, Mora stays silent. I wonder if she's processing her mortality, now that she has an unknown amount of time to get rid of her thorns. Has she figured out that we might not be able to replace her pen with ink again?

I follow her gaze to the tunnel's walls where carvings of wolves cover the stones. The art becomes more elaborate the further we go.

We jog.

And jog some more. Mora's hands fold imaginary origami with the bottom of her shirt when we take breaks. Is her pulse racing as fast as mine? Then we jog some more until my feet ache and I've given up hope that we'll ever make it out.

"I'm sorry, Mora. I don't know how to make this better."

"Let's just focus on your daughter."

She doesn't look my way. I follow her gaze to a large lump of fur where dozens of wolves are curled together on the ground. This cave holds so many families, mommas protecting their litters and the males protecting them all. I'm unable to do either.

A giant wolf, almost as tall as me, walks out from the

shadows. If he views us as harmful intruders to his pack, we don't stand a chance. All the other wolves watch for their alpha's reaction.

Surprisingly, the alpha wolf bows his head to Mora. She lets out a big breath and slowly moves forward, one arm outstretched, covered in scrapes. I should lend her my sweater, but I'm glued to the spot. I may crave adventure, but that doesn't mean I'm used to addressing wild creatures.

"Thank you," Mora whispers and pets his neck. "Can you give us a ride out of this tunnel?"

The wolf's ocean eyes shimmer. He must trust Mora's good intentions. Somehow, he understands. With grace, he lowers himself flat and Mora climbs atop his back—a mount fit for a queen.

"We can look into the enchanted glass back home to find Cat's location," Mora says softly.

I nod and approach the wolf, hoping I will be worthy of a ride as well. There's no time to waste and his gallops will be far faster than my attempts to sprint. He accepts me, and once I'm settled onto his back, a zap of desperation runs through my blood again. If Cat has been infected by a poisonous thorn already, how am I supposed to save her?

The wolf takes off through the tunnel.

"Brody, you need to hold these for me." Mora hands over both tiny orbs. "Keep them safe."

I want to ask her why she doesn't trust herself with them but now isn't the time. Mora only has two. Does she need possession of the other five for her magic to work?

A round hole ahead grows larger. An exit. As we enter daylight again, the wind whips my cheeks, and pine trees whiz by us in an eerie dream-like state, yet I'm stuck in a nightmare. How am I supposed to find Cat? Mora's unusual quiet also has me on edge. What is she thinking? Does she know something I don't?

The wolf's canter isn't as fluid as War's so I'm relieved when he slows down. In the forest ahead, there's a wall of mist rising from the snow. The wolf snorts and its ears perk forward. I'm very aware of his hard muscles under my leg, the cardinal's song in the distance, and the cold breeze trapping me in a death grip.

"This is all my fault," Mora whispers in front of me. "Maybe if I had confronted Kavianne years ago then she wouldn't have taken your daughter. She's only trying to hurt me."

Carefully, I help Mora shift so she's riding the wolf backward and facing me. Finally, her dark brown eyes meet mine. Despite all the chaos, I want to kiss away her pain and worries.

"This isn't your fault, but if we're going to figure this out, I need to know the whole story. Tell me what happened with your sisters."

Her gaze diverts to the trees again, but I move her chin so she can't avoid me any longer. A long sigh parts her lips and I can sense her entire past lingering on the tip of her tongue.

"It all started about seven or eight years ago when my magic became stronger than theirs." Her expression distorts into a grimace. "I was only seventeen and my powers developed so fast. The orbs and I connected so easily. Kavianne often jabbed me with her sarcastic comments, but I never assumed she truly meant me any harm. Lessie on the other hand was simply in awe. Every day she asked me to teach her different spells. Lessie turned into my devoted shadow. She absorbed any detail I taught her. I could've told her that the moon was made of paper and she'd believe me." Mora pauses.

The heaviness of her words isn't lost on me. I take her hands in mine, encouraging her to let it all out. "You're safe with me," I whisper.

She speaks again. "The only irritating thing about Lessie was her fear. She was so excited to learn new things but didn't have any inclination or confidence to try them. Once it took five days to convince her to try a simple transformation spell to turn a flower into a toad. Her reasoning for not trying was that she couldn't ask the flower permission. So she waited, wasting so much of my time. After she advanced, I wanted to teach her to hover in the air, but she was too scared of hurting a rock below if she failed and fell—" When Mora cuts herself off again, her eyes are locked on our joint entwined fingers. Her thumbs caress mine. "I was impatient," she continues, "and tired of waiting for Lessie to grow a pair. If she could do one super challenging skill, then she'd stop hesitating during the smaller tasks. So, one night, while Lessie was sleeping, I used a mind-control spell. Mora gulps and her eyes rise to mine, shimmering and full to the brim with unshed tears. "I wanted to prove to her she could do it. Right when I whispered the spell, I could feel the control I had over her mind. The power was…like nothing I've ever experienced. One of the first things I did was tell her to hover over the cliffside where we used to play as children."

I'll never forget the glossy look in her eyes. Mora pauses so long, I'm afraid she's done sharing. I wait. And wait. As Mora gathers the courage to continue, I lean closer, holding my breath.

"Lessie ran so fast, unnaturally fast through the forest and to the cliff. Something started to feel wrong in my gut, but I didn't know why. Part of me was nervous that Kavianne would be angry that I used a dangerous potion. And the other half was proud that I was the one to think of such a brilliant idea. Soon, they'd both be thanking me for getting Lessie over this hurdle of conquering her fears."

As Mora speaks, the mist completely envelopes us in the forest and all I can see is her face directly in front of mine, white as a ghost with haunted visions flooding her mind.

"Lessie made it to the top of the mountain. As I was chasing after her, a blade-sharp feeling twisted in my chest. Lessie wasn't slowing down. The cliffside grew closer and closer yet Lessie only sprinted faster and faster. At that rate, she wasn't going to only hover, she'd leap off the mountain and…" Mora's voice sounds far off, but her words come faster. "I knew in that moment that I mixed the potion too strongly. I was transfixed. Like focusing on a bubble, knowing any moment it's about to pop and there's nothing you can do to stop it. Those three seconds lasted a lifetime..." Mora's tears spill freely down her face. "I yelled for Lessie to stop…and she did. I was so grateful, so relieved that she hadn't leaped off, so glad I had control of her mind.

"But as Lessie took a single step toward me, her foot caught on a root full of thorns. She screamed out, twisted, and lost her balance. One moment, Lessie was in front of me, her dress blowing in the wind, her hair whipping behind her, and then she was gone. Her body fell over the cliff."

I have no words but my heart shatters for my Mora. Bringing her in for a long hug isn't enough to heal her wounds. She has carried this pain and blame for so long. I rub her back.

"Anyone could stumble on a vine or branch. You weren't the one to send her over the edge." I squeeze her tighter as she sobs into my chest. "Listen to me. It's not your fault. You stopped yourself. It wasn't your magic." I rock her gently. "Her death was an accident."

Mora leans back and wipes her bloodshot eyes with her shirt. "If I hadn't been so certain, then Lessie never would've been there in the first place."

"If you think like that," I say, tucking a wet, tear-streaked piece of hair behind her ear, "then I could go the same route and say that if I had tried harder to convince Dom to stay then my entire life would've been different. Or if I had left with them, or if I had reported Elizabeth to the authorities." I shake my head. "So many options can drive someone mad."

Mora sniffs and wipes her eyes again. I don't want to put the focus on me if Mora isn't done telling me about her sister, so instead, I slowly pull her to my chest again. Feeling her heartbeat thud against mine eases my breathing to a slower and steady rate. Within a few minutes of holding her, the mist reveals the snowy forest again. We're close to the mansion's front gates.

"You lost someone too." The top of Mora's head brushes against my chin as she asks softly, "Can you tell me about what happened with your daughter?"

"I don't remember what I've already told you, but it's a pretty short story." I slowly stroke her hair with one hand. "Dom's mom thought I was trash and prevented us from dating. When she heard of Dom's pregnancy, we had hopes that Elizabeth's outlook would turn around after the baby was born…that she'd turn into a doting grandmother who let go of all her hate." As I stare at the tree trunks surrounding us, the bark somehow morphs into the shape of my enemy's face. "Elizabeth despised Cat from the day she was born, claiming that since she was *my* offspring, she'd ruin Dom's entire life too. The woman spied on us to purposefully catch us in arguments, filmed them to use as proof that we weren't fit to raise a baby. She threatened us, saying that if we didn't give our baby up for adoption, we'd be sorry."

"Brody, that's terrible." Mora's hand finds my chest, and I notice another one of her thorns has disappeared. Maybe she has a chance to break the curse after all.

"At first Dom was in denial, but after her mother tried to break into our apartment one night, she decided to run away with Cat and for me to stay behind and convince Elizabeth that they both died in an accident. We even held a funeral. We planned that after six months, I'd meet them and we'd have a future together, but Dom never sent me their location. I never heard from her again. I've waited. Year after year I waited for a message, or for them to return home. I never…I never knew…" I become stuck on an icicle sharp sensation in my throat. "I never knew whether they were alive or not until I saw Catterina in your mirror."

Mora holds eye contact with me, which encourages me to relay my biggest fear—something I've never admitted to anyone. "Sometimes," my voice is so low, I'm unsure if Mora will be able to hear me, "sometimes, I wonder if I wished they had died because then that would mean they didn't abandon me. When I saw Catterina in your mirror, she was happy and healthy." I rub my newly formed beard with one hand. "What kind of father thinks that? What kind of dad would rather wish his child dead than imagine her happy without him?"

She takes both my shoulders in her hands. "Don't judge yourself. You love her. And we'll find her. Catterina will be okay."

Mora has to be right. We arrive at the front gates. Despite the suns shining on the other side of the treetops, under this canopy, all I feel is frigid sorrow and all I see is hard gloomy stone reflecting the state of my soul.

When the wolf stops, we slip off its back, and Mora bows. "Thank you."

The animal runs into the forest before I can show my appreciation. As Mora opens the creaky gate, a fairy flies out of the brick post and buzzes around our ears.

"Princess Preta?" Mora shields her eyes from the bright black glitter. "What's wrong? What are you doing out here?"

"One of the sick girls in the village died," Princess Preta says quickly. "No medicine worked and since my entire village is recovering, we don't have any other option. I know it's not fair to ask this of you, Miss Mora, but I need some of your stored roses for their doctors."

Mora's face whitens, so I tuck her into my side and speak up for her. "We have a few roses in her apothecary studio. You can come take a few, but every potion she has tried hasn't mixed well."

Princess Preta flutters by my face. "Thank you."

We trudge through the snow. It's like I'm dragging a human doll behind me because of Mora's incoherent posture. At first, I'm worried about hypothermia until I realize the real issue. She's blaming herself. Again.

"Mora, the girl didn't die because of you."

"My thorns. She died from my thorns," she whispers. "My thorns."

Shit. Everything is fucking falling apart. I can't take care of all these problems at once. I need help. I can't focus on Mora until I hear news of Cat first. So I face the fairy and ask, "Princess, have you heard of a girl named Catterina, or Cat? Her mother's name is Dom."

The fairy cringes. "Yes, there's already a search party out for the little one."

So, it's true. She's been taken. I slouch, a sickening pain in my stomach threatening to have me vomit.

"Catterina is your daughter, isn't she?" the fairy asks.

I nod, unable to speak.

"We will keep looking for her, but in the meantime, I'll bring you to her mother. She's waiting inside."

"Dom is here?"

CHAPTER 21

Mora

"Where is she?" Brody's demand slices through my thoughts. "Where's Dom? Take me to her."

His other ex? She's here? My gaze falls on my home, where a shadow paces behind a curtain. Surely Dom wouldn't come here, of all places. She doesn't have any way of knowing where I live or that Brody is here. The silhouette inside must be Feathi awaiting my return, but all my roommates know to stay away from the windows.

I stare in a trance. Nothing makes sense.

My thorns killed a little girl. Even from afar, I'm deadly. I have to stop this from happening again. Her poor parents probably cradled her limp body in their arms, unable to make sense of their loss. My legs tremble, but I won't let my knees give out. There are too many problems and not enough time. How am I supposed to find Brody's daughter and mix healing potions for the villagers at the same time?

Now that a ton of boulders have buried the ink pen far under the library, there's no point in focusing on my curse. But what if I don't have days left? What if I only have hours? What I need is time. Time. I immediately picture the fairy village underground, surrounded by those epic giant clocks. Time. I gasp. My magic can't help, but maybe the fairies' can.

I look to the fairy standing on Brody's finger, her black lace dress draped into his palm. They're mid-discussion but I only understand a few of Brody's rushed, scrambled words.

"Princess," I interrupt, "can you stop time?"

She snaps her fingers, and a strange sensation punches me. A forceful blow to the stomach. Preta stands on Brody's finger but his lips are moving in slow motion. When he bats his eyes, his long lashes fall to his cheeks like the blinds of a window slowly closing to the outside world.

"I can slow time in small increments," Preta gestures around her where snowflakes hover mid-air. "When I do this it costs a great deal."

I gulp, hyper-aware that my movements remain at normal speed. "What's the cost?"

"Every second slowed for you takes a year off the life of the one you love most."

"Bring us back!" I yell. "Now!"

She nods and snaps again. Brody's movements spring to life with urgency and desperation. I can't slow time because years will be taken from Brody. My heart hammers faster than it ever has in my life.

Fuck, I love him? No, I can't.

"You said Dom is here?" Brody asks frantically. "Where? How?"

"She's inside," Preta gestures to the door. "I'll bring you to her."

I tromp through the snow, up the icy stairs, and heave open the heavy iron doors. It creaks as I strain to push it against rusty hinges.

A woman with pink glasses that match her bright hair stands by the foyer's fireplace. Is that Dom? She paces in front of the flickering flames though I know she must be aware that we've entered. With her arms crossed, her expression mirrors Brody's.

"Dom!" Brody runs across the lobby entrance and wraps her in a hug. He holds her head to his chest and I wish I had the strength to look away, but the universe is run by cruel Goddesses who control my gaze and refuse to let me blink. The sight of them embracing is a sharp blade slowly slashing my throat, without the relief of death. Her red nail polish in his hair is the blood spurting out of my neck. Her arm around his back is a rope strangling me. And their comforting sighs while embracing are the gurgling sound I hear myself make, though I am not allowed to die.

I can't help but give her a once-over. The white dress hanging below her winter coat is torn and covered in dirt. What terrors did she face in the forest while traveling here? How long has their daughter been missing? Their daughter. Theirs. Because Dom and Brody are a family.

My stomach churns with nausea. I glance between Brody and Dom, picturing their past, their love, their connection, their bodies. There's no stopping my spine from curling in anguish.

"He took Cat," Dom says, and her voice matches her

features, quiet but challenging, small yet fierce. "I haven't been able to find her." She paces now, wringing her hands.

"We will," Brody says, and I may as well have turned invisible once they looked into each other's eyes. Two people who share the same priority, lost within each other's thoughts. I'm the outcast here.

My voice wants to protest their nearness. My arms want to put canyons between them. My legs want to kick her across the Barrett Sea. But I just stand and stare at the couple who share a history and, most likely, a future. Maybe this is how it was supposed to be. My punishment for Lessie's death hasn't been the curse all along; it's this torture in front of me, the fact that I can't have him. That must be the lesson Kavianne wanted me to learn. I took away the love of her life, her baby sister, so she wants to rip away my chance at love.

My hands curl into fists. No, I don't love him. I can't. And even if I did, it's just as easy to fall out of love. All I need is to focus on the next step. We need to find Cat. I'll fight to give Brody what he wants if it takes until my last breath.

"What did the man look like?" I step forward. "Did he take her into the forest? Which way did they go? Were they riding any type of animal or a hoverboard?"

"No, you don't understand." Dom sighs, as if annoyed, then points to the stairs. "The dog took her to a hiding spot somewhere in this huge house and we can't find her. We've been waiting for you to return, and I guess she got nervous and followed the damn puppy to some corner of this castle, but no matter how loud I call, she won't come out." Dom stomps toward the stairs again. "Get your butt down here, missy, or you won't have chocolate for the rest of your life!"

Speechless, Brody's eyes widen to the size of a full

moon. "She's here? She's safe…and she's *here*." His voice is so tender I want to capture the texture of it in one of my apothecary bottles to keep it for eternity. "Cat is *here*?" He spins in slow circles. "Right now? My daughter is here?"

Here. If she's here, then was the threatening note fake? Or maybe Dom isn't who she says she is? What if Kavianne is disguised as Dom? I jump between her and Brody and ask, "Why are you here?"

"We heard about the plague, so we rushed back home in case it happened to you." Dom puts both hands on her hips. "It's five years late for this argument, but you never called. You never came for us."

"What? I didn't have a number to call, Dominique!" Brody says. "You didn't want your mom to find it, remember?"

"I left you messages, though," she scrambles, unsure. "Plus, we said we'd meet in Runlose. You never showed up."

"No, we didn't decide on where. I wouldn't have forgotten that," Brody says, his voice calming. "And I didn't get a single message from you."

"But…how?" Dom's chest rises and falls fast, and a wash of confusion cascades over her face. "I was furious at you for so long."

"I never abandoned you. I've been waiting at home for years."

"You know why I couldn't return home, but then I heard about the plague and couldn't imagine you poisoned." She drops both hands. Her eyes start to water. "I'm glad you're here." Dom's voice starts shaking. "Brody, I'm so sorry. After a year went by, and you never came, I thought you just didn't want to be a part of our life." She starts sniffling. "I'm sorry, I'm so sorry. I love Cat so much and thought I was making the best choice for her."

They stare at each other, and I wonder what's being communicated in the silence.

"And just so you know, I didn't say one negative word about you," Dom adds. "Cat only knows you as a hero and had faith you'd find us. She can't wait to meet you, Brody, so Don't. You. Dare." Dom stabs his chest with her finger to punctuate each word. "Break. Her. Heart."

Goosebumps rise on my arms as his energy floats toward me. The utter and complete tornado of his emotions is a thick syrupy cream that I can taste. I don't move a muscle.

"Let's find her." I point him toward the stained glass window. If he asks it, the glass will work the same as the enchanted mirror and show him Catterina's location. Wait, he doesn't know that part of the magic.

I clear my throat and fixate on the glass, prepared to explain the rules to him. The image swirls into a scene of falling snow and I expect to see Lessie's final resting place again. Instead, a faint outline of Brody's sharp jawline, scruffy beard, and messy hair appears. My heart thunders in my chest as the glass shows me the man who already holds my heart in his pocket. Damn it. How did I let this happen? And if I'm in love but have thorns, then love doesn't break the curse. Why else have they been disappearing?

I clear my throat. "Brody, ask the glass to show you where Catterina is."

"Oh, it's like the mirror," he says without looking at me, completely entranced by the possibility of seeing his daughter again. Without a second's delay, his face twists into a smile as he stares at what I cannot see. Maybe after they all leave together I'll shatter every window in this house so I will never risk seeing his face again. I'm about to walk to my apothecary studio and let the two parents start their happily ever after when Brody grabs my hand.

"They're eating brownies off the kitchen floor. Come on, Mora," he says excitedly.

"What?"

"I said come on. Don't make me carry you again."

"But…" A lump the size of a book lodges in my throat. We lock eyes and I have to make sure I'm breathing. "You want me to come with you?"

His thumb grasps my chin. "If you keep looking at me like that, then there's no chance I'll win our no kissing bet." With intent, Brody pulls me to his side and wraps his arm around my waist. "And I promise I'll sweep you onto my back if you don't start moving, *Lulita*."

He emphasizes the last word and the wall encasing me in a prison of fear crumbles to the floor. My head has never spun this much, my heart has never felt so heavy and weightless at the same time, and my lips have never pulsed with tingly need. The way Brody looks at me changes reality, shifts all possibilities, and opens doors I've never known to exist. I love this man.

We hustle, but I doubt my feet touch the floor. Brody isn't holding Dom's hand, he's holding mine. As we pass the ticking clocks in the hallway, I'm vaguely aware of their voices in conversation, but I can only concentrate on Brody's fingers laced with mine, Brody's thumb rubbing my wrist, now more easily accessible with fewer thorns occupying it.

This is insanity. I should be comforting *him* right now. He's gone years without seeing his daughter and his entire life is about to change. Ahead, the kitchen door is open a crack, and light shines into the hall. I stop and pull Brody closer.

"Are you going to be okay? I mean, do you need a pep talk before meeting her?" I ask.

"A kiss could help distract me." He smiles with the wicked triumph of a winner in all his glory.

My cheeks burn hot since I'm wholly aware of Dom staring at us. I nudge him playfully. "I don't lose challenges," then whisper, "There's no chance I'm kissing you first."

He fidgets and cracks his neck. His eyes bounce to all the clocks behind me, then out the window. "What if…" he bites his lip. "What if Cat doesn't like me? What if she's scared of me? What if I say the wrong thing?"

I wrap my other hand around his. "Cat will be obsessed with you."

I can tell he's trying to resist the temptation, but his eyes flicker to Dom for reassurance, who helps in the best way possible by saying, "She's just like you, Brody: fearless, full of wild adventure and curiosity. Just get her talking about a treasure hunt."

His shoulders loosen and he visibly relaxes, yet his eyes roam the hallway, as if Cat herself will burst out of the stone walls. "Treasure, huh? I can handle that."

I nod my thanks to Dom, surprised when she smiles in return. Maybe this won't mirror those terrible romance novels where the two women are in competition. We could be friends. And if not, I'll still fight for Brody.

Brody moves toward the kitchen door, one hand outstretched. The same sensation cascades over me as when the fairy slowed time, but when a soft giggle slides out from the kitchen, it becomes painfully obvious that Brody is simply frozen in place.

Inhaling a deep breath, I take his hand once more and pull Brody through the door to the other side.

CHAPTER 22

Brody

Cat sits right in front of me. Am I dreaming? My daughter plays on the floor, her back to me. She wears overalls that cover a braid tucked underneath. She's bent forward, drawing a picture in the flour with her finger across the tile. I want to rush to her, but I can't move. On her left, Heathcliff's tail wags, sweeping flour back and forth. The pup has more courage than me.

A gentle tug from Mora pulls me forward. With each step, it becomes clearer that Cat's tangle of hair is the same dark brown as mine. When she turns, will she recognize me? Has Dom prepared her for this moment?

Still unaware of my presence, Cat starts to hum a song.

I've heard the melody once upon a time but can't place it. The purity of her voice strums at my heartstrings like an expert guitarist. My hands sweat so much that I drop my grip on Mora. I shuffle forward again. Freeze. Wait. Her name is stuck on the tip of my tongue.

Catterina.

She's here. Right now. Cat is here. I need to breathe.

"Catterina?"

My daughter turns slowly. First, I see tanned arms covered in flour. Then, her right ear, pierced with jewelry already. I wonder if it was her idea or Dom's. It doesn't matter, I could kiss that ear until it falls off. Next, her soft jawline. Her cheek. Suddenly, I'm face to face with the love of my life. Her emerald-rich, bright eyes shine with youth.

Cat tilts her head, her eyebrows scrunch up, and her nose wrinkles. Even her lips twist into a pouty mess. "Papi!" She spits out with the ferocity of a volcano and my heart melts faster than lava. "I'm gonna call you papi if you like it or not cuz Kwistyne fwom school has two daddies and they let her pick what she calls them when she moved in with them at the beginning of kinduhgawten so you will be Papi and you will love it so much. Huwwy though, we have a lot of wook to do." She stands and stomps over to me. "You need to help me with this map."

At some point, I fell to my knees because we're eye to eye. I'm gazing into the bright green color that holds the spark of a thousand stars. Goddess, I love her so much. When she grabs my hand, I remind myself to breathe.

"And you need to wite down all my favowite things, Papi. All of them, cuz if you fowget jelly on my sandwich then I won't let you tuck me in at night and Mommy keeps telling me how much you gonna wanna tuck me in." Cat pulls me to her powder chaos on the floor. "This is us and 'X' is wheyuh we need to go."

A tear falls down my cheek as I stare at her animated face. She has dramatic expressions meant for theater.

"See, Papi? Look heyuh. You see it, wight?" The genuine concern she demonstrates is all-consuming.

I try to answer, but only a frog's croak comes out. After I clear my throat, I try again. "Yes, Cat, I see. What's at the X?"

Her face brightens more as she claps her hands together. "The biggest tweasuh of all!"

What she doesn't know is I've already found my treasure.

"Maybe we can play hide and seek. No, wait, fiwst I need to show you my teddy, he's in my backpack." She rummages through a rainbow-colored, holey bag and tosses out several drawings of maps, a compass, a plastic spyglass, and a pack of crackers. "Heayuh he is! Guess his name! No, you won't evuh guess. His name is mistuh beah."

"Mister Bear?"

"Yeah! That's it. He wants a stowy. So, weady, set, go." She looks at me with doe eyes and I melt inside.

"Oh, I'm good at stories." I clear my throat and Mora rejoins my side in encouragement. "Once upon a time, there was a magical Book and an enchanted pen." Cat scoots closer on both knees, already enraptured. "The Book was good and evil at the same time."

Cat's jaw drops. "No way!"

"Well, the Book wrote about a powerful witch's life, which is an amazing thing to do. For years, her every move and thought was written on the pages of the Book, but if the pen ever ran out of ink, she'd turn into a monster forever."

Catterina gasps. "How tewwible!"

"I know. So, the only way the witch could win against the Book was to break her curse."

Cat gasps. "How?!"

"She has to find all her missing, magical, glowing orbs and use their magic."

"Why doesn't she know wheyuh they awe, Papi?" Catterina inches closer, eyebrows raised high. "Did she lose them?"

"Someone hid the orbs and we need to go on a scavenger hunt to find them all."

Catterina's face drops and she crosses her arms. "Papi, you can't twick me. That's not weal. I only hunt for weal tweasuh."

Mora speaks as she reaches into my pocket and pulls two of the small spheres out. "Oh, they're real."

"Wow!" Catterina reaches for one and I assume Mora will hide it away from her, but she shatters all my expectations and hands over her most valued possessions to a six-year-old. Cat holds it tenderly and stares into it like a snow globe. "Look, theyuh is swiwls inside, Papi!"

"Yes, those swirls are magic."

"I want magic," Catterina whines.

I pat my lap, hoping she'll sit on my leg without fear. She does, and looks at me from under long lashes. In that moment, I know without a doubt I'd move mountains for this girl, kill anyone for her, sacrifice my life again and again if necessary. She's all the suns condensed in one tiny body.

"Cat, you don't need magic. You ARE magic."

She rolls her eyes. "Mommy told me you'd say something like that and that I'm supposed to let you, but Papi, that's just silly. But you know what I've been waiting to tell you?"

"What's that?"

"My biwthday is soon and I want a huge pawty cuz it's the fiwst biwthday with you, Papi!"

I want to give her a pony, a thousand ponies, the entire ocean, but reality hits me like a bowling ball to pins. "I want to throw you the biggest party of them all someday. Everyone will wear their fanciest ball gowns and we will rent out a giant ballroom."

"Like in the movie, Hop Pop Goes the Weasel?" Her eyes light up more. "They all dance in teacup dwesses. But I've never dwinken tea. Mommy doesn't let me twy soda. You'd think one little dwop wouldn't be too bad, wouldn't ya, but nope, she said that soda and suguh would have to wait until I'm ten. But I look ten, wight? I'm fastuh than kids bigguh than me, and I can climb highuh. But I don't want to invite the big kids to my biwthday party, just you and Mommy." She pauses and glances to my side. "You can come too. You must come, as a biwthday rule. What's youh name?"

Mora places her hand back in mine and I kiss the back of her knuckles. "This is Mora and she'll be my date to your party, but I'm sorry, Cat, it won't be—"

"Brody…" Mora interrupts. When I look over, her eyes are full of unshed tears. She stares at my daughter in a way that would burst my heart apart if it hadn't already done so.

Slowly, Mora's head turns toward me. "Brody, I'm gonna kiss you now."

If Mora kisses me, she's agreeing to host the party here, at her house, full of strangers, who will see her remaining thorns. If she kisses me, it'll be her first time fully relinquishing control. If she kisses me, she's accepting my ideas instead of controlling the outcome, but, most importantly, if she kisses me, she will make me fall for her faster.

"Are you sure?"

Mora leans in and brushes her soft lips against mine. So

pillowy soft. How did I become the luckiest man to have two strong feminine souls on either side of me? A flash of our potential future takes over my thoughts, with images of Catterina's future summers, chasing her around an amusement park, Mora's apothecary shop in a Lacordian town, Mora teaching Cat how to fold origami, the three of us holding hands on the couch during a scary movie. I want it all.

"Ew, yuck," Catterina covers her eyes right as we end our kiss. "You looooove each othuh! Do I get thwee mommies now!?"

I keep my eyes trained on Mora. As if she's prepared to destroy all my self-control, she bites her lip when her cheeks flush pink. My life couldn't get any better than this exact moment. I shake off the giddy drug-like sensation. I love Mora. And I think she loves me.

"We'll be right back. We're going to tell your mommy about the party. Stay here."

I can't believe Catterina is here. My mind is spinning and my heart has walked out of my body and now sits on the floor of the kitchen. How am I supposed to live with my heart walking around this cruel world?

When we rejoin Dom on the other side of the door, it's obvious she heard the entire conversation. She nods in approval and then scans my hand around Mora's waist. A flicker of a smile flashes in her eyes and she's about to say something, but Gabrielle walks around the corner of the hallway. Her inhuman white teeth almost blind me.

"Oh, thank the Goddesses, we thought the witch ate you," Gabrielle says.

"How did you get here?" I ask.

"I'm not an idiot. I put a tracker on your Taj when you stayed at my house. I've been waiting for you to return on your own so I wouldn't have to trudge through the snowy woods. When Dom showed up out of the blue frantically searching for you, I offered to lead her here." Gabby glares at Dom as if she's already planning the woman's murder, with disgust dripping from her revolting eyeshadow. Each time Princess Preta buzzes by her ear, she tries to swat the fairy away.

Mora leans toward Preta and says, "Please spread the word that there will be a once in a lifetime party here. Anyone who brings a rose for admission can attend. I don't care if you create gossip, just get people to show up."

Gabrielle's angry stance relaxes a bit. "You'll need an event planner." When she looks at Mora, her eyes narrow and she leans forward.

"Um, excuse me!" Mora slides away.

Gabrielle reaches into her pocket, pulls something out, and quickly plucks the outlandishly long hair from Mora's chin.

"Ow!" One hand flies to her face. "What in the Abyss! Warn someone first."

"You're welcome," Gabrielle rolls her eyes.

I meet Mora's gaze and she's halfway furious and halfway about to start laughing, so I save her any further embarrassment and pretend that didn't happen.

"I'll cover the cost of the party," I say, ready to get back to my daughter's side. "Do it all, Gabby—decoration, food, music. Just make sure everyone knows they must have a rose."

She takes out her Taj device as if to take notes. "What's the dress code? Is there a theme?"

"I don't care. We just need the roses. It's important." I resist glancing behind me. "Oh, and Gabby, make sure the invitation is clear that magical creatures will be in attendance. I don't want anyone having a heart attack when they see Mora's roommates."

"Wait, Mora LIVES here?" Gabby's eyes widen. "You didn't say that." Her mouth drops open in question. I explain the basics of the situation, only giving essential details. No one else needs to know about Mora's curse. Since her few remaining thorns are hidden, there is a chance we can get rid of them before Cat even sees one.

"Brody, can we talk for a minute?" Dom asks.

I nod at Mora and she heads back into the kitchen. We stand under the open door.

"Catterina is amazing," I say, almost breathless while watching her.

"Yeah, she really is." Then I can feel her eyes on me again. "You like her."

"Of course I like her, I love her. She's magnificent, Dom. You did such a good job raising her."

"I meant the witch."

Mora's sitting with Cat on the floor, laughing and drawing in the flour too. A strand of hair falls over Mora's cheek.

I lean back against the wall where I can keep both eyes on my daughter through the doorway. "Dom, what we had in the past is exactly that, the past. We can only be friends."

She slaps my shoulder softly. "Shut up, I have a Partner. Her name is Stephanie, and we've been together for four years. She's the other reason I never came back to try and find you. I didn't know how you'd react."

Her honesty is probably the only thing that could peel my eyes off Cat and Mora playing thumb-war on the floor. "Are you happy with Stephanie?"

"Yes, we're having a Commitment Day. All the paperwork has been made official already and the party was planned, but then I heard about the plague and needed to make sure you were okay, so we postponed it."

Gently, I brush the back of her hand. "All that matters is

she's here now. Thank you for taking care of her so well. She's brilliant. And thank you for bringing her back to me."

"I know how I can apologize." Dom hops in place. "I'll make a dress for your girlfriend for the party."

"You don't have to design Mora a dress. There's not much time."

"Consider it done." Dom steps around me and squints through the door. "So, she's about five-six, curvy hips, small shoulders, I might not have to measure her size. It could be a surprise, a 'welcome to the family' gift."

I can't deny her after that show of genuine excitement. "Okay, Dom. Make a dress, but please use her favorite colors, dark crimson or gold."

Dom mumbles a plan to herself. We have so much to talk about, and tomorrow morning I'll have pages full of questions to ask Dom and Cat, but right now, I need time with Cat. What is she thinking right now?

"Catterina, stay with your daddy," Dom says. "I'm gonna go find where they keep fabric."

"His name is papi."

Dom shoots me a glance and I shrug. "Okay, then. Papi will play with you until bedtime."

Cat tugs my arm down and whispers into my ear, "I'll be dwagon and you'll be my pet fwog."

I kiss her forehead. "I'll be anything you want me to be, sweetie."

We spend over an hour playing make-believe, which eventually leads to hide and seek within the kitchen, and ends with an imaginary tea party in outer space. I can't stop grinning at Cat and all her amazing ideas. I catch Mora's eye after a while from where she sits at the counter watching us contently.

Dom walks back in and checks the closest grandfather clock. "Okay, it's time for bed Kitty Cat."

Catterina yawns and ruffles my hair. "Be a good fwog tonight, Papi. Don't get into twouble."

I drink in her scent as I lean in for a hug. "Goodnight Catterina. I love you."

She wrinkles her nose again. "Hhm, I think I love you too."

Dom holds out her hand and they disappear around the corner.

"She's absolutely amazing." Mora glides to my side. "I'm so glad she's here."

Goddess, she said the most perfect thing, exactly what I needed to hear.

I need her. I fucking need her to be mine and I can't wait any longer for her to know. I sandwich her waist with my hands and pull her closer. "Mora, I haven't known you very long."

She raises on her tiptoes and paints a tender kiss on my neck.

"Mmmm," I can barely speak when she moves her mouth along my jawline. "I'm feeling things for you that I haven't felt in a long…mmmm." My cock stiffens.

She sways back a little, so I can see her face, but keeps her hips pushed against my body. "My thorns are all gone," she says, so convincingly that I'd believe her if it weren't for the tiny movements of her fingers folding origami by my side. "Everything will be fine, now. It's a happily ever after."

I know she's lying, and she knows I know. If this is what she needs to say right now to feel secure, we can figure out a plan for how to get rid of the rest tomorrow.

"Mora, thank you for handling that all so well. I appreciate you and I've been wanting to say…" I take both her hands in mine.

"Just...wait on whatever you're about to say. There's no need to recite poetry or write a romantic movie."

Gently, I lift her chin. "It's okay if you're scared of what we could be. I'm terrified of us, but what I feel for you is real. Even though I'm afraid, I want to spend every moment I can with you. Starting in our bed."

"*My* bed." Her devious smirk is the final topping on the best day of my life.

"*Our* bed." I swoop her into my arms as she squeals. A sharp thorn in her side pierces my skin but I don't let her notice my quick intake of breath.

"Fine, *our* bed."

CHAPTER 23

Mora

After Brody starts a small fire in my bedroom's hearth, we find ourselves standing on opposite sides of my room, staring at each other. Despite the minimal light, I can see the hungry look in his eyes and the fast movements of his chest rising and falling with each breath. The icy cold wall behind my back seems to push me toward him, like this house has a mind of its own.

"Do you want to play a game?" he says, the fire highlights the little smirk rising on his face.

My fingers fold nonexistent origami by my side as I stay silent, awaiting his next move.

He runs a hand through his hair and if I hadn't been studying his expression, I wouldn't have detected the nervous look he's trying to hide. "How about for every truth confessed, we take a step forward."

That's when I notice him fiddling with a tool near his pocket. Is he as nervous as I am? "Fine, I'll play," I say.

He pockets his tool and all his focus is on me. He scans me from head to toe. No, the sensation is more physical than that. Brody's gaze is a feather sliding from the top of my neck, all the way down, not skipping an inch. It doesn't matter that I wear yoga pants and a hoodie, I feel more naked than I have in my entire life, and I want to give this man more of myself.

"What are you afraid of right now?" I ask, focusing on keeping my breathing steady.

"That you'll run from me." He says it so quickly it's as if he's already contemplated this. And when he takes his single step forward, lessening the space between us, a tingling travels up my spine one vertebrate at a time.

Maybe he should do us both a favor and pin me against the wall right now.

"My turn." Brody licks his lips. "Why did you kiss me downstairs? Why did you let me win?"

I swallow, my heart racing at the intensity of his stare. "Because when I saw you interact with Cat, I've never been more attracted to a man."

When I take a step closer to him, I swear he takes a sharp inhale. The fire crackles and embers spark but neither of us breaks eye contact. For a moment I study his outfit and decide the quickest way to tug off his t-shirt and yank off his pants. Is it buttons or zipper? Maybe he's strong enough to rip them off without having to undo any.

"Eyes up here, Lulita." I startle and meet his entertained gaze. "The last two times I had sex, I didn't even ask their names." He minimizes the gap between us after giving his truth, but this is taking too long.

"I like the name Heathcliff even though I pretended I didn't." Big step forward. "I want to meet your sisters." Another step forward, my hands shaking by my side. "I wish I had more time with you, but my curse isn't actually broken yet." I'm two feet away from him, but neither of us leaps into the other's arms.

His expression is a mix of desire, longing, passion, and tormented agony all rolled into one. "I ripped my boat ticket before Cat arrived."

My heart rate pounds in my chest as he takes a step closer. We're inches apart.

"Last question. What are *you* most afraid of, Mora?"

I wrap my hands around his broad back, pulling him into me. When I look up, the tenderness in his eyes urges me to answer. His look promises safety in his embrace, but I've never been afraid of him; he's not the cursed one. I'm terrified of myself, my beastly powers and monstrous potential.

"Nothing," I say cowardly.

"Liar," he says as his lips brush my neck. "I know you're afraid."

Every fiber of my being fears the 'what ifs' bouncing around in my head like ping pong balls. What if I slice his skin open during sex? What if he falls in love and I break his heart? What if I do leave him and confirm his worst fear?

"I'm afraid of hurting you," I whisper.

Brody strokes a hand through my hair. We're too close yet too far simultaneously. His fingers trail over my cheek.

"Listen to me, Mora. If I were to parasail, there's a chance I'd break my leg. If I were to scuba dive in Nerida, I could get tangled in seaweed. If I were to experience all my dreams and live a life full of great adventures, there's danger around each corner awaiting me. Figuring out ways to make your nose scrunch, firing comments back and forth, being by your side…loving you…it's the most perilous adventure of all, but I wouldn't miss it for anything. I'll be right here. Even if you threatened to rip me to shreds, I'm not scared of you."

"Maybe you should be."

He smiles, but I barely get to inspect the curve of his lips before they're planted on mine. Just like before, he tastes of moonlight and stars, of mountains and cliffside waterfalls. He couldn't cling tighter to me if he tried. We're a unique origami creation, with countless folds of arms and needs, kisses and moans, soft hands and sharp nails scratching backs.

Suddenly, my calves hit a piece of furniture. When did we move across the room? The devious gleam in his eyes tells me neither of us will be able to hold out much longer, but I still want to savor this moment, in case it's the only one we have.

His lips are a stamp across my collarbone. His fingertip is a pen writing a poem. His body is an envelope protecting me from the world. All my senses respond, alive, aware, and ready.

"What do you like?" Brody growls against my collarbone as his hands lift my hoodie over my head and the fabric flops to the floor. "I'll do whatever you like, just tell me, Lulita."

I tug at his shirt, but it gets stuck halfway over his head. He laughs and pulls it off the rest of the way. Goddess, he's gorgeous. He throws me on the mattress, swiping off my pants in an experienced sweep. His lips tickle my thigh. His fingertips circle my breasts softly.

"I'm taking these off too."

I watch him drink me in as he slides my underwear to my ankles. I lay bare below him. My heart rate skyrockets when his eyes darken further. The seriousness of his gaze is striking. No, I need a better word. He looks famished. Frenzied. The view of his chest shimmering in the firelight will be etched into my mind for eternity. Sculpted shoulders meet arms that have seen work, arms that have chiseled and sawed and scraped for a living.

He leans over me, but he doesn't end my misery with a kiss. Instead, he whispers in my ear, "Tell me what you like."

I fiddle with his pants buckle, struggling again, and grunt as I yank it side to side.

"Whoa, easy there. I might start to think you're impatient." His smile undoes me and I can't survive this torture any longer. As his fingertips trace masterworks of art an inch over my breast, I grunt in frustration.

"Take these off." I groan between words. "That's what I want. Please."

Brody moves to stand at the end of the bed, staring me down. I'm his next meal. The jeans drop to his ankles. Damn, I hadn't expected his legs to be so toned too. There must be a challenge in my eye because he tilts his head with a smirk.

Brody drops his boxers to the floor.

Yup, what he's got will definitely get the job done.

Brody clears his throat with a touch of laughter. "Well, my dear Mora, are we on equal ground now?"

I lift my knees and spread my legs.

"Fuck," he mutters.

He's on top of me before I can breathe. Brody's dark eyes hold an unfinished story, and for now, I'm happy enough to be a part of one chapter. We may as well make it a binge-worthy one.

"Tell me, Mora." His greedy hand hovers above my clit, not touching. "Tell me what you like."

What he doesn't know is he's already unraveling me. "I like…being teased," I whisper, sliding my fingers over his shoulders.

"Like this?" One fingertip rests on my clit but he doesn't move it. Doesn't circle. Doesn't massage. And I love it.

Slowly, I rotate my hips to rub against his touch.

He exhales deeply. "Shit, Mora. Look at you." Brody bends over me, eyes locked on mine, and hovers his lips over my nipple.

All I want is for him to kiss my breasts, lick, bite, but he holds there with the self-control of a god, to make me fall apart. His tongue dips, staying within an inch of my pointed mound, and I have to arch for us to meet.

He groans when his mouth becomes full of my breast. My eyes flutter closed, but I pry them open, unwilling to miss one of his expressions. He's so damned beautiful.

Brody moves to my neck, kissing with such soft touches—silk on silk. It's obvious how much he's holding back for me. That thought alone almost has me shattering.

His finger speeds between my legs and he adds one into the mix. "You're going to come for me before you feel me inside you."

I moan and clutch onto him. Every muscle clenches. I'm wound so tight, hot and coiled, ready to burst. His hand works me like his life depends on it, making my fists clamp the sheet into a ball in my hand.

I writhe against his movements. "I can't…" I pant. "I can't come like this."

"I've got you, Lulita." He positions himself over me and presses the tip of his cock against my folds. Oh my Goddess, nothing has felt better. "Fuck, Mora…" His eyes go wild. "…it feels like you already came for me."

My entire body shakes. I'm in divine agony without him even being inside me.

He circles his cock around my thighs, my entrance. I'm going insane. Sounds come out of me that shouldn't exist in real life. I desperately throw my arms back to grasp one of the posts of the bed.

Above me, the gravity of Brody's face and his complete concentration send my heart racing. I want this feeling, him, every day, forever.

"Ooh! Fuck!" I scream, moving in rhythm with his hips, but he hasn't even pushed into me yet. "Fuck!" I arch my back again, and again, needing him inside me. "Please!" I arch again, trying to push myself around him. "Brody, please!" I gasp.

"No, my little Lulita." His breath is ragged, his muscles strained, brows furrowed. "Come for me right now, then you can have all of me."

"Ahh! I can't!" I'm out of breath, muscles taut, so much tension built I can't stand it.

"Yes, you can. You will fuckin' come for me, my Mora. Let go." His hands pin my waist hard to the mattress and he holds his cock pressed against my entrance, teasing me with pleasure I've never experienced before. "Now, Mora!" he growls with such intensity I forget to breathe.

The room fades, his face becomes fuzzy, and a spot deep inside my core erupts into powerful waves of magic. There's so much pressure. Until everything inside me detonates violently. I shudder, clamping tight. A sensitive tingling climbs up my spine. It lasts so damn long. Finally, I release the breath I'd been holding.

When I open my eyes, panting, Brody's staring at me with the ferocity of a hunter. Without a word, ever so slowly, his cock slides into me. Just a little at a time until

I'm sure there can't be any more of him left. Then more fills me up.

"Oh. My. Goddess." My nails dig into his biceps.

His Adam's apple bobs and he squeezes his eyes shut for just a moment. "Hold on a second." His eyes flutter open again and they have that heavy look only meant for midnight. "Are you okay?"

Still completely out of breath, all I can do is nod. He thrusts once.

"Whoa." I brace myself.

Twice.

"Fuck, Brody, www-what…whoa…" I squeak out. Gooseflesh covers my arms.

He pulls all the way out, then slips in again. "Mora…this is…fuck…this is…oh, my God, holy, fuck."

"Oooh," I manage to say, "slow, just go slow."

Brody obliterates any standard of sex I'd ever considered. Fictional or real life, he outdoes every other man.

In and out, in and out.

My brain is mush, my mind only sees him, my heart is ready to explode. Nothing can compare.

In and out, in and out. I'm so full. He's so hard. So thick.

My body takes in his every movement, every kiss, every touch. He's driving me insane.

"Mora…" The intensity of my name is like a prayer in his deep voice.

Eventually, neither of us have the strength to hold my legs. He turns me, so we lay spooned with him sliding in and out like it's all that will ever matter. Like it's what he was born to do. He rubs my breast slowly. Even at this angle, I can't get enough of him. This can't ever end. I want him to live inside me.

Brody whispers into my ear, "I love this." He groans against my skin. "You're destroying me."

As much stamina as he's shown, if he goes on for much longer at this rate, one of us is likely to pass out. His sweaty chest sticks to my back when he reaches over and grabs my hand. His thrusts are never-fuckin-ending.

"Oooooh…come, Brody." I can barely speak.

He slows, the tip of his cock hovering outside of me once again. "You mean, inside you?"

"I whispered a spell. We're safe."

His hand tightens more around mine and he pushes into me like I'm his home. "Fuck, Mora."

"Deeper," is all I can say while gasping.

"Lulita." He gasps. "I can't go slow during this."

He feels so damn good inside me. I can't speak, can't say anything in return.

I grasp onto his forearm that's wrapped over my side. Grunting, he slams into me from behind again and again. His cock feels so thick that I'm in disbelief that he's gotten harder somehow. Goddess, he's amazing.

Completely cradled, I can only lay and take it at this point. His arm tightens around me. He gets louder and louder, sending all my senses into overdrive. I rotate my hips into him. Faster. Faster. So much pressure builds up that I can't tolerate it.

"Fuuuuuuuuck!" He combusts all at once and I've never felt another fit more perfect.

I love him. I love Brody Ricci. I love this man.

My vision blurs. Blotches like stars pulse. The explosion inside of me is nothing I've ever felt before. Breathless.

Fuck. Fuck. Fuck. Brody is everywhere. All at once. He's me and I'm him. My nails reach back to claw into his skin. So intense. Every muscle is tensed as I ride out the wave with him. I've never felt so good. Can't think. Can't move. He squeezes me tight and then slowly we both relax, lying in complete satisfaction.

Other than our panting, the room silences. His arm falls heavy over me. His chest rises and falls behind me. We're both so sweaty but he stays curled into my body, framing me from behind. Until slowly, his lullaby fingertips skim over my skin.

I stare at the origami tapestry I made, trying to calm my racing heart. High on adrenaline, I count each crease, recalling how long it took me to fold each piece together to create it. If I had to save one belonging in an emergency, it'd probably be this, despite being too heavy to carry if I'm fleeing for my life. The tapestry holds so many of my worst moments, weaved into its form. When I was feeling alone or depressed, I'd add another piece. During times I was annoyed with my roommates for not understanding my point of view, I'd hide away here in my room and fold another section. I remember a few times, years ago, when I'd dream of a non-existent boyfriend while creasing and joining the paper together.

To be honest, I'm a bit in shock that someone with such a pure heart as Brody sees good in me. For so long I was stuck in my ways, stubborn and unwilling to bend. And in a very short time, Brody has wiggled his way through the cracks of my armor and wedged himself between me and the shield I've been carrying.

Now I have more of a reason to break my curse. There are only three thorns left. If I focus on them, I may have a future. Slowly, I skim my hand down to my thorns and feel the curved barb, then prick my finger on the sharp point. There's the first one. I find the second and do the same. When I search for the third remaining thorn, only skin remains. I gulp, wondering if Brody noticed, and wonder when it disappeared.

Brody props himself on his elbow and rolls me over onto my back. His lips skate over mine and I sigh into his mouth.

"You are amazing," Body says, smiling sleepily.

"In general or at sex?"

"Both." He plants soft kisses on my cheek, my neck, my shoulders.

I'd go for round two if I were in better shape, but my man is probably in desperate need of hydration after that.

"Mmmm," I moan. "I used to hate the thought of people touching me."

"Good." He kisses me tenderly. "I want you to continue to hate the thought of people touching you. Because I'm not *people*. I'm yours."

I study his intense gaze, gratefulness and comfort washing over me.

"I could lay here all day staring at you," he says.

"But?" I laugh as he kisses me more.

"Wanna shower?" he asks, exhausted.

"Yes, then sleep," I chuckle. "In fact, my legs may not carry me to the bathroom."

The corners of his mouth rise again. "Are you claiming defeat for once? Have I won this battle?"

"I'll let you win every battle if they're all like that."

"I need that in writing." He laughs and scoops me into his arms.

Even though I squeal, he doesn't set me down until we're in the shower. Steam rises within seconds and covers the mirror. We rinse off in silence, the only sounds are tender kisses as water falls between us. It's so much more freeing and easy to move without the constant fear of jabbing someone.

"I'll share the bed, tonight." He hands me a towel and I can't help but admire his body before he wraps one around his waist.

I nudge his chest. "How generous of you."

I stand bare in front of him. His gaze drops to the two thorns. One of his fingers slowly slides up the curled claw of the larger one on my stomach. "What are we gonna do about these?"

"Let's talk about it tomorrow."

Something in his expression shifts and for only a moment I worry if tomorrow will bring a change in him. Will he regret his choices? Will our time together move us backward instead of forward? As we dry off, I try to savor the sensations that currently surround us in this steamy bubble. The thickness of the heat from the shower is heavy to breathe in. Brody's scent is masked by the new pineapple soap I opened last night. As for taste, all I want is to taste his kisses again and again.

"Will you be my date for Catterina's birthday party?" he asks quietly.

I pull him toward me. "I may need some more persuasion." I straddle him and run a hand along his jawline.

"I need some time to recover before more persuasion is attempted." Brody kisses my knuckles. "Tomorrow."

"Tomorrow," I repeat. Everything will be figured out tomorrow.

I could stay here with him in this moment forever. It's too bad my forever may be cut short.

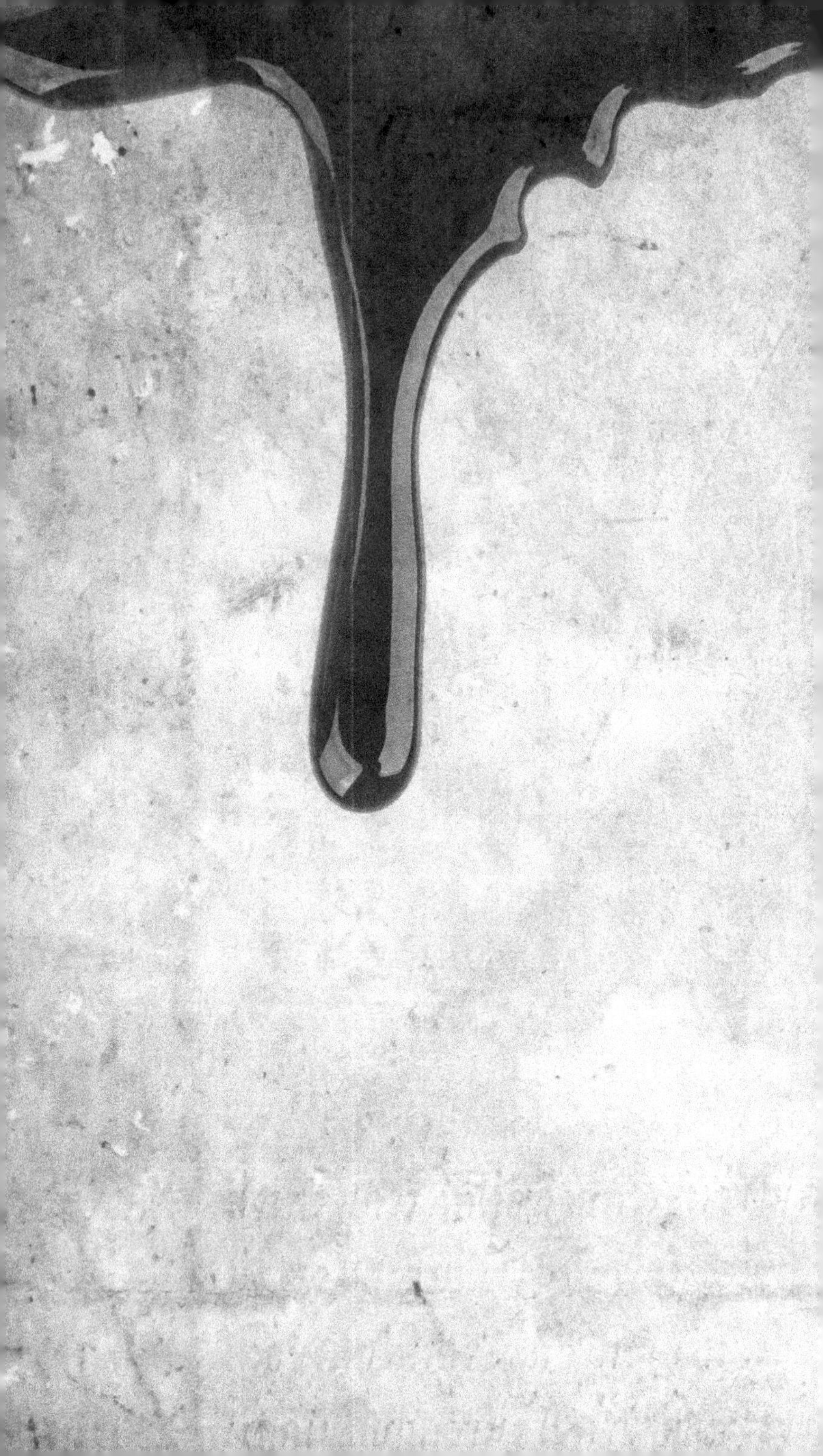

Recent excerpt from
The Book

The End.

Just kidding...

CHAPTER 24

Brody

The first of the suns' light pours through the bedroom window. I watch new snowflakes flutter outside, dancing free. Without waking Mora, I pull the blanket further over her bare shoulders so she isn't cold. One of her thorns digs into my hip, but I don't dare move an inch from her. In sleep, her soft face looks years younger.

What she went through when her sister died, and the time since, has been a heavy burden for her to carry alone. Has she been with any other man while locked away in hiding? If she was only eighteen when Lessie died, that means she's been cursed her entire adulthood. Has she ever had the opportunity to confess her feelings to someone?

How does she know if what we have is real without comparisons?

Her thick, messy hair covers my chest and I resist tucking a piece behind her ear so I can see her face more clearly. Goddess, she's so beautiful. I spot three tiny freckles on the side of her nose that I've never seen. Hopefully, I'll discover new bits and pieces of who she is every day for the rest of her life. And I need her life to be long.

Last night couldn't have gone any better. As carefully as possible, I reach over the side of the bed into my pack and fetch the page-turning device I have been working on—not that she requires it any longer. All the thorns have disappeared on her hands and fingers; she will be able to read in peace without my creation.

She stirs and moans quietly. That sound alone makes my dick hard. This woman will be my new beginning. From now on, life will be classified as a *before* Mora and an *after* Mora.

"Brody?" She softly moves her hand up my chest and traces circles with her fingertip along my skin.

Fuck. She's near perfect. If I think about her body too long then we'll be at it again. I'll never want to leave this bed.

"Good morning." I kiss her forehead and tug her closer. The massive bed frame creaks as she curls into my chest. "I have a present for you."

Her eyes snap open, meeting mine. I'll never tire of staring into that deep, endless brown. "You do?"

I hand over the little wooden device I made that can pinch objects. "Guess what it's for."

She inspects it from each angle, her brows knitting together in the cutest way. "Uh, is it tongs for cooking?"

"Nope, try again," I scoot her impossibly closer, hoping to meld us into one being.

"Tweezers to pluck my chin hairs?" She grins a sleepy smile and I want to devour every inch of her lips.

"Nope, I made it to help you turn pages so you could read without ripping your books."

Her mouth drops open as she meets my gaze again. "Thank you! This must've taken you a while, which means—"

"Which means I started it soon after I arrived here, yes." I kiss her lips this time. "You've enchanted me since the beginning. I just happened to enjoy bantering with you."

"Thank you. I'll keep it in my drawer." She leans over to the nightstand where six orbs sit on the top.

Mora swipes a piece of paper that reads, *"Polka dots are for the most generous of avocados, but not many baskets are aware of their smooth technique."*

"Yin must've dropped off the ones she found while we were sleeping," she mutters.

"So, you have most of them." I stare into the black swirls that look alive inside the spheres. "One more to go."

"Yeah, but Brody, I was thinking last night…" she starts.

"You were…thinking? During our world-altering sex?" I tease.

She nudges me playfully. "After the world-altering sex, when you passed out—"

"I did *not* pass out."

"Oh okay." She plants a kiss on my jawline and settles back onto my chest. "When you *weren't* passed out, I was thinking about your theory. It doesn't make sense that having all seven orbs is what will break my curse."

I swallow, worried that she'll say what I've already suspected. "Why?"

"Because I had all seven for the first few weeks after Lessie died before I had ever asked Feathi to hide them. If that's all it took, then my curse would've been broken long ago."

I slowly massage her shoulder. "Why do you think your thorns have disappeared then?"

"Honestly?" she pauses for a beat. Two beats. Three. "I thought Kavianne wanted me to fall in love to make them disappear."

"But you have two thorns left."

She nods. "I have two left."

A new fear arises. Maybe that means she doesn't care for me enough.

"I don't know how to get rid of them," she says.

Maybe we should look for the last orb, just in case. Though I doubt it'll make a difference and it could be wasting precious time.

We sit in silence, both our minds turning. The door squeaks open and little pitter patters scrape against the hardwood. Shortly after, a little yelp comes from the floor. I scoop up Heathcliff and let him snuggle between us, blending into the furry white blankets.

"He's a good pup." Mora runs a hand over his back. "But we should probably try to get him to stay with that pack we found."

I join in stroking his soft hair, letting any worries leave my fingertips with each pet.

"He needs a family in case I—" She stops herself.

"Last night we said we'd talk about us tomorrow," I whispered into her ear.

"It's not tomorrow yet." She hides her face so I can't see her expression. "How about we wait one more day."

"Mora, look at me," I plead and she does. "What are you thinking?"

Her gaze is layered with desire and fear, wants and

ideas. Within those layers, there's undeniable devotion, to me. And it looks good on her, more vulnerable, more real.

I'm such a lost cause. She has damaged me for any other relationship. It feels like every moment with her is a stolen bit of time I don't deserve that I'll keep treasured in a box. All of my hesitations and the parts of me that were broken have been mended. She deserves the type of man who can give her the greatest adventure of all, a shared life, and I'm finally ready for the task.

"I'm so scared, Brody. I don't have much time," she says. I'm about to interrupt her to reassure her, but she puts a finger against my lips. "I'm made to poison things, but that doesn't seem to bother you. I'm a better version of myself when you're around. With each day, I'm letting go a little bit more. You're helping me do that, Brody. So, maybe I'm only saying this for selfish reasons, but I'm not going to run." She swallows and tears form in her eyes. "Last night I told myself when we woke today, I'd promise you that though I don't know the answers or the right path, or how to fix everything, I'll stay by your side."

I kiss her again, and say, "Thank you."

I taste her tears on my lips. Hope. She's choosing hope. We can climb this mountain and conquer the peak. Together. Neither of us wants to say goodbye. Fighting to make this work is the only option. I refuse to throw away this feeling or let her deal with the curse alone. The word grateful doesn't cover how I feel that we're on the same page.

I wrap her into a hug and focus over her shoulder at the snow falling. I'll have to shovel a pathway for the guests to enter the front gates for the party.

"I forgot to tell you," I pull away and wipe the tears off her cheeks, "Dom is determined to design you a custom ball gown."

A true snort explodes from Mora. "Oh, that'll be a picture. Will there be two holes prepared for my thorns? She doesn't know I have any. Plus, I don't need a dress."

"Well, yes, I much prefer to dance with you naked all night, but I think jealousy will drive me wild if you're not clothed in front of the guests."

Pink flushes her cheeks and her gaze drops to my bare chest for a moment as she bites her lip. There's hunger in her eyes. "And what will my prince wear?"

"A surprise."

"Will it be a replica of the glamour I made you for the festival?" Her laugh is cinnamon sprinkled on hot cocoa. "That black spandex was definitely attractive on *these* quads." She grabs my upper legs and then runs a hand higher.

Any more moves like that will make us late for breakfast.

"I hope your sisters come to the party. I'd love to meet them." She shakes her head but then frowns. I'm still..." Mora's playful energy slips away from me. She scoots off the edge of the bed quickly and searches for clean clothes. "I don't have time to lay here, I'm sorry. Plus, Feathi, Nax, and Yin need to know about our visitors." She scrambles around the room and shoves one of her shoes on. "I can't believe I forgot to warn them. What if Gabrielle sees them? What if Catterina stumbles upon them and is scared?"

"Hey, hey, hey, take a breath." I'm by her side in a moment and help her ease a fresh sweater over her head. "I already told Dom and Gabrielle about your roommates' condition last night."

She freezes, terror claiming her face. "How did they respond?" Her hand covers her mouth.

"They had questions, but I didn't tell them about your

curse. I didn't think it'd matter, since we're going to break it today."

Her wide eyes soften, and she pushes her forehead straight against my chest. "Right."

"Did you hear Nax is going to propose to Feathi soon?"

She whips her gaze to mine again. "Really? How do I not know this?"

I dig in my bag for extra pants. "Nax has been asking me to help make him a ring, but I haven't had time."

"Shit, I feel terrible. That's probably what he's been wanting to talk to me about."

Outside our door, quick footsteps grow closer, faster. I expect it's my little Catterina who has probably been waiting to launch out at me since she awoke. Instead, Dom soars around the corner and runs in.

"Whoa, Dom, what is it?"

Panicked, with manic eyes, her voice shakes as she says, "Catterina's gone. She's been taken." Her shaky hand holds out a letter. "I CAN'T FIND HER ANYWHERE!" Dom screams, her voice echoing in the narrow hallway.

In the same scrawl as before, is written.

There's still ink in Mora's pen.
Your daughter will be the next to be poisoned.
Just as promised.
You have until the suns hit the middle of the sky.

"WHAT DOES THIS MEAN!" Dom screeches.

My chest seizes tight and I can't feel my legs. A thousand plans already rush through my mind in a battle of the best way to find Cat.

"She asked for three chocolate chip pancakes with a chocolate chip face for breakfast, so I went to the kitchen to see if this castle has any food and this note was sitting on the counter." Dom paces three steps one way, then turns and starts tugging on Brody's t-shirt. "It must be Elizabeth! My mom found us! I knew we never should've come back! But why would she want to poison our little girl? She's bluffing, right?!"

"Listen to me." I take Dom by both her shoulders and squeeze her harder than I should. "Did you see Cat this morning?"

"Yes," she starts to sob. "She wanted to play with the paper lady. Wait, did those creatures take her? Why would they want her?"

"No, it wasn't them." Mora starts jogging down the hallway and we follow.

"How much do you trust this place, Brody? It's haunted. You said there's strange magical things going on and I didn't believe you at first..." Her face is red as she runs next to me, but the tears have stopped.

I don't know what to think. Don't know what to say. I assumed everything would be okay and had convinced myself the threat was a fluke. Maybe I should've spilled Mora's ink when I had the chance. No, I can't choose one life over the other. I love them both and need to protect them both.

"It was Kavianne, my sister." Mora stops at the closest window and stares into the glass. "Show me my sister."

I see a different image than before. This time, Mora and Cat are huddled over paper, folding origami, but this can't represent reality because Mora is standing right in front of me, in a different outfit. And Cat looks older, taller. Could it show the future? Maybe it's trying to reassure and calm me. Or it's another trick of this wicked house.

"Ugh!" Mora shouts. "I can only see...never mind."

Dom has started crying again. "I see her, look. Cat is at our neighborhood park jumping in the fountain. That means she's safe, right? Wait, I've seen this before. That's her swimsuit from last year that she doesn't fit into anymore. Is this a memory maker?"

"No," Mora marches further into the hallway. "It's an enchanted glass that shows you who or what you love the most, but not always at the current moment."

Dom and I exchange a glance. We run down the hall, passing one, two, three grandfather clocks that all start chiming at the same time. Eight in the morning. Only four hours until Cat will be poisoned. Where do we start? Next to me, Dom is wheezing, but I need to focus on one thing at a time.

If Kavianne stole Cat before breakfast it means she's not far. Plus, how would she know if we empty the pen unless she is close by to check it? And, if she's that close, why doesn't she empty it herself? If Kavianne could access the pile of rubble underground, then she wouldn't need one of us to spill the ink. Which means someone might be helping her. Who?

"Stop!" I halt. "We need to split up!"

Both Dom and Mora are out of breath, glances darting from the clocks to each other.

"Mora, get War and search in the forest," I say and she's already sprinting away when I had expected her to argue.

"I'll look through the house again," Dom cracks her knuckles and wrings her hands. "If you swear we can trust the paper people then I'll ask for their help."

"Yes, you can trust them," I say and wave her off, "Go!"

"Wait!" She turns, and over her shoulder asks, "Where will *you* search?"

CHAPTER 25

Mora

I sprint into the malicious forest as Brody suggested. Another thorn vanishes from my body. Fetching War would have been smarter, but there's no time to get to the stables. Where would Kavianne take Cat?

Hopefully, Brody finds Cat first, safe and alone. Wait. If Brody has to fight Kavianne without my help, he won't win. My sister possesses powerful magic and she won't go easy on him. In that case, it needs to be me who finds poor Cat. The little one must be freezing if she's out here. If Kavianne has any decency, she'll have wrapped the girl in a coat at least.

The cold bites at my hands, ears, and cheeks as a wild winter wind whips through the pines. In broad daylight, the emptiness of the woods carries the same dark energy as at midnight. Maybe more so, since there's not an animal to be seen or heard. At least during the night, the owls hoot and the wolves howl to create a harmony for sleep. The silence that surrounds me now just puts me on edge.

My boots crunching through the snow sound louder than bombs exploding. Everything is too still, too quiet. It's like the forest is watching, listening, waiting for something big to happen. I pray to the Goddesses above for the opposite—a boring, uneventful rescue.

Or maybe the only way to end it all is to attack Kavianne before she can do more harm. All these years I've wanted to simply talk to her, but she hasn't given me the chance. Yes, my magic took away the person most important to her, but she's not the only one who has suffered.

Each step feels heavier than the last, and my calves become wet beneath my pants. Why did all of this have to happen on the coldest day of the season?

The rapid beating of my heart isn't warming my body. My hands have turned numb, and my earlobes sting. A shadow shifts to my left. Impossible. There isn't any sound. I would've heard something. I stop and hold my breath. Snowflakes flutter as if we're in a dreamscape romantic scene. Yet I can sense the danger lurking in the air.

Suddenly, there's a noticeable drop in air pressure. Another shadow creeps by my feet. I spin around. Then look up. A large vine has twisted around a trunk, with the tip twitching back and forth like a rattlesnake's stinger. My body tenses more.

"It's just a regular plant," I whisper to no one. "It's just a plant. It's not alive."

I brush snow off the vine then rip off one of its grotesque thorns as a potential weapon. Rotten black liquid oozes out of the decaying bark. Other than the orb in my pocket, this is the only defense I have.

I continue to weave through the trees. No tracks. Time is ticking. There are hundreds of acres of forest out here, with snow covering all the trails. I glance around, looking for familiar landmarks.

A twig snaps ahead, and someone coughs. I duck behind a thick pine. Heart thumping. I peek around the trunk. A woman stands with her back to me only a few feet away. Her dark brown hair is tied in a high bun. I know it's Kavianne from the arrow tattoo on the back of her neck.

Silently, I raise the sharp barb.

Before I can make the strike, Kavianne turns fast, holding a little girl in her clutches with a bag over her head. "Hello, sister," she hisses.

"Catterina! Are you okay?" When I try to take a step forward, Kavianne brings a blade to the girl's side. "Don't come closer."

I freeze, sucking in a painful breath. The girl wiggles a bit and mumbles, but it sounds like she's gagged. It's hard to tell through the bag.

"Stay still and she won't hurt you," I say with false confidence.

Kavianne grins. "You don't know me anymore, Mora. In fact, I don't think you ever did."

I ignore that, not willing to fall into a trap of distraction. "Don't worry, hun, I'll get you out of here."

"Sure, you can take her, but first you need to poison her." Kavianne's smile squirms like a deadly eel. "After, I'll tell you how to get rid of your thorns."

"Are you crazy? I'll *never* hurt her."

Kavianne's eyes grow twice their size. "Oh, but you'd hurt *me*, your flesh and blood, and you'd murder our sweet Lessie! Such a hypocritical witch you are."

I whisper, "We need to talk about the past. Just let her go."

"I don't think so." She tilts her head to the side. "I know you want the answer. You've been searching for a way to break the curse for so many years. It must eat you alive inside that I know the answer and you don't."

"Why are you doing this?" My voice cracks at the end.

"YOU KILLED MY BABY SISTER!" Kavianne shrieks.

"I'm sorry for what happened to Lessie, but this isn't the way to deal with it."

"Oh, no. I disagree. You need to feel what it's like to have the ground collapse from under you, for your heart to be nothing but a hole, for the pain to consume your every thought. I lost EVERYTHING when you forced Lessie over that cliff."

"I didn't mean to." My hands shake, and I want to reach out to my sister, ease her suffering, but she holds Cat in her grasp. "I'm sorry, Kavi, but you have me. You're not alone."

"Is that what you think?" She pauses and a foggy look covers her features. "When we were little, all I wanted was to be like you, spend time with you. But every hour, every day, you pushed me away because I wasn't worth your time. Your books were more important than me."

"That's not true."

"Oh, sister. Don't you remember our precious song?" She starts to sing, sounding like she's lost her mind.

"Thorns might block our path and tangle us in wrath.
But it has been foreseen, that..."
"...even death can turn green," we say in unison.

"Why did you say our song was a clue? We wrote that

song for our Commitment days. Was it about falling in love?"

Because I did fall. I love Brody more than all the letters that form all the words that fill every page of each book in our universe.

"Love? Are you crazy? No, of course not!" Kavianne hisses. "You're such a fool. I don't know why I ever admired you," she spits out. "You never saw me as a teammate or on equal ground with you. Until I cursed you. Let me guess, for seven years you've continued to do things *your* way, using *your* ideas, in *your* home, by *your* standards. Just like when we were kids."

I shake my head, but I can't form a response. Is this how she saw our past? Is any of it true?

"You said I have you left, but I never *had* you, and no one else will either." Kavianne nods to a specific tree next to us. "I'm surprised you haven't figured out that your roommates have been helping me. Even those closest to you can see how infested your heart is."

"What are you talking about?" I ask, confused.

"Brown is new to me," Yin says as she steps out from behind a trunk. "I'd rather call it chestnut or caramel because there's too many varieties of trees in this world. Be the tree today."

"Yin?" I shake my head. "What's going on?

"Be the tree, my friend." She smiles and I have no idea if she's self-aware anymore.

Then my heart shatters completely when Feathi joins her side with a blank ghostly stare. She doesn't look at me but is fixated on something behind me.

"Feathi?" I take a step forward, arms outstretched. "Feathi?"

"*You* did this to us," she says in a robotic voice. "Mora

Thomesse is responsible for our pain. *You* are why I'm made of paper."

Tears pool and threaten to fall down my cheeks, but I have to stay strong for Cat's sake. "I'm sorry, Feathi. I never wanted to hurt you, any of you."

Feathi doesn't so much as blink. Instead, she repeats the same thing with a flat voice. "You did this to us. Mora Thomesse is responsible for our pain. *You* are why I'm made of paper."

I wave my hand in front of my best friend's face. "Feathi? Please, look at me, wake up. I can help you."

"What time is it?" Feathi quickly glances at all her watches, then looks to Yin. "Who are you?"

I whip around to Kavianne. "What did you do to them?!"

"Tick tock goes the clock."

It feels like a lump the size of a boulder is lodged in my throat.

Kavianne winks at me. "I may have used a little spell on your roommates. It's not like she has long to live. Though, you could save them now. I'll tell you the secret of how to break your curse. All you have to do is stab this girl right now. She won't even die if the doctors find a cure soon."

"Then why force me hurt her?" I squeeze the barb tighter in my hand, unsure if it's to prepare to strike or for self-control not to.

"Because I want you to see what I already know. You'll *always* choose what you want over others. You're an arrogant, know-it-all who must have things *your* way and save who matters most to *you*. I've seen you with that man. Even though it'll devastate him, you won't pick what *he* wants by saving this girl. You'll choose the selfish way to gain the answers to your curse, just like you chose the selfish thing when you controlled Lessie."

I shake my head, unable to form a word. "Let Cat go. I'll give you anything."

"Stab her, then I'll let her go."

"If you want her poisoned so badly, *you* do it!" I stupidly throw the barb at Kavianne's feet.

"You're not listening. I'm in control now…" Kavianne pushes the tip of the blade against Cat's skin. "You used to be the master of our coven. *You* were the puppeteer. Not anymore. I'm in charge."

"Wait!" I drop to my knees. "Please, stop!"

"The girl either dies by my hand or gets poisoned by yours." Kavianne hisses. "Those are the only two choices, dear Mora. And either way, that man will see what kind of soul you have. No one could love such a wicked beast."

"What do you mean?" Tears flow down my cheeks as I crawl to the thorn.

Kavianne points to Feathi, who is holding a Taj99 device in her hand. The red light flashes, indicating that it is recording a video.

"Say goodbye to your daughter, Mr. Ricci." Kavianne's hand tightens around the blade.

I can't let Cat die.

I lunge for the thorn. Swipe it through the air. Stab it straight into Cat's thigh. She crumbles to the ground with a stifled moan. I gasp. My heart beats wildly. What have I done?

When she hits the ground, the bag falls off her head. It's not Cat at all.

Ryanne, the girl from the village, lies bleeding on the forest floor. I gather her in my arms, cradling her as I rise on trembling legs.

"You, bitch!" I scream and back away from Kavianne. "Where is Catterina?"

Kavianne's laughter makes the icicles snap off branches

and cascade to our feet like daggers falling from the sky. "Send that video to her boy toy," Kavianne commands Feathi, "but edit out the last few seconds that show this girl's face."

"I'm sorry," I say to Ryanne while I peel the tape off her mouth in a quick motion.

Tear streaks stain her cheeks.

"Ssh, it'll be okay."

I help Ryanne quickly and gently pull her into the forest. The girl must be in shock to act like she trusts me. We stumble over roots and vines but manage to stay upright.

"I'll see you soon, Sister!" Kavianne cackles behind us. "If you think I'm a monster, then we're one and the same, Mora."

She's wrong. I'll never be as cruel and heartless as her.

As we stumble further from Kavianne, she continues to yell cold obscenities through the flurries, but my sister doesn't chase. What is her plan? Where is Catterina?

Breathe in. Breathe out.

"Does it hurt?" I ask Ryanne.

She bites her lip and doesn't respond.

Fuck. I had to poison her. Otherwise, Kavianne would've killed her. Breathe in. Breathe out. Need to keep moving. Get away. Move faster. Find Brody. Breathe in. Find Cat. Breathe out.

"Miss," Ryanne mumbles at my side and drags a hand over her thigh. "Miss, I feel...dizzy."

In the hole of her jeans, instead of blood trickling out, thick black goop gurgles and spills at an alarming rate down her pants. I freeze in place.

"Goddess, I'm so sorry, Ryanne. I'll carry you." However, I'm unsure if I can because though she's young, the girl is probably already half my weight.

Her eyes roll so I can only see the whites and her head lobs to the side. I catch her in my arms. "Shit." I try to plop her onto my back, but the angle is too awkward.

"Help!" I scream toward my house, unsure how far I've traveled. "War!" I begin dragging Ryanne's feet, making an easily traceable trail in the snow. "Nax! Brody?! Heathcliff! Anyone!"

My head throbs and my ears ring. I take another step. Heave. Her weight feels like hauling a boulder.

Black glitter sprinkles down, intermingling with the snow and landing on Ryanne's hair. I whip my gaze to see Princess Preta flying above.

"Your….pocket…" Preta's voice is so quiet, and the wind steals half her words.

"What?" I lean in, out of breath.

Princess Preta cups her hands around her mouth. "Your orb! Your pocket, Mora!"

I had totally forgotten. It's been so long since I've used magic that I'm not used to relying on my powers. I reach into my pocket and palm the sphere. Immediately, the strands within swirl to life. Closing my eyes, I whisper an easy spell so I don't have to carry her. Now, Ryanne, unconscious, hovers horizontally in the air, as if sleeping on a cloud.

I sprint toward my home, her body soaring beside me. Princess Preta probably trails, but I don't dare look back. There's not a second to waste. Everyone needs me. Brody. Cat. Feathi. Yin. Ryanne. The other poisoned children.

Hopefully, the orb will have enough time to recharge by the time I need it again. Because this battle is far from over. And not for the first time, I have no idea what to do.

CHAPTER 26

Brody

My muscles scream from digging for so long. But I must keep hauling out the debris that collapsed on the West Wing. Every neuron is firing and I may have broken a finger a few minutes ago. This pain is only temporary. I have to get to Cat. My gut tells me she's below with Kavianne. The only way Kavianne would know the pen isn't empty is if she had checked it.

Tick-tock. Tick-tock. An hour could've passed already but there are no clocks near.

Sweat drips down my temple the lower I go, especially because the humidity from the hot springs has started creeping up through the cracks of the pile. I push another rock to the side.

I shout as I heave with all my strength, shaking. My back flexes. I clench my teeth and shove another boulder. It can't be much longer now. My biggest concern is that moving a specific boulder might accidentally start a rockslide and kill Cat if she's under there.

Finally, a blue light shines through a hole, and steam curls around my boots. My entire body begs to collapse from exhaustion, but I push the remaining boulder further to create a space big enough for me to drop through. I fall about five feet and my boots thud on the stone of the underground cavern. My legs almost give out, but I catch my balance on a nearby rock.

"Well, that took you long enough," a familiar high-pitched voice rings out.

"Gabby?" I ask, wiping my brow. "How did you get here?" I glance around for any sign of my daughter restrained by a witch. "Have you found Cat?"

"I have." The way she says it, so matter-of-fact and devoid of emotion, makes my spine straighten. "But first, tell me, what is she worth to you?"

What the Abyss does she mean? I stare at the woman in front of me. Even underground Gabrielle is as put together as a model plastered on the front of Ozaron's most popular magazine. She runs a hand through her blonde hair, then crosses her arms.

"Gabrielle, I don't have time for this." I curl my hand into a fist at my side. Loosen. Curl. Loosen. "Tell me where Cat is. Now."

"You don't know her, Brody. You and I have a history, a story worth telling, and all my friends can see our future together. Even your mam approves. Once we put all this drama behind us, you and I can have our own daughter. I'll give you a herd of them."

I breathe out. One. Two. Three. Gabrielle seems to be teetering on the edge of a delusion, so I can't push her too far when she has the answer I need.

"I'm going to walk this way…" I say calmly, slowly, "… around the corner and look for Cat. I want you to stay here."

"No!" She stomps her foot and blocks my access to the hot springs entrance.

The only way around her would be to literally lift her and the last thing I want to do is touch this woman.

"Why don't you want me? First, you get Dom pregnant, who isn't that pretty, and now you want a disgusting, cursed witch! How can I knock some sense into you!"

My patience fades like the dust speckles floating in the blue light. "Don't talk about Mora."

Gabrielle sighs. "She has lied to you, Brody. She has used you. Mora is a murderer and has been manipulating you from the very beginning. I know you have such a golden heart, but you need to understand, that once someone turns dark, there's no saving them." Gabrielle tries to take my hand, but I don't let her. "Mora's sister explained everything to me. Listen to me. She's a beast!"

"Let me pass or I'm picking you up."

"Didn't you hear me?" She lays a hand on my chest. "She's a monster."

"She's *my* monster!" I scream. "*My* Lulita."

Suddenly, everything becomes so crystal clear, at the worst possible time. Committing to a Partner isn't the end of the world if it's the right person. I'm not afraid of belonging to Mora, I crave it. I had simply feared Commitment to the wrong woman. I don't need to travel the world and distract myself with foreign adventures to find happiness. As long as I have Mora and Cat in my life, everything will be okay.

"The witch has been lying to you this whole time," Gabrielle says. "I bet you don't know that if Mora collects enough blood from children, she'll double her powers. Mora has been controlling that plant, commanding it to strike children. Her goal was to get you to trust her, so she could get close to Cat and collect her blood too." Gabrielle pauses. "Well, from the look on your face, I guess you didn't know that.

"This whole story is so sad," she continues. "You'd think people would learn over time and change their toxic ways. Maybe it's just too much to ask for Mora to consider not having power. All that witch wants is control over you."

"I don't believe you."

This time when Gabrielle reaches out, her hand grazes my arm. "Then why are you already questioning if I'm right? I know you, Brody. I can see your wheels spinning. You're wondering if it's true. You're picturing her leaving her haunted mansion at night to cast spells on the vine creature. You're asking how you didn't see the signs sooner."

I take a step back.

Gabby pushes a little knob in the wall that I hadn't seen. The stones move, revealing another hidden entrance. More light spills out.

"I'll show you proof," Gabrielle says as she walks through the sheen.

I can't help but step inside, following Gabrielle into the unknown. It smells similar to a greenhouse. Once we walk through the mist to the other side, I don't see pools of steaming water. I gasp. My heart stops. In front of us, there are thousands of red roses, fresh and gorgeous, climbing up vines along the wall.

"No." I push a hand against my temple. "This isn't possible. Mora couldn't have known these were here."

"Oh, really?" Gabrielle brushes against me, her hand on my chest. "Your precious witch doesn't know what lies below her own home?"

Hundreds of vials of liquid sit on shelves in the shadows. Crimson red. Someone has been collecting blood. It couldn't have been Mora. She wouldn't do this. It doesn't make sense. My Mora loves origami and her roommates and baby wolves and reading. Mora doesn't hurt others, or hunt down the young, leaving them to a nasty fate or to store their blood for her own gain.

I keep shaking my head as Gabrielle speaks again. "See, she's hoarded enough roses that she could have healed the sick kids the whole time, but she didn't want to use the flowers for others. That witch is selfish, and arrogant, and needs to be stopped. She's been keeping them for herself."

"No…" I say, my chest rising and falling fast. "I saw her pen and how low it was on ink."

"Just a mirage." Gabrielle starts massaging my shoulders. "She's a witch, sweetie. Of course she cast a spell on you, to make you see what she wanted."

I shrug off her touch.

A beeping sound interrupts us.

"I have service down here?" Gabrielle pulls out a Taj and taps a few buttons. "Oh, no…Brody. I can't let you see this."

I swipe it from her grip and stare at a thumbnail-sized frozen video on the screen. Something I couldn't ever have prepared myself for. My vision blurs, and I sway until my side hits the cave wall.

"Brody, don't watch that. You shouldn't see this."

I push start and as the scene starts to unfold, it feels like someone has clawed my organs and shredded them to bits.

In the snowy forest, Mora is on her knees. Kavianne grips a small child, with a bag over their head.

"Cat!" I yell at the screen.

"...either way, that man will understand what kind of soul you have. No one can love such a wicked beast..." Kavianne says. There are crackling sounds and the video goes fuzzy for a moment.

"Cat!" I yell and grip the Taj harder.

When the image refocuses, Mora lunges for something on the ground. A giant thorn. She slashes it through the air and then clearly stabs it straight into Cat's thigh. My daughter crumbles to the ground with a stifled moan.

"No!!" My voice booms off the cavern's walls. "Where is Cat!? WHAT HAPPENED!? BRING ME TO HER!"

Gabrielle slips closer. "Of course, but first Commit to me officially."

"Are you fuckin' insane?" I almost smack the phone out of her hand. "MOVE OUT OF MY WAY!"

"It'll all be fine." She pushes her phone in my face. "Just sign here for the first step."

My jaw clamps and I need to work it loose before speaking. "Do you think *THIS* is going to make me love you? I didn't like you before!" I throw both my hands in the air.

"We don't have much time before the poison sets in." Gabrielle tilts her head. "Do you want her to die while debating this?"

"Fine, okay! I'll do whatever you want right after you bring me to her! Hurry!"

"No, do it now." Gabrielle's hand slides up my sweaty

back, sticking to my shirt. "Commit to me, here and now, then Cat will be given a potion to stop her symptoms."

"Fuck you, Gabrielle...Fine, I don't care what you do to me. Just please, please, take me to my Catterina now."

"Okay, you don't have to beg, sweetie." She plugs in a sequence on her Taj and forms pop up. "Sign here," Gabrielle says with a smile.

I scribble my name quickly, heart pounding insanely, ready to burst.

"And sign here."

I'm stuck in a nightmare.

"And lastly, we have to video this part to make it legal." She hits a record button "I, Gabrielle Maria LeGume do willingly and passionately take Brody Kain Ricci to be my Committed Life Partner for the rest of my days."

I wince but repeat the same promise. "I, Brody Kain Ricci, do willingly take Gabrielle Maria LeGume to be my Committed Life Partner for the rest of my days."

Gabrielle lowers her phone and lunges at me for a kiss but I dodge her. "You got what you wanted. I'm your prisoner. Forever. Now, please take me to Cat."

The roses in the back corner rustle and out steps Kavianne from the thicket. She's holding my sleeping daughter in her arms. "We barely escaped from my deranged sister. As I ran away Mora kept screaming *'Give me Lessie!'* She is hallucinating."

"Cat!" I rush forward. "Let me have her." I curl my unconscious child against my chest. Her breathing is slow and soft. "Cat, wake up," I cry, with a lump in my throat. "Please, Cat, wake up. I'm here. I won't let you out of my sight again. Wake up, please."

She drools against my shirt but doesn't show any signs of hearing me. I shake her gently.

It feels like a wormhole is sucking me into another

dimension. Weight stacks against my chest. What do I do? As I glance around, I search for a fast escape. Last time I was stuck down here we had to walk down a tunnel for an hour, leading away from the house and into the forest. The opening led to the pack of wolves. We don't have time to venture that far. What if Cat grows weaker, or stops breathing?

Right now, the two wicked women in front of me are my only option for answers.

"Why won't she wake up?"

"She needs a healing potion," Kavianne's tone is thick and gurgled, reminding me of the black ooze from the poisoned puddle. "Do you know where my sister's hidden apothecary studio is? We can heal her there."

"Yeah," I say reluctantly. "It's on the first floor, behind a hidden door."

"What if Mora is in there?" Gabrielle's eyes widen with fear. "She could kill us all."

"Mora won't hurt us," I spit out with confidence. If anyone is our enemy, it's the two women in front of me.

Kavianne pulls out a tiny orb, with swirling red ribbons of magic inside. Wordlessly, Kavianne points it toward the ceiling, and my feet float off the ground. I tighten my hold on Cat as we hover mid-air. The magic moves us as a group around the bend and then we rise toward the library. Why is she helping us? What's in it for her?

Cat doesn't stir once as we rise. I won't let myself think the worst. After so many years, she came back to me. I can't lose my daughter again.

Once we land in the library, I run toward the apothecary studio with Cat in my arms. The maze of these halls clicks into a completed puzzle. I've walked this path with Mora at my side countless times. Her apple cinnamon scent is fresh in the air.

Behind me, the two women trail silently. The tension is thick. A sharp pain pierces my chest. I won't lose her. I can't.

Out of breath, we arrive at the apothecary studio door. It's already open; clinking sounds come from inside. I breathe a sigh of relief. Only one person would be in there. Before I have the chance to move inside, my foot crunches on glass. I peer down into the pieces and an enchanted image reflects.

Mora's sleepy eyes bat slowly as she lays next to me in our bed. I can feel the soft way she holds my hand and the secrets she has told me. Our shared kisses. Joined bodies. Love.

I love her. I love Mora. Fuck. Beast or not, guilty or not, I need to protect her too.

I burst through the door, Catterina still a limp doll in my arms. "Mora! She needs a healing potion!"

Mora works over a girl who lies asleep on the work table. Wait, she's the same one I freed my first night here. What was her name? Rachel? Ryelle? Ryanne.

Mora tightens binds at the girl's ankles and wrists. She leans over Ryanne's body with an empty jar in hand. Blood pours from the open wound in the girl's thigh.

"Brody! You found her!" Mora holds her arms out.

My gaze flickers between Mora…Ryanne…then Mora…then the jar.

Gabrielle's warnings come flooding back. *'I bet you don't know that if Mora collects enough blood from innocents, she'll double her powers... Mora has been controlling that plant ... All that witch wants is control.'*

The only thing is, she'd never hurt Cat intentionally. They're lying to me. With Cat in my arms, I quickly close the door behind me, locking out Kavianne and Gabrielle.

"How can I help?"

CHAPTER 27

Mora

Brody locks the door behind him and then lays Catterina on the old chair in the corner. A giant wave of relief washes over me that he found his daughter. But why is she unconscious?

The room buzzes like a guitar string pulled too tightly.

"What happened?" He looks at Ryanne with obvious concern.

"Kavianne said she'd kill her if I didn't poison her. I had no choice. She's been hallucinating and her leg looks terrible," she says, while pulling the small blanket further over the girl's leg. "I had to tie her down because she was thrashing around, but I think I made a healing potion that works."

"Do you have any more for Cat?" he asks quickly.

A loud pounding comes from the other side of the door. "Brody, my love! Let me in! This isn't the best way to treat your new *Partner*," a woman shouts through the door. "Unless this is foreplay for later," she continues. "You'll love my outfit, if you could call some little lace strings an outfit."

"Just ignore Gabrielle. She blackmailed me to sign Commitment papers as her new Life Partner," Brody says, in a rushed voice.

My breathing accelerates, but I don't want to act stricken. I need to stay in control. His jaw grinds and I can't tell what he's thinking. Immediately, my mouth turns desert dry. He's Committed. And Cat is unconscious. What the fuck? Our eyes lock for too many moments of silence, too many unspoken tense words hover in the air.

"I'm sorry I don't have time to talk about this right now," he says. "Do you have enough potion for Cat?"

"I need more roses," I mumble, "Ryanne happened to have one in her pocket. I would need more."

"I can't leave Cat but I know where you can find some close." Brody grips my shoulders a little too roughly and looks me straight in the eye. "Someone has grown hundreds of them under your house in a hidden room, by the hot springs room."

I shake my head. "That's not possible."

"I saw them."

"I don't know where to look."

"It's in a tunnel, down by the Book. Mora, you're the most badass person I've ever met. You can do this. Please. Cat didn't do anything wrong. She doesn't deserve this, and I refuse to leave her. Go get the roses, I believe in you."

I quickly gather as many of the bottles of halfway-finished potions as I can and gently place them in my bag. "Do you know how she got hurt?"

"No, just hurry!"

"Okay." I gulp. "Ryanne has already drunk her healing potion. She should be fine. And I'll be back soon."

There's no chance I can leave through the main door with Gabrielle waiting on the other side. That's not something I can deal with right now. My heart feels like a sponge being squeezed until it's empty and dry.

My hand brushes against a hidden lever on the cold stone wall. All I want is for Brody to wrap his arms around me, for him to tell me everything will be okay, but that's not possible. Everything is falling apart, and the safety of his daughter lies in my hands.

With a swift movement, I push the lever and slip behind the revolving stone. I speed down the tunnel faster than I've moved in my entire life. Then I hear soft breathing beside me.

"Rainbow sprinkles flutter like wings."

It's Yin. Somehow my friend joined me, but I curse internally. She may be under Kavianne's control still and I don't want any danger to come to her. I palm the sphere in my pocket. Energy thrums from the orb, but I can tell it hasn't fully recharged yet. Its faint light lets us see without tripping.

Step after step I run farther from Brody, yet closer and closer to the solution. This plan will work. It has to. Some of the bottles in my bag clink together. Finally, the tunnel under my home ends. My legs burn and I fumble against the rock wall, groping for the exit lever.

"Silver snakes secret sashes around their slippers," Yin says and points to a spot on the wall.

My finger snags on something sharp and I pull away, hissing. I know it's bleeding. "Damn it."

Outside, the soft light of the dusk confuses me. How long had I been working on potions in my studio? Time doesn't seem to have meaning anymore. I don't know where Feathi or Nax are during this chaos. At least Yin is okay, here beside me, instead of being manipulated by my sister again.

Under the orange haze of the setting suns, I frantically glance around the world of snow, unsure where the secret entrance is to the tunnel we had used before. My legs have started shaking and a strange queasiness roils through my stomach.

"Do you know where the other tunnel entrance is? All the trees are starting to look the same."

"Mauve moves memories to make multiple manic mannequins," Yin says smiling.

A migraine forms. A ringing in my ears starts so violently I scream into the forest. What's going on? Is my body in shock from all the adrenaline? No, I felt fine in my studio. Well, not exactly fine, but my body was functioning. My vision zooms in and out of focus and I look down. Black ooze goops out of the new scratch on my finger.

"Shit!" I flick my hand and black gunk spurts onto the snow below. No, no, this can't be happening. This shouldn't affect me. I AM the thorns. I AM the monster.

Suddenly a thundering sound crashes behind us. We turn. A pack of wolves stampede straight at us. I try to jump behind a tree, but my boot gets stuck on a root. I fall straight into the snow. Paws pound the ground. Yin screams somewhere close.

"Yin!"

I look up, though snow is being kicked in my eyes. All I see is a mix of brown and white. Up and down. Back and forth. Brown and white. Yin reaches down to untangle me.

"Thank you." I turn to her, but she's not there. My heart slams against my ribs.

I peek around the tree.

Yin is stuck between sprinting beasts. One howls in an ear-splitting pitch. It stops right in front of Yin.

"Yin! Move!" I scream.

Its paws rise from the ground.

"Yin!" My hands clutch the bark of the tree.

The wolf's paws slam down, pounding into Yin's chest.

"No!" I scream.

Yin's body deflates into a flat paper sheet. It's too late. I know she's dead before I can crawl to her.

The last wolf runs off, leaving me in silence. I stare at her flattened form.

"Help!" I scream.

This isn't possible. Yin was just here. Now she's not. There must be magic to make her chest rise again. I dare to look at her pale paper skin, sprinkled in snowflakes. Before I can try to save her, the snow transforms what's left of my friend into a pile of mush.

"No!" I scream again, my voice bouncing off the pines. No one in the forest responds. I can't hold Yin's hand. She's gone. Tears burst into a sob. I can't even say goodbye.

"Come back!" I hover my hand over the wet paper pieces, unsure what to do.

She's another soul I led to their grave. My heart seizes uncontrollably. Yin shouldn't have helped me. I should be the one trampled. I'm the one that causes endless problems. But I'm here, and she's not. All I can do is breathe through the pain.

What do I do now?

I don't dare move before checking the potions in my backpack. When I reach around to unzip my bag, I gasp at the state of my finger. Instead of the nasty black crap dripping from my skin, my entire finger has turned to a black vine, with three thorns curling out. I stare. Flex my vine finger. Bend it. It feels the same, but where flesh and blood used to be, now is only a plant.

It's happening. I'm changing. Time has run out for me. The pen must be empty.

Part of me feels relieved. It's over. I did all I could.

"MORA!" Brody's voice calls from behind and heavy clomps follow.

He came after me? He'd never leave Cat in her state, so, why is he here?

"MORA!" Brody bellows, closer.

I can't think, can't move. Should I tell him about Yin? Should I show him my vine-finger?

"Mora! Thank Goddess, there you are," he says, dropping off his mount, and kneeling in the snow beside me. "Are you okay?"

"Where's Cat?" I hide my hands behind me and find that I can't look at him.

"Kavianne used magic and took her again. I need your help."

The damage is done. "I wish I could. It's over, Brody." I whisper, staring at a tree behind his head. It's the only way to keep my eyes open at this point. A piercing prick is zinging back and forth in my skull, barely tolerable.

He shakes his head. "What do you mean? I need your help! I need you!" His voice stutters and I want to support him through his pain, but my head droops to the side. "Mora? What's wrong? Where are you hurt?"

He sounds fuzzy, thick, like he's on the other side of the wall, but that doesn't matter because I see Lessie. Right in front of me, plain as day, my dead baby sister stands in her favorite summer dress as it blows in the wind. Her hair also whips around and when she smiles, the clouds part for her.

"Mora! Your hand!" someone shouts, but I keep waving at my Lessie, my sister, my heart.

"I'm picking you up."

What is happening? I try to move my legs. They're numb. Did I become paralyzed? How? Strange movements. Lifted. Whatever is happening doesn't matter because as I move through a land of white, my sister soars next to me. She whispers softly, "E*ven death can turn green."*

'Lessie, I'm so sorry,' I think. *'The most important apology note I should've written was to you. I'm sorry that I tried to control your mind with a spell. I'm sorry I thought you needed to learn my way. I'm sorry I thought I was right. I'm sorry I didn't listen. I'm sorry I killed you. I'm sorry.'*

Somewhere far away I hear a wolf's familiar huff. I dream of sitting in a saddle. Strange movements. Bouncing. I can't open my eyes, but Lessie stays with me the whole time. Everything gets colder and colder. Hands touch me, lift me. Loud shouts echo.

Lessie smiles at me and whispers again, "E*ven death can turn green."*

"Fetch Doctor Hajil," a man close by yells in my ear. "Hurry!"

"He's out of town," another voice.

"What?" The deep voice sounds panicked.

All I care about is Lessie as her hand grazes my cheek.

"Is that my Brody?" The voice of an older woman. "Son, what's going on? Oh dear, what is happening to her arms? Poor thing, bring her inside."

'Lessie you'll come with me, right?' I try to ask but her silhouette flickers in and out.

Someone rushes me into a warm house. No! I need my

Lessie. Bring me back to my sister! Kicking and punching aren't working against whoever is holding me.

"Sssh, Lulita, it'll be okay. I'm here."

I'm laid onto something hard and flat.

"Lessie!" My voice cracks, or something cracks.

A zipper zips. Yin is gone too.

Glasses clink together. Yin, come back. Lessie, I need you.

"Mora, drink one of these." A bottle is put to my lips. Sweet, syrupy liquid glides down my throat and I want more. More.

"More," I croak. "More."

"No, that's enough." A deep, bold, assertive voice commands, but I can't see who it is with the intense, blinding pain striking behind my eyes. "She'd want the rest to go to the sick children. Sofia, go deliver these to the families who need a healing potion. Trust me, it'll work. No, I'm not leaving her side. Go!"

Nothing makes sense. Who is talking? Where am I?

"Yin!" I sit up and hit my head against a chandelier.

"Mora, ssshh. I'm here. Lay back down," Brody says.

Brody. It's my Brody. He's here. But Yin isn't. Lessie isn't.

"Wh-wha?" My fingertips slide over the sheet below me, but something feels different. Something's not right. "What's happening?"

"Mora," Brody's voice is full of anguish. "The ink, Mora." He takes a deep breath in. "It seems as if your pen ran out of ink. We don't have any time left."

CHAPTER 28

Brody

Time has seemed to stop.

Please, I beg silently to any Goddess who will listen, *Please, wake her up.*

Mora lays unconscious on Mam's kitchen table. New holes appear in her clothes every minute. Sometimes a sharp barb will protrude, other times an entire vine will slither out from her body as if a plant has always lived inside her. Is she in pain? Can she hear us? How can I stop it from spreading? How can I wake her?

"You need to eat something, Son." Mam offers her homemade bread, but I shake my head. If I tried to speak, it'd be layered with shaky desperation.

So, my mother continues to fret over Mora, waving

every spice and herb she owns under Mora's nose to rouse her. As Mam speaks a mile a minute to my sisters, I tread marks into her hardwood floor with the steady back and forth of my boots. For a few minutes, I allow myself to relish in the comfort of home—the hideously perfect floral wallpaper that has an air pocket bump in the upper right corner. When we were kids, my sisters and I would throw toys at the wall and see who could get the wallpaper to peel off. Year after year that stupid, stubborn paper held up. Now, whenever I dream of this childhood home, the wallpaper is the highlighted feature. Each year passed, the wallpaper stood the test of time, strong and steady, even after I left.

Someone enters through the front door, making me jump. It's Sofia. She brushes snow off her boots and sets down the backpack. Before I can ask if all the potions were delivered to the sick kids, she nods a confirmation. Her gaze asks an unspoken question, of whether Mora has shown any improvements. I think it's obvious by the tension in the air, so I don't respond. My ten-year-old sister walks over to me and slowly unclenches my tight fists that I hadn't realized were balled. One finger at a time, she uncurls them, easing some of my anguish.

"It'll be okay," Sofia whispers, "she'll wake up."

My thoughts aren't coming clearly. There are too many unknowns. I try to make sense of the last few hours.

Cat has been taken. Again. I couldn't protect her. I don't know where she is. I need Mora to help me fight Kavianne.

Clunk. Clunk of my boots.

Mora is becoming a vicious plant. She's leaving me too.

Clunk. Clunk.

The love of my life is out of time.

My body shudders from shoulders to toes. How the fuck am I supposed to fix this? I press both palms against my forehead. Mora is the clever one. I need her here. For the first time, I want a Partner, yet she's not alert enough for me to tell her that. Though, now, I can never have a true relationship with Mora even if she wants one. Commitment to Gabrielle will be a life of torture.

I shake my head in rage. Sure, I won't have to ever sleep with Gabrielle, but for the rest of our lives, the bond we made will wind around us like a rope, suffocating me. I'd rather never have sex again than share Gabrielle's bed. I'm trapped. It's like the ground has been ripped out from under me.

It wouldn't be a cage with the right person—with Mora.

"Brody, would you stop pacing?" Mam says in a worried tone. "You'll pull a muscle and don't get me started on your old boots. Five-year-old boots are not suitable."

"I don't care about my damn shoes, Mam! I just need Mora to wake up!" I scream and all my sisters' eyes go wide. It's probably the first time a male has raised his voice in this house.

After a few tense moments, my mother focuses her attention back on Mora. "We should close the curtains," Mam continues. "If Bill finds out he'll start a petition to burn her."

Did she just say burn? I become lightheaded and have to use the wall for support. The only way to stop the *Vignamassi* the first time was with fire. I can't burn Mora—that's insane.

A clattering of utensils competes with multiple female shrills behind me. I turn around as Mam lifts a steak knife and holds it over Mora's wrist, or the vine that used to be her wrist.

"No!" I leap across the kitchen and snatch it away. "Don't cut her. What are you doing?"

"I just thought, maybe they'll stop growing if we chop it off." Mam's bottom lip quivers.

"No, it grows back stronger and it'll ooze toxic liquid."

"Well, what are we supposed to *do* with her, Brody?" Mam throws up both her arms. "We can't keep something poisonous at the place we eat."

"She's not some *thing*. She's my…she's my everything," I mutter as I curl myself into a chair in the corner of the room.

My stomach roils as if I'm about to puke, but I ignore the nausea. If the Goddesses want to make me sick every day for the rest of my life, I'll bargain my health for Mora's safety.

"You look terrible. Listen, let's all get some sleep," Mam suggests. "We've spent hours trying to wake her up. We need our rest and maybe someone will have a new idea in the morning."

We don't have that kind of time. At the rate Mora is transforming, she could be a full *Vignamassi* when we wake. But as soon as Mam turns toward her bedroom, all my sisters follow her lead. I guess it'll only be me staying up.

What would Mora do? If only she'd wake up. Unless… maybe if she stays asleep, she has a smaller chance of hurting anyone. What if the only way to save the people from further suffering is to lock Mora away in a place that invasive plants can't escape? Does a cage like that exist? If it does, I'd likely never see her again.

At this rate, if she heals, we may not have a chance of a future together anyways. The bonds of Commitment are an ironclad sacred agreement tied through magic. Once made, the only way out of my arrangement with Gabrielle is to sacrifice my most desired dream.

What is my biggest dream? If someone were to ask me

weeks ago, I'd naively respond with a quote from some traveler about exploring the world, but I've changed so much during my time at Chambrea. Now, my dream would be to wish Cat a long and happy life where I can see her every day or for Mora to be free of this curse. In this situation, I'd only be able to choose one. So, if I were to break the bond with Gabrielle, only one of those would be granted. Which do I want more—for Mora to be healed or for Cat to return?

I love them both. With everything I have. The clock on the wall ticks the seconds. Tick-tock. Tick-tock.

I slam a fist into the damn wallpaper, forming a hole in its floral pattern. A strangled scream rips my throat and I punch the wall once more. A crack runs up the pattern, like a vine connecting the flowers.

CHAPTER 29

Mora

My eyes are open but I can't move. I can hear and feel everything but each limb is too heavy to lift or move. There's so much pain radiating down my body. I use every ounce of strength to focus on Brody, otherwise my spirit will break. Yin is dead. If I'm officially the beast then Feathi and Nax might be gone already too. It's all over.

Hopeless.

Brody's eyes are wide and haunted, like he's unable to blink. His eyebrows are pulled together, the crease between them deep. Sitting on the chair next to the kitchen table, he drags one hand down his cheek. It's like he's unable to sit as I'm paralyzed.

Another sharp twinge shoots up my back. Fuck. I can't shout out in pain.

I'm caged.

Earlier, each time Brody spoke to his dear mother, his voice broke and it shattered my heart. I need to move, do something, calm him. As therapeutic as it might be for him to shred the wallpaper, his desperate behavior is only further tormenting me.

The pounding in my head, like a crazed drum, strikes harder and faster to crack through my skull. No, no, no, no. Please stop.

Stuck.

Snow falls inside, and the cottage kitchen shifts into a prairie. Lessie lies flat on her back making snow angels and I'm rearranging my favorite yellow gloves, the ones with the puppies on the side. On the top of the hill in the distance, Kavianne jumps on a sled and I can hear her shout with glee.

Then floral wallpaper returns.

Brody's eyes keep looking at the clock hung on the wall until his posture collapses, unable to hold his weight. I want to run a hand over his chest, soothe his rapid breathing, but I'm frozen like a statue.

Trapped.

Soon my body won't belong to me. I need him to leave, to run as far from me as possible. His entire family needs to flee. The whole village needs to hide. Soon I'll have the strength to murder them all.

My left calf cramps and spasms. If I could just stretch it or massage it or change positions. This vegetative state is worse than any of my past injuries combined.

With each passing hour, I long to shout for help, to break free of this hold the spell has on my physical form.

Impossible. It feels as if my heart is hammering. I see spots in my vision and feel dizzier. Tingling intensifies in my fingers. My toes go numb. The taste of dirt coats my tongue, choking me. I swallow down a clump of soil.

Please, Goddess above, make the pain stop. Something…just help me.

"We'll always be together, right Sissy?" Lessie shows off her toothless grin and tosses a snowball at my scarf.

"Maybe. If you do what I say," I respond, throwing a snowball back. It hits her straight in the stomach.

"Hey! That wasn't very nice." Her pink nose scrunches in a twist. "Say, you're sorry!" Lessie chucks a bigger snowball at my face.

"No, way, I'm never wrong!" My baby sister throws another snowball, then another. "Goddess, Lessie, when did you get so strong!"

She glances down at her tiny biceps wrapped in a winter coat. "You think so?"

"Yeah! We'll have to form a secret strong club. I'll be the leader and you'll do whatever I say, but don't tell Kavianne yet."

"Why not?" Lessie tilts her head to the side.

"Because she has to prove her strength to the leader first."

The snowfall fades away. If I was that much of a controlling bitch at such a young age, no wonder Kavianne despises me. I can imagine Kavianne smiling at the sight of me now. I may have acted wicked once upon a time as a child, but no one deserves *this*.

Suddenly, my right forearm snaps at a ninety-degree angle—the bones no longer existent. Tears would be streaming down my face if possible. I'd have lost my voice from screaming, but there's no outlet for this excruciating pain.

The room goes hot and cold at the same time. I wish

the transition would finish and end this agony. All my energy has been drained, stolen, taken. Please, just let me pass out. Please, please let me slip away.

Brody knocks around a few bottles of alcohol, pours himself a glass, and chugs the contents. "You're leaving me," he grumbles and leans over me with hands—even the one holding his glass—on either side of my ears. No, I don't want him to see me this weak. A strand of his unruly dark hair falls over my face, inches from my nose. "I don't think I'll ever get over it if I lose you too."

I'm shutting down. My body is probably going into shock. I can't tolerate much more. In fact, it'd be better if I didn't survive.

Once I had asked Brody to end my life if I turned into the beast that hurt others. Does he love me enough to do it? If he asked the same of me, could I slit his throat or poison his drink or…in this case, set him afire?

No, never. It's an impossible ask.

Bearing down with all my might, I force my gaze to make eye contact with him.

Brody gasps. Drops his drink. Glass shatters everywhere.

"Shit! You moved! Can you hear me? Have you been awake this whole time?" His eyes grow wet. "Oh, Goddess, this can't be happening. You've got to be in so much pain. If you can hear me blink twice for yes."

I blink twice.

"FUCK! Oh my Goddess. Are you in pain?"

I blink twice.

The plant growing inside me feels like it's stretching me out like a rubber band, then flipping my skin inside out.

"FUCK!" he bellows with rasping breaths. "SHIT! I'm so sorry, Mora." With flaring nostrils and bulging eyes, he starts rummaging through cabinets in the kitchen. "FUCK!

I can't do it," he blubbers, repeating it over and over. "I can't do it. I can't." He bumps into chairs, knocking things over in the cabinets.

When he turns, he holds a lighter. Chest heaving. His eyes scan my body from head to toe, or thorn to vine for all I know.

"I can't," Brody pleads but steps closer. "Fuck...you're suffering," he flicks the lighter so a flame appears at the end. "You're wrong, Mora. I can't do this."

He's too good for me. Our first encounter flashes like a video on the wall. I thought Brody had no right storming into my house and making demands, but of course, anyone would try to save an innocent child.

"You've made a big mistake coming in here," I had said to Brody that night.

"You're wrong," Brody had spat out the words like poison. Those two words are what completely undid me. Because I couldn't face my fears or consider being out of control.

I stare into Brody's dark eyes, wanting them to be the last thing I see before the afterlife.

"Don't make me do this. Please." Tears begin to slide down his cheek. "Tell me you'll fix it."

I can't fix this. I have no brilliant ideas, no suggestions, no magic, no miracles at the tip of my fingers. Even if I did, it's time I let someone else have control. If Brody truly believes the best option for my beastly state is to be scorched, I trust him completely.

Heat nears my wrist, but I refuse to look away from Brody.

It's okay. I'll spend time with my friends in the next stage. It's okay, let me go.

I wish he could hear me.

It's okay.
Light me up.

CHAPTER 30

Brody

Mora stares at me, pleading with her eyes. I drop the lighter to the table, hands shaking, and lean over her paralyzed body. "Don't hate me." A couple of tears drop onto her shirt. "I can't do it. I'm sorry. I'll find another way to stop your pain."

Another thorn protrudes next to her ears. I watch it slowly creep out of her skin, clawing through her muscles and flesh.

Even if killing Mora saves a village or an entire universe, I refuse to let her go. She can't leave me. I may not know where Cat is, but I'm here with Mora now. I can help her. She's the type of person to challenge a *Vignamassi* to save a pup, so I vow to be the type of person strong enough to protect her from danger.

Saving her is the only option. But how?

Ryanne bursts through the front door, panting, her forehead glistening with sweat. She bends over, puts her hands on her knees, and sucks in deep breaths. The girl slides onto a nearby stool and tries to mime something circular.

"I overheard them talking," she manages to say while pushing against a stitch in her side. "They said they're going to give Mora a taste of her own medicine by brainwashing everyone she cares about."

My fists clench.

Ryanne pants, trying to catch her breath, and bends over in half.

"Ms. LeGume was there too, Mr. Ricci, remember her from our garden? She wants the witch to give her a mind-control spell so she can make you fall in love with her. And that's not all, Ms. Legume wants to erase your memories of Ms. Mora and your past too."

Rage boils hot in my blood, but I let her continue without interrupting.

"And the witch said she has lots of bottles of blood saved in a safe place for a dangerous potion. We can stop them though. I took these when they were distracted."

She unzips a bag at her feet. Roses spill out. Hundreds of them, big and small. A few petals detach and flutter to the floor. My heart also flutters. Hope.

"I followed those nasty women to a stash hidden underground," Ryanne sputters, obviously exhausted. She lifts an armful and lays them on Mora's stomach. "Don't just stand there, help me. She saved my life, twice. So, help me put these on her."

I jump into action. In the back of my mind, I believe the

roses alone won't make a difference. They probably need to be mixed into a potion, with ingredients only Mora knows.

Bright red roses, curled at their edges, cover Mora from head to toe. Many of them slip off her forearms and lay on the wooden table. How will this help? I'm not a witch and Ryanne doesn't have any powers. Even if we had a spell book, neither of us knows how to recite one. My body starts to shake when I see Mora's eyes have closed. Hopefully she can't feel pain anymore.

I place two rose petals over Mora's closed eyelids. "Please," I whisper.

Our time together has been short but it all flashes in my mind.

Her fierce eyes had captured my attention from the first minute. I had studied the way her expressions shifted so slightly, trying to determine if she was a threat. Her sarcastic tone when bantering. The way she didn't want to keep Heathcliff though she was enamored at first glance.

All of the memories make me unable to swallow. I don't know if she will ever ride War again, or find other secret tunnels under her home, or throw snowballs, or fold origami, or read a book. A tear slides down my cheek as I hold her limp hand in mine.

"Heal," I whisper. "Please, for me."

More flashes of our adventures play like a video.

The first time I witnessed her sip hot cocoa. The way Mora's lips felt against mine. Her devotion to her friends. The sheer awe we experienced together at finding the fairy village.

Wait. I drop her hand accidentally.

"The fairies," I say.

Ryanne looks up. "What?"

"An old fairy told me something right before we left her

village." I start to pace and push against my temple. "What was it? Something about roses and...I remember!"

"What do you remember?" Ryanne's eyes are wide and excited.

"She asked what my biggest treasure is. And that one day, I may need an answer for the roses. What if that day is now?" I stop pacing and lean over Mora. "Yes, this is it, but how do I talk to a rose?"

Young Ryanne smiles. "I heard you have a daughter a little younger than me. Haven't you ever played make-believe with her?"

"Not yet."

"Here, watch me." Ryanne lays her hands over the roses that cover Mora's knees. "Roses are red, violets are blue. Your heart is my treasure because I wanna hug you." She lifts her hands and nods in encouragement for me to try.

I don't know any poems, but one line keeps repeating in my head. *'It has been foreseen, even death can turn green.'* It's the song she had sung to me, a tune from her childhood. For some reason, it has stuck with me, but I need to tell her my most valuable treasure.

So, I take a deep breath and lay my hands on Mora's stomach, then squeeze my eyes shut. I imagine Mora's smile when she first hurled snowballs at me at the festival.

"If you can hear me," I clear my throat, "my treasure is you, Mora; your future, your happiness, your smile, your joy. I'd hunt for a billion roses and set fire to all the enchanted forests if it meant keeping you safe. I'd fold origami until my hands were bloody and raw if it meant your freedom. You need to come back to me. Please," I whisper, "even death can turn green."

Another tear falls, but I keep my eyes clenched shut. I don't feel her fingertips twitch against mine. I don't hear any shuffling of her body against the table. Nothing changes. It didn't work.

"Mr. Ricci!" Ryanne gasps.

I open my eyes and startle backward. My heels ram into a chair and I almost topple over. The black vines and thorns entwined around Mora's body are fading away to flesh again. Her eyes are sealed, but an obvious transformation is happening, stealing my breath. Most of her limbs and skin are returning to normal.

"Wait, what are those?"

Intricate tattoos begin to cover every inch of flesh. They crawl like phantom ink over her legs, drawing shapes of flowers, branches, twisting tree trunks, roots entangled together, and thorny vines. All the plants decorate her skin in a web of greenery.

I hold her hand the whole time. Finally, her finger twitches and then her eyes snap open.

I don't dare breathe.

Mora coughs and a little black puff of dirt flies out of her mouth. She spits and makes a disgusted face that makes me want to sweep her into my arms. She's here. Mora is okay.

Her eyes find mine. Thank Goddess. I thought I had lost her.

"You're here." I cradle her head against my chest. "You're here."

"Yin is dead," she says slowly, the first words out of her mouth. "I couldn't save her."

My heart breaks for her. Should I ask what happened or would that make her grief worse? Does she know how long she's been unconscious for? Is she aware that more than half of her body had turned into the *Vignamassi*?

"I'm sorry, Lulita." I hold her tighter, so glad that it's a possibility. "I know how much you love Yin." I'm afraid to ask the next question but do anyways. "Do you think your curse is broken?"

"No," Mora shakes her head. "Something is missing, but I didn't expect these tattoos. They feel like magic too."

"What kind of magic?" I ask, releasing her from our hug.

"I'm not sure, but I'm not back to normal," she says gesturing to the tattoos on her body. "So, what do we do now?" Her brown eyes shimmer with unshed tears. "I don't know what comes next. Just tell me what to do. Just tell me the answers to fix all this."

I kiss her forehead softly. "I've got this, Lulita. Don't worry."

Ryanne quietly scurries around the kitchen to grab Mora a glass of water. I stare at the crooked clock on the wall, next to Mam's shelf of lit vintage candles. Time and fire. Time is precious. And fire is the only thing that defeated the *Vignamassi* the first time around.

The seconds hand circles a couple of times before anyone speaks. I form a plan in my mind. "Okay, this is what we'll do." I lift one finger to keep track. "First, we go back to your house and collect all your orbs."

No rebuttal so far. Mora looks at me with interest.

"Secondly, we'll find Kavianne and force her to both give us Cat and tell us how to permanently break your spell."

"How? She'll never agree."

"You have six total orbs, right?"

"Yes."

"That means you have six attempts to use magic. I know you don't like to use them, but one spell could be used for a truth spell on Kavianne."

She nods and digs inside her pocket. "I have one orb with me. Should we use this one now?"

"Perfect!" I kiss the top of her head again. "Call War with that one. We need to hurry, and he will help us move faster."

With the orb in hand, Mora mumbles under her breath. The black swirls inside suddenly move faster while glittering like they've come alive.

"Done." She pockets the orb since it needs time to recharge and tries to stand.

I support her body as she sucks in a deep breath and puts weight on both feet. Hesitantly, I let go. "You okay?"

Without a response, she moves toward the window on shaky legs. "We used one orb, and one will be for making Kavianne give us answers. So, what will the others be used for?"

"Okay, the second to free Cat. The third to help Feathi. The fourth to annul my Commitment."

She cuts me off, sighing. "Magic won't work for an annulment. You need to sacrifice your most desired dream."

My chest tightens. I don't want to think about that right now. It's either living a life with Mora or living a life with Cat. "Okay, forget that one. With one, you could make an army of origami people."

Her face looks confused.

"Trust me. Origami is made of paper, right? I bet it's within your ability to turn one of the trees into a thousand origami soldiers to be on our side. It'll only be temporary, to serve as a distraction against Kavianne."

"Okay. What about the last orb?"

I pause, mentally list off multiple scenarios that might happen, and say, "We should probably plan for a way to detain Kavianne. So that once she's forced to tell us the answers, we have somewhere to put her so she can't hurt anyone else."

"Like create a magic-proof cage?"

"Something like that."

War roars outside the window, followed by loud paws crunching over snow.

I snatch a lighter off the shelf and shove it in my pocket —just in case.

I help Mora hobble outside, wondering if we should use one of the orbs to give her extra strength. Kavianne won't go down without a fight. War snorts, blowing hot, visible air in front of my face. We move fast, with purpose. There's no time to tell Mora everything on my heart and mind. Hopefully, she knows how much she means to me.

"Here, you take the reins," she says.

"Are you sure?"

"Yes, I trust you, Brody."

I steer War straight to her home, into the soon-to-be-setting suns, unwilling to lose any time. This plan feels impossible, but we have to try. Everyone we care about is relying on us. I dig my heels into War's side in hopes he'll move faster.

CHAPTER 31

Mora

The suns set behind us, casting a strange hue between the snow-covered pines. Once we arrive at my home, nothing looks the same. It's been a whole day since Brody carried me to his Mam's house. The iron gate protecting the front entrance is bent at strange angles as if a bulldozer had smashed through it. Mud tracks infect the snow, creating a dirty brown sludge over the front stairs. Most of the stone statues are split in half. My favorite one that resembles War is cracked in pieces, spread helplessly along the cobbled pathway. I scan the façade of our house, noticing long curtains blowing eerily through broken windows.

"Goddess, what did she do?" Brody whispers as he slows War's momentum.

Even the animal's ears flick back and forth, searching for the threat's location. The air is too quiet.

"When crossroads split to black, I will have your back," a high-pitched, quiet voice whispers in between the snowflakes.

"Kavianne," I carefully dismount, not wanting my sore bruises to protest. "I'm not afraid of you!"

A whoosh sound comes from my right. I spin around but see only pine trees swaying.

Another sound hisses by my left ear. I turn fast but only spot Brody dismounting War. The hair on my arms rises. The gooseflesh isn't from the lack of a sweater but from the terror of what Kavianne is capable of. I don't want Brody to be in danger, but I can't refuse his help anymore. He deserves to have a say, a choice.

"Together we are whole, shielded tightly in one soul." This time Kavianne's voice sounds as if she's coming from everywhere at once.

Her voice grows louder as she repeats the phrase. Louder. It attacks us like a blast of wind. Brody covers his ears and winces. War runs off into the woods. It's just us two—a dreamer and an injured witch.

What could Kavianne possibly want from me? She is already taking my life. Her plan will torture me for eternity. Hasn't she gotten enough revenge? Isn't she satisfied with all she will be ripping away? Before my time runs out, I must try to stop her. I can't give up.

"Can't go through the front door," I whisper to Brody and scan the other entrances that Kavianne may or may not know about.

"Isn't that a tunnel entrance?" Brody points. "It let out right there?"

"Perfect. I think that one leads straight to my room." I grab his hand just as he reaches for mine.

Another loud whoosh pierces my ears, followed by a chorus of voices singing in unison, "Shielded tightly in one soul."

I turn around and see Kavianne, inches from my face. "What the fuck?!" I stagger back, slamming into Brody's chest.

Brody catches me. "Whoa, it's just a mirror."

I peek around his waist. "It's not just a mirror. The voice is coming from inside the glass."

Blocking me from moving, Brody steps forward carefully. The mirror is framed by familiar intricate details that match the smaller one I used to own. This bigger replica leans against a thick tree trunk.

"It's beautiful," Brody says, reaching out.

I smack his hand down. "It doesn't feel safe. Don't you hear those voices? They're singing like sirens."

He tilts his head, as if in a trance, staring at the mirror. His fingertips hover over the intricate flowery carving around the border.

"Brody! Don't touch it!"

But it's too late. His hand swipes over the wooden frame.

"Fuck." I want to rush to him.

He stares into the mirror. A human hand reaches out of the glass, holding a bottle of crimson liquid. I know those slender fingers, and the rings that rest upon each. Kavianne. How is she doing this?

"Brody! Look at me!"

Hypnotized, Brody stares at the red liquid sloshing around inside the glass bottle.

And I can't fucking move my feet forward. I strain against whatever power holds me in place. His hand caresses Kavianne's, softer than a lover's touch, and he takes the bottle for himself.

"Brody! Put it down!"

I'm trapped, having to watch him raise it to his lips.

"No! Brody! Stop!" All I can do is yell, but he ignores me.

It's like I don't exist. I'm already a ghost. He grins at the mirror, then drinks straight from the bottle. He empties the contents in one long gulp.

"Make yourself puke," I beg, "Listen to me, please."

His muscles become clearly strained and his body goes rigid. The empty bottle drops into the snow, disappearing silently. Unexpectedly, he turns toward me, murder in his eyes.

"You!" he spits out. "You killed Cat!"

"No, Brody." I keep my voice calm. "It isn't real. She's controlling you."

"You took her from me!" he bellows.

"No!" I take a step back, heart pounding.

Brody grabs the mirror in fury and slams it against the tree trunk. It shatters into a thousand sharp pieces. Snow falls from nearby branches. Light from the setting suns reflect off the pieces of glass shimmering in the snow. The number of singing voices from within them increases. This time the lyrics change and shift like they're a part of the breeze.

"We shattered from one soul. Shattered. You took a soul. Shattered. I'll take your soul. Shattered."

I should run. Instead, I take a broken glass piece from the broken mirror. I'm supposed to see who I love most in this world. Kavianne appears. She's ten years younger, in her favorite gray dress with long hair bouncing down her back. My sister runs in a sunflower field but with each step, she multiplies. Two Kaviannes turn to four. Four of them double to eight. Exact replicas of the same girl, jogging among the prairie grasses.

"Take your soul," she echoes. "Take your soul."

I drop the glass into the snow. It's dark magic. What has she done? I look over and Brody has fallen to his knees, head buried in his hands, shoulders slumped.

"She's gone. Cat's gone. Gone!" The raw sounds that must scratch his throat tear my heart apart.

"Brody!" I throw a snowball at him, too scared to move closer.

His head snaps up and the pure agony written on his face is immediately replaced by rage. Brody staggers to his feet and charges at me. I don't wait. The only way to save Brody's mind is to use my orbs, but they're upstairs. I lunge toward the tunnel entrance. Sprint. Trip in the snow. Hands sting. My knee hits something hard.

Brody's heavy breathing chases behind. "Come here, you witch!"

I get up. Run. My lungs burn. Wind slashes my face. He's right behind me. I chuck the orb from my pocket at his legs, whispering a spell. He falls.

Quickly, I jam my palm into a specific stone. A hole opens. I rush through. The door closes. I'm alone in near darkness. My breathing comes hard, labored, heavy. Brody starts banging on the other side.

"You killed her! I saw it! What have you done to my baby!?"

Tears slide down my cheeks at hearing his pained voice. My heart hurts for him. Even though it's not real, the hallucination feels real to him.

Taking a deep breath, I jog down the dark tunnel and leave Brody behind. *Thud. Thud. Thud.* My boots echo in the tight space. All my nerves are frayed. I shake my head and focus on one thing. Get the orbs. Get the orbs. It was stupid to throw the only one I had.

My lungs are on fire and my muscles scream in protest. I'm shutting down from exhaustion. What am I supposed to do once I get the orbs? What if Kavianne is too powerful? What if my body changes back into a plant?

I stop in my tracks, forming a plan.

"That's it!" I speak into the darkness. "That's what will save them!"

When the time comes, if my orbs aren't enough, I'll *choose* to change into the *Vignamassi* voluntarily. Maybe I can pull off the impossible. If I can control it, the strength from the monstrous plant will be enough to destroy Kavianne. I'll have to trust that I won't hurt those I love.

Ahead, someone else's labored breathing in the darkness makes me jerk to a stop. Maybe I'm imagining it. I count to three.

One.

Someone exhales.

Two.

Someone coughs.

Three.

A dog whines.

"Heathcliff?"

"Mora?" Nax calls out, voice strained and tortured.

"Nax!" I rush over to my roommate.

If he's still here, it means the pen hasn't fully run out of ink yet. He's crumpled over in a pile of pieces of paper. His mouth moves, but I'm certain it's not connected to the rest of his face. Some body parts I can't distinguish from the others. This shapeless mess of my friend brings me to a new shower of tears.

"Nax! What happened?"

"Mora...your puppy is okay." His eyes close.

I want to hug him, but am terrified of ripping any more parts off his body. “Forgive me, Nax. I’m so sorry,” I plead, unsure what to do, how to help him.

The orbs. I can use one to save him. We had an extra one planned for emergencies like this.

I reach around Nax’s non-waist to the entrance of my room. Jiggle the handle. Locked. I turn it again and again. Useless. I slam my fists against it. Shove my elbows. Kick it hard. Pointless. We’re trapped.

“Kavi took the other…” Nax wheezes, “…orbs from your nightstand.”

“No, no, no, no. I need those.” I hover my hand over him. “Nax? What do I do?”

Slowly, the pieces of his body shift and rotate until a tiny ring clatters to the rock ground at my knees. Dirt covers the jewelry, so I brush my finger over it. Underneath the coat of grime, shows my last, most powerful orb, as the centerpiece of a Commitment Ring.

“Can you…”—wheeze—“give this…”—wheeze—“to my Feathi? Tell her I… ” Nax never finishes.

The remaining upright pieces of his paper body deflate and flatten to the ground. Dead. Gone.

I can’t breathe. I can’t think. At the top of my lungs, I wail and scream. Every muscle clenches tight. I cry for him, for Yin, and for the village girl who died by my thorns without receiving a healing potion in time. I sob for Brody losing Cat. For all the pain.

I pound the tunnel’s wall with my fist. I kick the wall. Scream. Scream! And SCREAM!

No more tears are left to fall. There’s only one last thing to keep me together. Brody and Feathi are the only ones left. I still have the strongest orb now from Nax’s Commitment ring.

When I squeeze the powerful, tiny orb in my hand,

warm liquid runs down my palm. Blood. I had punched the wall too hard too many times. I wipe it on my shirt, realizing that it's Brody's clothes I'm wearing. I steal a single moment by sniffing his scent, relishing this comfort. At the end of this tunnel, he's probably still slamming against the wall, trying to enter and hunt me down.

If Brody's still under Kavianne's control, I may need to fight against the love of my life.

CHAPTER 32

Mora

I thrash, kick, and punch at the wall. A thunderous rumble echoes as stones shift and fall. I cover my head and curl into a ball. Debris rains down onto my back and neck. Pebbles, dust, and soot bury themselves in my hair. Is it over?

Faint light shines through a new opening in the tunnel. Heathcliff shoots out like a rocket and runs across the snow. I peek through the hole, and then check left and right for any sign of Kavianne. Maybe she's stuck inside that mirror, and I won't have to deal with her again. That'd be too lucky.

I glance back at Nax once more, wishing I could lay his body to rest somehow. A sharp ping zaps up my forearm.

"Ouch!"

The last of the suns' rays cast light along my new tattoos. The dark green vines, thorns, and flowers inked into my skin slowly shift to black. My gut tells me this is bad—very bad.

I don't have time to wonder what it means, so I slip out of the tunnel and run.

"Mooooooora?" Feathi's voice rings through the treetops, swirling around me like a tornado. "Mooooooora? Where are you?"

"I'm here!" I turn right.

"Mooooooooora? I'm in the courtyard."

I turn left.

"Mooooooooora? I'm in our garden. Come find me."

I turn around on my heels, ready to go anywhere Feathi tells me. At this point, I have nothing else to lose.

"Mora!? Help me!" Feathi screams into the crisp evening air.

A flock of ravens perched on a branch flies off together, leaving me alone. I see no one. Feathi's voice left as quickly as it had appeared.

"Oh, sister," Kavianne calls from beside my home, where the balconies overlook the cliffside, my least favorite spot on our property. It reminds me too much of the past. "Come join us for a little game."

Snow flurries begin to fall. My fingers are turning numb, but I plow through the snow straight toward her voice. I squint into the whipping wind, hunching my shoulders to shield my neck from the sting. Each step brings me closer and closer to the cliff's edge. Ahead, the drop is a straight plummet for hundreds of feet.

When the hazy cloud of white clears, I see two silhouettes floating mid-air. Brody and Feathi hang, dangerously suspended. I gasp. Stop in my tracks. A trembling hand covers my mouth.

"Bring them down!" I scream.

The two people I love more than life itself dangle directly over the abyss.

"Brody!" I yell.

He wears a new expression of pity within his glossed-over eyes. "You thought I'd never figure out your plan to use me?" His question attacks me in a bitter voice that doesn't sound like his own. "I never would've stayed with you. It's outrageous for you to consider that we could've lived a Partnership side by side. A *cursed* witch only infects. Your ideas, your thoughts, your magic, it's all been poison. No wonder you tried to control others for so long. It's the only way you feel good about yourself."

I refuse to cry. I know he's being manipulated by Kavianne and that his accusations are only half-truths. It's not only his words that hurt though, but the possibility that he'll be under her spell forevermore—brainwashed.

I glance over to Feathi, who brings more harsh tones when she adds, "He's right. I've hated living in that despicable house where you treated me more like a servant than a friend. Never grateful, you acted like a queen, entitled to be worshiped, and I've had enough. Good luck cooking your own dinners, you bitch!"

Feathi's right. I made too many mistakes. I can do better. Unsure where my sister is hiding, I yell, "Kavianne, let them go!"

Midair, Brody's body drops a bit and I scream, reaching forward.

"Beg on your knees, pretty Sister," Kavianne hisses. This time I follow the sound of her voice coming from a high tree branch. She isn't sitting on a branch as expected.

Dozens of broken mirror pieces hang like icicles next to the pinecones. When they sway in the wind, I catch glimpses of my sister's smiling face within each of the reflections.

I drop to my knees in the snow. "Please, don't hurt them. I'll be your puppet, but let them go. You can make all the choices. I'll do what you say. I won't fight back. Please, Kavi."

I meet her eyes in a mirror, then the one next to it, then the third, and fourth.

"You killed our sister! Lessie is gone!"

"It was an accident, Kavi! I didn't mean to hurt her!"

All she does is narrow her glare more intensely. She won't be convinced. It's a lost cause. My heart pounds. What the fuck am I supposed to do? I lock eyes with Brody and the eyes I've memorized return for a split second. The man I've fallen in love with has returned. I see him and he sees me.

"Mora?" His body tenses.

"Brody!"

Despite his shock at hovering, he starts to fight against Kavianne's hold, wiggling and writhing. Until he suddenly stops. He stares at the glass pieces holding Kavi. It's as if he's listening to some secret I can't hear. Terror washes over his face, then a sad acceptance. My Brody looks at me again, his gaze begging for something I don't understand.

"I would've spent all my adventures with you," he says with a sad, weak smile.

Then Brody drops out of sight. He falls into the canyon.

My breath is torn out of my lungs. There's a buzzing in my ears and my vision goes hazy.

Only when my palms burn do I realize I'm frantically crawling to the cliff's edge. I lay flat on my stomach. Peer over the side. All I see is white. I can't scream his name. I can't speak. I can't think. He fell. He dropped. That can't be right. Brody was just here. Now he's not. I was looking at him, listening to his words.

He's not here. It doesn't make sense.

He's not here.

How am I supposed to apologize?

Here's not here. What if he's cold where he landed? What if he needs me? What if I need *him*?

He's not here.

A howling sound rips my attention toward the woods. A shadowed clump of gray flickers behind the wall of white snow falling harder.

"You don't look too good, Sis," Kavianne says, "but I guess someone cursed with thorns can't ever be attractive."

A massive animal stalks out from between the forest trees. The alpha wolf who once gave me a ride steps out into the clearing. He howls, roars, and paws the snow, possessed. His pack emerges behind him, ready to attack me. They all have glossed over all-white eyes that make them look otherworldly, haunted. More grunts rumble in my bones and send a spike of fear up my spine.

"I bet you wish you were as fatal as a poisonous plant now, don't you?" Kavianne laughs, then commands, "Go get her, pups."

The pack lurches forward. I run toward the edge of the cliff, only thinking of Brody.

A faint flapping sound comes from my left. I turn. Hundreds of fairies charge the wolves. Their black glitter sparkles off their tiny wings and sprinkles to the snow, dusting the white in a dark powder. Princess Preta leads her army.

There's a clash of magic versus muscle. Beams of light shoot from the fairies' fingertips at the brutes. A wolf goes sailing into my home. Glass smashes. Brick and stone crumble into the snow.

I turn away from the chaos. I must find Brody. I crawl closer to the edge. Screams, hollers, and growls all mix into a crazed battle, but I must get to him.

"Wicked girl," Feathi's voice, coming from above, sounds like a snake.

I glance up. She's too far to reach. Sweat drips down my temple.

"Feathi!" I scream above the noise. "Can you swing your body to me?"

A ray of light bounces off one of the mirror shards. The glass piece falls into the snow. In that moment, Kavianne's control over Feathi's mind wavers too because I can detect a hint of Feathi's normal expression. She shakes her head and stares at me.

"Mora?" Then she glances around and screams, waving her arms wildly as she looks below her suspended feet. "Help!"

"Don't look down." I inch forward a little more, hoping the rock holds my weight. "Look at me, Feathi! I'm right here!"

"I need Nax," she says as tears stream down her red, terrified face. "Please, please, where's Nax?"

I swallow. This is it. I can lie and tell her everything will be okay to keep her with me until my last moment or I can give her the choice. The way her watery eyes plead with me makes the task seem harder. There is no easy answer.

"He died. Just a few minutes ago in the tunnel. I'm sorry, Feathi." I won't give up on her without a fight though. "Will you stay with me, still? Will you fight this? Please, Feathi?" My shoulders strain from trying to grab her body.

"No."

"No?" My arms shake. My voice shakes. Everything trembles.

My beautiful, sweet, loving friend stares at me. "I can't. I love you, Mora, but I can't." Tears streak her cheeks. "Please don't make me stay without him. Let me go."

"I can't say goodbye." Tension coils in my gut.

"Please, Mora. I want to go to him," Feathi says, her eyes dropping to the ring on my finger, the one Nax had picked out for her.

There's no point in telling her what she already knows. I rub the little orb in the center, squeeze my eyes shut, and make the hardest decision of my life. I mumble the strongest spell I can recall, one that might fully cut Kavianne's control over Feathi.

In a heartbeat, Feathi plummets down, out of sight. Just like that—gone. I've lost everything.

I stare at the empty space where she used to hover.

A wolf roars, but I have no energy to defend myself. It's over. More of the tattoos zing with a fierce stabbing sensation. I don't care. It doesn't matter what overtakes me.

There's nothing left. Yin's gone. Nax. Brody. Now Feathi. All I have is Kavianne and she despises me.

My sister's voice shrieks in an inhumanly high pitch. There's no point in responding. Directly in front of me, where Feathi's body used to hover, the many broken shards of mirror float together to reunite. The pieces of Kavianne form together into a whole unit.

She walks out of the mirror and her body hovers above mine. Kavianne smiles. Maybe she was right and I've been the villain all along, ignoring others' needs solely to do things *my* way, on *my* time, the way *I* wanted it.

"Together we are whole, shielded tightly in *one* soul." Kavianne reaches out to me. She doesn't need to further explain her intentions. My little sister is clearly telling me to follow her blindly and bid her wishes. This could be my way out of the curse. She may grant me freedom if I do exactly what she says, but I refuse.

"No, Kavianne."

Her eyes narrow. Her shoulders tighten. "Fine," Kavianne smiles wickedly, mid-air. "Have it *your* way. Just like always, but all these deaths will be on *your* conscience."

She raises both hands in the air and the snow stops. The wind ceases. The pine trees are still. Silhouettes form in the mirror. At first, it looks like an army of shadows, but as they move closer, growing larger with each step, I recognize Ryanne. Her face is expressionless, in a zombie state as she walks closer and closer to the mirror face. Next to her is Brody's little sister, Sofia, and his Mam walking forward like mindless ghosts.

"What are you doing?" I scream at Kavianne, my throat already raw. "Stop!"

"You forced Lessie off the cliffside." Kavianne hissed. "Now you'll see what it feels like to watch everyone be commanded to their death."

A man I recognize from the winter festival steps in front of the others. His pace quickens. When he reaches the edge of the mirror, he falls out of that dimension, through the glass, and hurtles straight down into the canyon.

"No!"

And then I see little Cat among the hypnotized crowd. My heart fucking stops. My blood burns hot. I see red. My body reacts before my mind.

I don't need any fuckin' orbs. With fists clenched tight, I call to my forest at the top of my lungs. The plants answer. Leaves snap off branches and cover my shirt. Twigs rise from under mounds of snow and twist into my hair. My tattoos spread further over my hands. Swirls of inky vines wrap around each finger. Roots explode from below the earth and curl around my waist.

In the mirror, the other townspeople move closer and closer to the edge.

There's only one way to stop Kavianne. My life will be forfeit, but this plan could save them all. I summon the thorns that have been buried deep within my flesh, commanding them to return. My muscles flex and my legs are in a stance ready to transform. A loud rushing sound floods my ears. I blow out a deep breath and prepare for the pain of transformation, but none comes.

Thorns burst from my wrists, forearms, and neck. They split my clothes and grow longer. I can do this. My heart slams against my chest. Warmth spreads over my body and I have a sudden urge to tear off my clothes, to be one with nature. There's no need because another rip slices down my shirt. A giant vine shoots out of my chest. Still no pain. Raw power consumes me. A second, longer one juts out from my stomach. I need more, all of them.

My breath is bottled in my chest, so I release a roar that stops the wolves from charging. Adrenaline rushes through my body.

"Kavianne!" The ground shakes when I shout.

A look of fear flickers through her eyes before she masks it. I swipe a long deadly vine-arm straight at her neck. She dodges.

"You care about nothing!" I wail and take a large stride closer to her.

The roots connected to me won't let me fall over the cliffside. I can reach her. I'm invincible. Kavianne bares her teeth at me and snarls but moves a step back. The people in the mirror continue to walk. They're only steps away from the edge.

"I never meant to hurt you," I say softly to my little sister.

Then I raise a barbed vine for the killing blow.

She freezes. At first, I assume she's cowering, but I'm *also* unable to move. The villagers are as still as a statue.

Time has stopped.

Princess Preta flutters in front of my face, but I can't blink to check if what I'm seeing is real. Everything behind her has ceased moving, yet her wings continue to flap. I can't open my lips to ask what's happening.

"We are stopping time for sixty seconds, Mora," she says softly, sadly. "It'll take sixty years off the lifespan of the one soul you love most at this moment."

I want to tell the princess there's no one left for me to love, but that'd be a lie. I don't want to kill my sister. I love her. I always have and always will. No matter what, we are a part of each other.

I struggle against the hold Preta has on my body. I have no control, I lock eyes with my sister. Fear is plastered on her face. Ten seconds have passed. She already looks older. How? Kavianne may have plotted to destroy me, but I love her. Only able to use my eyes, I glance between Preta and Kavianne. Preta gently shakes her head and lays a tiny hand over mine. A sharp hitching in my chest is a thousand swords to my heart.

Ten more seconds pass.

Kavianne's eyes widen. It's obvious she feels a difference. Is aging painful? My head pounds, unable to help. A thickening in my throat makes it hard to breathe.

Ten more seconds pass.

I want to cover my face with both hands, but I'm stuck in this torture of witnessing her decay. Kavianne's gape widens. Her eyes fill with unshed tears.

Ten more seconds go by.

There's so much that needs to be said. I want to turn and hide, to deny that this is happening. I want to run toward her and take away her discomfort. I want to go back in time to a decade ago and choose differently. I'm sorry, Kavianne. I didn't mean for this to happen.

I can't believe what I'm seeing. Her shoulders visibly slouch even though she's stuck in place, and she seems to shrink before my eyes.

Ten more seconds pass.

I glance down at my hands. Despite the thorns curling out, my skin is young. Across the way, Kavianne is covered in wrinkles, with sagging skin on her neck. Her eyes droop with dark circles underneath. I should've told her what she means to me long ago. Dizziness takes over as Kavianne meets my eyes again. For the last time.

Princess Preta releases the time freeze. I can move again. I reach forward to my sister as Kavianne lets go of one last breath and dissolves into glowing specs. The wind immediately carries her away.

I want her back. I want them all back. An all-consuming fire flares intensely in my chest. My bones quake and my muscles seethe with insane ferocity. A rage deep within has been triggered. I *am* the *Vignamassi*. And it is me. We are one.

"Together we are whole, shielded tightly in *one* soul."

CHAPTER 33

Mora

A few of Kavianne's glowing specs land on my hands. Like a crack of lightning, something snaps inside of me. Strength pulses through me. Power rushes like a river. It's fucking intoxicating. I suck in a lungful of crisp, freezing air. When I roar, screaming out the grief trapped inside, hundreds of decayed flowers explode from my mouth.

I'm famished.

The wolf pack scurries into the woods while the fairies fly toward the mirror holding all the townspeople. They flick their wrists in unison and a bridge immediately forms. It connects the floating mirror to the side of the cliff. Delicious humans pour out of the mirror onto the bridge. I smile. Lick my lips. They'll all be fine fertilizer once buried under my roots.

Darkness squeezes with a tight grip on my heart, crushing my insides with so much strength that I relish the sensation. Pure intensity swirls within me. Raising a vine high into the air, I strike at the enchanted bridge. The pathetic humans all wail as half of it crumbles into the vast canyon below. I smile. They're so weak. Their fear fuels my rage. Something was taken from me. I may not remember what it was, but I want it back.

All these small humans will suffer and bleed into my earth until I feel whole again. My tentacled limbs swing wildly. One slams into the ground. It sends snow soaring over the cliffside. I can't help but laugh. Punishment is needed. My forest will thrive as their flesh rots beneath precious trees.

A wolf attacks my trunk but I stab him with a thorn. He howls as a festering boil surfaces from under his dark fur. Good. He deserves it. There's no point in battling me. By the second, I grow larger, stronger, taller, and indestructible.

My branches whip toward the bridge again. I'm ready to taste their blood for my next meal. As the people panic, another large section collapses into the abyss. This game of torturing them is so damned amusing.

In the distance, a small girl waves her arms. She steps out from the others with a defiant look on her face. Perfect —someone brave to make an example of. The young one holds something wooden in her hand like a weapon. She wants to fight? I can smell her human blood streaming through her veins. Some brutal bruises and broken bones might teach her a lesson before her untimely death.

I crunch through the wicked snow, shaking the ground

beneath me. Someone so insignificant can't wound me. I am unstoppable. She doesn't back down. The stupid girl keeps waving the play sword in her hand. I squint. Then lean forward. My branches creak with the movement. It's not a sword, but a small wooden device. Something about it looks familiar.

"Mora!" the tiny voice yells.

Who is she talking about? And why am I giving her any time to speak? The only logical action is to crush, drag, and smash this tiny human. They deserve to die. Someone stole my everything, my future, my life, my love.

"Stop! This isn't you. Wemembuh? My papi made this for you." The girl looks shocked, eyes wide as she fixates on something behind me.

I no longer have to worry about any wolves since they've all fled, but still, I turn around to check what she could possibly be staring at. A man covered in scratches lifts a lighter into the air. His fierce gaze challenges mine as a flame flickers brightly.

"Mora, release the poison," the man says. "Don't try to control it. Just let it go."

"It's too late," I say to the man, unsure what I mean.

"I don't want to hurt you," he moves the flame and lights the nearest branch, holding it out toward me "Come back to me, Mora."

Without hesitating, I whip a long vine in his direction. It slams a few feet to the left. He can't use fire. It'll destroy me.

"Please, Mora," he raises the blazing branch to the tip of my vine. "Remember who you are. Your favorite colors are crimson and gold."

I project another limb straight at the man. It catapults into the snow to his right. Next time, I won't miss.

"You adopted a puppy named Heathcliff!" he screams at me. "And let him sleep in your bed."

His fire grows too hot, too large. When the man takes a step forward with the branch raised between us, I roar again. Hundreds of roses spill out of my mouth, falling into the snow like red jewels decorating white.

"You're angry and hurt and confused!" he bellows with strength, "but you're not alone. Remember the origami snowflakes, Mora!"

One of my deathly tentacles stops mid-air, a bit above his head. He hadn't cowered or ducked out of the way. Who is this man? Why doesn't he fear me? Something about the wildness of his eyes tells me I'm forgetting something important.

"My Mora," the confidence in his voice returns, and the corner of his lip ticks up slightly.

Slower than death, the man pushes the lighter into his pocket and raises both hands in surrender. He kneels in front of me, brown eyes trained on me the whole time. Curiosity gets the best of me. What human would sacrifice themself? Is he volunteering himself as an offering? For some reason, I want to taste him more than I want to kill him. I feel myself lowering, the snow becoming closer. I stare at the black poison dripping down from my limbs. Drip. Drip. Drip.

My thickest vine reaches out. My sharpest thorn hovers by the man's neck. It'd only take one quick stab and his blood would belong to me.

"Trust me. Release the poison, my Lulita," he whispers. "You don't scare me. Since your thorns are a part of you, they don't worry me."

I shake my head. Blink. Once. Twice. It's Brody. Brody stands near the base of where my feet should be but instead of feet, I have a twisted trunk. He's alive. I've never felt such a relief as knowing that fact. He'll be okay even if I'm not. I was never intended for a happily ever after.

His eyes widen larger than seems possible. My body creaks and cracks strangely. When I look down, my form is a mess of warped vines, thorns, and bramble. I glance around at the destruction surrounding me and my home. What have I done?

This is his chance to save them all. Whatever plan he chooses, I support. I give him full control. Brody looks at me once more. I hope he can't tell that I recognize him. I know him. I see him. Thank you. I love you.

All at once, I do what he says. I let go. I throw up all my vines in the air at once and scream a deadly cry of joy. I can viscerally feel the poison exploding out of me like a volcanic eruption, but all the humans below cower and cover their ears.

Brody bites his lip and throws the fiery branch at me.

I watch him stare at me in horror. Heat blazes. It burns. I try to ignore the scorching sensation because nothing is as painful as memorizing the devastation on Brody's face. I want to tell him that it's okay, that he has saved everyone. A golden glow stretches and crawls higher to my stomach. The smell of the rising smoke suffocates my very breath. Yet it's Brody's tears that incinerate me. I hold in my screams, not wanting to torment him. I drop to my knees, or what's left of them. The snow sizzles part of the flames, but this isn't something I can fight or stop.

Everything hurts. Sharp shooting needles devour me from head to toe. My bark dries, splits, and cracks. I blacken and char. Just let it be over. Please, I'll do anything to make the torment stop. My body crackles as it falls apart.

I try to find Brody once more through the smoke, but there's only gray. My head swirls and I collapse to my side in a thunderous thud. When I'm reduced to ashes, I hope he knows I love him. I love him.

"I trust you," I say instead, and close my eyes.

CHAPTER 34

Brody

Mora lies in the snow as a half-*Vignamassi,* with parts of her plant body unrecognizable. I hate myself. I despise what I did, but I know she'd never forgive herself for hurting innocent people. The monstrous side had taken over her mind, but I know her heart.

I rush over to her. Snow falls, extinguishing the fire atop her. Broken branches lay scattered. I jump over each one, praying to any Goddess that she's alive. Since she listened to my command and released her venom, there's a chance she's still in there somewhere.

The fairies fly beside me, carrying a large sack among them.

"Hurry. Hurry with the potion!" one says as they topple out the contents and a dozen bottles slide out. Each holds a crimson liquid.

I carefully gather Mora's head in my arms, her ear made of bark scratches against my skin. Her chest—or what I think is her chest—doesn't move. No breath comes from her flowery mouth. I've lost her. Bile rises in my throat, but I don't let myself vomit. My heart physically aches as if there's a hole in my chest. I need her. Intense, unyielding pressure builds in my gut. I forget to breathe.

The fairies pour four of the vials over her branches and vines. Some of her remaining poison sizzles in protest, but the potion seems to be doing something because thorns start to disappear into her skin. Princess Preta tries to pour the last bottle into Mora's mouth but it only dribbles down her cheek into the snow. Red blots splatter the pristine snow in severe contrast.

My shoulders crumble and it feels like my chest has caved in on itself. I hang my head and let out a strangled cry. My breath is shallow, stuttered, forced. I tip my head back to look at the sky and want to curse the freshly falling snow. It all happened too quickly.

"Oh Goddess, no, no, no, no."

My plan was supposed to work. Mora's chest doesn't rise and fall. I stare. And stare. This can't be real. We were supposed to dance at Cat's party together. She hasn't taught me how to fold a swan shape yet. There hasn't been time to teach her how to train Heathcliff. How am I supposed to find any adventure without her? This is it. She's gone. I can't live without her.

"Mora," I say, rocking her gently. "Wake up. I need you to wake up."

The fairies shake their heads silently and retreat. I'm alone with the love of my life, but she's gone. Mora looks so peaceful in death, eyelashes long, resting against her cheek. A single snowflake lands on her eyelid. A sob jerks from my chest and I fall atop her.

She's gone. This can't be happening.

"Wake up!" I yell, my throat feels so thick I can barely swallow.

She didn't know how much I love her, so I tell her now.

"You make me smile for no reason." I choke on my tears. "Sometimes my cheeks hurt just being around you. Every time your deep brown eyes capture mine, you imprison me in your energy. I want to share all my dreams with you, Lulita. I want to sit on the couch with you and fight over the blanket," I say, barely able to breathe through the tightness in my chest. "I want to make fun of you for the books you like, and tickle you on dates, and hear your moans from my kisses under the moonlight. I can't live without you, Mora. Please, come back." I grip her tighter.

"Don't leave me. I love you."

My eyes grow wet and my vision blurs. I do not attempt to wipe my loose tears away. I haven't cried like this in years. Everything drains out of me and my heartbeat feels painful with each thud, a drumming of defeat.

What am I supposed to do now? Slowly, I lift my head to memorize the curves of her face. I'd kiss her once more, but something about it doesn't feel right. She's already gone. I wouldn't be kissing Mora anymore. A sharpness bites at my chest at the thought of never kissing her again, never seeing her eyes open, never hearing her laugh. What am I supposed to do?

"I love you. I only want you as my Partner."

I tenderly try to wipe away my tears from her collarbone. They glisten like rain on her new tattoos.

When my hand clears her shoulder, a faint green courses through the line of her tattoo like a river. I blink. It's gone.

"Mora!?" I shake her gently. Nothing happens.

Again, I swipe my hand to rub any leftover tears into her skin. Another part of her tattoo glitters to life. I gasp. This time, it stays green.

"Please, please, please," I beg, wanting to squeeze her hand, to see if she can hear me but her body slowly rises from the snow.

"Mora?" My body freezes in place.

Just a few feet off the ground, still unconscious, Mora floats in the air. In slow motion, her body twists like a wrapping vine. Her bark, vines, and leaves turn back to flesh. There isn't one burn mark on her skin, only the new rose and thorn tattoos. With each passing second, the snow falls harder and her tattoo glows brighter. The green spreads from her arm to her throat, up her neck, and behind her ear.

It can't be possible. I don't understand. What am I seeing? I must be hallucinating. How is this happening?

Slowly, her body lowers back into the snow, and she looks just as peaceful as before.

"What just...Mora?" I cradle her head in my hand, waiting for her to wake up.

She doesn't even stir. Until her eyes flutter open. Wide and alert and alive, they focus on me, and a strangled sound comes from my throat as I gaze at the dark brown eyes that have taken me captive.

"Mora!" I'm unsure if I say it aloud before my lips are on hers.

Warmth floods my veins. She kisses me back like no time has passed at all. I want to drink in the moment, to remember this feeling forever. I'll do anything for this woman. All the tension in my body releases. Her lips claim me. Her breath mixes with mine. I hold her longer than necessary until I have to come up for air.

"Your speech of love sounded like something from a novel," she whispers, followed by a soft laugh.

"Mora!" I gently swipe a piece of her hair behind her ear.

"Call me Lulita."

I half laugh half cough. "I thought you hated that nickname?"

She smiles, softly, weakly and lays one shaky hand on mine. "I can't hate a nickname from the man I love."

I pull her into my chest, never willing to let go. My heart pounds behind my ribs. Is this real?

She groans. "Brody, you're squeezing too hard."

Attentively, I reposition her on my lap. When she raises her chin toward me again, I can't help myself. My lips find hers. I cover her mouth with delicate kisses, softer than rose petals. I don't know how she's alive, and I don't care.

We'll be okay. An overall feeling of weightlessness takes over my body and I want to shout into the forest how much I love this woman.

"I love you, I love you, I love you." I sprinkle kisses on her forehead, her cheeks, and the tip of her nose.

"I love you, too," Mora says, her voice rich with emotion.

She clutches me tightly, her eyes soft and filled with an inner glow. Pink flushes her cheeks and I swear my grin won't ever leave. I'm too elated to think straight. It's like a cloud has carried me away and all strength has rushed back into my body, like I could hike the highest peak. Everything will be okay. Mora hugs me again, and when I'm snug against her body, I know where I belong for the rest of my days. I never want to let go. Tears well up behind my eyelids, which seems impossible for already crying more than I ever have.

"You're here. I'm so glad you're okay." I kiss promises to her cheeks, in a relieved trance of sorts.

I take hold of her face and growl, "Don't you ever EVER do that to me again!"

She half cries half laughs again. "I'll do my best." Mora takes a deep breath. Her lips part and she lets her head fall back. I hear her mutter a soft spell to the sky and remind myself to ask her later what it was.

"Brody, I'm...I'm cold," she laughs shakily and sags over a little.

"Right, let's get you warm. Can you stand?" I don't bother waiting for a reply before gently pulling her to her feet.

She scans the wreckage around us and gulps, then stares at me, "How did you survive the fall? One moment you were hovering over the canyon, and then you were just...gone."

"You wouldn't believe me if I told you," I say.

Her nose scrunches in that adorable way. "Seriously? I just spurt roses out of my mouth like a volcano shoots out lava, and you're saying I won't believe you?"

I rub a hand down my face, dumbfounded that she's making jokes already. "It was your damn origami blanket. It caught me."

She stares. Her mouth opens in question, then closes. "My. Origami. Blanket. Caught you?"

"The one you made that hung from your bed canopy," I say while leading her through the snow.

"Yeah, I get it. That's the only one I've made." She looks at me in disbelief.

"I told you it doesn't make sense."

"Well, I definitely wouldn't have guessed that." She runs

a finger over my wrist. "I'm glad you're safe. That you're still ..."

"I know," I say, kissing her forehead. "Me too."

After I pretend like my legs aren't wobbly and my knees aren't threatening to buckle, we move past the destruction.

"Cat, come here!" I shout into the crowd in the distance.

She rushes over. "I think you might want this back." Cat hands over the page-turning device I crafted.

"Thank you." Mora smiles weakly. It doesn't quite meet her eyes.

She glances at the cliffside where I had been dropped—where Feathi plummeted—where Kavianne disintegrated into black glitter. I don't have any words of comfort. It'll take her time to heal, but I vow to be her family, to spend every day trying to make her happy.

"I think..." she swallows. "I think I'll need a funeral for Yin, Feathi and Nax."

"Why?" Cat leans in with her brows knitted together. "I don't think they will want that when they awe gonna go to my biwthday pawty."

"Honey, let's talk about this later," I say.

"No. It's not faiyuh." She stomps. "I'll go ask them wite now."

"Wait, Cat," I say, trying to reach out and stop her as Cat runs into the crowd of villagers. She doesn't understand that they're gone.

My elation that Mora is here with me alive is quickly being overtaken by exhaustion. My body turns heavy. So I spend my energy staring at Mora's perfect face. Unable to take my eyes off Mora's soft features, I startle when her eyes double in size.

"WHAT?!" Mora nearly falls into the snow. "WHAT? It can't be!"

I follow her gaze. Cat walks toward us holding hands

with a woman who looks familiar. She's tall, thin, blonde with light eyes, with both arms covered in unique watches. I stare at the woman, speechless.

Mora pulls me forward. "Feathi!" She half runs half falls.

I chase after, helping her each time she sways sideways.

"Are you real?" She hugs Feathi, almost knocking her over.

She nods, cheeks pink, and squeals with delight. Cat's eyes are wide and glowing. She skips around the duo in a circle whooping loudly.

Mora turns them around and pokes at her non-paper body. "How is this possible? Wait…where's Yin?

Feathi shakes her head. "I was stuck in the in-between for a bit. Yin can't come back."

"Why?" Mora drops her friend's hands.

"Because she didn't die by Kavianne's magic. The wolf was a natural cause."

"What about Nax?" Mora looks behind Feathi.

Feathi points into the crowd. "He's feeding Heathcliff. I think he'll fight you to keep that pup for himself."

Mora leans her body into my chest for support and I wrap my arms around her frame. "Feathi, you're human again. That means the curse has truly been broken."

CHAPTER 35

Mora

The crimson dress swishes as I sway my hips in front of the floor mirror. In the reflection, I take a moment to stare at the Book, no longer magical. It rests on my desk, next to the pen. Maybe one day I'll write the next chapter next to the phantom ink of previous pages.

Cat jumps in the room, springing onto the master bed. She throws pieces of food to Heathcliff.

"You're going to mess your hair," I say, unable to hold back a laugh.

She sticks her tongue out and purposefully pulls at the braid Feathi twisted earlier. "I'm the biwthday giwl, I can be a messy pwincess."

"Quit moving, Mora, or your hair will be a disaster too." Feathi grins in the mirror.

For a moment, we stare at each other, a thousand conversations bouncing back and forth in that single heartbeat. There's so much we haven't needed to say to each other, already understanding the other through the hardships of grieving Yin's loss. Each week she has stayed by my side as I've processed the trauma we all went through. With her help, I've broken down the biggest lesson, the specific reason I think the curse was broken—I needed to learn to let go of control. I learned I can let others take the reins and listen to their ideas. I think it was broken when I let Brody decide my fate, when I trusted him to make the best choice, even if it didn't benefit me. At that moment, I had felt a second lightning bolt zap through my body, like everything was buzzed with a shock of energy.

Looking back, Kavianne seemed more angry about not feeling heard when I made her do everything my way. I did it out of love, not knowing how much I was hurting her. After discussing this pattern with Feathi, she pointed out that my thorns disappeared each time I relinquished my power over others and let them take the reins. I may never know if that lesson was Kavianne's true intent, but it seems to be the right answer.

Feathi spins me around by both my shoulders. "Let me get a good look at you."

I curtsy clumsily, almost tripping on one of Heathcliff's bones. We sigh at the same time, then both start laughing.

"Are you happy?" I ask my best friend.

She nods, with a little gleam in her eyes. "Yes, Mora. I have everything I want. Now, it's time to get your happily ever after."

It's not possible. "Brody is Committed to Gabrielle. I'll never ask him to relinquish his biggest dream for me."

Feathi fixes a loose bobby-pin in my hair and takes her time before speaking. "Would you give up *your* biggest dream for him?"

I sigh and tell Feathi the truth. "Brody *is* my biggest dream. He's all my dreams, but I can't ask him to make a sacrifice."

"What if it's not your choice?" She picks a little lint off my dress before turning away, not giving me a chance to respond. "Let's go, Cat, I believe everyone is awaiting your grand entrance in the ballroom."

"Did you hear that Heathcliff? Theys a ballwoom foh me!"

They shuffle out, chatter echoing down the hall. The stroke of a grandfather clock teases me with the joy of a party downstairs. But tonight, my heart is torn. I find a moment of freedom as I spin in this dress because no thorns tear at the fabric. There are no longer barbs that twist at a deadly angle. My life is completely changed, but it's not full.

Brody isn't mine. Just thinking of him makes my heart spasm. This isn't how love is supposed to work. If I go every day thinking of 'what if' then how will I ever get over him?

I move to a window, nearly tripping over piles of Heathcliff's blankets, and gently pull it open relishing the freezing air that brushes against my face. After Brody spent weeks reconstructing the damage to my home, the statues below are clean and shiny.

The landscape design in the snow is breathtaking. Soft flakes pile on the new fountain and bench near another trellis. They all form a welcoming entrance for visitors who come from the town for a variety of potions. After

Ryanne mentioned her idea it didn't take me long to become comfortable with helping those in need, as long as I had a say in what type of potions I administered.

High on this hill, I look at the rooftops of the tallest building in the valley. The streets will be empty on a celebratory night like this when everyone is invited to the grandest event in the most mysterious home in Ozaron.

An owl's hoot from the nearby pines jolts me back into my reality. My hand wearing the smallest orb in a new ring is shaking as I close the window.

The soft creak of hardwood echoes down the hall and the sound of a door squeaking sends my heart racing. I know it's him, so I don't dare turn around. I may not survive the image of Brody in a handsome tux with his newly shortened beard accenting the look. I clench my eyes shut and try to shake the idea of his arms wrapped around my waist, of him pulling me close to his body. I can't want him. I have to move on. Maybe it's time to leave Ozaron and start a new life where memories can be replaced.

"I'm not a very patient man, Lulita," he says behind me in a stern voice, but I can immediately tell he's not angry. He's in the same agony as I am, unable to act on the chemistry between us. He needs to stop calling me that beautiful nickname, or my heart will never let go.

I suck in a deep breath but don't dare turn to face him.

"What's wrong, Mora? Is the dress too tight? I can help you with that, you know," he says.

I can hear the wink between his words. I can imagine one of his hands braced on the doorframe, his muscles clenched in restraint. It's too much. I spin around and stifle a gasp. He is definitely not wearing a tux, but instead, a replica costume of the glamour I had designed for him at the festival. From head to toe, Brody sports an entirely black, spandex outfit, decorated with gold paper roses. How long had it taken him to fold each of those origami flowers? He had to have help. Were my friends in on it? Why would they torture me with a gesture that only gives me false hope? Why would he do something that makes me love him more?

"It's a bit tight in the crotch, if you know what I mean," he says.

Goddess, this man will undo me.

My mind is determined. I'll tell him that I'm leaving after the party. He can even have the house if he wants, as long as he's okay with sharing the space with my roommates since Feathi and Nax want to settle here.

"Brody, stop."

"I can't stop when it comes to you." He takes a step forward. "I know what you're asking me." Another step forward. "You want me to stop flirting. Stop being mesmerized by you. And stop fantasizing about your smile." Another step toward me closes our distance. He continues. "You're asking me to do the impossible, Lulita. You're asking me to stop loving you. I can't stop."

He's an inch from me now. My hands hover right over his chest. If I lean in, I'll want to kiss him. That's a lie. I already want to kiss him, strip off his shirt, whisper everything I adore about him into his ear.

"Brody," I whisper, "You're Committed to Gabrielle."

"Says who?" He tilts his head to the side so one of the longer strands of his messy hair falls in front of his eyes. "I don't think that's true anymore."

My heart skips a beat. I study his face. "Wh-what did you do?" Suddenly, I become angry. If he jeopardized his relationship with Cat, I'll summon the power of the forest through my tattoos and shred him to pieces myself. "What did you do?"

His hands cup my elbows, softly. "I love you when you're furious, but it's okay. I know what you're thinking, and me and Cat will still see each other."

I take a step back, shaking my head. "What is your biggest dream, Brody?" Unable to hold back, I slap his chest. "What did you give up?"

Brody softly lifts my chin. "Apparently, our Commitment is broken." So much tension has left his shoulders. He stands taller, more relaxed than he has been in weeks.

"What? How?"

"My guess is …" He rolls in his lips and waits too long.

"What is it Brody? Just tell me." I can barely breathe.

"My guess is when I lit you on fire, it was a big enough sacrifice to cancel the terms." His finger trails over my collarbone.

I don't know what to think, what to say. It would sound crazy to thank him for making such a large sacrifice. A relieved sigh leaks out. There's no need to worry about Gabrielle any more.

"So, you'll have some competition tonight since I'm the most eligible bachelor at this party," he says teasingly.

"And do these women have the power to do this?" I ask, calling roses to crawl out of my tattoos. They're followed by long stems that wrap all the way up my arms and connect to the bustline of my dress.

Brody's eyes darken and he leans over to kiss the tattoos trailing down my neck. His lips are softer than a raven's feather, more luscious than my cake. Finally, he's mine. Slowly, he backs me across the room until my back is pressed against the floor mirror. He groans against my skin.

"Mora, say you're mine."

"Maybe," I practically moan as his tongue strokes my

neck, "I'm the most eligible bachelorette at the party tonight, so you have some competition."

He presses against me with such longing that the mirror behind me breaks.

My high heels crunch over pieces of broken glass. If I were to look into a similar mirror, enchanted to show me who or what I love most in this realm, it would be this man. Brody saved me. It may not have been love that broke my curse, but I only survived because of his devotion, his ideas, his determination.

When I kiss him again, he groans against my mouth. "I guess it's time for our next adventure."

EPILOGUE

Mora

2 years later

The Barrett Sea is miles behind us. After hiking for hours along a mountainside in Lacordia, Brody skips, hops, and prances to my side like a rabbit on steroids.

"Will you let me carry your backpack?" he asks while adjusting the strap on the side. "We can move faster that way."

"No. You already have to carry Cat's." I nod toward the two backpacks over his shoulders, one decorated in unicorns and rainbows.

"I think I need to invest in a matching one. We could be nicknamed the Rainbow Rioters."

"That's a terrible name, Papi," Cat teases from ahead. She jumps from boulder to boulder as we scale a steep hill.

At least I'm in the best shape of my life. After training to scuba dive last year, my lung capacity has improved drastically. That doesn't mean I'll ever be in love with hard-core fitness.

"How much longer?" I groan and shield my eyes from the unrelenting suns. Their heat burns my exposed shoulders.

"I told you to wear sunscreen." Brody smiles, casting me under a spell, then wags a finger at me.

"I am!" I nudge him playfully, careful to not push too hard so he doesn't topple to the gravel. "It's my tattoos. They seem to absorb sunlight like a frickin' plant!"

"Ohhhhh! Mora said a bad word!" Cat laughs ahead. In between her giggles, she glances back at us. "Frickin'! Frickin'! Frickin' plants!"

I love watching her on each new adventure we experience. Not to mention that the first time she sees new waterfalls, is exposed to new cultures, and hears a new language, it's my first time too. We're walking through life together. And I wouldn't have it any other way. When Cat stays with Dom, I crave the moment when she returns. Every morning that Brody and I wake with Cat in our lives, I relish the uniquely clever ideas she shares. Her positive spirit and excitement is not only mesmerizing but absolutely contagious.

"Why the grumpy face, Lulita?" Brody smirks. "Forget about the backpack; maybe I should carry *you* until we get to the jungle?"

I clap slowly. "Ha. Ha. Very funny."

He waves a hand, then winks. "Oh, you're just flattering me."

On my worst days, Brody has a way of brightening my mood. We never truly figure out what the tattoos mean, but they seem to only enhance my power and I'm not mad about it.

"I hope we get there soon too, Papi," Cat calls out. "My water bottle emptied ten minutes ago."

Brody huffs. "Okay, ladies. Team meeting, come on, let's take a break."

I immediately flop my backpack to the ground and collapse atop a giant rock.

"No way, I'll never sit again for the rest of my days!" Cat hollers happily.

He chuckles and pats a boulder. "Come join us."

"I'm not tired!" she yells with more energy than I can imagine.

"Fine," Brody basically sings back to her. "Just stay close, where you can see us."

He scoots next to me and wraps his arms around me in a hug. Though it's too hot to be this close, I lean into him. It's not fair that he smells good when sweaty. I lace my fingers with his as we survey the scenery. High on a summit, we overlook a Lacordian jungle below. I'd have to check the map to remember which one. If I weren't too exhausted to reach for my Taj, I'd take a picture to savor this view forever. Instead, I turn and snap a mental image of the look of awe on Brody's face. The way he soaks in the new sights will never get old.

"It's astounding, isn't it?" he asks.

"Mhm," I say, unable to take my eyes off him. Goddess, I love him so much.

"How many lizards do you think are out there?" He

leans forward as if he'd be able to see them miles away, under the canopy of greenery.

"Probably ten."

He snorts again, a cute quirk he seems to do only when Cat visits us, as if his body knows she's close and blends with her traits.

"Do you think the legends are true? Do you think we'll find one of the hidden caves or any treasure? Do you think Pixie is real? What about the never hour?" he asks excitedly. "I wonder if we'll see a real shadow wielder. Plus, it's been a year since we ran into a pirate. Maybe—"

I squeeze his hand. "Babe, I can't possibly answer all those questions at once."

"You're right." He scoots closer to the unknown again. "I bet Axton and Eribelle were right when they suggested we take this route."

I can't help but grin, since I don't believe any of the things he mentioned exist. Yes, magic of course is real, but the stories he speaks of are just that, stories. I highly doubt that there is a giant treehouse purely made of crow and raven feathers. For now, I'll let him wonder.

"I'm sure we'll find everything you're searching for. It may just take a while," I say.

Finally, Brody turns and faces me. "I already have everything I need, Lulita."

When he brushes his lips against mine, I give him the reins.

PEOPLE AND PLACES

Brody Kain Ricci- hero, carpenter
Catterina- Brody's 5-year-old daughter
Chambrea Fortress- Mora's home
Dom- Brody's ex
Elizabeth- Dom's mother
Feathi- Mora's origami best friend
Gabrielle- Brody's "Gaston"
Heathcliff- wolf puppy
Kavianne Thomesse- Mora's younger sister
Lessie Thomesse- Mora's deceased youngest sister
Mam- Brody's mother
Mora Thomesse- witch heroine
Nax- Mora's male origami friend/roommate
Ozaron- their country
Preta- fairy princess
Ryanne- little girl from Villeneuve
Sofia- Brody's 10-year-old sister
Villeneuve- Brody's hometown in the valley
War- wolf that helps Mora
Yin- Mora's origami friend/roommate

The Wicked Blue

Prequel

Cassie Swindon

THE WICKED BLUE PREQUEL

A SHORT STORY

"Eribelle's Dream"
By Cassie Swindon

CHAPTER 1

How can I paint the taste of saltwater? I swipe more colors from my palate to stroke the beach I'm overlooking. How will the viewer experience the taste of the sea?

I've been raised to fear the waters and detest the merfolk who lurk Below. Yet I find myself licking my lips to savor a little flavor from the forbidden.

Standing on my balcony, gazing at the crimson horizon, wind whips my hair. Sometimes I have a strange compulsion to lean forward, slightly too far over the balcony's edge. Do the wind nymphs detect the confusing longing that teases me to test the boundaries and dip my toes in the waves just once? If I fall over this balcony, will those very nymphs catch me and carry me to the tides to please my soul?

I brush another curve on my canvas, then try to move a stray hair out of my face with my forearm. Otherwise, my hands would be responsible for a cluster of pinks and oranges smeared across my forehead.

Bending sideways, I survey the landscape from a

different angle. What would it be like to sail on a ship to where the sky kisses the luminous blues? I may never have been aboard a boat, but I can envision every shade the ocean would have to offer, from navy to cerulean to teal and cobalt.

I finish painting, I wait for Sampson's design in which he promised me the same colors for his latest fashion genius. I glance around my studio, past the other two easels and the mess across my bed to where my best friend sits at a desk. His back is turned toward me as he furiously scribbles his vision on paper.

"Done yet?" I set down my palate and try not to trip over the half-hazard books strewn around my rug.

"Don't rush me, Eribelle," Sampson mumbles, but I can hear the smile in his voice. That's good news. If he's smiling, he likes what he has created. "And don't brag that you finished first."

I have half a mind to throw a pillow at his back but wouldn't want to mess up his drawing. He groans, then flips the pencil over to erase something. In his frantic movements, he accidentally knocks eyeliner and eyeshadow onto the floor. Among my disastrous domain, they may be lost forever more.

"Done!" He twirls around fast in the spinny chair, holding his paper to his chest so I can't see. "Show me yours first."

"No way!" I block his view to the balcony where my painting is drying. "This was your idea, so you go first."

He huffs. A burst of air blows a long lock of brown hair puff up for a moment. "Fine. But it'll be better when its finished, I swear."

As he turns it toward me, I gasp, and walk toward the beautiful outfit he drew. "Sampson! It's perfect!"

"I hate that word. Nothing is supposed to be perfect. In

fact, maybe I'll rip the seam a little once you put it on just to teach you a thing or two."

"You wouldn't dare!" I grab his notebook.

The intricate detail of the outfit for my upcoming twenty-first birthday is breathtaking. Sampson used shades belonging to the sea: indigo, denim and berry. Blues shift and slide against each other in both contrast and balance.

"If I wear this, Dad will arrest you," I choose to, in fact, throw the pillow in question to his head.

"Hey! The crop top isn't *that* tight. And it'll let you throw up your arms while dancing without any precious treasure falling out."

I agree. But it's the high-rise skirt that I can't take my eyes off of– a piece made from liquid heaven. The way the fabric glides mirrors the fluidity of the ocean. It's as if Sampson knows the one and only secret, I've kept from him–my longing to explore the sea. Yet, he's also my only confidant who understands the harsh punishment Dad would lash out at if I were to be caught in the waters.

I should have better sense than to wish to explore the Below. Apparently, my stupid genes have won in a battle against my survival instincts because I'm seriously considering changing my plans tonight and taking the risk.

"So…? You like it?" Sampson's biting his nail, while his knees are curled into his chest.

"No! I love it! Don't change a single thing." I point to the blue skirt. "What material do you have in mind? This looks like silk."

"I'll surprise you." He winks and takes his notebook back. "Well, Sugar Pants, what time are you leaving?"

I dramatically collapse on Sampson's lap. "Do I *have* to go?"

"Eribelle, Eribelle, Eribelle…" he starts with an

outrageous fake accent, "you, m'lady are the most popular, most anticipated person at the ball tonight. Of course, you have to go, unless..." Sampson loops and twists my hair into an updo with mastery skill, despite my odd angle of hanging off his lap. "Unless you are planning any shenanigans. I think I can get on board with shenanigans, especially if they involve Kilka milkshakes."

Sampson taps the Taj99 device on his wrist and pushes a few buttons until a milkshake recipe is projected against my wall, with a very high level of alcohol mix required.

"Holy Abyss, Sampson, do you plan on killing me with that?" I topple off his lap onto the floor and begin cleaning some of the mess. "If I drink that much, I might make out with *you* tonight."

He makes a gag face and rolls his eyes. "Fine, I'll go easy on the Kilka this time." Sampson slaps my ass while he moves toward my bedroom door. "You need to get ready and I need to find a snack, which I won't be sharing."

"You have so much hatred."

"I said what I said." He glides out the door, humming a recent Talia Sanchez song that echoes down the hallway.

Alone, I groan and check the time on my own Taj99. Only an hour until the guests expect my grand entrance. Maybe I can convince Dad to let me skip this event. Not a second goes by until I laugh away at that possibility. Possible buyers from Khajit, Gonia and Ozaron will be in attendance, and they all expect to see Finley Erickson's famous daughter– the only human known to have blue eyes. If Dad has any chance of selling more yachts than last year, I should play my part.

A strong cinnamon aroma wafts through my doorway and footsteps thud against the hardwood, growing louder with each step.

"Damn it," I quickly crawl to toss a blanket over my

most recent painting and shove my paintbrushes under my bed.

"Eribelle?" Dad's voice booms like a giant. "What are you doing spread out on the floor like that?"

I bend into a yoga pose, one foot and one hand off the ground, then take a centering breath.

"Ah, that's my girl. It's good to brag about your flexibility."

I almost puke. Maybe I should. Then perhaps I can get out of this party if I fake an illness.

"I brought your favorite snack," Dad says, offering a cinnamon bun mid-air.

There's no point in correcting him with my intense chocolate obsession since he'd forget by tomorrow. Dad starts talking business and his expectations for my behavior tonight, but I tune him out and listen to the waves crashing into the pier outside. Seagulls squawk and the familiar shouts of fishermen greeting each other all blend into a painting in my mind. If I close my eyes, I can see the white foam making shapes on the seashells and footprints pushed into the sand. The textures, shapes, and colors all form an image of freedom.

"... Eribelle? So, what do you think?" Dad checks his Taj as an incoming message alert him with a beep. "Can I count on you to do that, tonight?"

"Uh, yeah. Definitely."

"That's my good girl. I'm so lucky. You'll be my biggest prize." Dad turns away, his shoulder width barely fitting through the doorway. "Oh, and if the mayor of Runlose cozies up to you, just play along. We wouldn't want a repeat of last year, do we?"

My insides turn to mush. Of course, I'm a prize. Of course, he backhandedly threatens me. Of course, I'm forced to attend another boring event with a silent competition of whose wallet is bigger than whose. Of course, I'll be used by Dad to make more sales.

As his footsteps fade away, I shove a bit of a delicious cinnamon roll in my mouth. Sugar probably coats my lips, but it's not as if I'll be putting on lipstick anymore. There's no way in Abyss I'm going tonight. I leave the rest of the dessert for Sampson to finish off when he returns. But by then, I'll be gone. I can't send him a Taj message because Sampson sucks at lying.

Quickly. I tug on the straps of a backpack. It's buckle sticks on something under my bed. I yank and pull until it comes flying at me and I somersault backwards. As I shove a few essentials inside the bag, our three suns setting change the shape of the shadows within my room. I follow their rays to the open doors leading to my balcony. Running out the front door of Dad's estate isn't an option. Too many of his employees will ask why I haven't yet changed into a ballgown. Or they'd take the opportunity to politely congratulate me on my appearance on the new billboard downtown. I'd have to flash another fake smile and gently bob my head until they'd eventually mosey away.

I carefully move my still-wet painting inside in case this fierce wind is followed by a storm later. My balcony doors lock from the inside once closed so if close them, there's no turning back. I suck in a deep breath and shut them softly.

Warmth caresses my cheeks when I step out of the shade. Carefully, I peek over the edge. Heights haven't ever scared me, but I've also never considered scaling the side of a four-story mansion before. Voices holler and laugh far below. If I fall, there aren't any wind nymphs to save me. This could be the most moronic choice I've ever made.

Heart pounding, I straddle the railing and wipe my

sweaty hands on my t-shirt. Hoverboards rush by below but thankfully no rider has noticed me yet. I say a useless prayer to whatever Goddess might be watching over me and swing my legs over. The stone exterior creates many divets for someone experienced to latch their fingertips and toes on, but I'm no professional.

My shoe slides off its spot.

"Fuck!"

The muscles in my arms scream in protest. I manage to balance and gather my breath. *I can't fall. Keep going. Don't fall.* At a torturous speed, I scale down one stone at a time and somehow stay alive. Left foot. Right foot. Left arm. Right arm. Sweat drips down my temple. My pulse races.

Finally, my sneakers hit the pavement and my knees buckle. Shaking, my trembling hands hover over the street. I gulp and give myself three moments of panic. One. *I can't believe I just did that.* Two. *If Dad finds out...* Three. *Sampson will think I'm a rockstar.*

Pressing off the ground, I straighten, walking taller, more confident than ever before. With each step, the waves pounding against the boulders roar louder. I'm almost there. A couple holding hands passes by me without a glance in my direction. They both seem captivated by the cheery song blasting from their Taj. I start walking to the beat with a bounce in my step, believing for the first time that I'll swim in the ocean that has called me my entire life.

Why have I been such a coward? I should've tried this long ago. A bird swoops low, white wings outstretched, then lands to my right. Some of my classmates at university have rambled on when drunk or high about wanting to be a bird to soar through the open skies. I've never understood that desire. If given the chance, I'd be any sea creature besides a merfolk– perhaps a dolphin. I'd glide in the murky depths to experience a new life, where no one could tell me how to act or what to say or wear.

At last, the sounds from the bars down the street dissolve into distant hums and thumping beats. Ahead, the suns dip lower, ready to skim the horizon. My gaze locks onto a sail and I wonder if they're headed to Ozaron, the city famous for its art and deep forests. Slipping my shoes off, I wiggle my toes in the sand. Do I dare enter? I scan for any signs of creepy merfolk spying on me. No one.

I toss my backpack where it'll remain dry then slowly wade in the water. Ankles deep. I hold my breath. Water reaches my knees. Nothing catastrophic has happened yet. Maybe all the years of fears being carved into my mind were pointless.

I cringe. If Dad ever knew my thoughts, he'd ...well, he wouldn't listen to my pleas for the finances necessary to attend art school.

The water reaches my hips and I bask in the sensation of being halfway submerged. As corrupted as the merfolk are, I wonder what it'd be like to live like them– under the sea. Do they have any form of art that could survive the elements of the wicked deep?

"ERIBELLE!" The familiar voice skids like scissors sliding against metal. "ERIBELLE! Get out of the water!" Sampson yells, his calls growing louder and closer.

I should've explained to him, but this may be my only chance. Headfirst, I dive under. The icy cold doesn't hit me as harshly as I expected. Instead, it's soothing, like I've been meant to swim. But it's not where I belong since I can't paint here.

Sampson's muffled demands come from Above and I almost turn around. Unfortunately, I can't hold my breath forever, so I swim as far as possible then breech to suck in a lungful of air. The waves rock me and water splashes my cheeks. I smile. Perfection. I don't care if Sampson hates that word. This moment, right here, during the last moments of the setting suns, drenched from head to toe in the ocean is my perfect paradise.

Another scream comes from further out. In a small canoe, a woman bends over the side grabbing at the water like a lunatic. What is she doing? Did her hand get caught in her fishing net? I swim closer, faster, ready to help.

"Nate!" She peers over the side with wide eyes. "Nate!"

Immediately, I freeze. A high pithed sound rings in my ears. Shit. Someone has fallen overboard. I dip under but don't see a sinking body nearby.

"Hey!" I yell but the lady doesn't seem to hear me. "Hey!"

"Nate! No, no, they took him."

My heart stops. They? I glance back to the shore. Sampson is jumping, waving both hands in the air and wildly pointing behind me.

I spin. Bright scales shimmer. Merfolk. Many of them. Terror clenches my gut. I don't stand a chance of outswimming them. If I can pull myself into the canoe, maybe the two of us can paddle back faster.

"Hey! Help me up!"

In a daze, the woman stands, paying me no attention and stares at the sky. I guess I'm on my own. Struggling, I heave myself into the boat despite it rocking back and forth.

"Nate," she sits on a crate and mumbles the name, "Nate, my Nate."

Regret floods me before I act but I slap the stranger's face. She whirls at me, noticing me for the first time.

"Take an oar!" I say, while paddling myself. "Come on!"

We move in a circle, the waves rocking us. What the Abyss was I thinking coming out here?

"Hey! I place my hands on either side of her face and stare into her brown eyes. "You need to row. We're going to land. And you need to row now, understand?"

Slowly, she nods, tears running down her face. As she lifts an oar, slippery pale arms slide over the side of the canoe. Arms made of nightmares wrap tightly around my boatmate's waist.

Screaming. Someone's screaming. It might be me.

I clutch the oar and smack the merman's arms until he let's go.

A loud horn blares and bright headlights blind me for a few seconds. The merfolk all instantly swim away. We're safe–for now. Shielding my eyes, I catch the name of the yacht drifting toward us, *'The Eribelle.'* Dad's boat. Double triple fucking shit.

ABOUT CASSIE SWINDON

Cassie Swindon loathes wet socks, leaf blower machines, tight hugs, and rickety fans. Things she might murder for: a free massage, cuddles from a kitten, chocolate milkshakes, and long naps. Some of her favorite activities include decorating for the holidays, playing board games, and avoiding phone calls. She has four more ideas for upcoming books so sign up for her newsletter below.

Check out free short stories as prequels to my upcoming works in progress and also sign up for my newsletter here: https://cassieswindon.com/

facebook.com/cassie.swindon.3
twitter.com/CassieSwindon
instagram.com/cassie_swindon_author
bookbub.com/profile/cassie-swindon
amazon.com/stores/author/B091N72414
goodreads.com/cassieswindonauthor
tiktok.com/@cassieswindon

FAIRY TALE FLIP SERIES
CASSIE SWINDON
CASSIE SWINDON
THE WICKED BLUE
CASSIE SWINDON
THE PHANTOM INK
CASSIE SWINDON
THE NEVER HOUR

THE LINKED TRILOGY
CASSIE SWINDON
CASSIE SWINDON
SCORCHED
CASSIE SWINDON
SEVERED
CASSIE SWINDON
SHATTERED

GOLDEN CHAINS TRILOGY
CASSIE SWINDON
BREAK THE STONE
CASSIE SWINDON
HUNT THE STORM
CASSIE SWINDON
STOP THE CLOCK
CASSIE SWINDON

www.ingramcontent.com/pod-product-compliance
Lightning Source LLC
Chambersburg PA
CBHW070547310726
48982CB00011B/1483/J
9781737346999